DANGEROUS TIMES ON DRESSMAKERS' ALLEY

ROSIE CLARKE

Boldwood

First published in Great Britain in 2024 by Boldwood Books Ltd.

Copyright © Rosie Clarke, 2024

Cover Design by Colin Thomas

Cover Photography: Colin Thomas

A CIP catalogue record for this book is available from the British Library.

Paperback ISBN 978-1-78513-139-4

Large Print ISBN 978-1-78513-140-0

Hardback ISBN 978-1-78513-138-7

Ebook ISBN 978-1-78513-141-7

Kindle ISBN 978-1-78513-142-4

Audio CD ISBN 978-1-78513-133-2

MP3 CD ISBN 978-1-78513-134-9

Digital audio download ISBN 978-1-78513-136-3

Boldwood Books Ltd
23 Bowerdean Street
London SW6 3TN
www.boldwoodbooks.com

PROLOGUE

There had always been dressmakers in the alley. At one time, when a mad – or very sick – king sat on the throne of England, and the regent ruled in his stead, the desire for extravagant clothing had been at its height. At least ten seamstresses had worked here then, side by side in their small terraced houses, bent over the opulent clothes ordered by the *haut ton*. Their work meant hours of backs aching and eyes stinging from tiredness, as they struggled to see by the poor light of tallow candles, their pay for all this effort, a tiny fraction of what Madame would charge for the wonderful creations they produced.

Madame, a French émigré, who had barely escaped the guillotine with scarcely a rag on her back, now had an important establishment, in a far nicer situation in town, receiving her wealthy clients in an atmosphere of comfort, with no hint of the sweat and tears that went into producing their expensive clothes. The unfortunate girls of Dressmakers' Alley were her dirty little secret, the murky base on which she had built her empire, and if one of them died of malnutrition or illness, who knew or cared?

Much had changed by the spring of 1923. Madame was long gone; her seamstresses and their toils forgotten. A terrible war had rent the world apart, resulting in huge loss of life, sweeping away much of the old way of things, and bringing heartache and loss in its wake. After the war had come a terrible sickness that men called the Spanish flu; it had taken many souls. Then came the years of depression, finishing, with the end of rationing, in 1921, but now a change had begun as life started to improve and people could learn to forget the pain and grief of those years in the new prosperity.

For the young, it was the Jazz Age, a time to have fun and snatch what they could from life, half-fearing to look over their shoulders; the start of what they were told – and wanted to believe – would be a golden age. Bonar Law was Prime Minister and King George V was on the throne. A war had been won and surely life was theirs for the taking?

Yet here in Dressmakers' Alley in London's East End, there was scant sign of that golden promise. Here, little had altered; the people still worked for wages that were barely above the poverty line, lived in bad housing and saw nothing of that glittering new future.

Yes, there had been a few changes since the days of the regent at the beginning of the century. Some of the old terraced houses were still there, but the fronts had big glass windows and several had been knocked together – two or three combined into one – to become shops with windows filled with interesting items, from the second-hand jewellers at numbers 5 to 8 and the flower shop at the corner, which was one of the newcomers – no more than a year since it opened. On one side of the alley was a clothing workshop – or, if you spoke plainly, a sweatshop – where young women sat for hours on end churning out garments that would sell at high prices in the West End stores.

They were not much better paid than the seamstresses of old, if the truth were known, working long hours for perhaps twenty shillings a week – or thirty-one shillings and sixpence, for more specialised work that involved careful hand sewing. At least they had better light than the women who had worked here before them, but life was much the same as it had been for those poor seamstresses of the nineteenth century, except that they used treadle machines mostly rather than sewing by hand.

Yet on this day in March 1923, when a pale sun struggled to make itself felt, a swirl of mischievous wind was blowing, playfully catching up fallen debris and sweeping it along, only to drop it elsewhere. Change was in the air. Change was coming. Unknown and unbeckoned, it was on its way...

1

'I have a task for you,' Mary Winston announced to her young friend, Winnie, that springlike morning in March 1923. 'It is something that should suit you because you like making clothes and you're good at it.'

'That was one thing Mum taught me,' Winnie Brown replied, looking at Mary curiously. 'She worked as a seamstress for a while and I can at least sew a straight seam.' She waited, but though Mary's eyes sparkled, she said nothing. 'Well, go on! Tell me...' With her thick, rather unruly dark hair swept back off her face with combs, Winnie was attractive rather than pretty, but her eyes were bright and alert as she looked at her friend. 'Don't keep me in suspense!'

Mary laughed at her impatience. 'I – or rather the Movement – want you to work in a clothing workshop for a while, perhaps only a few weeks – perhaps longer.'

'But why?' Winnie looked at her, puzzled. They were both members of the Women's Movement. Winnie lived in a hostel provided by the Movement and worked a few hours each day in their office just around the corner from Oxford Street. She received only a small wage and her lodgings in remuneration, but it suited her and she liked the friendship she'd found with the other volunteers. 'Is it important?'

'Yes, Winnie, it is.' Mary smiled at her. 'One of the most important things we've asked of you so far...'

'You know I would do anything for the cause – and for you.' Winnie had marched, protested, and shouted outside the Houses of Parliament and Buckingham Palace; she'd stood on cold street corners with flags and a collecting tin and spent ages addressing envelopes to be sent out to supporters, but this sounded very different.

Mary was Winnie's true friend. Without her, she might have ended up struggling for a living and perhaps driven to things beyond the imagining of a decent girl. She would be happy to do whatever was asked of her.

'We want you to do some investigating for us, Winnie. We have decided to highlight the terrible conditions that some women are forced to work in. It isn't enough simply to campaign for equality, though we have made some headway recently. The Matrimonial Causes Bill will be a triumph when it goes through – if it does. Now, at last, women will be able divorce an unfaithful husband, whereas before it was only the husband who could apply to the courts.'

The recent bill, introduced in February by a private member, was a huge victory for women's rights and they'd celebrated it, although it had not yet passed parliament, everyone believed it must.

'However, we should not rest on our laurels. Girls are being exploited by their employers. It is time that some of these wicked establishments, who pay so poorly, were held up to the light – exposed for what they are – little more than slave drivers!' Mary looked angry. 'Yes, I know it is better than the workhouse, and the laundry maids in big country houses are worked just as hard, but that doesn't make it any better – does it?' Winnie shook her head and Mary smiled. 'I know you feel as I do and I shouldn't ask so much of you – but it needs to be exposed. We have to make people in high places sit up and notice.'

'You know I'll do anything for you, Mary,' Winnie said instantly. 'I owe you so much. I don't know what I'd have done if you hadn't helped me when you did. I was so miserable – so ashamed.'

Constable Winston, Mary's devoted husband, had found Winnie the night she'd broken the window at Harpers Emporium in Oxford Street. She'd done it in a spirit of angry defiance – and because of her shame at what she'd done; a wicked spiteful thing. She'd stolen some jewellery from her employer, and that wasn't the worst of it! She had been jealous and infatuated with Ben Harper, her employer's husband, so she'd written them both horrid letters. She'd accused Ben Harper of having an affair with Lilly Ross, who worked in Harpers' flower department, and she'd said Sally Harper was having an affair with one of her male friends.

None of it was true and Winnie had wished afterwards that she hadn't done it. When she knew she had to leave her job, and the Harper children she'd begun to love during the time she had looked after them, she'd taken the jewellery in a stupid moment of rage and despair. Her home life had always been miserable and so when her mother screamed at her for leaving the Harpers, she'd run away from home with no thought for her future. Only when she was alone on the streets with hardly any money, no job and nowhere to go did Winnie suddenly realise the enormity of her mistakes. She'd been filled with rage and misery that had culminated in a burst of frustration, and she had smashed the store window with the heel of her shoe.

After breaking the window at Harpers Emporium, she'd run off into the night, pursued by a police officer. Lost in a dark lane that she didn't know, she was attacked by a man who'd tried to rape her. Winnie's screams as she had fought him off had brought the police to her rescue – and the first on the scene was Constable Winston.

Instead of reporting her for the broken window, Constable Winston had taken Winnie home to his wife. Theirs was a happy home, but childless, and in Winnie, Mary had seen something that touched her heart. Mary had listened to Winnie's story and sympathised, but she'd made her return to the Harpers' house, where she had given back the stolen items and apologised. She had been lucky to escape prosecution for what she'd done – and even luckier that she'd found such a good friend.

For some weeks, she had lived in their home, then she'd been offered a room in the hostel and part-time work at the office of the Women's Movement in Oxford Street. It didn't pay very much, but Winnie felt independent and happier than she had since her father had died, leaving her alone with a mother who did nothing but scold and complain. In Mary, she had found a family and her life had become richer and better.

She visited Mary's home most weekends and had Sunday lunch with her and Constable Winston, becoming firm friends with both of them. It was therefore a given that if Mary wanted her to do something for the cause, Winnie would oblige. Of course she was going to do as Mary requested. Mary was devoted to the cause and Winnie felt that it was a community belonged in and it gave her a chance to help other young women in similar circumstances.

'Where is this workshop?' she asked.

'Good girl,' Mary continued with a smile. 'It is in Dressmakers' Alley, which is within walking distance of Commercial

Road, and we want you to apply for a job there – so that you can discover the truth about its working practices. We've heard rumours that women and girls are being exploited; the owner pays some young women far less than he should and uses them almost as slaves. We've heard that some of them sleep on the premises, upstairs, and are not allowed to leave. If this is true, it is a scandal and should be exposed – but although we have been told of these young women, or girls some of them, less than fourteen, I've been told; we can't prove anything yet.'

'You think if I work there for a while, I can discover the truth?' Winnie stared at her uneasily. 'But, Mary, I can't sew well enough to do it professionally—'

'I think you will find you can – and you can use my machine for practice,' Mary offered. 'I don't want you to be outstanding at it, Winnie, just one of the girls. This job is only for a few weeks – or however long it takes you to discover if the stories we've been told are true.'

'Supposing I can't discover anything?' Winnie asked, her stomach clenching. She didn't much like the idea of working in a place like that, especially if some sort of illegal exploitation was going on. She'd been prepared for demonstrating with placards against the government, chaining herself to railings and throwing eggs at important people, even imprisonment, because that was part of the campaign to make those in power take notice of the Movement – but this sounded dangerous.

She knew that Mary and others like her had not been satisfied with the act that had allowed women over the age of thirty to vote; they could vote now, but only providing they were married to a member of the local government register, or a member of some such body themselves. That meant many women still did not qualify and that was not fair. The Movement's work would go on until every woman and man had the

same rights, because some men did not have the right to vote
either. Winnie wanted to do her best for the Movement and
Mary – and yet... a little shiver of fear touched her nape,
warning her.

'If you work there for six weeks and see nothing untoward,
you can leave,' Mary promised. She'd seen Winnie's doubts
cross over her friend's face, because she took hold of her arm
and pressed it. 'You can leave at any time if you feel they suspect
you and you are in some danger. I recommended you for this
job, Winnie, because I know you feel strongly about the misuse
of power by those who have it. Don't you think that if girls are
being held against their will, they should be freed?'

When Mary asked her such a question, Winnie could give
only one answer. Of course she wanted to help any young
woman forced to work against her will, or exploited with low
wages. Besides, Winnie could not refuse to do what Mary asked
of her – she owed her new life to her generosity and she truly
liked what she was doing. It would be a wrench to leave the busy
campaign office, where she had been at the heart of all that was
going on, but in a way, it was quite exciting. If she was successful
in exposing illegal practices, her name would be in the papers
and she would become a leading light in the Movement.

* * *

Winnie had agreed to try to do what Mary asked; there had
never truly been any doubt that she would. Now, here she was,
standing in Dressmakers' Alley, outside the workshop of
Madame Pauline, her knees a little trembly and her heart
thumping. She looked around nervously. It was a dingy street,
peeling paint on window frames and some of the windows were
dirty, though the flower shop on the corner looked bright and

clean, and the glass had been recently washed at Madame Pauline's.

Winnie wondered if her one-time employer, Sally Harper, bought clothes for Harpers Emporium here. She surely wouldn't if she heard that the seamstresses were being exploited. Dismissing her thoughts, she took a step towards the door and halted, wondering if she ought to turn and run away quickly – but she couldn't. She'd given her promise to Mary.

Winnie swallowed nervously as she opened the door and entered. The reception area was pleasant enough, a plain beige carpet on the floor, a large mahogany desk behind which a stout, very respectable-looking woman with spectacles sat typing. There were also several mannequins with examples of the dresses and suits made on the premises, one of which displayed a suit that looked much like the new, shorter fashion the French designer Coco Chanel had made so popular this last year or so. It had the same loose jacket and a relaxed style, which was so much more comfortable than the tight corsets they had been forced to wear before the war. Winnie thought the fashion was almost a symbol of the new-found freedom many women now enjoyed.

The woman behind the desk looked up as Winnie entered, staring at her for a moment in silence. She had been told to wear her oldest working dress, ankle-length, and to carry nothing that could expose her as being a young woman who had been holding down a responsible job for some months.

'We want them to think you are desperate for work,' Mary had warned her. 'You wouldn't be asking for a job there if you had money in your pocket – so try to look humble.'

'Yes?' the woman asked after a few seconds of silence. 'What can I do for you, miss?'

'I wondered if there was any work?' Winnie said in a small

voice. She felt a shiver down her spine as the woman's eyes narrowed behind the heavy-framed spectacles. 'I can sew, but I'll learn to do anything...'

'Need a job badly, do you?' There was a brief glimmer of sympathy in the woman's eyes.

Winnie took a deep breath. 'I got turned off from my last place...'

'What did you do – steal something?'

It was so close to the truth that Winnie flushed bright red as she invented her tale. 'No... the master fancied me and the mistress didn't want me in the house. I... I was a parlourmaid. She won't give me a reference, so I can't get another job in service... and I heard there was work here.'

'There is for good workers.'

The woman stared at her for a couple of minutes in silence, making Winnie's nerves tingle. Had she guessed the truth?

'I'll speak to Mr Barrow. Sit over there – and don't touch anything. I've got a good memory for faces and if you pinch something, you'll be sorry.' She pointed to a spindly chair that looked as if it might have belonged in an earlier age.

Winnie sensed the menace behind the words. She perched nervously on her chair as the woman disappeared through a door behind the desk area. Winnie wouldn't have dared to try to steal one of the dresses from the dressmaker's dummies, even if she'd wanted to, which she didn't. They were expensive items, she didn't doubt that. A black evening dress made of some filmy material with heavy fringing and lots of beadwork was exquisite, almost what one would expect of a French designer, but it would not suit her. The other two dresses were plainer, but matronly, ankle-length, and not to her taste at all. Everything looked so middle class and respectable that she wondered if Mary had got it all wrong. Was she even in the right place?

The brand name was *Madame Pauline*, but Winnie didn't think the owner could be French if he was called Mr Barrow. Catching her breath as the woman returned and a man followed, Winnie wished she was anywhere but here. The woman was respectable, but the man sent tingles of fear up her spine. Tall and heavy-set, he had a swarthy complexion and black hair, his eyes a cold grey that were not smiling as he looked at her, his mouth a thin line of disapproval.

'Yer wanted a job?' he asked, in his thick London accent. 'What's yer name and where did yer come from?'

'I have a room in a hostel,' Winnie replied nervously. She wanted to turn and run, but her loyalty to Mary held her where she stood. 'I was in service – but I was let go...'

'Show me yer hands,' he demanded and Winnie obeyed. He gave a snort of disgust. 'These hands have never scrubbed a floor in their lives. So what's the truth?'

'I didn't do the rough work, just helped my mistress and light work, fetching tea to the parlour...' Winnie held her breath as his gaze narrowed, seeming to pierce her. 'I really need a job...'

'You're lyin' to me,' he muttered 'But we need all the girls we can get these days and half of 'em think they're too good for this kind of work. I reckon you've been in trouble – but I'll give yer a trial. What's yer name then?'

'Winnie Brown. Thank you. I promise I'll work hard.'

'Yer will that or answer to me,' he grunted. 'How old are you?'

'Nineteen,' Winnie quavered nervously.

He nodded. 'That sounds about right. Come on through then. I'll show yer where you'll work and you can start right away. We've got a rush order on. It's twenty bob a week if yer over eighteen and any good – maybe more once I'm satisfied.' He gave her a hard stare.

Winnie quailed. She could imagine how young girls desperate for work must feel. There was still so much poverty in this part of London, even though the depression was supposed to be over. Perhaps it was for the rich and privileged, but the working classes hadn't seen much change.

'I thought it was thirty shillings...' she said, feeling she ought to say something, because the wage he'd offered was low, considering the hours the seamstresses worked. He hadn't mentioned the hours, but Mary had told her they would be long – perhaps eight in the morning until gone six at night, from what she'd gleaned so far.

'Mebbe, when I say, and if yer good enough,' he told her. 'Do you want a trial or not?'

'Oh, yes, please,' Winnie said quickly. She was finding it difficult to breathe as they passed through a narrow corridor into a large workroom. There were four rows of tables, at which women of all ages sat, their heads bent over as they sewed, the noise of their machines loud to her unaccustomed ears. Not one of them looked up as he summoned someone and a woman of perhaps fifty got up and came towards them. She was thin-faced and looked nervous, her hair scraped back into a tight bun.

'Yes, Mr Barrow,' she said apprehensively. 'I think the order will be on time.'

'I never asked yer that, but it had better be, Betty. Or I'll want ter know why not.' His gaze narrowed and he gave Winnie a push towards her. 'I want you to set this one a trial. I doubt she'll be good for anything but a simple hem, but see what you can make of her.'

'If I take time out to show her...' Betty's protest died as he looked at her. 'I'll see the order goes out on time.' She beckoned to Winnie grudgingly. 'Follow me. I hope you can sew, because we're pushed for time as it is – and he's got the boss on his back.

He gets the flak if we let him down and then he takes it out on us.'

'Mr Barrow isn't the boss then?' Winnie asked and Betty gave a crack of derisive laughter.

'Him the boss? Not bloomin' likely. He's a bloody slave driver, but he ain't got the wit to run a place like this… not to get the fancy orders anyway, nor ain't Mrs Jarvis out front. He just stands guard over us and he's good at fixing the machines if they clog up.'

Winnie nodded. She'd noticed that their supervisor had gone through a door at the end of the large room. 'Where does that go?' she asked.

'Nosy ain't yer?' Betty said. 'It's the cutting room, if you must know, and where they do the fancy stuff. You won't be working in there, so you don't need to know anything about it.' She gave Winnie a sharp look. 'It's best not to ask questions round here, understand?'

Winnie nodded. They'd got back to Betty's worktable and she saw she'd been sewing the hem of what was clearly one of the matronly dresses she'd noticed out the front. It was a dark blue and fine wool suiting, but too warm for summer wear so that was perhaps why they wanted it out before the weather changed for the better.

'I can finish that seam for you,' she offered.

Betty indicated she should sit and Winnie finished the short seam that had been left when the supervisor was summoned to Mr Barrow.

Betty took the garment from the machine and inspected Winnie's work.

'Is it all right?' She felt nervous as the sharp eyes scrutinised her stitching.

'It's straight at least,' Betty said. 'Now do the other side and the hem and pass it to the station in front of you.'

'You don't want me to set the sleeves?'

'No, that's Yvonne's work,' Betty told her. 'She is skilled and fast. It takes her half the time it would take most of us. I just do seams and hems and supervise – that's my real job, when we have enough girls.'

She nodded as Winnie hemmed the other side and then began the bottom hem.

'Yes, not bad. Bit slower than most, but neat. If I can leave you to get on – there's a pile of pieces on the bench over there.' She pointed to one end of the room. 'They are all together – so one pile is what you need for one dress – got it? Bring one at a time and do the seams and hems and pass on. I'll come back in a while, but I need to check the finished work for mistakes.'

'What happens if someone sews a crooked seam?' Winnie asked.

'Depends,' Betty said. 'We can't unpick and resew most things, especially in fine material – it shows whatever you do, so that garment becomes *cabbage*... and don't ask because I've got work to do.'

Winnie had no idea what she meant by *cabbage*, but supposed it was just a name for spoiled garments – the kind that ended up on the market selling for a fraction of the shop price.

Winnie nodded and went to pick a bundle from the bench that held the cut garments ready for sewing.

Another girl arrived at the bench at the same time. She shot a shy smile at her. 'I'm Daisy,' she whispered. 'No chance to talk now, but I'll see you when we finish this evening.'

'Don't we get a lunch break?' Winnie questioned, realising that she hadn't asked about her hours when Mr Barrow offered her the job. She was already beginning to feel hungry.

Daisy shook her head and went back to her workstation.

Well, that was the first thing she would report to Mary! No lunch break – that was surely not legal for a start.

Winnie selected the next bundle and took it back to her station. She hemmed the seams, glancing up only when she changed the position of the material in the machine. After she'd passed the garment on and fetched another, she saw that a girl had got up and gone to the far end of the room, disappearing through yet another door. She returned moments later, carrying a tray with mugs of what looked like strong tea, which she then distributed to the girls at their stations. They all drank it and went on with their work.

'I'm hungry,' Winnie said when the girl got to her. 'Do we get any food?'

'No, just tea,' the girl replied. 'You should bring your own food and eat it when he isn't looking – or when you have permission to go for a toilet break. You can't have more than four of them a day and you are allowed five minutes...' She passed by, leaving Winnie to drink her tea and place her cup on the floor beside her, as the other women did.

Later, the same girl came and picked them up, taking the tray out to what must be a kitchen, before returning to her work.

Winnie frowned. She couldn't believe that women were willing to work in such wretched conditions. It was stuffy in the room, because there were no windows to open, and, at one end, there was a big steam iron where the garments were pressed before being taken away by Mr Barrow, the smell of damp cloth adding to the claustrophobic atmosphere.

She managed another word with Daisy at the collecting point and asked where he took the finished items. 'To the packing room,' Daisy told her. 'I go sometimes and help with that – we put them in tissue and boxes, five garments to a box and a van comes to take them away.'

'Where do they go?' Winnie asked.

'All over – London and other places,' Daisy said. 'Don't know much, but I saw a couple of invoices. They charge a lot of money for the best dresses.'

'Where are the invoices made up? And what is *cabbage*?' Winnie asked, but Daisy had gone back to her station and started work.

There was no chance to speak to her again, until she requested a toilet break and Winnie asked for one too a few seconds later.

'Remember to be quick about it,' Betty told her. 'We need to get this order out by four this afternoon.'

Winnie mumbled something, got up and went out of the door she'd seen Daisy use a moment earlier. It led into a dark and dingy hall, the walls painted a dull cream that had turned brown with age, and at the end was a notice on the wall saying:

TOILETS

Just beyond the toilets, there was a short staircase that reached a small landing and then went to the left so that it wasn't possible to see what was at the top of the stairs. Winnie approached the bottom of the stairs and put a foot on the first, but as she did so, Daisy came out and called to her.

'Winnie! You're not allowed up there.'

Winnie halted and went back to her. 'Where does it go? What's up there?'

'I don't know…' Daisy glanced over her shoulder nervously. 'One of the girls went up there a few weeks back and listened at the door at the top. Mr Barrow caught her and she was sacked immediately. He was furious and she was frightened and in tears when she left. He frightens most of us. He's got a shocking temper.'

'Oh, I see...' Winnie spoke as if it did not matter, but she felt a tingle at her nape. Mary was right. Something bad was going on and Winnie was suddenly determined to discover the truth. Her fear and slight resentment at being sent here vanished. She did not like Mr Barrow and it was wrong that the girls who worked here should be in fear of his wrath. 'Oh, before you go, what's *cabbage?*' she asked.

'It's garments that can't be sold as perfect. There's always more material ordered than necessary to fill an order, so any spoiled ones are sold cheap to the market boys on the side. It don't cost the boss nuthin', 'cos they charge the customer for the cloth... but they fine us anyway. We hardly ever get our full wage at the end of the week.'

'That's a bit unfair,' Winnie objected.

'There's a lot worse round 'ere. We get fined for lots of stuff. Last week, I earned twelve shillings and sixpence, 'cos I was late a couple of times. You'd better hurry up,' Daisy said. 'You'll be late back.'

She walked hurriedly down the hall and into the workroom.

Winnie hesitated. She was debating whether to risk running up the stairs when Mr Barrow came into the hall. It would have to wait for another day, but she would do it soon, because she would be glad to leave this place once she had the information they needed.

2

Lady Diane Cooper seized on the distinctive box as her maid entered her bedroom, crowing in delight. 'It's here,' she cried. 'Oh, Susie, it's my dress from Worth. It was based on one of their own models, but I asked for certain changes so that it would be quite unique; my own design. I ordered it when we were in Paris last month. I shall be able to wear it for the party this evening.'

'Yes, my lady,' Susie replied with a smile. 'It is very exciting.'

Miss Susie Collins, dresser and personal maid to the young and beautiful wife of Lord Henry Cooper – a man some twenty years her senior and previously a widower and father of three sons, presently all at Eton – looked fondly at her mistress. She was an enchanting creature, with glossy dark hair and hazel eyes, and the darling of the society gossip columns. Her rise to fame had been swift after the marriage had shocked many and made others smile and nod in a knowing way. *He* was considered a sly dog for snaring such a charming beauty, and *she* had clearly married for his fortune – and who should blame her?

Only, it wasn't that way at all, as Susie well knew. She had witnessed more hugs and kisses than any of the gossips would credit and knew it was a love match. That Lord Henry should adore his fascinating bride was no wonder, but perhaps that she should love him as much as she so clearly did was harder to understand – unless you knew Lady Diane.

Her title was her own. She had sprung from aristocratic parents, both of whom had died when she was a small child. Raised by a strict aunt, who never ceased to tell her how fortunate she was to have been taken in, and reminded her often that her parents had left her nothing but a ramshackle property in the country that would be better sold rather than left to dissipate what little fortune she had from her grandmother, Lady Diane had thirsted for love and kindness. This she had found in abundance in her doting husband. From the moment they had met on her first visit to London to buy clothes, the attraction had been mutual and strong. The cynical would say that if it wasn't his fortune, it was that she needed a substitute father, but Lord Henry was, at the age of forty-two, a charming man. His dark hair might be slightly silvered at the temples, but his features were strong – attractive rather than handsome – and he had a deep cleft in his chin. He was also healthy and energetic, perhaps due to his love of walking and riding when in the country, as well as being a keen cricket player in season. It was, in fact, a true love match.

Susie had placed the box with its distinct Worth label on the peach satin bed quilt.

Lady Diane lifted the lid and then gave a little gasp of dismay. She glanced at Susie in a puzzled way. 'Did you have cause to open this, Susie?'

'No, my lady.' Susie moved forward and saw what had disturbed Lady Diane. The top layer of tissue paper was normally sealed neatly, but it had been crumpled and was slightly torn. 'That is strange. Anything from Worth is always beautifully packed.'

'Yes, it is, normally.' It was typical of her that she accepted Susie's word instantly. 'I did not think it was you who opened it, Susie, for you know I would wish to be the first to see... but someone has done so.'

'You are right, my lady,' Susie replied. She could see as clearly as Lady Diane that someone had taken out the dress and refolded it and replaced it, but not as carefully or as expertly as the original packers.

'Who took this from the carrier?' Lady Diane asked. The gown had not been ready when she and Lord Henry had returned to London, but she'd been assured it would be sent by an exclusive and secure carrier.

'I had it from Molton, my lady, but I will enquire who fetched it from the carrier.' Susie frowned. 'If it was one of the footmen, they will be spoken to sharply.' The household at Grosvenor Square was presided over by the butler, Molton, who ruled his various underlings with a rod of iron, and woe betide whoever had dared to open Lady Diane's special box.

Lady Diane removed the dress from its box and her frown disappeared. It was fashioned of a silk organdie in white, with a silver tunic of softest silk beneath. The straps were thin lines of sparkling crystals, and matching crystals were worked down the deep V-neck at both the front and back in a geometric pattern; the skirt was designed to finish at mid-calf and the workmanship was exquisite. She held it up and both she and Susie examined it for faults but could find nothing to mar its perfection.

'It is not harmed,' Lady Diane breathed a sigh of relief. 'I do not know why anyone should wish to take it out, but they were careful. However, in future either you or Molton will fetch any packages from the carrier.'

'I will discover who fetched it, my lady,' Susie said. 'It is so beautiful. Will you try it on now?'

'It is slightly creased at the hem,' Lady Diane observed critically. 'You will press it for me, please, Susie, and I shall wear it to the party this evening. I am sure the fit will be perfect for they have never let me down yet – but you will also press my yellow silk just in case.'

'Yes, my lady,' Susie replied. 'Is there anything else?'

Lady Diane looked at her wistfully. 'Only that I wish you would call me Diane.'

'It wouldn't be right,' Susie said but smiled, because she knew it was her employer's true wish. 'No, not even in private, for if I did so, I should be sure to forget and say it properly in public.'

'Very well.' Lady Diane sighed. 'You've been my friend for such a long time, Susie. You know I trust you implicitly. I hope I did not offend you by asking if you had opened the box?'

'No, my lady. It had been opened and that is very wrong. Such things are special and for *you* to have the pleasure of opening. I knew you would take my word, for you always do; you know that I will never lie to you or let you down.'

'Yes, I know that well,' Lady Diane said. 'There was a time when I was very unhappy and you were my only solace, Susie. I have no secrets from you.' She sighed. 'I shall certainly be very careful about who delivers my dress for the royal garden party, though.'

'I shall fetch it myself.' She smiled at her mistress.

It was true they were friends, though Susie was ten years her senior and had been employed as a parlourmaid by Lady Diane's formidable aunt. She'd always had a talent for dressing hair and for neat sewing and had jumped at the chance to become Lady Diane's maid when she married.

'Have you ordered your dress for the wedding of Prince Albert to Elizabeth Bowes-Lyon yet?' Prince Albert was the younger brother of Prince David, and reputed to be shy. Some people said that he had a stammer, but those who knew the truth did not speak about it. It was Prince David who would succeed his father as king one day, and the newspapers always had lots of pictures of the handsome young man. Prince Albert was normally accorded respectful privacy, but his wedding was another matter and there were many pictures of the beautiful young woman who would be his bride.

'Not yet; I have time, it is not until April.' She smiled at Susie. 'I showed you the invitation Lord Henry and I received, did I not?'

'Oh yes, my lady. It was such a privilege to see it – and to think you will be there.'

'Not one of the principal guests, but we shall see them wed.' Lady Diane smiled.

'You will tell me everything,' Susie said. 'It is so exciting.'

'Yes, I think so,' Lady Diane replied. 'That is all for now, Susie. Go and do whatever you need to. I am going to send for the car and go shopping. It is Henry's birthday soon and I have ordered something special for him from Asprey.'

She placed a charming hat on her head; Susie helped her pin it, held her fashionable coat for her and handed her gloves and a small leather bag. As Lady Diane went off with a smile on her face, Susie took the new gown and the yellow silk down to the ironing room to be pressed. She frowned as she walked down the back stairs at the end of a long hall; someone had opened that box and she intended to get to the bottom of it...

* * *

'I am not perfectly sure who fetched the package from the carrier,' Molton said, looking outraged at the suggestion that one of his footmen might have dared to open the box and take out a dress belonging to her ladyship. 'I believe young Fox handed it to me – but he had been cleaning silver in the pantry all morning. I know that, because there was a smear on his uniform and I rebuked him for it. He knows full well that he must wear an apron when cleaning the silver.'

'Someone opened it after it left Worth's establishment,' Susie said firmly. 'I intend to discover who fetched it from the carrier – will you please ask Fox who handed it to him at the door? I do not think it can have been delivered by someone employed by Worth – and it normally is—'

'I will enquire,' Molton said.

He went off, his back stiff with annoyance and Susie knew that whoever was responsible was in trouble.

* * *

Susie carried the gowns she had carefully pressed back to her ladyship's dressing room and hung them up ready for Lady Diane's approval that evening.

As she was about to leave, his lordship walked in. He was carrying a slim leather box that looked as if it might contain a necklace.

'Is her ladyship in, Miss Collins?'

'No, my lord. I believe she may have gone shopping – but I think she intended to be back for tea.'

'Ah, good.' He smiled and placed the box on the dressing table. 'Will you see she gets this, please? I do not know what she intends to wear this evening, but it is a trinket she might like...'

'Her new gown arrived from Worth,' Susie told him. 'I believe she may wear that if it pleases her.'

'Ah, good, Sinclair did say he would fetch it from the carrier personally.' Lord Henry smiled and nodded. 'When the message came that it was ready for collection, I mentioned it to him and he said he would be in the vicinity and that he would bring it straight round.'

'Mr Sinclair, my lord?' Mr Sinclair was Lord Henry's land agent; he looked after his lordship's estate and property, over-seeing the payment of rents and all manner of business. He was highly respected and trusted, and it surprised Susie that he should have offered to fetch a package when it should surely have been one of the footmen's job. 'Worth's carrier normally delivers their clothing themselves...'

'Yes, there was some problem,' Lord Henry said. 'I forget what – but no matter. The dress was safely delivered.'

'Yes, my lord.' She did not feel it her place to tell his lordship it had been opened on its way here. Lady Diane would do that if she wished him to know.

Susie bobbed a curtsy and received a dismissive waved hand.

'No need for that, Miss Collins. I assure you I neither want nor need such ceremony.'

He left the room, leaving Susie to put the box away safely. She would normally have left it where he had placed it, but after the incident with the new dress, she was uneasy. If his lordship's agent had fetched the box from Worth, he must be above suspicion. He'd been with the family for some years – so who was the culprit? Mr Fox, the young footman who had handed it to Mr Molton – or an inquisitive maid? Had it been placed somewhere unattended until Susie had taken it up to her ladyship?

Susie had not even been tempted to look in the box his lord-ship had left. It was for Lady Diane to show her the gift – but were there maids in the house who were less scrupulous? To take an expensive dress out and handle it – with hands that may have been less than clean! It was a shocking crime that would have earned instant dismissal in some households – or would have before the war. These days, it was harder to find girls willing to enter service; the life was hard, the hours long, and young girls today preferred more freedom.

Susie frowned. She thought it was far more likely to be one of the maids than the footman, for what would he want with a dress? However, the label would tempt some pert young girl who could never hope to wear such a garment. Young Dot might be such a one, or Mabel the second parlourmaid… but Susie must not jump to conclusions. Yet, surely it had to be one of the maids. It could not possibly have been the respectable Mr Sinclair. He was his lordship's man and he could not be a suspect.

3

The sewing room was busier than ever the next morning when Winnie arrived at seven o'clock, by the back door this time. She hadn't known where to go, but Daisy showed her the narrow passage to reach the rear entrance, used by the seamstresses. A rush order had come in that morning. Someone wanted a particular dress out in the shops by the next day and there was a buzz of excitement in the room as Betty told them there would be an extra threepence in their wages for each garment they managed to complete.

'Does this happen often?' Winnie asked Betty when she was told of the bonus.

'Not often, but it depends on our getting this out before anyone else,' Betty told her.

'Why the rush?' Winnie was curious, but Betty just shook her head and told her to get on with it.

She went to the collection bench and selected a pack of pieces, puzzled at first, because there were no sleeves, but then she saw that it was an evening dress of white silk with an organdie overlay and tiny beaded straps; the straps had already been sewn with crystals, and there were crystal strips to sew onto the dress once it was seamed. Yvonne was sewing the strips of crystals on to the V-neckline, which allowed Winnie some relief as she wasn't sure she could make a neat job of it.

Because the design wasn't darted, relying on its clever cut to make it hang loose to the hips, where it would cling enticingly, it was a simple case of three seams and a hem. Winnie was getting quicker after several hours' work the previous day. She soon had her first finished and passed on to Yvonne, who did the more complicated task of embellishment. Though with the straps and strips of crystals already having been prepared, it took far less time than it would take a skilled seamstress to sew them on by hand, which was how a dress like this would have been made by one of the prestige designers like Worth, Patou, Fortuny – or the new darling of fashion, Chanel.

When the girl came round with their mug of tea, a lot of the women ignored it. The lure of an extra threepence was of more interest than a hot drink. Winnie took hers and drank it quickly. She heard a sigh of exasperation from Yvonne when she turned and the next dress wasn't ready but ignored it. She wasn't keeping her waiting more than a second or two, which was much better than the previous day.

'Come on, Winnie,' Yvonne said. 'I can do with a few bob extra in my pay.'

Winnie nodded and bent her head to the task again. She noticed that no one in the room had asked to go to the toilet that morning. However, an hour later, she was forced to ask if she could be excused. Yvonne glared at her as she left, then got up and went to fetch another bundle of cloth, clearly feeling she could do the whole job in the time Winnie was gone.

* * *

Winnie visited the toilet. When she came out, she hesitated, looking over her shoulder. This was probably as good a time as any to investigate the top of the stairs, since the women were all too busy to take a break.

She ran lightly up to the top of the first few stairs, just before the bend and then froze as she heard the men's voices.

'Never ask me to do that again, Bert,' one of them said in an angry tone. It wasn't a London accent, Winnie noticed at once. 'If he discovered what I'd done, I'd be out of a job—'

'How can he?' That was Barrow's voice answering. 'It could 'ave been anyone from the Worth's workshops or a maid after it arrived at milady's. You're above suspicion, Cyril. Anyway, it will only put her high-and-mighty nose out a bit, if she sees someone wearing a copy of her dress. Besides, you owed me for what I done for yer.'

'I know, but I would have made it right in time. You may be my brother and partner here, but—'

Hearing footsteps coming down the stairs, Winnie turned and flew back the way she'd come. If Mr Barrow caught her being nosy, he would sack her immediately, but he might do more if he knew what she'd overheard.

Worth's workshops! Winnie was an intelligent girl and suddenly she understood why all the urgency in the sewing room that morning – and the bonus if they could get the dresses out in the shops the next day. She had always taken an interest in the latest fashions and, whenever she could, read the magazines that reported on society affairs. The gorgeous and exclusive gowns the wealthy aristocracy and – sometimes famous actresses – wore to special occasions were described in detail and photographed. Before long, cheaper copies of those gowns would be on sale in dress shops all over London, and in time the provincial towns, too. Winnie had herself bought a copy of an elegant day dress that she'd seen one of the famous film stars wearing – only a few weeks after she'd appeared in it in public. There were a few differences – there had to be if the manufacturer wished to escape being sued for copying an exclusive design – but everyone knew it was a copy.

It sounded as if Barrow had persuaded his brother, Cyril, to somehow divert an expensive gown on its way from the exclusive couturier before it reached its destination. And Cyril was afraid of losing his job! He must work for a rich man – a titled one too. Mr Barrow had mocked her ladyship, the true owner of the dress. What a horrid man he was!

Yvonne glared at Winnie as she got back to her station. 'You're late,' she hissed. 'I've done two garments since you left. Betty will fine you if you do it again. She don't know I did all the work.'

'Thanks. Sorry...' Winnie murmured, but she wasn't. She was burning with suppressed excitement as she started work again. Only her second day at Madame Pauline's and she'd already discovered one secret. She couldn't wait until that evening when she would be able to report her findings to Mary Winston.

'You took your time!' Betty said, coming up to her and making her jump. 'Do it again and I'll stop a morning's pay.'

'That's not fair,' Winnie complained. 'I was only a few seconds longer – and it's my time of the month.'

'That's not my worry,' Betty said sharply. 'You work to the rules or you're out – understand?'

Winnie nodded but made no reply. Betty was clearly completely on her employer's side and didn't care about the girls. It was so unfair that working girls should be subjected to this kind of treatment. She had friends and somewhere to go if she lost her job, but many young women did not and would feel bullied, desperately afraid of losing their job. The next step from here might be scrubbing floors – or, worse, a life on the streets.

Frowning as she hemmed the next dress, Winnie wondered what was at the top of those stairs. Was it another workroom, where the beading was done – or something else? Someone had worked on all those beaded straps and the strips of crystals. They had appeared overnight. Had the girls who were not allowed to leave worked all night? If that was the case, it was outrageous! The sooner Winnie exposed them, the better!

* * *

'That is illegal for a start,' Mary exclaimed when Winnie told her what she'd discovered. 'Whoever the lady was that ordered an exclusive design from Worth would be so disappointed to see a cheap copy in the shops, perhaps even before she'd worn it.'

'Would they dare to sell it before she'd worn it in public?' Winnie asked, wrinkling her forehead. 'I think some of those dresses cost hundreds of pounds.'

'I am sure they do, even more sometimes,' Mary agreed. 'I suppose the manufacturers get away with it by changing small things – but, nevertheless, if you've paid a fortune for a dress, you don't want to see someone else wearing a cheap copy a few days later.'

'I think whoever wore it must have done so recently,' Winnie said thoughtfully. 'They were in such a hurry to get it finished by this evening that they paid us threepence per garment. I earned an extra four shillings and sixpence and some of the girls earned more.'

'Well, that can't be called a bad thing,' Mary agreed. 'And yet it doesn't seem fair to the person who paid so much money for the real dress.'

'Is it lawful, though? Could we make trouble for them because of it?'

'I shouldn't think it is enough to get them closed down,' Mary said, looking thoughtful. 'I doubt there is an actual law against it – unless, the designer had a copyright on it, and I'm not sure you can do that...'

'I'll just have to keep looking then,' Winnie said with a sigh. 'By the sound of Mr Barrow's brother, he was very angry with him. I think he is the real boss, though he said his brother was his partner. I don't believe there is a Madame Pauline, if there ever was. Mr Barrow's brother, Cyril, said if it was discovered that he'd shown them – whatever it was, and I guessed it was the special dress – he would lose his job.'

'He deserves to,' Mary said. 'If he used his privilege to sneak that dress out, it was an abuse of trust.'

'Yes, it was – but I just wonder who he works for that he was able to get his hands on such a valuable thing. It must have cost the lady who ordered it a small fortune – perhaps three hundred pounds.' She hazarded a guess.

'More if all those crystals were hand-sewn, which they must have been if it came from Worth.' Mary frowned. 'What did the crystal embroidery look like – just so I can recognise it if I see it anywhere?'

'They were little circles...' Winnie frowned. 'It was the only thing that let the dress down. I didn't think they looked the same quality as the fabric.'

'Did you ask where they came from?' Mary asked curiously.

'I asked Betty later and she said they bought them in, as they always do that kind of thing. I wondered if she was lying and the girls upstairs worked through the night to do them. Unless... Well, I don't know when they saw the original or how long they had been in the making...' Winnie frowned. 'You'd think Betty would be more considerate of the girls, but all she seems to care about is pleasing Mr Barrow.'

'Probably her job depends on it. You can never tell what goes on in other folks' lives.'

'I suppose what I heard hasn't helped us much?' Winnie was disappointed.

'No...' Mary sighed. 'We don't have enough to make a stir. We need proof that something more is going on there, Winnie. The wages they pay are disgraceful, but we need to know if young girls are being exploited in other ways.'

'Can't the police raid them?' Winnie asked hopefully. Mary's husband was a police constable after all.

'For what reason? They must get a warrant to raid anywhere and that isn't easy. It takes a lot of proof for the chief constable to allow it.'

'Supposing I see or hear something that we think points to a nasty racket going on in the upstairs room? Will I need proof – or will Constable Winston take my word for it?'

'If he doesn't, he'll hear from me,' Mary said. 'Ah, here he comes... I can hear his key in the door. We'll ask him about copying that gown... and then you should get home and go to bed or you will be tired in the morning.'

* * *

Constable Winston had listened to Winnie's tale and shaken his head over it. 'It is a bad thing to do and very annoying for Worth or whoever it came from, also the designer and the lady who paid hundreds of pounds for an exclusive dress – but it goes on all the time. If you – or she – happen to spot the dress in a shop, there will be certain differences and so they get away with it. It ought to be a prosecutable offence, but it happens a lot. No sooner does a lady of quality wear an exclusive dress at a big occasion, like a royal garden party or to the opera, than someone copies it.'

'It seems very unfair that they get away with it,' Winnie replied.

'I fear they get away with far worse things,' he replied. 'Some of them are not fitting for a young lady's ears – but you just be careful, Winnie. It's all very well, you spying on these people, but if you get caught, there is no telling what they might do. I don't want you listed as missing without trace and ending up in some potentate's private harem.'

'Bill! Don't frighten her,' Mary commanded. 'There's nothing like that to worry about, Winnie. It's far more likely to be a case of underpayment of wages than anything sordid.'

'I'm not so sure. You just be careful,' Constable Winston told her. 'I'd best call you a cab to get you home. It is getting late.'

'I'll be all right...' Winnie protested, but he refused to listen and went out into the street to hail a cab for her, seeing her into it himself a few minutes later.

He pressed her arm as he helped her in. 'I've been working on some nasty cases recently, Winnie. Young girls coming to harm. We fished a young woman out of the river today with her neck broken – and I shouldn't like it to happen to you. Mary is so fond of you. Just take care.'

Winnie promised she would and climbed into the cab, sitting back with her eyes closed as she made the short journey through poorly lit streets to the women's hostel where she lived. She paid the driver when she got down, thanked him, and went into the large building, which was bathed in light inside, the laughter of other young women in the sitting room relaxing her as she went up to her room.

* * *

Winnie lived in comfortable accommodation, with a bed, wardrobe and writing table, together with a large elbow chair where she could sit by the window and read when she had time to relax. Not that she often did these days. When she worked for the Movement, her days were spent talking and laughing with friends as she typed and filed and made drinks for the other young women. There was always something new to plan and little triumphs to celebrate when someone made the newspapers after a daring exploit and an article in support of the Movement appeared.

Working at Madame Pauline's was much harder and no fun at all. Winnie did not mind the sewing, but she hated the atmosphere of fear and oppression. It was clear to her that the girls were frightened of Mr Barrow – even Betty appeared nervous when he summoned her. Daisy had whispered to her that he had been known to slap a girl into obedience and she'd looked terrified when she'd confided on a hurried toilet visit that one of the girls had recently disappeared.

'I went to Jean's lodgings to take her the money she was owed, but she wasn't there. I tried three times over the next two weeks and her landlady said she'd gone to the police because it wasn't like Jean to go off owing money—'

'Did she leave London to look for work – go home to her family perhaps?'

'I don't know – but afore she left, she told Mr Barrow she would make trouble for him and he slapped her – said she'd forfeited her wages due, but the next day he told me to take the money to her.'

'What did he say when you told him she had disappeared?'

'I didn't – I gave the money to her landlady to keep for her if she returned.'

Winnie had told Mary about that whispered conversation, but she thought the girl had probably done a runner because she couldn't pay her rent. 'It happens all the time,' she'd said. 'Stands to reason, your Mr Barrow knew nothing about her disappearance or he wouldn't have given Daisy the money to pay her.'

Winnie had accepted her solution to the small mystery, but now she wished that she'd told Constable Winston. He had spoken of girls coming to harm – and perhaps one of them might be the girl that Daisy had whispered of. Supposing she'd been murdered? She had been heard to threaten Mr Barrow. Was that enough for him – or someone he knew – to kill her?

Winnie shivered as she undressed and jumped hastily into bed. If she thought Mr Barrow was a murderer, she wasn't sure she would dare to continue working at Madame Pauline's. Yet if he disposed of all the girls he disapproved of, he would soon have no workforce to make the clothes.

She was making too much of Daisy's story. The girl probably liked attention and had made it sound much worse than it was. People didn't go around murdering others just because they had dared to cheek them... Unless, Jean had discovered something she wasn't supposed to know.

Pulling the covers over her head, Winnie tried to block out the terrifying thoughts. What might Mr Barrow do to her if he caught her poking her nose in where it wasn't wanted?

4

'Look at this.' Lady Diane showed Susie a picture of herself at one of the most select evening parties of the year in the society column of *The Times* newspaper. 'Doesn't the dress look wonderful? I am so glad it arrived in time for the occasion.'

'It is really elegant,' Susie replied. 'It is such a pity that you tore the skirt when you came home.'

'I must have caught it on the car door as I got out,' Lady Diane said. 'I do not know how I could have done so, but I suppose it may be mended.'

'I could do it, my lady – or return it to Worth for you?'

'I am not sure I should wear it again if it were repaired,' Lady Diane replied. 'I should always be conscious of it – in case someone noticed. Because of the simplicity of the design, it would be impossible to replace the section – unlike removing a whole panel and replacing it.'

Susie nodded. 'You only wore it once – and it is so beautiful. It seems such a shame.'

'Perhaps Worth's workshop could do something – redesign it somehow,' Lady Diane reflected. 'The beading is so particularly pleasing – the geometrical design was much liked by my friends. I suppose the bodice might be removed and used again with a skirt and jacket, or some such thing.'

'You could design an outfit in satin to complement it,' Susie suggested and smiled. 'I dare say some of your ladyship's friends wished to know where it came from.'

'I told them Worth, of course, but they do not know that much of it was my design.' Lady Diane laughed, her face alight with mischief. 'I do so wish I might set up my own fashion house, Susie. I have so many ideas teeming in my head – but I fear my dearest Henry would not care for it. Nor would my aunt – though I care nothing for her opinion.'

And everything for my lord's, Susie thought, though no words left her mouth, for she would not overstep the mark, even though her lady insisted on treating her as a friend rather than a servant.

'Why do you not offer to design a few gowns for your friends, my lady?' she asked. 'Would it not amuse you to do so?'

'Perhaps,' Lady Diane laughed. 'I am not certain that the House of Worth would appreciate being given designs to copy too often. My gown was a one-off and much admired when I showed my drawing to Madame Felicity. She said it would be an honour to have it made up for me, but I do not think they would wish to do it all the time. Their designs are a part of their reputation after all.'

'Yes, I understand,' Susie nodded her agreement. 'It is a pity you cannot find some way of expressing your talent, my lady.'

'To do it commercially would smell too much of trade,' Lady Diane remarked. 'I should not regard it myself – but I do not imagine Henry would like it. There has never been anything of that nature in his family, I am sure.'

Unlike many aristocratic families, who had married into the

bourgeoisie class to save themselves from ruin, the Cooper dynasty had remained aloof, investing in land and property, and trusting to good management to keep them from decline. Lord Henry had also, quite recently, unknown to his wife, invested a good part of his fortune into shares – some of which might have smelled faintly of the shop, but since his wife knew nothing of it, she was blithely content to accept that it was invested in the 'five per cents', as her Aunt Camelia had told her was the right way for a lady or gentleman.

'He might help you to do it in a very discreet manner...' Susie attempted, but Lady Diane shook her head.

'No, I must not think of it, Susie. Please do not tempt me – besides, if I did my duty, I should be increasing by now.' There was not the least need for her to give Lord Henry a child, since he already had three grown sons, but Lady Diane felt her lack, believing that he would like a daughter – as she would herself. Perhaps a little girl she could dress in pretty clothes would solve the slight boredom she felt at times when Lord Henry was busy. A little sigh escaped her. 'I think I should change my dress. Miss Amelia Clarkson is coming to tea. I think the peach silk tea-gown...'

* * *

'Oh, Diane... that dress of yours was so gorgeous. Did Worth truly make it for you?' Amelia asked as she sipped her tea and nibbled a tiny almond cake. 'It must have cost a thousand pounds – at least that is what Mrs Weatherspoon claimed.' Amelia was a pretty, dark-haired girl of good family, but did not have the natural style of Lady Diane.

'I am not entirely sure what it cost,' Lady Diane replied and laughed. 'I do not think it was anything like that much – but then it was, in part, my own design.'

'No! Really…?' Amelia frowned. 'I thought it was wonderful… but… Mrs Weatherspoon told Mama that she saw a gown very like it in Oxford Street this morning. She said that it was the same – with that very low dip at the back, which she thought shocking – but that there was something different about the embroidery.'

'Surely it could not have been so similar?' Lady Diane frowned. 'It is only two days since I wore it – and the picture in *The Times* did not appear until this morning. I know that gowns are sometimes copied cheaply, but the beading alone took hours. Madame Felicity assured me that it would take two weeks for their seamstresses to complete…'

'Perhaps it wasn't the same,' Amelia soothed as she saw Lady Diane's annoyance. 'Mrs Weatherspoon went in and looked at it. She told Mama that it was very cheaply made, no proper finishing inside and the crystals of inferior quality. It was selling for twenty guineas and advertised as "worn in high society".'

'I imagine it must be very inferior,' Lady Diane said. 'They could never use the same silks and organdie for that price. It would cost far more even for the materials and the crystals.'

'Well, it is annoying,' Amelia replied. 'I wanted a dress from Worth for my dance this summer, but Mama says now that she is not sure if it is the right thing to do. Why pay such high prices if you will only wear it once – for how could one wear it again if it was being sold cheaply on the High Street? She thinks we could have some pleasant gowns made up by an English seamstress far more cheaply.'

'That is very true,' Lady Diane agreed. 'It is most irritating to think that it can be done so quickly. If the copy does not appear for some weeks, the dress may have been worn sufficiently that it no longer matters.'

'Yes – but a few days is a different matter.'

'Well, in this case it doesn't signify,' Lady Diane said, deciding not to let it upset her further. 'I happened to tear the skirt when I got out of the car, though I did not notice it at the time. I had already made up my mind to have it altered, so I shall do so... but I shall ask Madame Felicity how it could appear just days after I first wore it, before it was even shown in the magazine.'

* * *

In the event, Lady Diane was not put to the trouble of visiting or writing to the exclusive couturier. Madame Felicity happened to be in England on a business trip and had chanced to see the copy herself. She came to Lady Diane's home and begged for a moment of her time. She brought with her one of the infamous copies she had collected herself from Bond Street only that very day, which she showed to her valued customer with abject apologies.

'It was brought to my notice almost at once, my lady,' she said in shocked accents. 'The House of Worth has suffered such piracy in the past, as have most exclusive houses, but normally after some weeks have passed and I fear that once a dress has been featured in the society columns it cannot be avoided. However, as you will see, there are several differences.'

She showed Lady Diane the seaming, which was hastily done and not finished folded under as the best seamstresses did, also the inferior crystals that had been machine-stitched on to a strip of gauze and not hand-sewn painstakingly onto silk.

'As you can see, the dipping-V at the back is too low,'

Madame Felicity told her. 'It has not been cut skilfully and will gape. Yours hangs perfectly and you can be certain that nothing will be revealed that ought not – as I fear is the case with this monstrosity.' She crumpled the offending garment in her hands and pushed it into the paper bag. 'I cannot imagine how someone was able to penetrate our security, my lady. It has never happened before and we shall be doubly careful that it does not happen in future.'

'Please do not disturb yourself, Madame,' Lady Diane bestowed her charming smile on her. 'I am not at all certain the breach occurred at your workrooms. I believe it may have occurred after your courier handed it to my husband's agent – Miss Collins suspects one of the maids, but we are keeping an open mind.'

'If your ladyship trusts us with another commission, I shall personally see that it is delivered to Miss Collins,' Madame Felicity vowed.

'Oh, I attach no blame to you,' Lady Diane replied. 'I am designing a ball gown I shall need this summer, which I will bring to you when I am satisfied. Also, I tore the gown that was so clumsily copied and was wondering what to do with it, as I do not believe a repair to the skirt would be invisible. I thought that perhaps it could be remodelled as a blouse to wear under a jacket?'

'I am sure that would be perfectly possible,' Madame assured her. 'We can certainly reuse the beading. It will also be done at no cost to you, for I do not hold myself blameless.'

Lady Diane thanked her and she departed. The meeting was reported to Susie, who wondered if, after all, the breach of security had occurred at the exclusive workshops or with the carrier.

'She must feel it may be her fault or she would not come in person, my lady,' Susie said and frowned. 'I have questioned Dot twice and I believe that she is innocent. I would not put it past her to look in the box, but I have discovered that she has a sickly mother to support and I think she would hardly dare to do anything that might lead to dismissal.'

'Then we must give up the puzzle. It hardly matters now that I have torn the gown, for I should never wear it again, or not without alteration.'

* * *

Lady Diane might have dismissed the incident, but Susie was unable to put it out of her mind. It annoyed her that she could not discover who the culprit was, even after questioning Mr Fox, who had taken it from Mr Sinclair at the door. She was ten years older than her mistress and protective of her, as well as grateful for the elevation to her present position. She told the unfortunate Mr Fox in a sharp tone that in future anything that was delivered for her ladyship was to be put into her hands only.

'Not that Mr Molton would have presumed to open the box, but I dare say it was laid down for a moment and some person betrayed her ladyship's trust.'

'Come off it, Miss Collins,' Mr Fox replied. 'No need to get that lofty tone with me. I certainly didn't open the box and I don't believe anyone in this house would do so either. Lady Diane is highly thought of by us all.'

'Someone did,' Susie retorted, cheeks pink.

'Well, it wasn't me – nor Dot neither, so you can stop looking at me like that, as if I would do such a thing. None of us would. We know what is due to her ladyship – and no one is more pleasant to work for than she…'

'I am not blaming any of you, but I feel I've let her down.'

'Stands to reason it happened before it arrived,' Mr Fox told her. 'Either on the way or at the workshop.'

Susie nodded. It seemed the only explanation. Yet she knew the security was strict in all the exclusive fashion houses when working on a new collection or for commissions for clients. Lady Diane was a special client, for not only did she buy several gowns a year, but she was also beautiful and a darling of society. Her talent at designing clothes was also quite special and had she not been the wife of a titled man, it might have earned her a place in the workrooms of Worth or another respected house. Her photograph wearing any designer's gowns would appear in the society column of various newspapers, plus magazines that attracted the notice of women everywhere. It could only do any fashion house good for it to be noted that her latest spectacular gown had come from them. If a copy was made before the client wore it, that would do harm to its maker and could lead to loss of business.

However, there was nothing more to be done. Spring was a busy time for Lady Diane, because she attended many fashionable parties, accompanied his lordship to the races, which was a passion of his, enjoyed weekends in the country, and visited the opera and theatre. Her wardrobe was extensive, most of it made specially for her, and it was Susie's job to keep everything fresh and ready. She had little enough time to spare and so the dress faded into the background over the busy weeks – and then, at the end of March, something so wonderful happened that it was forgotten altogether.

5

Winnie stopped to look in the flower shop on the corner of Dressmakers' Alley. One of the better properties in the area, with green-painted woodwork, it looked inviting. The window was always so tastefully arranged, with pretty displays of flowers and she'd noticed recently that it seemed busy whenever she passed it on her way home from work. The lights were still on and she could see someone inside, buying flowers from the young woman even though it was half-past six. It seemed she worked longer hours than Winnie – though the shop wasn't open when she passed on her way to work.

A young man left the shop carrying a bunch of spring flowers and looking pleased with himself. He was just an ordinary working man. Winnie had seen him passing through the alley and knew that he worked in the cobblers just around the corner. Yet he had stopped to buy flowers for his sweetheart on his way home.

'They look lovely,' she said, then blushed at herself, but he smiled and nodded.

'For my mother. It's her birthday today and she loves

anemones; they are her favourites. I always buy her some – and Lilly got them in specially for me. She sells them cheaper than the big shops; that means I can give Mum some fudge too.'

'I'm so glad,' Winnie replied and blushed again, wondering what had made her say such a thing. He would think her very forward. However, he had stopped walking and was smiling in a pleasant friendly way.

'I've seen you before,' he said. 'You work at that Madame Pauline's, don't you?'

'Yes, I do,' Winnie said and smiled as he extended his hand for her to shake. 'I think you work around the corner.'

'I'm the cobbler – my name is Sam Collins.'

'Oh – I'm Winnie Brown...' She liked his firm clasp. 'I mustn't stop you, Mr Collins. Your mother will be waiting for you.'

'Yes, she will,' he agreed and nodded. About to walk off, he thought of something and stopped to look at her. 'Are you getting on all right there...?' He jerked his head towards her workplace. 'I've heard a few stories about that Mr Barrow. You take care, miss – and if you ever need a friend, you know where I am.' His cheeks heated then and he walked off quickly, as though he'd said too much.

Winnie stared after him. She felt a chill at her nape and shivered. Then, seeing a young woman come to the door of the flower shop and look out, she stared at her in surprise. Surely that was the girl from the flower shop at Harpers! A feeling of guilt crept over Winnie. Had Lilly been dismissed because of something she'd done – those spiteful, deceitful letters she'd written to Mr and Mrs Harper in a moment of jealousy? She'd hinted that Lilly was involved with Ben Harper and now felt dreadful about it.

'Hello,' Lilly spoke to her, smiling. 'Do you like flowers? I often see you looking in our window.'

Winnie approached her. 'Is this your shop?'

'It belongs to my husband, Jeb, but I run it for him,' Lilly said. 'If you want to buy flowers but can't always spare the money, I sell them cheaply at this time of night. If the flowers might not last much longer, I let folk have them for next to nothing – it is better than seeing them waste in the shop.'

'You used to work in Harpers, didn't you?'

'Yes, I did.' Lilly smiled happily. 'I only left there quite recently because I waited for them to replace me – but now Jeb is free to do other jobs. He likes to earn money and works all hours; it's why I don't mind working late.'

Winnie nodded her head. She had recognised Lilly but there was no reason the other girl would remember her. They had only met once when Winnie had bought a single red rose from Harpers. She could see that Lilly enjoyed her life, so there was no need for guilt. 'Have you got any cheap flowers this evening?'

'Yes, I've got some violets,' Lilly said. 'Would you like them? You can have them for nothing. With luck, they will last another day or so, but no longer.'

'You are very kind...' Winnie followed her into the little shop. Buckets and vases of flowers filled every available space and the smell was wonderful. 'You won't earn much profit if you do this too often...' she remarked as Lilly handed her a bunch of violets.

'Flowers are to be enjoyed,' Lilly told her. 'I've sold most of them – and the last ones I'll take home to my mother. I'm going there now before I get tea ready. Jeb won't be in for another hour.'

'I'll buy some another day,' Winnie promised and they parted at the door.

Lilly was locking up as Winnie left the alley and walked on towards the Commercial Road, past Mulberry Lane, and the busy pub at the corner. A few men lingered outside the Pig &

Whistle, waiting for it to open. One of them called a greeting, but Winnie ignored him.

* * *

Stopping at a small corner shop, Winnie went in to buy an evening paper, which she placed in her basket, on top of the pie and chips she'd purchased a few minutes previously. The headlines were about the royal wedding of the Duke of York and the Lady Elizabeth Bowes-Lyon, which would take place later in April. Winnie smiled, because the pictures of the young woman smiling were happy and everyone one wished them well. She tucked it in her basket to read later.

She crossed the street, turned left and walked on through the busy streets until she reached the door of the hostel. The violets had a sweet smell and would brighten up her little room. Winnie felt tired and a little dispirited as she let herself in and switched on the light. Her job at Madame Pauline's was hard and unrewarding and, since the little bit of excitement, when they'd rushed that dress into the shops, rather boring. Each day was the same. Nothing out of the ordinary happened and she was beginning to despair that it ever would. She'd been there for four weeks now and it seemed longer.

She hadn't been up the stairs again, because each time she went for her toilet break one of the other girls followed her out and she did not dare to let them see her attempt it. With all the noise of the sewing room, it was impossible to hear if anything was going on above them, and Winnie knew that unless she could explore further, she would never discover anything.

The truth was that she was a little afraid of Mr Barrow. He'd looked at her once or twice and it had sent a shiver down her spine. He seemed to have all the women who worked for him cowed, even Betty and Mrs Jarvis in reception. That seemed a little strange to her, for why did they continue to work for him?

She frowned as she remembered the warning from her new acquaintance, Mr Sam Collins. If he'd heard things about her manager and told her to be careful that meant something bad might truly be going on behind the scenes and she wondered what it could be. Somehow, she must try to get to the top of the stairs and listen at the door that must be there. Were there really girls imprisoned up there? Or was it just a story Mary had heard?

Sighing, Winnie unwrapped the pie and chips she'd bought on the way home. It was never truly hot when she ate it, but she couldn't afford to eat in cafés and there were no cooking facilities in her room. The hostel had a canteen where she could buy a cup of tea, something on toast or a ham roll, but she didn't much like the food served there. She wished herself back at her old job, where a lunch had been provided. She did want to succeed in her first real mission for the Women's Movement, and to please Mary, but it wasn't a very enjoyable way to live. Winnie was aware of feeling lonely. She missed her job at the busy office of the Women's Movement, but she told herself she was doing important work for the cause by staying at Madame Pauline's. She must carry on until she either discovered something or Mary told her to leave.

Her thoughts turned back to the young man she'd met earlier. He'd had such a lovely smile, too, and seemed nice. Perhaps she would meet him again another day.

* * *

Sam called out as he opened the back door of his mother's house and went into the tiny dark hall. 'Are you there, Mum? I've come to wish you happy birthday...'

'I'm in the kitchen, love, and your sister is here,' his mother's voice replied. She sounded cheerful and that made Sam smile as he went into the warm room that smelled of baking and herbs. Her life had been hard since his father had died, when Susie was still at school, and Sam not much more than a toddler; she'd brought them up single-handedly and been a good mother – something neither he nor his sister ever forgot. 'Isn't this a lovely surprise, Sam?'

'Hello, Susie, good to see you,' Sam said, looking at his elder sister with affection. 'Managed to get the night off then...?'

'Lady Diane isn't going out this evening and she said I might have a few hours off to visit Mum – so here I am.'

'And she brought us a wonderful cake – and this shawl...' Mrs Collins showed it off proudly. It was a proper birthday cake with icing and marzipan and decorated with sugar flowers. 'Her ladyship sent the shawl, when she knew it was my birthday... Wasn't that kind of her?'

Sam nodded. The shawl was paisley and of a heavy silk, very expensive. It made his gift of flowers and fudge seem insignificant, but his mother received them with every sign of pleasure, inhaling the scent of the blooms.

'My favourite – and fudge too. I am so lucky.'

'We're lucky, Mum, and you deserve much more,' Sam said and kissed her cheek again.

'I bought Mum the cake,' Susie told him, an apology in her eyes. He knew she couldn't have afforded the shawl any more than he could, for though she was paid more than he earned, it would still cost too much. 'Lady Diane bought the shawl but didn't care for it. She never wore it – so she said I might have it and I thought it would keep Mum warm.'

'Yes, it will,' Sam agreed and it was kind of her. 'Well, Susie, how are you? I know you don't get much time off – but you enjoy your work, don't you?'

'It's the best job in the world,' Susie told him and rushed to give him a hug. 'She is so lovely to work for, Sam. She treats me like a friend, always has – everyone loves her, which makes it so strange—' She broke off and shook her head. 'It doesn't matter...'

'What's bothering you?' Sam asked as he took off his jacket and went to make up the fire. 'You may as well tell us – you know we don't blab.'

'Yes, I know,' Susie agreed. 'It happened some weeks ago – a dress of hers was somehow diverted and copied and into the shops within a day or so. It came from Worth, sent by special courier, and cost a small fortune.'

'She didn't blame you – you haven't been dismissed?' Mrs Collins asked anxiously. Both Susie and Sam contributed to her welfare and Sam could never have afforded to make up the difference.

'No, she knew I would never do such a thing. I was so angry. Why would anyone do that? I don't understand.'

'For money,' Sam told her. 'I bet it sold like hot cakes. Anything she wears is bound to appeal to lots of women who could never afford the real thing.'

'Yes, I know,' Susie agreed. 'There are firms that do it all the time; once it has been seen in public, an original design is bound to be copied – but how could they have got it so quickly? I'm almost certain it didn't happen once it got to his lordship's house.'

'It must have been copied in the workshop surely?' her mother said. 'What an unpleasant thing...'

'I don't know. They have tight security. I suspect it happened at the courier. Well, it doesn't matter now,' Susie said. 'We have more exciting things to think about.' She shook her head as her mother looked at her curiously. 'No, I can't tell you yet, Mum. I will next time perhaps...'

'I've just remembered.' Sam was frowning. 'I heard something a few weeks or so ago – about a special dress being copied at a workshop near me. I know the woman who oversees the girls and she comes into the shop to have her shoes repaired. She told me they'd been working flat out to get it into the shops before anyone else could – and she'd got a bonus. Pleased with herself she was.'

Susie stared at him. 'Can you find out more?' she asked. 'Will you ask her if it was a white silk dress?'

'I think it might make her clam up if I asked for details,' Sam said thoughtfully. 'I'll ask if she's had another bonus and see if she is inclined to chat, but if she thought I was curious, she wouldn't tell me anything. I do know she fears her manager, Mr Barrow. I believe him to be a nasty customer. One or two of the girls have left because they were scared.'

'Of what?' Susie asked. 'His temper – he can't harm them, surely?'

'One girl came in to collect a pair of shoes a couple of weeks after she'd quit. She was out of work and asked if she could pay me later and I asked why she'd left.' He frowned. 'She told me he'd got angry with her for asking questions and he'd taken her by the throat and threatened her. She left that night. Never went back for her wages and was finding it hard to get work without a reference from her last employer.'

'Poor girl,' Susie said. 'She ought to have gone to the police.'

'She was too scared. They wouldn't have helped her much anyway,' Sam remarked. 'She had no proof, so they couldn't do anything. Besides, how would that help her find work? I told her about a job at a pub I'd heard of. She came in a week later and paid me for the repair I'd done, happy as a lark with her new life.'

'That was good, Sam,' his mother gazed at him fondly. 'I'm glad neither of you needs to work at a place like that. I've heard of them, of course. They don't pay the girls properly and they fine them for the least little thing – and sometimes worse.'

'Yes, there are worse things,' Sam agreed, looking solemn, because he couldn't tell them the girl had since disappeared. He wasn't sure enough of his facts. She might have left her job at the pub and gone off, and yet she'd seemed to love it. 'And they're not fit for a lady's ears, so I shan't repeat them.'

'Don't,' his mother said. 'Let's have a nice piece of hot buttered toast and some cheese and enjoy ourselves – and that cake. There's trouble enough without us looking for more.'

Sam agreed, but something lingered at the back of his mind. He remembered the girl he'd spoken to outside the florist's. It wasn't the first time Sam had seen her, but he'd been too reserved to speak to her before, and then she'd spoken to him about the flowers. She seemed as nice as she was attractive and he was conscious of a niggle of worry about her. It was odd, because he didn't know her – but he wouldn't like to think of young Winnie in trouble at that place...

6

'They both look so happy, so suited to one another,' Lady Diane said when Susie took the tray of hot chocolate and buttered muffins into her bedroom the next morning. She lay down her newspaper; she had been reading of the wedding of the Duke of York and Elizabeth Bowes-Lyon, at which she and Lord Henry had been present. The Duchess had placed her wedding bouquet on the tomb of the Unknown Warrior. 'She is rather lovely, isn't she?'

'Oh yes, my lady. You told me it was a marvellous occasion – but rather tiring.'

'In my condition, yes,' Lady Diane agreed. 'We stayed only a little while at the reception, before Henry brought me home.'

'I remember you were very tired that evening,' Susie replied.

'Well, I have had time to rest now – and I feel very well.' She smiled.

'Tell me, did your mother have a pleasant birthday?'

'Oh yes, my lady, we had a happy evening. She loved that shawl you sent her and my brother brought her some of her favourite flowers and a bag of fudge. We all had supper together and a glass of port and lemonade.'

'That sounds nice,' Lady Diane said, slightly wistful. 'I hardly remember my parents now. My aunt never encouraged such intimacies...' A sigh escaped her and was banished in an instant. 'It will be different for my children! Lord Henry already has his heir, so he doesn't mind what I have, but I would like a daughter first and then a boy – that will do very nicely.' She patted herself with a look of contentment, for although the merest rounding of her normally flat tummy was just visible, she held her first child wrapped safely within her womb.

'It is so exciting,' Susie said, smiling at her happiness which radiated light like a beacon. 'His lordship must be delighted.'

'Oh, he is,' Lady Diane said and sipped her hot chocolate. 'This is delicious, Susie. Did you prepare it?'

'Yes, my lady. Cook was busy, so I took the liberty.'

'I knew you had; you do it so much better...' Lady Diane looked at her, gaze suddenly focused. 'What is it, Susie? You want to say something but aren't sure if you should.'

Susie hesitated. She hadn't wanted to spoil her ladyship's content by mentioning what she'd heard. 'I wasn't sure whether to say – but my brother heard something that might interest you, my lady.'

'Tell me, please.'

'He works around the corner from Dressmakers' Alley and there's an establishment called Madame Pauline's...'

Lady Diane sat forward, suddenly alert. 'This is about my dress, isn't it?'

'Well, it might be...' Susie told her what Sam had heard and she nodded. 'I asked him to discover what he could but...'

'Yes, go on. Don't think I've forgotten it, Susie. I put the annoyance out of my mind, because it does not do to dwell on these things, but I am still angry that it happened. Had I not worn that dress to the party that night, I might never have worn it at all.'

'I think they had seen the garment prior to its arrival and copied it,' Susie said. 'That was blatant theft of your original design, my lady.'

'Yes, I agree. What did your brother say to your request?'

'That he would ask the person in question when she next came to the shop, but she might clam up and not tell him anything. He was going to chat to her and see if she let anything slip.'

'Yes... perhaps we might investigate a little further...' Lady Diane's eyes sparkled with mischief. 'Shall we do a little snooping ourselves?'

'What do you mean?' Susie looked at her in surprise.

'We must think of an excuse to visit this place – if it makes clothes, then it must sell them. Does it have a showroom?'

Susie hesitated, then, 'I think it must,' she said. 'I could investigate that when I visit my mother next Sunday... but how would that help us to discover anything?'

'I don't know yet,' Lady Diane admitted, looking thoughtful. 'But we might pretend to have a clothes shop and be looking for a new supplier...'

'We? You'll never go there?' Susie frowned. 'It isn't a fit area for you, my lady. Lord Henry would not approve if I let you visit a place like that – and they might recognise you...'

'Not if I wore clothes that a working woman might wear.' Lady Diane gurgled with mirth as she warmed to her theme. 'You can dress up in something smart and I'll come as your assistant. We will say that we are opening a large store and want a regular supply of good-quality but inexpensive clothes. Then you can demand to see them being made and we'll get into the workrooms.'

'Oh, my lady...' Susie stared in astonishment. 'It's such a risk. If anything were to happen to you – and in your delicate condition—'

'Pfft! I am not in the least delicate at the moment,' Lady Diane laughed but looked determined. 'It will be fun and I shall enjoy tricking them – if they have cheated me, then they deserve it.'

'And if it wasn't them?'

'Then I shall give them a small order for something plain and sensible and give it to a charity – there must be plenty of women in need of a new dress.'

'How will you know?' Susie sought desperately for something to dissuade her mistress from what she thought a dangerous scheme. 'I doubt they will have kept a copy of your dress. It isn't one they will repeat.'

'I think we'll know if something unpleasant is going on,' Lady Diane replied. 'In any case, it will be amusing. It will give me something to do when Lord Henry is away. He is going down to the country for a few days. I had thought I might accompany him, but I shall make an excuse to stay here. It is merely estate business and not at all necessary that I should go.' Her eyes gleamed and it was clear she had made up her mind.

'Very well, my lady. I will investigate the establishment this Sunday.'

Susie could think of no way of changing her purpose for the moment, though she felt uneasy and half-wished she had not told her. If anything were to happen to her ladyship, she would feel responsible. However, she knew Lady Diane to be stubborn and, at times, headstrong. When she got a bee in her bonnet, there was no changing her.

Lady Diane, remembering an appointment to lunch with her husband at Claridge's, was suddenly in a hurry to dress and be off, since she wanted to shop first, and the subject was dropped – but not forgotten.

* * *

Why did one's people always disapprove of anything that hinted at a little spice or danger? Lady Diane was piqued but not annoyed with her personal maid. She understood Susie was protective of her and, also, extremely fond of her.

However, she had not brought Susie with her, nor had she told her where she was going that afternoon, despite her liking for the woman who took such good care of her. Lady Diane had had few people in her life to show her affection and loyalty and Susie had been more like, not a mother, for the age gap was not sufficient to be maternal – but a sister. It was necessary for a woman in her position to keep a certain formality, though she pushed the boundaries as far as possible. She would very much have liked to claim her as a friend, but Susie knew her place and could not be coerced into forgetting herself. She considered herself privileged to have her ladyship's confidence, but even though they often laughed together, there was a line beyond which she would not go.

At one time, Lady Diane had been very lonely. Susie and an old nurse – who now resided in Lord Henry's country house – had been the only ones she could turn to when her heart ached, as it often did in her teenage years. Nanny Ruth had held her as she had wept many a time, soothing her and telling her that it would all come right for her. With Susie, she had laughed at small triumphs over a tyrannical guardian, and she'd shared her joy at finding love with both her fierce protectors. Such happiness as she'd known with her husband of nearly two years now was more than she had ever expected.

Living in London as an adored and thoroughly spoiled wife, Lady Diane had blossomed, enjoying the round of social events: the weekends in the country, the shooting parties, the races and cricket matches, the balls, theatres, museums and shops and, of course, the wonderful royal occasions. However, she did now and then long for something more – which was extremely bad of her when she had been given so much. She felt herself to be idle and imagined that it was because she was yet childless. Now, at last, it seemed she was to be given the missing piece that would make her life complete – and yet... still she felt there was something. Something she yearned for, though she had no idea what it might be.

When, on rare occasions, she was forced to stay at home with no engagements, she often designed clothes for herself. She liked to turn on the wireless, on which the newly formed BBC had quite recently broadcast *The Magic Flute* from the Royal Opera House, and draw as she listened, though, as yet, the broadcasts were infrequent. Sometimes, if she was particularly pleased with something, she would take her designs to a fashion house and ask them to make it up for her. Nothing exceeded her pleasure than to see them finished. It was so exciting – almost like giving birth to a child, she thought, making herself laugh aloud.

'You may set me down in Oxford Street, Stevens,' she said, leaning forward to speak to her chauffeur.

'Oxford Street, my lady?' He sounded surprised at her destination.

'Yes, and I shall not need you again. I will have any packages sent to me and I'll take a cab for my lunch appointment.'

'Very well, my lady.' Surprised he might be, but he was Lord Henry's man and accustomed to obeying orders without question. He would have been most surprised if she'd addressed him by his first name, as she did Susie and her beloved Nanny.

Oxford Street was one of the locations that her dress had been seen in one of the windows, though it must have been all over London. Lady Diane thought there could be no harm in casting a curious eye at their rails to discover if any other recognisable gowns were on their rails. She paused outside the impressive shopfront, Harpers Emporium. While she had never shopped there herself, she knew of some wealthy women who did so, perhaps not for their best evening gowns, but certainly for tea-gowns and morning wear.

Entering, she was impressed by what she felt at once to be a welcoming atmosphere. The lighting was good and she liked the way the glass counters were arranged so informally. Yes, it was a pleasant shop.

The young man who politely asked what floor she wished to visit when she stepped into the lift was scarred, most likely from the war, but he smiled in a friendly manner and she felt he could only be an asset to the company. He opened the door for her at the first floor and directed her to the dress department.

Lady Diane liked the way it was set out, with three comfortable chairs for clients waiting to be served or when their companions were trying on clothes. However, a look through the rails revealed nothing she thought might help her quest for a sighting of her gown. She did see a smart navy-blue suit in the style that Chanel had made popular these past two years that she thought would fit Susie. She thought it would be perfect for the part of a well-off, middle-class woman, who intended to open her own business. Dressed in this suit, Susie could carry it off perfectly. Ordering it in her maid's size, she gave her address in Grosvenor Square. The package to be sent to Lady Diane Cooper. She smiled; her little plan was taking shape...

'I thought I had seen your picture,' the smiling assistant told her. 'You were wearing a beautiful dress. We had something similar here a few weeks ago – but it was inferior quality and Mrs Harper told me she would not buy from that firm again. She tried a single garment, but once she saw the dress for herself, she instructed Mr Marco to take it out of the window. "We don't sell that shoddy stuff here" – that's what she said, and very angry she was too.'

'Is Mrs Harper in the shop today?' Lady Diane enquired, thinking she would like to meet her.

'I don't think so, my lady. She usually visits the department first thing when she comes, but that isn't every day.'

Lady Diane thanked her and walked away. The assistant was friendly and had been very helpful, but there was no point in asking her questions she couldn't answer. It was possible she might contact Mrs Harper at home, if she could discover her phone number. Although if the mystery was solved too easily, it would be unnecessary to go through the little masquerade she'd planned – and she was looking forward to it. Her life had always been ordered and well-mannered and it amused her to do something slightly shocking. If her friends saw her dressed as a servant, they would think she had run mad – or was involved in a clandestine affair; if they recognised her, of course, and she thought they would not, if she purchased a fair wig to hide her glossy dark locks that could look slightly red when caught in a bright light. A little smile played about her perfect bow-shaped lips, a smile that those who knew her best would recognise instantly.

In Oxford Street, she hired a cab to take her to Dressmakers' Alley. She would simply drive past the establishment she sought. To go in would be to risk being recognised when they returned as potential buyers... Besides, she did not have time if she was not to keep her husband waiting at Claridge's.

7

Winnie took her shoes into the cobblers on her way to work. The soles had almost worn through and the heel had come away at one side. She'd been forced to wear a better pair of shoes that morning, but if anyone commented, she would say she'd got them cheap on the second-hand stall on the market.

Sam Collins was working away at his bench at the front of the shop, which smelled of leather and glue. He looked up, putting down the gentleman's boot he was repairing and smiled at her.

'Miss Brown, isn't it? What can I do for you today?'

'I wondered if these were beyond repair?' Winnie asked, offering the work shoes she hated but was forced to wear. 'I'm having to wear my best ones today and they are too good for every day.'

Sam glanced at her highly polished patent court shoes. 'Yes, they are,' he agreed, brow wrinkled as he examined her work shoes. 'I think these are hardly worth repairing – the uppers have split here, see...?' Hearing her little gasp of dismay, he said quickly, 'If you would wear them, I have a pair of shoes in your size – comfortable shoes that would make life easier for you working all day at that treadle machine. They belonged to a lady who died before she collected them, some two years back, and, as the repair was not paid, I suppose I am within my rights to dispose of them for the cost of the fee – which is five shillings.' He delved under the counter, hunted for a moment, and then brought up a pair of soft suede shoes with a rubber sole. 'They are nice and clean inside, for I put a new lining in...'

Winnie opened her purse and looked inside. 'I only have half-a-crown with me this morning, and a shilling for my supper. Will you trust me to pay the rest of the money at the end of the week, please?'

'Yes,' he said instantly. 'No rush. Bring it in when you are ready – a shilling at a time if you wish.'

'You are very kind,' Winnie told him and tried on the shoes. They fitted perfectly and were so comfortable. She looked at her own shoes. 'May I leave these with you and collect them this evening, please? I don't want to take them to work with me.'

Sam accepted her money and the shoes, putting them under the counter. 'They will be here for you when you come,' he said and smiled. 'How are you liking it at Madame Pauline's?'

Winnie hesitated, then, 'Not very much, if I speak the truth. It is little more than slave labour. We hardly get any breaks all day. They expect us to work flat out and if we take too long in the ladies' room or make a mistake, they fine us.'

'Why do you stay there?' Sam asked.

'Oh, I have no choice for the moment, but I shan't stay forever – only until—' She broke off with a sigh. 'It isn't a nice place to work, Mr Collins.'

'No, I've heard things before,' he said sympathetically. 'You haven't been threatened with violence?'

'No – but Mr Barrow was very angry with one of the girls

yesterday. I don't know why. She'd done something wrong and I think she cheeked him. He held his fist up to her but then thought better of it. She was given the push that evening – and that meant the rest of us had to work harder because they had a special order to get out.'

'Unfortunate for you and the girl,' he said. 'Do you know her name?'

'She is called Daisy and I liked talking to her when I got a chance,' Winnie sighed. 'Most of the girls aren't friendly; they are too busy to chat, but Daisy liked to gossip when we went to the ladies' room or after work.'

'You'll miss her then,' Sam suggested and she nodded.

'I'd best go or I'll be late. Thank you for your help, Mr Collins.'

'If you need anything else, I'm always here – seven-thirty in the morning until six in the evening, with a short break for lunch.'

'Thank you.' Winnie smiled gratefully. She did not know why she felt it comforting to have found a friend just around the corner from her workplace, but she did.

Betty greeted her with a sullen look as Winnie hung up her coat and went into the sewing room. 'You're late,' she said and looked pointedly at the clock. 'It is a quarter to eight. You were told to be here by half-past seven, because we're short-handed.'

'You didn't tell me,' Winnie protested.

Betty glared at her but said no more as she took her station.

Daisy's station was vacant so it was clear that they hadn't hired anyone else. If Mr Collins had heard bad things about this place, others had too and girls who had a choice would probably not wish to work here. Winnie couldn't wait to leave, but Mary wanted her to stay.

'It was never going to be handed to you on a plate, Winnie love,' she'd told her the previous evening, when she had complained it was a waste of her time. 'You know there is something up those stairs they don't want you to see – so you have to get up there and find out what is going on.'

'I almost got caught twice,' Winnie had frowned. 'I went up to the bend in the stairs a couple of times and I think I heard a scream...'

'A woman's scream?'

'Yes, but I wasn't sure and then I heard the door open and I ran back quickly.'

'You must try to be braver, Winnie, dear. If there are girls imprisoned up there you must find out. They won't harm you.'

'Mr Barrow might,' Winnie had replied. 'We never hear anything in the sewing room, it is too noisy, but Daisy may have heard something. I think she wanted to tell me, but she didn't get the chance.'

'He dismissed her?' Winnie had nodded. 'So if he dismissed her because he thought she'd discovered something, why are you nervous? If he sends you off, that will be the end of it for you. We'll have to find someone else willing to try.'

Winnie didn't think Mary quite understood how difficult it was to do anything but sit and sew garment after garment. If she took too long on her break, Yvonne frowned at her and she was fined by Betty, but unless she made more of an effort, Mary would be disappointed in her.

* * *

Later that morning, Winnie drank a little of the tea that Jenny brought her and then set it down, before asking Betty if she could take a break. Permission was grudgingly given and Winnie went out into the hall. She paused for a second outside the toilets, but no one followed, then she took a deep breath and ran up to the bend in the stairs and turned onto the small landing. A steep flight of stairs led up to a dark oak door at the top – a very solid door with a brass handle and a big lock.

Deciding it was now or never, Winnie ran to the top of the stairs and breathed deeply before trying the handle. It was locked, but she could hear sounds inside. Women talking and crying! She could hear someone crying inside the room!

Her fear forgotten all at once, she tugged at the handle and called out, 'Are you in trouble? Can I help you? Are you a prisoner in there?'

The voices stopped and it was suddenly quiet, then she heard what sounded like a struggle and something was knocked over. A voice called out, 'Help us, please—!' but it was cut off in an instant.

Winnie tugged at the handle again. 'Should I call the police? Who is keeping you prisoner?'

Silence again and then a different female voice, close to the door. 'Go away, please, whoever you are. If you cause trouble, he will kill us...'

'But why does he keep you here against your will?'

'Go away or he'll kill us and dispose of our bodies...'

'I'll get help – but not the police,' Winnie promised.

She heard another muffled cry for help, as if someone had put a hand over a girl's mouth, and then she turned and ran down the stairs. She went quickly into the toilets, leaning against the door to calm her thudding heart, and then, when she could breathe again, she washed her face with cold water at the cracked and stained basin.

Those girls were in fear of their lives! Mary had been right. But one of them had begged her to do nothing. She was obviously terrified of retribution if any attempt was made to rescue them.

Was Mr Barrow such a monster that he would kill those girls and dispose of the evidence rather than suffer the consequences of his evil actions? Winnie was incensed that he dared do such a terrible thing and she wanted to march up to him and accuse him of his crime, but that might cause the very tragedy she must avoid at all cost.

She paused for a moment to gather her thoughts. Now that she had discovered what Mary wanted to know, could she leave here and not return – or would that endanger all the girls?

She decided that she must finish out the day as normal. It would not do to arouse his suspicions.

* * *

As Winnie entered the sewing room, she was aware of several pairs of eyes watching her as she walked to her station. Betty was working at Daisy's table and, apart from a ferocious glance, said nothing until midday when more tea was brought round. She approached Winnie purposefully, her eyes glacial.

'What do you think you're here for?' she demanded. 'You were gone nearly ten minutes. Yvonne was twiddling her thumbs and threatening to leave unless I moved her. She could get a job almost anywhere and I don't want to lose her.'

'I was unwell,' Winnie lied easily. Her first panic had receded. 'I was sick twice and I had to wash my face. I think I might be going down with the influenza.'

Betty's frown deepened. 'I hope you haven't infected the rest of us,' she said, no sympathy whatsoever in her voice. 'Are you able to work or do you want to go home?'

Winnie swallowed hard. 'I think I might be sick again,' she said, holding a handkerchief to her mouth. 'Perhaps I should go...'

'And perhaps you should stay away,' Betty said unkindly. 'You've never been able to keep up with the rest of us. We'd do just as well without you.'

'Are you dismissing me?' Winnie managed to sound upset at the idea.

'Yes, and don't expect any wages for the week. You've forfeited them all for lateness and being absent without cause from your station.'

'You can't do that!' Winnie cried, stung by the unfairness. 'I'm owed fifteen bob at least—'

'Too bad,' Betty told her a gleam of triumph in her eyes. 'Ask Mr Barrow for it if you dare...'

'Where is he?' Winnie asked. 'In the cutting room?'

She jumped up and strode towards it, anger overriding her fear. Thrusting open the door, she went in. Her first impression was of bales of cloth stacked everywhere; the floor littered with scraps of material. The large room was occupied by two men, who were bent over the cutting table, engrossed in their work, and two others who stood talking.

'What do you think yer doin' comin' in 'ere without permission?' Mr Barrow demanded angrily as he saw her.

The man with him glanced at her and frowned, but the cutters didn't look up.

'I've been unfairly sacked without pay,' Winnie said, 'and I demand my fifteen bob that's owed me.'

'If you've been sacked by Betty yer must 'ave done somethin' to annoy her,' he muttered. 'You'd best clear orf before I raise me 'and ter yer.'

'No, I shan't.' Winnie stood her ground and glared at him. 'You are not the boss of this firm. I shall go to him and complain, and if he doesn't pay me, I'll go to the police.'

'You little slut!' Mr Barrow snarled at her, fists balling at his sides. 'Who says I'm not the boss? I'll teach you some manners.'

He raised his hand to strike her, but his arm was caught by the man he'd been talking to.

'No, Bert,' he said in a softer voice – a voice that could be taken for a gentleman's. He was dressed in a suit, too, his thinning hair slightly grey, his nose pinched above a hard mouth, and he was clearly older than Mr Barrow. 'He wouldn't like it if there was trouble...'

Winnie wasn't completely sure but believed she'd heard that voice before – on the stairs. He was Mr Barrow's brother, Cyril – but they were very different to look at and in the way they spoke.

'I thought he didn't know about this place?' Barrow grunted.

'It's in his portfolio, but he knows nothing of...' The other man lowered his voice, but Winnie could still hear. 'He doesn't know what goes on here yet – but yesterday he sent word that he wants a list of his properties and I've to take them to the house when he returns from his trip out of town. If there was a scandal, he'd want to know a lot more and then we'll both be in trouble...' He inserted his hand into his jacket pocket and took out a wallet. Extracting a pound note, he gave it to Winnie. 'Here, take it and go, girl.'

'You only owe me fifteen bob...'

'Keep the rest as compensation for any unpleasantness.'

'Are you the boss?' Winnie asked, stubbornness keeping her here, though her stomach caught with fear as Barrow's eyes narrowed.

The other man looked at her oddly. 'No, but I am here in his stead... take your money and go.'

He was lying. Winnie knew it immediately. He was the boss but didn't want it known – but who was the other man he was afraid might find out what was going on here?

Winnie decided that she had better leave as Betty entered the room. She thrust Winnie's coat at her, looking a bit scared. 'I'm sorry, Mr Barrow. She's defiant and not good at her work.'

Winnie gave her a look that spoke volumes, accepted her coat and left without another word. She had discovered some important things today and they'd dismissed her, so the girls upstairs wouldn't be harmed because she wasn't going to be there any longer. All she wanted now was to reach Mary's house and tell her all she knew.

The shoes she'd left at Mr Collins' shop were, for the moment, forgotten.

8

'What happened?' Mary asked as Winnie burst into her kitchen, her colour heightened and clearly excited. 'Home in the middle of the day?'

'Oh, Mary, you were right,' Winnie said, suddenly breathless. 'I'd begun to think they were just a bit crooked – copying that dress and fining girls for tiny faults out of a pittance of a wage, but it is more than that—'

'Come and sit down,' Mary invited. 'I was just making a cup of tea and there are some buns I baked earlier. You look as if you've been through a hedge backwards...'

Winnie put up a hand to her hair. 'It is all over the place, but I left my hat behind and it was windy. Mary! I heard a girl crying behind the door at the top of those stairs. I rattled the handle and it was locked. One of the girls cried out for help – but then another one stopped her. She came to the door and told me to go away, because if *he* suspected anything he would kill them...'

The colour left Mary's face. 'Winnie! She never did...? Oh, my Lord! I knew these things went on, for Constable Winston comes across it in his job, but when I sent you there, I thought it was just a case of forcing girls to work for low pay...'

'He wouldn't kill them just for that,' Winnie said. 'It must be something more...'

'It must be prostitution,' Mary said, shocked to the core. 'I should have guessed, but I didn't want to believe that sort of thing could happen now. In Victorian days or earlier, yes, but this is 1923. We have music on the wireless from the BBC; and we have moving pictures, cars, and electric light. Some women even have the vote. How could it go on these days? Girls forced to do that against their will... it doesn't bear thinking of!'

'I think there is a lot of bad stuff going on there,' Winnie said and explained how she'd been turned out without her money and how she'd stormed into the inner sanctum of the cutting room to discover Mr Barrow in conversation with another man. 'I recognised his voice. He was the one I overheard on the stairs that first time – the one I think diverted that dress to them to copy. His name is Cyril and I think he is Mr Barrow's half-brother, rather than full, because they are so different in appearance and manner. He told Mr Barrow to be careful because someone – I think it must be an important person – wanted to know about his properties and if there was a scandal it would go ill for them both.'

'You did that – after you discovered what was going on?' Mary looked at her with respect. 'I think I might have left immediately.'

'If I'd done that, something bad might have happened to those girls. As it was, I was dismissed and they won't suspect I know anything – unless one of the girls tells Mr Barrow.'

'They won't do that if they are in fear of their lives,' Mary said decisively. 'No, it worked out very fortunately for you, my love. You can move back to our hostel and take up your job in the office. You've done your part. Now it is over to my husband and his colleagues.'

Winnie hesitated. 'I said I would go to the police and the girl who told me to go away said that if there was trouble, he would kill them and dispose of their bodies.'

'Well, he won't know,' Mary said. 'The police had their suspicions before this, but with nothing to go on, it wasn't possible to do anything – but now they know they'll find something, they can apply for the warrant.'

'It would be terrible if it leaked out that they were planning a raid,' Winnie said. 'If those girls disappeared without trace…'

'Now, don't you go imagining things,' Mary told her. 'It won't happen. The police know how to plan these things, believe me.' She placed a cup of tea and a plate of rock buns in front of Winnie. 'I know you hated it there, but you've done well. You can go back to work in the office – until we have another assignment for you.'

'It will get into the papers, won't it?' Winnie said. 'The police will be pleased with the Movement for helping to expose this awful crime.'

'We shall make sure there is a big fuss about it,' Mary said. 'There are influential people who are on our side, Winnie. This is just one small part of what we do. People who believe we simply parade up and down and chain ourselves to railings know nothing of the secret lives we lead, exposing the illegal treatment of women wherever we find it.'

Winnie nodded. 'I had no idea of how much went on behind the scenes, all the lobbying, the letters to parliament, the persuasive arguments we make to bring the inequality of women's rights to the fore.'

Mary looked stern. 'Getting the vote will avail us little until we can make society understand that women should be given equal rights with men. Even now that a woman can divorce her husband, it is always *she* that bears the shame. Either she is a "flighty piece" or "cold and unfeeling", and her husband justified in casting her off. More often, it is impossible for a woman to get free of an unhappy marriage. Her husband fears being ridiculed and what she suffers in the bedroom is perfectly legal. Only if physical violence goes too far will the law intervene – and then it is probably too late, for the woman has died of her injuries. And sometimes the verbal abuse is even harder to bear.'

Winnie nodded. 'Even if there is no physical cruelty, the bullying, controlling, kind of man can make his wife's life a misery with his threats and his scorn and even the withholding of sufficient money. The women cannot escape a life of drudgery because they do not have the funds.'

'We all know of these cases,' Mary agreed. 'Too often, there is little we can do to help. They must try to leave the home before we can step in and find them a new one. Otherwise, we might be accused of coercion.'

'That isn't always easy,' Winnie said. 'My father wasn't a violent man – in fact, I loved him, but he drank too often and did not give my mother the money she needed to live decently. When he died, she received a small pension from his work and was better off than she'd ever been – but it made her bitter and...' She shook her head.

Mary gave her a look of understanding. 'I know you had a hard time and it has lit a fire in you, my girl. The man you marry must be a good, honest man, and you only need to look at my own dear husband to know there are some.'

'You are lucky, Mary,' Winnie said and smiled. 'Constable Winston *is* a good man. I'm not sure I shall ever marry. Why should I when I have the Movement to fight for? They have given me a home and a job.'

'Indeed – but do you not sometimes think you would like a home of your own and a family?'

'Not if it became a life of drudgery and misery,' Winnie said. 'It is not only in the poorest homes that women suffer, Mary. I know that some entirely respectable men treat their wives badly; they hold prominent positions and are not poor and yet they make their wives unhappy.'

'They are the worst – the ones I despise,' Mary told her. 'They hold up their heads and pretend to be so good and decent – and yet behind closed doors...' She shook her head. 'Only when women have equality and can live a proper happy life as their own mistress shall we see a change. When a woman can divorce a violent man and not be penalised and a court treats her fairly, then she may dare to seek justice.'

'Perhaps not even then, for how can she live if she has not been used to work?' Winnie replied. 'No, I do not think I shall marry. How could I ever trust any man enough?'

Mary smiled at her. 'One day you may fall in love, and then you will see it is quite easy.'

Winnie was about to refute it when she suddenly remembered her shoes. 'I will allow that some men are kind,' she said, and to change the subject, 'These buns are lovely, Mary. May I take one with me to eat later?'

'Why don't you come to supper with us? Constable Winston will want to hear everything for himself.'

* * *

'Well, I think that is what we've been waiting for,' Constable Winston told Winnie when she had recounted her story. 'I believe I can persuade my boss to raid that place now. You've done a good job – but you mustn't go back there to fetch your hat. It might be dangerous if they should suspect anything.'

'Will they all be arrested?' Mary asked him.

'This Mr Barrow certainly will be – and the other man if he happens to be there when we find the girls, but it would be difficult to bring a charge against that supervisor. She almost certainly knows, but she would plead ignorance and say she feared her manager.'

'Yes, she would,' Winnie agreed. 'I think she knows what is going on up there, but I can't be certain. Yet when the sewing room is silent, it must be possible to hear movement upstairs... I would be curious if I were her and she is the first in and the last out, so she must know.'

'I dare say she is paid to keep her mouth shut,' Constable Winston said, shaking his head in sorrow. 'It is a sad thing that money persuades many to look aside.'

'I don't think the man who owns the property knows anything illegal is going on. They didn't mention his name, but that he was taking an interest and intending to inspect his properties and that had made Mr Barrow's brother nervous.' She frowned. 'Do you think he is an agent or some such?'

'He could very well be.' Constable Winston looked at her thoughtfully. 'Sometimes, these very wealthy men own a great number of properties and know nothing of what goes on in them. They employ men to collect their rents and are ignorant – or uncaring – of what goes on. There are many such properties on the docks, a number used by unscrupulous rogues who use their employees badly, forcing them to work in terrible conditions. We are always being called out when there are accidents; someone has fallen from a roof because there was no safety measure to prevent it, a winch rope has frayed and a heavy object crushed a man beneath its load, and others are exposed to harmful substances that make them ill and likely to die long before their time.'

'There is so much injustice in the world,' Mary said, looking at her husband fondly. 'It is why my Bill is a constable. He wants to right all the wrongs, but it is an impossible job, isn't it, love?'

'It is that, Mary. A constant battle. Some of those tenement buildings in Poplar need to be pulled down and decent housing built. There are rats, cockroaches, and bad drains, to say nothing of the damp coming through the walls. Some of the landlords charge extortionate rents for houses that aren't fit to live in. We can't do a thing about it, unless it's in danger of falling down and then we ask the council to take a look. Even if they condemn it, folk find their way back inside. I suppose even a crumbling building is better than sleeping on the streets at night.'

'Do you think the landlords always know about the high rents and the terrible conditions?' Winnie asked. 'If there are unscrupulous agents, perhaps skimming the cream off the top for themselves...'

'That goes on, too,' Constable Winston agreed. 'It may very well be the case at Madame Pauline's for all we know – but if we find those girls, we'll get to the bottom of it. The bullies are mostly cowards once they know we've got them cornered.'

'I hope you do,' Winnie said, then, remembering, 'I left some shoes at the cobblers around the corner and I owe him two shillings and sixpence. I thought I might fetch them tomorrow – but perhaps I should stay away for the time being?'

'Might be best to go tomorrow,' Constable Winston said. 'It will take a day or two to get that warrant – stay away from the area after we raid, just in case.'

'In case they are still around, but won't they be in prison?' Mary asked.

'Providing we find the girls upstairs,' he replied grimly. 'It strikes me that if this brother of Mr Barrow's was feeling jumpy, because his employer knows nothing of their existence; they might decide to move them to a new location.'

'Oh no!' Winnie exclaimed. 'You don't mean murder them?'

'That would be a last resort, I imagine,' he said grimly. 'It's more likely they consider those girls to be a source of profit and will merely move them somewhere until the owner's inspection is over...'

'So they will get away with it?' Winnie stared at him in dismay.

'If I had my way, I'd raid them tonight,' he said, 'but I'm only one small cog in the machine of the law. If we're lucky, they won't do anything precipitate but...'

'How frustrating,' his wife said. 'And after Winnie risked so much to discover if there was any truth in the rumours.'

Constable Winston nodded. 'At least we have a chance and we'll do what we can – but it sounds as if we might be too late this time...'

Winnie found it hard to sleep that night. She'd been shocked by the cry for help and believed that rescue was at hand for those poor girls, but after what Constable Winston had suggested at supper, she wondered if she'd waited too long to pluck up her courage. If the girls were harmed or moved, she would blame herself.

Feeling restless the next morning, she walked to the cobblers and paid for her shoes. Not knowing why she should but perhaps because she liked him, Winnie told Mr Collins that she had been dismissed and would not be working in Dressmakers'

Alley in future. She saw a look of what might have been disappointment in his eyes and then he frowned.

'If you don't mind my asking, miss – did they pay you what they ought? Only I've heard some bad things about that place...'

She shook her head. 'It isn't a nice place to work,' Winnie replied. 'If you know someone thinking of it, I would advise against it.'

He inclined his head. 'I think there are some odd things go on there, miss – you are well out of it, I reckon.' He hesitated then, 'Perhaps I'll see you again when your shoes need repair?'

'Yes, perhaps...' Winnie hesitated, then, 'I work for the Women's Movement. My job here was just temporary. If you should see or hear anything you think suspicious, would you let me know? I could come every now and then, but it might be dangerous for me.'

He looked at her in silence for a moment and then smiled. 'I thought you were different, a cut above the girls that usually work there. I did wonder what an intelligent girl like you was doing in a place like that.'

'You won't tell anyone?'

'Of course not. My sister comes to some of your meetings. She doesn't approve of everything you do, but she thinks the women who endure prison for the sake of their cause are very brave. I do too...'

'Thank you.' Having gone thus far, Winnie was about to say more when the door opened and Betty entered. She was carrying a pair of shoes, but she frowned when she saw Winnie.

'What are you doin' 'ere?' she demanded.

'Just fetching my shoes,' Winnie said and departed.

She wondered if she had been indiscreet, but she believed she could trust Mr Collins not to say anything to Betty. He'd warned her more than once to take care and was clearly suspicious about the clothing factory. She wished now that she'd asked him what he'd heard and made up her mind that, despite the risk, she would visit his shop again when she had a free afternoon. If Constable Winston's raid was unsuccessful, they might have to begin all over again.

9

Betty was overseeing a new employee's work when Mrs Jarvis came through from reception. Betty was frowning. The new girl was nowhere near up to standard and it was getting harder to find decent seamstresses – even the one she'd sacked was better than this, she thought ruefully.

'Yes, Mrs Jarvis?' she asked, annoyed that she was hovering. 'We're behind with an order...'

'Mr Barrow stepped out a few minutes ago,' the receptionist told her. 'I have two women waiting. They say they may wish to order from us – but they want to look at our work... in here. The boss says she wants to make sure that the garments are properly finished. She says she is opening a shop in Oxford Street and could be a good customer. Do you want me to bring her through?'

'I don't know. I don't reckon Barrow would like it—' Betty began but stared with her mouth open as two women walked through from reception without waiting for an invitation. ''Ere, missus – you ain't allowed in 'ere,' she blustered belatedly.

'Whyever not?' The woman who was clearly the boss and

dressed in a very smart suit, almost certainly from one of the better-class shops, asked in a haughty tone. 'I always inspect the workshops of any firm I deal with. There is never any trouble – unless they have something to hide...' Her eyes swept the room. 'Do you have something you wish to conceal?' Her voice was like cut glass and she was clearly an educated and wealthy woman.

Betty quailed inwardly, knowing that she would be in trouble if Mr Barrow returned to find strangers in his workshop. While she dithered, unable to decide what to do, the other woman – obviously working class and not well-dressed – had wandered down the aisles looking at garments being sewn and had stopping to speak to some of the girls. For some reason, the girls had ceased working and looked up, smiling. Whoever the woman was, she seemed to have a way with her, Betty thought sullenly.

'Well, I believe your attitude tells me all I need to know,' the authoritative woman said, recalling Betty's attention to her. 'I had hoped we might give you a substantial order, but I think not. Good day, madam.'

'I don't even know your name,' Betty blustered as the woman swept out, followed by her assistant or maid, or whatever she was. 'What am I supposed to tell my boss?'

No answer came and Mrs Jarvis hurriedly followed them into reception. Betty followed her, but the women had already gone.

'What do you make of that?' Betty asked. 'They hardly looked at anything...'

'I think the other one – not the boss – picked something out of the scraps bin,' Mrs Jarvis said. She looked nervous. 'I think they were spies, Betty. They want to copy our designs. What shall we do? If Mr Barrow knows we let a competitor in, he will be so angry.'

'You reckon they were from another manufacturer?' Betty nodded. It was not unknown for one clothing firm to spy on another – and after the killing they'd made with that white dress, which had sold several hundred in a week, it might be that another firm wanted to see if they had anything else like it on the go. She firmed her mouth resolutely, 'We don't tell him, Mrs Jarvis. He'll likely sack you for letting them through. You're the one he'll blame...' Betty knew she would catch it, too, but if Mrs Jarvis thought she was in trouble, she'd keep her mouth shut.

'Oh, I shan't tell him,' she said with a little shudder. 'You know, Betty, I'd leave if I didn't think he might make it difficult... I thought he was all right when he asked me to come here, but...'

'We both know too much,' Betty agreed. 'One of these days I won't come back – when I've got enough money to get right away, but in the meantime, I just keep my head down.'

'I wish I'd never come here,' Mrs Jarvis said. 'But when my Dave died and I was left with nothing, Mr Barrow was kind to me. He said he needed someone like me to front this place for him – someone respectable. I thought it was a compliment. I didn't know then what was going on upstairs.'

Betty nodded. 'It wasn't like that for a start, Mrs Jarvis. It was just a sweatshop when I came, but this other business... I don't know where they got the idea, but I blame the other one. I reckon Mr Barrow's brother is behind all that stuff...'

'He seems such a gentleman, too,' Mrs Jarvis replied. 'You wouldn't think they were brothers. They don't look anything like each other, nor do they speak the same.'

'Half-brothers is the right of it,' Betty said. 'Different fathers. She came down in the world after her husband died, their mother – Mr Barrow was born out of wedlock so I've heard, and she died in the workhouse. I was told she had the pox...'

'Well, I never. I didn't know that, Betty.' Mrs Jarvis looked shocked.

'I'd best get back to work before they all start slacking,' Betty said. 'Mum's the word then – it never 'appened, right?'

'Oh yes, you can rely on me,' Mrs Jarvis agreed. 'I don't like this job – but I don't know what I'd do if I was turned out of my house... and Mr Barrow hinted it might happen if I let him down.'

Betty made a sound of disgust but went back to her work. There was a buzz of voices as she entered the room, but the next moment nothing but the whirr of two dozen sewing machines. She nodded her satisfaction; they were all there. None of them had slipped out while her back was turned. Betty was always strict on the amount of time she gave them for their comfort breaks. She lived in fear that one of them would venture up the stairs and discover what was going on on the top floor. She feared that if the police arrested Mr Barrow, they would arrest her too.

It wasn't her fault that he'd got greedy and decided the young destitute girls who had been housed and employed to do their fancy sewing could be used for other purposes. Betty thought the idea had come from his brother, but, when it came down to it, there wasn't much to choose between the pair – except that one of them spoke and dressed like a gentleman. Well, he'd been born in the country, educated and brought up by the family that had taken him in when his mother abandoned him, and he worked for a gentleman – a toff, so Betty understood.

Why should she pay for their crimes? She hadn't the courage to break away – she knew what Mr Barrow was capable of... and if he knew she'd guessed what had happened to that girl upstairs, she might find a watery grave waited for her, too.

* * *

'Oh, my lady!' Susie gasped with laughter as they relaxed in the back of the cab they'd picked up at the corner of Commercial Road. 'Her face was a picture! She was so indignant, I thought she would burst...'

'Yes, it was amusing,' Lady Diane said, taking off her wig and smoothing her own dark chestnut hair into place. 'I talked to one or two of the girls, you know – asked them if they were treated well and they all shook their heads or looked down.'

'What did you pick up just before you made the signal to leave?' Susie asked.

'I think we have our proof that they were the culprits,' Lady Diane said and took a scrap of white material with beading on it from her coat pocket. 'This exactly matches the decoration on that dress Madame Felicity showed me. It had been abandoned in the bin that they use for discarded scraps. Your brother was right, Susie; they did copy my dress.'

Susie took the scrap and examined it. 'I think it almost certainly proves that they made the dress – but I am not sure it would stand up in court, my lady. This decoration could have been pre-made – in which case, other manufacturers could buy it and use it.'

'It satisfies me,' Lady Diane said. 'I feel sure they were responsible – the fact that they were unwilling to grant us access, the atmosphere there; those girls were afraid of something. I believe we have found our culprits.'

'What will you do?'

'I am not sure we can do anything,' Lady Diane replied. 'I wanted to be sure who had copied the dress – and I shall certainly tell Lord Henry on his return from the country this afternoon, but I dare say nothing can be done about it.'

'Oh… that is a pity,' Susie said. 'I didn't like that woman – the one the receptionist called Betty. I think those people are not good people and I should like to think they might be punished.'

'If it were possible, yes.'

They relapsed into silence, both busy with their thoughts and it was not until later when they had reached the house, been admitted by a surprised-looking Molton, who had not seen them leave earlier that morning, and reached her ladyship's room that the conversation continued.

As Susie was helping Lady Diane off with her coat, she said suddenly and with some heat, 'The one I should like to see punished is whoever took my dress to that establishment. He or she was the one who let me down, for the manufacturers were bound to take advantage. Someone deliberately betrayed my trust and, as yet, we have no idea who that might be.'

'I'm not sure how that could be discovered,' Susie said thoughtfully. 'I do not think it was anyone in the house, my lady.'

'Nor I,' Lady Diane agreed. 'Indeed, I can only think of one possible solution. Madame Felicity assured me that her courier, who has worked with them for years, would never open a box meant for a client like me – that leaves Mr Sinclair.'

Silence followed this shocking statement.

Susie stared at her in amazement. 'Surely not – he is his lordship's man and has been for many years.'

'Yes…' Lady Diane hesitated. 'I would never share this with anyone else, Susie – but I have never liked or trusted that man.'

'My lady!' Susie was stunned, for her mistress had never said such a thing before. She was always gracious and generous when speaking of others, even certain haughty ladies of society that she did not particularly care to meet. 'I did not suspect… I know that Molton does not like him much, but on the rare occasions I have spoken with him, he has always been polite.'

'I dare say that there have not been more than half a dozen times,' Lady Diane remarked. 'When in the country, I have had cause to observe and to speak to him on many occasions and he is, as you say, always polite, but there is no warmth in his eyes. Have you not noticed they are cold – emotionless, one might say?'

'I had not noticed.' Susie was thoughtful. 'Would he risk taking your dress to that place? I believe Lord Henry would dismiss him if he knew.'

'Perhaps. He would be very angry. It is a betrayal of trust.' Lady Diane frowned. 'I suppose I ought to have made more fuss about it when I discovered what had happened, but Lord Henry has seemed a little distracted of late and I did not wish to bother him with what he must feel a trifling thing. However, I now believe that it was almost certainly Mr Sinclair who was at fault – and that is a different matter. Had it been a curious maid, simply wishing to look, I should have reprimanded her and forgotten it – but that dress was copied so quickly. If Mr Sinclair took it to that place, it was a deliberate act. Done for profit, I imagine. I do wonder whether Lord Henry is right to trust him with his business.'

'Oh, my lady...' Susie looked at her in dismay. 'If he could do that... he might do anything.'

'Yes, that is my thought,' Lady Diane replied, looking puzzled. 'I cannot understand why he was willing to take the risk of losing his job.'

She said no more, turning instead to what she intended to wear that evening.

Susie understood the implication of what had been left unsaid. If Mr Sinclair had done something that could risk his employment, was he guilty of far worse offences? Was he now in fear of being discovered of those wrongdoings?

A shiver ran down Susie's spine. It was an unpleasant thought that a trusted employee like Mr Sinclair might be capable of such betrayal – and yet perhaps Lady Diane had it wrong? Susie wished she thought so... but she had a horrid feeling that this was just the tip of the iceberg. Something much more important than the theft of a design was being hidden, of that she was suddenly very certain.

10

'Why tonight?' Bert Barrow demanded of his brother, when he arrived unexpectedly at the workshop just as Bert was about to lock up. 'Why do we have to move the girls tonight?'

'Because my boss is coming to inspect the damned place!' Cyril grunted his reply. 'They need to be gone and all their stuff.'

'I have arranged to meet someone at the greyhound racing this evening. I had a sure thing,' Bert grumbled.

'Gambling is a mug's game,' Cyril replied in a surly tone. 'Damn it, haven't you learned from what happened to me?'

'That was big money,' his brother said, 'and you gambled with the wrong people.' Cyril had got into a card game well above his league and found himself unable to pay. Pressed for the money he owed, he'd had to find ways to pay his debts, one of them being the girls above Madame Pauline's. 'I only have a pound on the races now and then – and I pay my dues.'

'Hell and damnation! Don't you think I've paid my debt in more ways than one – and you've benefited from our little side-line, so don't act high and mighty with me, Bert.'

'Only sayin',' Bert grumbled but in a low tone this time. Cyril had a violent temper when aroused. Bert wasn't afraid to stand up to him, but Cyril could be unpredictable, and Bert had his own reasons for wanting to keep things steady. 'It's about time we moved those girls anyway. Betty is jumpy – says more than one of the seamstresses are suspicious. They've heard crying and screaming when they go to the toilet.'

'Is it that red-haired one again? I thought I'd cured her of causing trouble.' Cyril frowned. 'I might have to teach her another lesson...'

'Like you did her older sister?' Bert remarked sarcastically and heard his brother swear beneath his breath. 'I'm not blamin' yer for what 'appened, Cyril, but it was me that had to clear up the mess.'

'She was a bitch and deserved what she got. Perhaps I should break the redhead's neck too – or yours?' He leered nastily at his brother.

'Don't bleedin' try it,' Bert growled. It was an empty threat – he was stronger than Cyril, and his brother knew it, but it annoyed him. Cyril should be more grateful for all he'd done to help him. Yes, he'd set Bert up in business and he'd directed the first clients to Madame Pauline's, but he kept a firm hand on the reins and took more than half the profits. Bert knew that he had quite a few schemes going on. He wasn't exactly sure what they were, because Cyril kept his business close to his chest – but he knew he worked for a toff and that he was skimming the cream from the business he handled for him. How was another matter – and who the toff was, was even more puzzling. Had Bert been able to fathom all his brother's secrets, he might have wangled more money out of him. Madame Pauline's earned him a living but not enough for him to retire in comfort one day, and he didn't hold with what went on upstairs, but kept his mouth shut rather than lose everything. 'We'd best get on with it then. Where are we taking them?'

'You just do as I tell you,' Cyril muttered. 'The less you know, the better – especially when he comes poking his nose in. He's coming back to London today, so you can expect him on Monday. And keep your mouth shut if you know what is good for you.'

Bert reckoned it was time to shut it and get on with it. He led the way upstairs and took out the large key, inserting it in the lock, but first he banged on the door. 'We're coming in – behave or you'll be sorry.'

As he opened the door, the stale smell of sweat and cheap perfume assailed him and he wrinkled his nose. Bert didn't use prostitutes himself. He had a nice little widow he visited whenever he felt in the mood for feminine company – but Cyril had a taste for them, as did the other men he often brought to visit. Bert wasn't sure, but he had an idea they needed stimulants that he thought of as perverted and there was a part of him that felt sorry for the girls he kept locked up for Cyril and his friends. He'd had to help Cyril out of a mess, after what he'd done, but he wouldn't be sorry to see it over and finished – as far as he was concerned anyway. Cyril would carry on as always but away from Bert's business.

One of the girls was tall and blonde, and very bold in her manner. She smiled coldly when she saw them, tapping her thigh with the whip she held in her right hand. Her name was Nell and she had been living on the street when Cyril had found her, near to starving. She was the only one allowed some freedom. There were two others at the moment: Nimah and Jinny. Nimah was red-haired and had a temper to match her fiery looks – but Jinny was young and delicate and she was the one who cried all the time.

Bert winced as he saw the state of her. She had a bruise on the side of her face the size of his fist. He wasn't above slapping the girls if they made him angry, but Jinny had been beaten – and she hadn't washed in days by the look of her. Her eyes as she stared at them were hopeless and Bert felt his stomach turn. He'd always thought of himself as a hard man – and he was in most ways, but what kind of a man took pleasure in beating a girl who looked as if she might snap if you blew hard enough?

'Put some clothes on,' he said brusquely, ashamed of his weak feelings. He couldn't afford to go soft or feel sorry for the girls. When Cyril had found him, he'd just got out of prison for stealing and no one would employ him. Yet his side of the story had never been heard, how he'd been sacked for no good reason, and had turned to petty crime to keep himself alive. Bert would have starved if his brother hadn't taken him on, set him up in business – but he hadn't known then that he would be asked to do all Cyril's dirty business.

'Why do you want us dressed?' Nimah asked, suddenly fearful. 'Are you going to kill us, too – like you did Jinny's sister?'

'We're taking you somewhere,' Bert said gruffly.

'Why?' Nimah persisted, looking stubborn.

'Shut up!' Nell snapped at her. She looked at Cyril. 'Where are you taking us?'

'To better accommodation,' he said. 'This was always temporary – you will be in a comfortable house near the river, much nicer.'

'Why?' Nell asked, eyes narrowing in suspicion. 'Why do you suddenly care how we feel?' She slapped the whip against the palm of her hand.

'I haven't got time to play games now,' Cyril said abruptly. 'Later – be a good girl, Nell, and see they behave themselves – or it will be the worse for you.'

'And if I do?' she said, a sly smile on her painted lips. 'What do I get for being a good girl?'

Cyril laughed. 'I prefer you to be a bad girl,' he replied, then, coldly, 'Do as I tell you and they won't get hurt – and maybe there will be something for you.'

Nell nodded. 'Come on, put some clothes on like he says,' Nell said and Nimah started to pull on a dress and a coat over it.

Jinny shivered and hugged herself, shaking her head.

'Come on, Jinny, there's a good girl,' Nell coaxed. 'You know what happened the last time you refused.'

Jinny gave a choking cry and suddenly rushed to the window, throwing up the heavy blind and beating at the glass with her fists as she screamed for help.

Bert swore and made a dash for her, dragging her away. He saw a man in the street looking up. 'You silly bitch,' he muttered, pinioning her arms. 'Cause trouble and I won't answer for what happens to you... Remember what happened to your sister...?' Bert said close to her ear. 'Be quiet and maybe I'll help you.'

Jinny went slack in his arms and he had to hold her to stop her falling.

'She's fainted,' he said. 'I'll carry her down. Give me that blanket to wrap round her and pack her things. You two – don't give us any trouble or you might not see Jinny again.'

With that threat, he started down the stairs, only to hear a crashing noise at the front door. Someone – probably the man he'd seen looking up at the window when Jinny threw up the blind – was trying to break down the door. Bert stood on the stairs listening. The door was solid. It wouldn't give to a man's shoulder. They would need a battering ram to break it down – the police could do it...

Cyril was on the stairs, with the girls just ahead of him. 'What are you waiting for?' he demanded.

'Someone saw Jinny at the window and the damned fool is trying to break the front door down.'

'We're going out the back way, so get going,' Cyril muttered. 'He'll likely go to the cops. Don't wait for the bleeders to arrive. I want to be away before they turn up.'

'What about me if they break in? They'll know what's been goin' on upstairs.'

'Get rid of their stuff quick,' Cyril said. 'If they check and discover who this property belongs to, they'll think he's had one too many... and if the cops do come, they won't find anything.'

Bert grunted. Jinny moaned faintly in his arms. He moved quickly down the stairs and through the hall into the sewing room and then the cutting room and then out of the back door. It led into another alley and a van was parked outside waiting.

A man jumped out of the driver's seat and unlocked the back door. Bert placed Jinny inside on the floor and saw that a figure already lay there covered by a blanket. He frowned as he realised it was probably another girl they'd either kidnapped or drugged – another victim of their selfish cruelty, unconscious for now. Bert said nothing as Cyril pushed the other two girls towards the opening, making them climb in. Nimah tried to run, but he grabbed her, slapped her, and thrust her inside. Nell just climbed in herself; she had nowhere to go anyway, except back to the streets.

Cyril turned to him. 'Get back inside and clean up – make sure nothing is left for the police to find if they come. If they find evidence, you'll be the one going down. They can't prove I had anything to do with your little sideline. I am a respectable man. With your background, they wouldn't believe I was your brother. We don't even have the same name...' Cyril laughed nastily and climbed into the front of the van, telling the driver to go. 'Don't drive fast,' he ordered. 'We don't want to attract attention.'

* * *

Bert stood watching as the van drove off, fury mounting inside him. The utter bastard! His gratitude was wearing thin and if Cyril thought he would keep his mouth shut, he could think again – and yet he knew that his brother had spoken the truth. No one would believe him.

He turned and went back into the building. If the police came, he would never be able to get rid of all the evidence in time. Like a bloomin' harem it was up there – beds and clothes and all kinds of things that made Bert shiver. Cyril and his friends were perverts, the lot of them! He wished to goodness he'd never met him. Yet the clothing business was a decent one and growing. If he lost it, he would be back on the streets again...

Bert unlocked the window at the back of the big room to let in some fresh air. Then he stripped the beds and bundled them together with all the girls' clothes into a large bin and carried it downstairs to the cutting room. The beds, chairs, sofas, and small tables had to remain. He couldn't clear them alone, nor did he have time.

When he heard the screech of brakes outside and then whistles, he knew it was the police and just managed to escape down the stairs and out into the back alley, walking away into the dark night. He could hear shouting and crashing and knew they would break the door down. They would know that someone had lived upstairs, but in the morning, he could spin a tale of girls who needed a home living there for a time – yes, that must be his story. He couldn't pretend no one had lived there – but the police would not find it easy to prove that girls had been kept there against their will.

* * *

The next morning, on her arrival, Betty stared at the smashed door in dismay. A police constable was standing outside and he put out an arm to stop her when she attempted to go inside.

'What happened?' she demanded. 'I work here. I've got orders to go out and girls coming into work...'

'My orders are that no one goes in until I'm told different.'

'Where is Mr Barrow?' Betty asked, a cold shiver at her nape. 'Does he know what has happened here?'

'That's what we'd like to know,' the police constable said. 'You're Mrs Betty Wright, the supervisor. We shall be asking you to step down to the station, madam.'

'Why?' she blustered. Her knees felt suddenly weak, but she knew she must try to bluff her way out of it. 'I ain't done nothin' wrong. I just work here.'

'You are often the first in and last out?' he questioned.

'Nah. Shows all you know,' she said boldly. 'Mr Barrow don't give his keys to no one.'

'You're here first this morning.'

'It ain't like him, that's all I can say.' She stared at him belligerently. 'Are yer goin' ter let me in then?'

'No, madam. I am not. We have a team in there going through the place and no one goes in until they say.' He eyed her coldly. 'You'd best go home or take yourself down to the station and ask to speak to Constable Winston – tell him your story.'

'Nothing to tell,' Betty retorted. 'Mr Barrow ain't goin' ter be pleased over lost orders – but it ain't my fault.' With that, she turned and stalked off, but when she gained the corner, she leaned against the wall, feeling her heart race. She saw Mrs Jarvis coming and went to stop her. 'You'll never guess what's 'appened,' she blurted out. 'The coppers 'ave only raided the place—'

'Oh, thank goodness,' Mrs Jarvis gasped. 'I hope those poor girls are safe now, Betty.' She suddenly turned pale. 'But shall we be arrested?'

'We stick together,' Betty said firmly. 'Neither of us knew a thing – and we was both afraid of Mr Barrow. The copper on the door told me to go down the station. I reckon we should have a cup of tea to calm our nerves and then go together. We'll get our story right and if we stick to it, they can't prove nothin'.'

11

'You are wanted in reception, Winnie,' Miss Rosalind Carlisle said, coming through to the back office. 'A young man...' She arched her fine brows, her laughing brown eyes hinting at a romance.

Winnie shook her head and hurried through to the small reception area. Her heart gave a little jump as she saw who was standing there. She'd guessed it must be him, but hadn't been sure; she hadn't expected him to seek her out here, even though she'd told him where she worked.

'Mr Collins. How are you? May I help you?'

'I have something to tell you, Miss Brown. If you would step outside – I thought we might go for a cup of tea?'

'Yes, why not?' Winnie didn't need a coat, because it was a warm day, but she returned to the office door, looked in and met Miss Carlisle's enquiring eyes. 'I am popping out for a moment, Rosalind.'

'Very well. I'll hold the fort – don't do anything wicked, will you?'

Winnie smiled. Rosalind often teased her about her secret

boyfriend, though there had been no evidence of a romance. She'd insisted there must be someone, and now she would give her no peace until she knew who Sam Collins was and why he'd come.

Winnie joined him and they went out, crossing the quiet street to a little restaurant opposite. 'It's nice in here,' he remarked as they found a table in the corner. The restaurant had only one customer, as it was a while before their busy lunchtime. 'I haven't been before, but it looked clean and quiet from outside, and I wanted to talk to you in private.'

'Have you discovered something?' Winnie asked.

'Well, yes, I think I might have,' Sam said. 'I mended some shoes for my sister, which she intended to pick up from my mother's house on her evening off – but I forgot to take them when I left yesterday evening.' He paused, then, 'I ate my supper with Mum and then went back to fetch the shoes. It was as I passed Madame Pauline's, on my way to the shop, that I saw a light in an upstairs window.'

'But those windows are blocked out by heavy blinds...'

'Yes, as a rule. They have very heavy blinds that would not show a light – but they had been thrown up and I saw a girl standing there...' He hesitated. 'She was wearing very little and beating her fists on the glass, clearly in some distress. I watched for a moment and was about to investigate further when she was dragged away from the window and the blinds pulled down.'

'Oh, the poor girl!' Winnie cried but said no more as the waitress approached and took their order for a pot of tea for two and departed. 'What did you do then?'

'I went to the door and tried it, but it was locked. Then I attempted to break it down with my shoulder, but it was useless.' He took a deep breath, rubbing his shoulder ruefully. 'I could do nothing without help – so I ran to the nearest police station and told them what I'd seen. As soon as I told them where it was, they told me they would investigate immediately...'

'And did they?' Winnie asked.

'I don't know... they told me to go home and leave it to them...' He looked apologetic. 'I returned to my shop, but Madame Pauline's was in darkness as I passed it. I have been fretting over it ever since, wondering if the girl was all right – and that's why I came to see you.' His expression was anxious, uncertain.

'Do you feel as if you let that girl down?' Winnie asked and he nodded, a shamed expression in his eyes. 'You must not! It is the law that should be blamed. I told them several days ago that girls were being held there against their will – had they acted on my evidence, they might have helped them before now.'

He looked at her but showed no surprise. 'I suspected you had discovered something. It is why I came to you – because I saw, when I passed it this morning, that the front door of Madame Pauline's had been smashed open. I supposed that it must have been the police. I am almost sure of it for a constable stood outside.'

'I do hope it was,' Winnie said fervently. 'I shall ask some friends of mine – they helped me when I had nowhere to go. He is a policeman and she is a member of the Movement.'

Sam nodded, his eyes never leaving her face. 'I knew there was something special about you from the very first, Miss Brown. You must be very brave to work at that place when you knew something wicked was going on.'

'It was suspected but they needed proof,' Winnie told him, enjoying the admiration in his look. She'd been feeling a bit deflated as nothing had happened after she'd delivered her information, but she now felt vindicated. 'I discovered that at least one girl was being held against her will in the room at the top of the stairs. I gave my friend the information he needed and he promised to get a warrant to raid it – but there were complications...' She bit her lip. 'I don't know all of it, but I understand the property belongs to an important person and he is a friend of the chief constable. They wanted to contact him but he was thought to be at his country home...'

'That is ridiculous!' Sam cried, making the waitress startle as she brought them their tea. 'Sorry, miss, not you...' he apologised and she looked relieved as she put down the tray and went off. 'It was wrong of them to delay for that reason...' he said in a low voice. 'Surely, girls' safety is more important.'

Winnie nodded. 'That is what Mary and I both said, but Constable Winston said my information wasn't enough for him to take it above his chief's head. Indeed, how could he?'

'It is that kind of thing that makes me furious,' Sam replied. 'Yet I think they acted last night after my visit...'

'I wonder if they were in time,' Winnie mused thoughtfully. 'I thought they might move the girls, but if they were still there last night...'

'Can you ask your friend? Will he tell you?'

'I shall certainly ask him this evening,' Winnie said. 'I dare say he will tell me – as much as he can anyway.'

'Will you let me know?' Sam asked. 'I've spoken to a few shopkeepers in the lane, but no one knows anything other than there was a disturbance last night, and Madame Pauline's is closed this morning. No one was allowed in, so the constable said, but I could not tell if it was a raid that caused the damage or someone else had broken down the door.'

'It sounds as if they acted on your information.' Winnie agreed. 'I am glad the police took more notice of you than they did of me.'

'I am glad you had left that place,' Sam spoke softly. 'I wonder what will happen to the girls who work there now?'

Winnie frowned. 'I am glad that the police visited them – but it must be hard for the girls if they have lost their jobs. I do not see how the business could continue if the police found something illegal going on, can you?'

'No, I can't,' he replied. 'Yet, it was not a good place to work, was it?'

'Not at all,' Winnie agreed. 'I was glad to leave, but the others might not feel the same. Why else would they continue to work for that firm if they did not desperately need their jobs?'

* * *

Winnie could hardly wait for the day to finish so that she could hurry round to her friends' house and ask Mary and Constable Winston what had happened.

Mary was setting the table and she smiled as Winnie entered the back door.

'I thought you would come as soon as you heard that the police had raided Madame Pauline's workshop.'

'Mr Collins thought it was the police...' Winnie said and blushed as Mary's eyebrows lifted. 'He has the cobblers around the corner. We talked when I took my shoes there and it was Mr Collins who went to the station last night and reported a girl in distress there. He tried to break the door down but it would not budge, so he informed the police.'

'It's a pity he didn't do that first,' Mary grumbled, 'because they were aware they'd been rumbled and got the girls away before Constable Winston and his colleagues could get there.'

'I was afraid of that,' Winnie said. 'But it was the fault of the police for not acting on my information immediately.'

'That is what my Bill says.' Mary nodded her agreement. 'He is as angry as you are, Winnie. They found evidence that girls had been living there – but the man who runs it says they housed some seamstresses who had nowhere else to live for a time, but he swears they left to find work elsewhere.'

'Surely they know he is lying?'

'Well, of course they do. But proving it is another matter. Had they found girls there in distress they could have acted, but as it is...' She sighed and shook her head. 'Apparently Mr Barrow walked into the station and asked why his place had been raided, bold as brass. They questioned him for several hours, but his story remained the same.'

She was interrupted by the arrival of Constable Winston.

He looked at Winnie and shook his head. 'We've let them slip through our fingers again,' he said. 'After all you did – but the chief wouldn't act until he'd spoken to his lordship. Said he was a good man and there was no way he would allow that sort of thing to go on in one of his properties...'

'That isn't right. They should have acted immediately. The owner probably didn't even know...' Mary exclaimed and Constable Winston nodded.

'You are quite right. His lordship had returned from the country, and he was contacted by telephone; he gave permission immediately. He said he had reason to believe his agent had been acting illegally and was about to confront him. He also said he hoped proof would be found of the man's wrongdoing.'

'I told you – he said if his employer discovered what was going on he would be dismissed... the man on the stairs...' Winnie cried excitedly. 'When I confronted Mr Barrow in the cutting room, I saw him. He is Mr Barrow's brother, I think – but looks and sounds nothing like him. You would take him for a gentleman at first glance – or a gentleman's agent...'

Constable Winston looked at her sharply. 'You may be called upon to testify in court that you saw this man, Winnie. Can you describe him?'

'I think so – thinning brown hair with grey at the sides, a narrow face and wiry figure. That isn't much to go on – but I would recognise him if I saw him again. Have you arrested him?'

'Not yet,' Constable Winston replied. 'His lordship says he believes he has been defrauding him for a long time. He did not discover it until his eldest son asked if he could learn about the estate and properties his father owns. Apparently, the son is a brilliant mathematician and spotted the discrepancies immediately. That made his lordship suspicious and when he visited his country estate, he discovered several disturbing things had been going on there. He telephoned his agent and told him he would be inspecting all his properties in London on his return.'

'*I* told you that bit...' Winnie put in and then apologised as he frowned. 'Sorry. Please continue, sir.'

'There isn't much more to tell,' he said heavily. 'If Mr Sinclair returns to his job, his lordship will tell us and we'll have him followed. Our only hope of finding those girls alive is if this agent chappie doesn't suspect he's been rumbled.'

'He has a different name,' Winnie cried. 'Is it assumed or did he have a different father to Mr Barrow?'

'Our Mr Barrow was born in London. His mother may have been married previously, but we know nothing of her before she turned up in the East End and worked the streets. She called herself Ellen Barrow and she died of the— well, an unpleasant disease. Albert Barrow was fourteen when his mother died in the workhouse infirmary. He lived and worked on the streets and got into trouble several times, before he was sent to prison for ten years.' Constable Winston frowned. 'After he came out...

it seems that he went straight and opened a business. His name is on the rent book anyway...'

'Betty said he didn't own it,' Winnie told him. 'I asked her when I started there and she said he wasn't clever enough to get the orders.'

'A front man for his brother probably,' Constable Winston nodded his agreement. 'It explains how he was able to get hold of that dress they copied... it belonged to his employer's wife and he was entrusted to fetch it from the courier.'

'That was surely enough to get him dismissed if he was caught,' Mary said. 'It makes you wonder why he did it...'

'Mr Barrow said he was owed,' Winnie reminded her of the conversation she'd overheard. 'I wonder what service Mr Barrow did for his half-brother that warranted such a risk...'

'That is a good question,' Constable Winston said, looking at her. 'I doubt our Mr Sinclair does much for anyone other than himself – so why did he do it? It must have been something beyond the call of duty...'

No one replied instantly but there was a chill in the air and both Winnie and Mary shivered at the implication.

Then, Winnie thought of something, 'Daisy told me that one of the seamstresses had gone missing after she was dismissed. Mr Barrow refused to pay her, but the next day he gave Daisy her money to take round to her lodgings, but she wasn't there and she was still missing a week later. Her landlady was going to report it to the police...'

'That's right, she did,' Constable Winston said. 'We did have a small investigation but nothing was found – and she wasn't the girl that washed up near the Embankment either.'

'Two missing girls,' Mary said, looking distressed. 'And now the girls Winnie heard in the upstairs room of Madame Pauline's have gone missing, too.'

'Aye. It's our worry that they'll wash up in the river an' all, if this Sinclair gets scared that he's been rumbled.'

'Surely his lordship will dismiss him?' Mary looked at her husband for confirmation, but he shook his head.

'I've told you all I can,' he said. 'Probably more than I should. Both of you are sworn to secrecy, mind. If word got out of our suspicions... well, I'd be in trouble for a start and I hate to think of the fate of those poor girls.'

'Of course we shan't say a word,' Mary exclaimed.

Winnie's nod was momentarily delayed for she had meant to tell Mr Collins, but then she agreed. 'Of course I understand. Those girls may still be alive. We must do nothing that would put them at risk.'

Constable Winston smiled. 'We've done all we can for the moment, but don't think it ends there, because the chief won't let this rest now. His lordship was put out that he hadn't moved in sooner...'

12

'Of all the incompetent idiots,' Lord Henry exclaimed as he replaced the telephone receiver and turned to see his wife watching him, an anxious look in her eyes. 'Just some business, dearest. Nothing for you to worry your head over.'

'You are worried, though; you have been for a while,' Lady Diane said and moved towards him, hands outstretched. 'I knew there was something when you left town – but I thought it all settled when you returned?'

'Some part of it at least,' he assured her and sat down on the large comfortable sofa that stood under the bay windows in his study. 'Come, sit with me, and I'll explain as much as I can – if you wish to know?'

'Yes, I do, Henry,' she assured him and touched her gently rounded navel. 'Don't worry about this one, she is quite comfortable and won't be disturbed by anything you tell me.'

He laughed, delighted with her plain speaking, which was one of the things that had decided him to ask for her hand, when he'd wondered if he was not a little too old for the charming Lady Diane. It had taken him only a few days to know his own heart, but some weeks before he could reconcile his conscience to asking her to marry him despite the age gap.

'Matthew asked me a few months back if he could help to run the estate for me. He wanted to take over the accounts and I gave them to him gladly. I hardly had time to do more than glance at them, because of other commitments.'

'Yes, you told me you were pleased that he was showing an interest. He could have done anything – followed a career in politics or law...'

'He is an intelligent lad, but it turns out he is brilliant at mathematics. It didn't take him long to spot the discrepancies... to discover, in fact, that my agent has been cheating me for some years.'

'Mr Sinclair? Yes, I can quite believe it,' she replied, surprising him. 'I never liked him, Henry. Something in his manner – a hidden insolence beneath the charming smiles. Besides, I believe he was the one that sold my dress design to that awful firm—'

'Your dress design?' He arched his fine brow. 'Have you mentioned this before?'

'I may have said how annoying it was that someone had copied my dress within two days of my wearing it, but I did not worry you with it too much,' she replied. 'Then Susie heard something and we did a little investigating – and we believe Mr Sinclair showed someone my dress when he fetched it from the courier.'

'Was it a firm by the name of Madame Pauline's?' he enquired.

'Yes... How did you know? Did someone tell you what we did?' She gave a little giggle of mischief. 'We visited it when you were in the country, Henry. Susie pretended she was setting up a dress shop and I acted as her assistant. I found a scrap of material that seems to prove our suspicions about the dress were right... but that is hardly important compared to your news. What will you do about Mr Sinclair?'

He looked at her hesitantly. 'Would you be very shocked if I told you something unpleasant was going on at that place – far worse than the copying of an original gown?'

'No, for I could see the girls were scared and unhappy,' she replied. 'I felt so sorry for them, Henry. Why, they work under such conditions...' She sighed. 'I suppose they have no choice, but it ought to be different, do you not think so? I am sure they were paid a pittance and that cannot be right, do you not agree?'

'I most certainly do, my love,' he agreed instantly. 'Perhaps their distressing circumstances will be finished now, for the place is temporarily closed. That business ought to be shut down for good and its owner arrested, but the idiots have let him go...'

'Is there proof of wrongdoing?' she asked.

Lord Henry frowned, wondering how much to tell her, and then decided that the truth was best, however shocking. 'The police believed that girls were kept in an upstairs room and made to... to work against their will.'

She stared at him in horror, guessing what he would not say. 'Oh, Henry, you mean... those poor girls! Were slaves for the pleasure of men? That is terrible, but surely, they will arrest that man?'

'The girls had gone by the time the police raided and there wasn't enough proof. That is why I was angry when you saw me put down the phone... and the worst of it is that I feel responsible.'

'You?' She looked at him in bewilderment. 'What had you to do with it, Henry?'

'I own that piece of property, along with many others in

London,' he replied grimly. 'Some of them have been a part of the family portfolio since my grandfather's time. I was aware of East End properties, but they were just a part of the rents that came in. I did know more about this place though because I'd had cause to look at some of the deeds and it was amongst them. I was satisfied it was let to a business and that was it – but Chief Constable Heatherington also knew I owned the property. He refused to allow his men to raid without contacting me – and I was in the country. I have never installed the telephone at Westward Park because I prefer to be quiet in the country. However, I should perhaps do so now. Heatherington didn't like to bother me, believed there was plenty of time to discuss it when I returned. I told him he should have spoken to the local magistrate, for Sir Philip would have found me wherever I was.'

'Surely, he knew that you were ignorant of anything illegal?' she exclaimed.

'One would hope so,' he replied with an odd smile. 'However, I assured him that if anything was suspected I wanted it stopped – and then they received further information and acted, but—' He sighed heavily.

'Too late?'

'Yes. The girls had gone. The story was that they had housed some destitute girls for a while, giving them sewing work until they moved on – but a bin of used clothes and bed clothes was found hidden in a backroom downstairs. Heatherington says they are pretty sure what was going on – and their worry now is—'

'For the safety of those girls,' Lady Diane said and looked distressed.

'You must not upset yourself,' he cautioned. 'Perhaps I ought not to have told you but... I do not like to shut you out, dearest. Some would say I should protect you from anything so sordid, that women do not understand these things – but I do not believe you ignorant of the world and refuse to treat you like a child.'

'Oh, Henry, of course I understand, and please do not exclude me from your worries. What will you do now?'

'What would you have me do?' he asked. 'This man, Barrow, has a lease signed by Sinclair. As my business agent, he had the right to lease the property – if he has a silent partnership in the business that is against the principles I expect from my employees, and another reason I wish to be rid of him... when I can.'

'Surely you can dismiss him?' she asked.

He hesitated. 'He may be the only one who knows where those girls were taken – at least that is what Heatherington believes. I have agreed to give Sinclair a little time while they try to discover their whereabouts...'

'So you can't just throw this Mr Barrow out and take that workshop over then?' she questioned. 'Only... if you could, Henry, I should like to have it for my own...'

'You? What on earth are you talking about?' he demanded, startled. 'You couldn't run a business like that, my dearest. It takes time and dedication – and you are in no condition to have the worry of it.'

'Oh no, I did not mean to run it myself – but I should like to have my own design business. Naturally, I would have a manager to oversee it for me and the girls I employed to make the clothes...'

'Not to be thought of, my love,' her adoring husband took her hand and kissed it. 'You do have talent for designing, Diane, and I should not object to your indulging your whim in some way – but to run what in common parlance is a sweatshop! No, indeed.'

'Don't be a stuffed shirt, Henry,' Diane retorted, a little stung by his answer. 'It wouldn't be like that if it was mine to order as I wished. Do you imagine I would permit my employees to be treated so dreadfully?' There was a touch of asperity in her tone now.

'No, of course not.' He shook his head, smiled, and took her hand once more, playing with her fingers. 'I know it sounds very stuffy of me, my darling – but my grandfather would turn in his grave at the idea of such a thing. Your own family would not approve either.'

'I care nothing for my aunt's opinion, but would not wish to displease you, dearest,' she said and laughed. 'Well, it is something that would please me – but I shan't tease you over it for a while. Not until all this unpleasant business with Mr Sinclair is cleared up, for I know that must vex you sorely.'

'It does,' he agreed. 'Let's leave this wish of yours for the moment, my love. Let me see what I can think of that would amuse you without involving you in too much work. I know that you are younger than I and perhaps need something to fill your time when I am busy... but you will be a mother soon and may find you are no longer interested.'

'You may be right, Henry,' she agreed sunnily, but there was a look in her eyes that told him she would not forget. He did not know how long the idea had been simmering but he did know that she seldom mentioned something that was not important to her. She was an ideal wife, loving, as well as intelligent and beautiful, and he hated to disappoint her, but he found the idea of his wife in business disturbing; it went against everything he'd been taught to expect with his family name. Yet perhaps that was old-fashioned of him?

His doubts reared once more. Had he done right to marry her? She was much younger and perhaps bored by a husband who was set in his ways. Could women of her class run a business? Was the notion that they should be cherished and protected from anything that might harm them outdated?

His grandfather would have told his grandmother nothing of what had transpired with his rascally agent; he would have thought it beyond the reasoning of a woman, too shocking for her sensibilities. Henry's first wife would not have been interested. Yet he knew that women were far more active since the war, in politics and other things. Henry would not insult his wife by keeping things from her – but run her own dress designer business in the East End of London? Surely, it was just a whim that she would forget once her child was born?

* * *

Lady Diane lost no time in telling Susie that they had been perfectly right to suspect Mr Sinclair of being less than honest.

'Well, my lady, it is a shocking thing,' Susie replied after she had been told it all in confidence. 'You do surprise me – but I cannot imagine what his lordship must feel to be so let down. He trusted Mr Sinclair all those years.'

'It is certainly unpleasant. His deceit was cleverly done and might never have been discovered had Matthew not been such a genius at mathematics,' Lady Diane said. 'We have always known that Matthew was studious, but he picked out the discrepancies almost at once, it seems. It is why Henry had to return to the estate straight after the royal wedding. I wondered why he found it necessary, but all the tenants had to be consulted... it was truly shocking.'

'So what will his lordship do, my lady?'

'Once the police have had time to discover the whereabouts of those girls – dismiss him, of course. I am not sure whether he will bring charges against him. The idea of a scandal and court case is wholly repugnant and, if he is involved in this other business, may not be necessary, as the police will charge him with his crimes.'

'Indeed it is most unpleasant for his lordship. Mr Sinclair's behaviour is despicable – to betray his position like that is disgusting,' Susie said, a note of anger in her voice.

'I hope he will be made to pay,' Lady Diane said. 'You do understand that you cannot tell your brother of this, Susie. If word were to reach Mr Sinclair – he might cut and run, as they say, and those innocent girls could suffer. It would be quite shocking if anything we did caused them to come to harm.'

'Yes, of course, my lady. I quite see that we must carry on as normal, if his lordship thinks that best.'

'Well, he must be the judge of it,' Lady Diane murmured. 'Though he is not right in all things...' Something flickered defiantly in her eyes and then she asked, 'What do you know of dressmaking, Susie – cutting out and making up garments? I know you are very good at mending and taking things in – or letting them out...' She laughed and looked at herself in the cheval mirror placed near her dressing-room door. 'I shall certainly need you to do so quite soon.'

'Dressmaking?' Susie was surprised at the abrupt turn of subject. 'I am quite good at it, my lady. Would you like me to make you something comfortable for your confinement?'

'Oh, as to that, I will decide later...' Lady Diane said. 'No, what I meant to ask, could you watch a person do those things and know whether they were competent?'

Susie was puzzled. 'I am not sure, my lady, what you mean exactly?'

'If I wanted to employ a seamstress or a cutter for instance – would you be able to judge if they knew their trade?'

'Yes, I believe so, but...?' Susie was bewildered. 'I still don't understand?'

'Neither do I, for it only occurred to me this morning,' Lady Diane replied with a naughty smile. 'It is just something I am considering, Susie. I will think about it some more and tell you another day.'

'What are you up to, my lady?' Susie looked at her askance. 'You can't be thinking what I suspect you are...'

'Oh, it is just a little whim,' Lady Diane replied with a casual air that was much studied and not to be believed. 'An idea I'd had for a while that was just a dream that I now think might be possible.'

'And does his lordship know of this whim, my lady?' Susie gave her a straight look.

'Yes...' Lady Diane responded with one of her irresistible smiles. 'At the moment he says no – but then, he has said no before when I suggested something, like when I wanted to learn to drive a motorcar, and has been known to change his mind...' She had her own little car, which she drove when they were in the country, though not in town. 'There is not much he would deny me.'

'Oh, my lady,' Susie said. 'Think what everyone would say...'

'As if I should care,' Lady Diane replied airily. 'Besides, they would never know. It would not be my name over the door naturally...' She gave a little giggle of pure mischief. 'I think I shall call it Miss Susie... now, isn't that a clever idea?'

Susie stared at her in shock. 'My lady...' she said but saw the dancing imps in her lady's eyes. '*When* you have his lordship's permission, I shall be pleased to help you all I can—'

'Spoilsport!' Lady Diane exclaimed but laughed. 'Now, what am I going to wear for Mrs Trefoir's evening party? Shall it be the peach silk or my pink...?'

13

'So it was you that reported seeing a girl in trouble,' Susie exclaimed as her brother finished telling her his story, when they met at their mother's home later that week. 'My lady heard some of it from his lordship, but she didn't know who went to the police. His lordship heard the story from his friend, Chief Constable Heatherington. They didn't find much when they raided, did they?' She was cautious not to reveal the more delicate details Lady Diane had told her, but the next moment wondered why she'd bothered, for he seemed to know more than she did.

'Winnie went to the police several days earlier, but they wouldn't act because they were waiting for some important person to return from the country. Apparently, he owned the property – though Winnie wasn't supposed to tell me that bit...'

'Who is Winnie?'

'I told you about her the other week when you came for supper – at least I thought I did. She worked at Madame Pauline's for a while, but she was really there as a spy for the Women's Movement. They had heard stories about girls being held prisoner, but they didn't guess the whole truth... then she heard a girl crying. She begged Winnie to help her.'

'Ah, yes, I remember you mentioning her, but I don't think you used her name then and you didn't mention she'd heard a girl crying.'

'Winnie didn't tell me that until recently. I've seen her a couple of times since your last visit.'

'Ah, I see...' Susie noticed a faint colour in his cheeks. 'Do you rather like Winnie, Sam?' She did so hope he had found a girl he liked at last! Both she and their mother had almost given up hope of it.

'She is a nice girl,' he replied. 'I was anxious for her when she worked at Madame Pauline's – because I'd heard whispers about something being not right there.'

'The girls had gone when the police raided,' Susie said. 'I don't suppose you've heard where they are?' He shook his head. 'It must be frustrating for the police to be so close to finding them and then discover they'd gone.'

Sam nodded, looking thoughtful. 'The place is still closed. Someone arranged for the door to be repaired, but it hasn't reopened. Several of the seamstresses have been into the shop this week. I've mended shoes for them and they can't pay, because they are owed wages and they don't know when they can return to work.'

'That is unfortunate for them,' Susie replied. 'Surely there are other manufacturers they could work for in the area?'

'I was speaking to one of the girls – she'd applied at three different firms this past week, but there were no vacancies. I suppose that is why they stayed there in the first place, despite the poor wages.'

Susie nodded. 'Do you let them take their shoes without paying?'

'Mostly,' he confirmed. 'I feel sorry for them, Susie. They didn't get paid much in the first place, but now they have nothing. Some of them will be on the streets before long if they can't find work.'

'Sam, don't say such things,' his mother reproved, having listened in silence until then.

'It is a horrible thing to say!' Susie exclaimed, but she knew her brother was right. There wasn't much choice for women if they had no husbands to keep them and were forced to work for their living; if they failed to find work, eventually they would either starve or be reduced to begging on the streets or, even worse, prostitution. 'Those girls who were kept on the top floor – how do you suppose they got there? Were they persuaded to go – or were they kidnapped?'

'I dare say some may have been willing to work in exchange for food, clothing and a place to sleep – but the girl who Winnie heard crying certainly wasn't happy.'

'Why didn't the police close the place down if she gave them evidence like that?' Susie asked and he shook his head.

'Not enough proof, so Winnie says,' he replied. 'They need to find the girls if they want to send the culprits down for a long time – but if you ask me, they don't have a hope of finding them alive.'

'Sam! Don't say such things,' his mother warned, looking upset.

Susie looked at him, shocked by the anger in his voice and then she inclined her head. 'He is right, Mum. The kind of men who would keep girls prisoner like that would kill them before they let them give evidence against them.'

'That is wicked,' her mother said.

'I hope they catch them and make them suffer,' Sam said fiercely. 'But I doubt they will. The police always seem one step behind the criminals; there's far more goes on in the underworld than either of you know or want to know...' He thought for a moment. 'I haven't seen Barrow since the raid. If I caught sight of him, I might have a go at getting something out of him myself...'

'And then he might kill those girls.'

Sam looked at Susie and frowned. 'He's a brute, but I don't think he is a killer. He might hit someone who stepped out of line – but I once saw him feed a stray dog in the street. I reckon whoever was behind it all is the dangerous one.'

'Just because he likes dogs doesn't make him a good man,' his mother commented.

Susie was tempted to tell Sam about his lordship's agent but she kept her silence and merely nodded. It gave her the shivers to think what that Mr Sinclair might be capable of and hoped he wouldn't come to the house ever again. To think that they'd all trusted him!

Bert cursed as he let himself into the empty building. It was dark and smelled musty after being shut up for more than two weeks. He needed to get it up and running again or he would lose his one chance of ever owning anything. Most of the money had gone into Cyril's pocket, damn him! Bert had done the work and taken the risks, and for what?

A shudder went through him as he remembered the hours of questioning he'd endured at the police station. He'd expected to be locked up for at least ten years, and the thought had scared him, but then they'd suddenly let him go. Bert had stuck to his story of having given some seamstresses a place to stay and, in the end, it seemed they'd accepted it. At least, he'd been given back his possessions and told he could leave.

What was he going to do now? Bert knew the cash he still had in his safe was barely enough to start up again. He hadn't been paid for the last two orders before the police raid and wasn't sure he would get the money now. Cyril had brought most of the orders in and been paid in cash, giving Bert his share and enough money to purchase materials and pay wages. He wasn't even sure who the last order had gone to. It would be in the order books – if he could find them after the mess the coppers had left behind them.

Looking around the sewing room, at tables overturned and bins lying on their sides, he cursed and started to pick up the pieces. Once he had it straight, he'd go looking for Betty and Mrs Jarvis, and persuade them to come back. Everyone had been questioned by the police and some would resent that. The seam-stresses would be glad enough of the work once he had the place open again, and he was fairly sure he could talk Betty and Mrs Jarvis round – but he wasn't so sure about the cutters. Joseph and Carl were skilled men and could find work anywhere.

Bert could cut garments himself if pushed to it; he'd worked for a tailor for a couple of years, before he'd got into trouble with the law. It wasn't ideal, but he would do it if he had to – but did he have enough money to carry on, and what about the orders? Gossip about the raid would have spread by now. Would the shops they'd sold to still want to buy from Madame Pauline's? Maybe, he'd have to change the name.

He wished Cyril had been in touch, but he'd heard nothing from him since the night of the raid. Was he keeping out of the way for fear of his boss getting wind of what he'd been up to? Bert cursed savagely. He wished he'd never met the man, but he'd believed his lucky day had come when Cyril had found him, claiming to be his half-brother and offering to set him up in business. Bert hadn't known then what a devil Cyril was – a man with perverted habits and a temper that had led him to kill when thwarted. Bert had thought himself a hard man, but he wasn't evil the way Cyril was; he hadn't killed a girl. It was Bert who'd had to clear up his brother's mess.

He wouldn't do it again, he decided. If Cyril came back and demanded he allow girls in the top floor for the pleasure of his brother and his friends, he'd say no. Bert was going to try to run this place straight this time. It was what he'd always wanted, a business of his own – if he could just get it going again...

Betty and Mrs Jarvis were the key. He would persuade them to return and then open his doors again. Maybe he wouldn't push the girls so much this time – he didn't need to work them so hard if he didn't have Cyril at his shoulder, telling him he had to get more orders out. Bert swore loudly as he fetched a brush and began to sweep the floor. Cyril had taken the cream off the top but that would not happen in future, because Bert was going to do this for himself. He'd gone along with his half-brother but now he would show him that he couldn't be pushed around. If he argued, when he came for the rent, he'd give him a fist in the face...

Yeah. Bert smiled, feeling better than he had in weeks. He'd had enough of being bullied by Cyril. It was time he asserted himself. He could get the orders – or Mrs Jarvis could. She had a way about her when she chose, which was why he'd asked her to sit in the reception and look after customers.

14

'He is here again,' Rosalind said as she entered the busy office and found Winnie filing reports at the tall cabinet. 'He seems nice. When are you going to marry him?' Her smile was teasing, but her words made Winnie's heart skip a beat.

'Don't be daft, Rosalind,' she said. 'I told you, Mr Collins is just a friend.'

'If you say so...' Rosalind's look showed that she didn't believe her, but Sam Collins *was* just a friend – and Winnie schooled herself not to blush as she went through into reception. She did like him but they hardly knew each other and Rosalind was just a tease.

'Mr Collins...' she greeted him with a smile. 'Have you got news for me?'

'Yes – not news that will please you,' he said, a look in his eyes that told her much. 'Do you have time for a cup of tea?'

'Yes, why not?' She nodded and went to fetch her light jacket as, despite the sunshine, there was a cool breeze, even though they were now well into June. She returned and they went out into the street and across to the café, moving towards the little table in the corner that they had used twice before now.

'I thought you would want to know that they've opened that place up again,' Sam told her when they'd taken their seats. 'He has a new sign over the door. It's still called Madame Pauline's, but there is a sign in the window that says, "Under New Management", but I've seen Mr Barrow going in and out and the same receptionist is sitting out front. I went in and asked her if they were offering work and she said they wanted seamstresses and a cutter.'

Winnie shook her head in dismay. 'So he has simply got away with it,' she said, anger beginning to build inside her. 'He ought to be in prison. Mrs Jarvis and Betty may be guilty of condoning what went on – but he is the one who should be punished.'

'There's another one behind it, I reckon,' Sam told her. 'I think he was responsible for what went on upstairs, but I've no idea who he was...'

Winnie bit her lip. She so wanted to tell him, but she'd given her promise that she wouldn't reveal the privileged information Constable Winston had given her. 'I think you are right,' she said carefully. 'Mr Barrow was a bully boy but... there was another man with him when I demanded my wages. He seemed to be in charge, a soft-spoken man you might take for a gentleman. I daresay he is the culprit.'

'I wonder if that is it...?' Sam mused, breaking off as the waitress came to take their order for a pot of tea. 'Can we have two of those iced buns as well, please, miss?' He smiled at her and she nodded, blushed slightly, and went off again. 'Do you think the police let Mr Barrow go in order to catch the other one?'

Winnie stared at him. She hadn't even hinted at it, but he'd worked it out for himself. 'I think that might be the case,' she agreed cautiously.

Sam nodded, looking eager. 'I'll bet that is what they are waiting for – a tip-off that he is sniffing around again. And he will if there is money involved, he will want his dues.'

'If it wasn't such a horrid place to work, I'd suggest sending another of our girls there...' Winnie said thoughtfully. 'They wouldn't have me or I'd volunteer.'

'Oh no, you mustn't run any risks,' Sam said quickly and then a flush ran up his neck into his cheeks. 'I beg your pardon – it's just that I... I couldn't be comfortable if I thought you were in danger.'

Winnie's eyes met his and then she was blushing, too, because his expression was so tender that she caught her breath. 'They wouldn't have me,' she said softly. 'I'm not sure I'd want to risk any girl's safety by sending them there – but we have lots of volunteers and we might organise a sort of spy team to watch the alley and see if he goes there...'

'How would the other girls know this man?' Sam asked her.

'Well, I could describe him – but we could keep notes and if the same man went in and out too many times, we'd know.'

'Does anyone have a Kodak box camera?' Sam asked. 'If the girls took a picture of anyone entering the premises and you looked at the photographs, you would recognise him, wouldn't you?'

'Oh yes, I am certain I would,' Winnie cried in delight just as the waitress brought their tea and buns. 'How lovely they look, so sugary and delicious.'

'I thought we'd have a little treat,' Sam told her. 'Do you have such a camera?'

'Not personally, but I know the Movement has more than one. We take pictures when we are demonstrating sometimes –

in case we are unjustly attacked or blamed for something we did not do.' She sighed. 'Before the war, our members were arrested all the time and the way they were treated was iniquitous.' The prison warders had been instructed to force-feed suffragettes if they protested by going on hunger strike. The process could be repeated more than once, which was why it was called *The Cat and Mouse* law, and was extremely cruel.

'Good, if you have a camera, then perhaps your idea would work. Your girls can walk past Madame Pauline's every half an hour or so and if they see a man entering or leaving, they just take a picture. Once you eliminate Mr Barrow, they will know to watch out for a different man.'

Winnie beamed at him. 'I will go with them for a start,' she said. 'I can do that, for why should I not visit the flower shop or the second-hand jewellers – or walk around the corner to the cobbler.'

'It may be best if sometimes there are two girls and some-times only one,' Sam suggested. 'But will the Movement give permission for their members to take part in such a scheme?'

'I will speak to Mary Winston,' Winnie said. 'If she thinks it is a good idea, I am sure the girls will love it. We all like to be out doing a worthwhile job – especially when the weather is so pleasant, and we are certain to spot him long before the winter.'

Sam looked at her and then reached out to touch her hand briefly. 'You will take the greatest care not to be noticed, Winnie? Don't make yourself conspicuous by hanging around too long.'

Winnie nodded, her heart beating so fast at the touch of his hand and the use of her first name that she hardly registered what he'd just said. 'Yes, of course... Sam,' she replied, and in that moment, she knew that they were going to be more than friends one day. 'Thank you for... for caring.'

'I do care, Winnie,' he said in a warm, deep voice filled with emotion. 'I've been wanting to ask – would you come to the theatre with me one evening? I thought you might enjoy an old-fashioned Music Hall night?'

'Oh yes,' she exclaimed in delight. 'I should like that very much. When shall we go?'

'On Saturday?' he asked. 'I close at lunchtime – so we might go to tea somewhere and then to the early-evening performance?'

'That will be lovely,' she said. 'I shall look forward to it.'

'So shall I,' he replied and smiled. 'Shall we eat our buns? They do look rather good.'

* * *

Mary looked at Winnie when she outlined her plan later that day. For a few moments, she was thoughtful, undecided, and then nodded her head in appreciation of the idea.

'I don't think Constable Winston would approve,' she said slowly. 'He might think we are interfering in police business – but it made me angry that you took so much risk and they waited too long. If your friend Mr Collins hadn't reported seeing a girl in distress, they wouldn't have moved in then – and now that firm is back up and running again. It isn't right.'

'When Sam... Mr Collins told me that Mr Barrow had opened up for business again, I felt cheated,' Winnie confessed. 'He should be in prison after what went on there. Mr Collins felt there was someone else behind the illegal stuff – and so I told him of the man in the cutting room. The one the police think is Mr Sinclair.'

'You didn't tell your friend who he was?'

'No, he had already guessed there must be someone else

involved. I mentioned no names, only that I'd seen another man in the cutting room and that he seemed to be in charge.'

'Yes, that is best,' Mary told her. 'We have to be careful, for there is as yet no proof that Mr Sinclair was involved in that nasty business upstairs at Madame Pauline's.'

'I know. That's why Sam thought of a camera. The Movement owns more than one Kodak box camera, doesn't it?'

'Yes, indeed we do, and very useful they have been when false accusations have been made against us. We are fortunate to have such things, Winnie. When I was a child the old tripod cameras were so difficult to use properly and you could never have concealed them – and that is what you and the girls must do. Whoever has the camera must carry it in a basket or a large bag. Be careful not to be seen taking pictures – and do so only when necessary.'

'Yes, of course,' Winnie replied. 'So may I ask some of the volunteers to help me keep watch at Madame Pauline's?'

'Are you sure you want to take part yourself?' Mary asked. 'If you were seen taking a picture, you might be in some danger. Having worked there, they might be more aware of you, Winnie.'

'But I shall be dressed differently and my hair was always dragged back for work...' She took a deep breath. 'I think I might have it cut in a new bob style.'

'Oh, Winnie! Your lovely hair,' Mary exclaimed, because it was thick and long, suiting her perfectly when she wore it in soft waves about her face and caught up at the back in a bun. 'Surely it isn't necessary to sacrifice your hair?'

'I've been thinking it might suit me,' Winnie replied. 'It is very fashionable to have shorter hair now.'

'I suppose it might suit you,' Mary said, looking at her. She touched her own abundant dark hair, which was rolled up in a large chignon at the back. 'My Bill likes my hair long – but it would be so much easier if it were shorter, I suppose.'

'It suits you the way you wear it, all combed back like that, but I think mine would look smarter in the new fashion.' Winnie blushed. 'Mr Collins mentioned over tea that he thought it was a nice look. He said that he admired the young women, like me, who were working for equality. I told him that we campaign for fairness, for the working man as well as women. They don't have all the rights they should either.' She raised her eyes to Mary's. 'We meet now and then – and he is taking me out this Saturday...'

'Well, I never,' Mary said softly. 'That is a change for the better, Winnie. I hoped you would find a nice young man, my dear, but I wasn't sure it would happen. So many young men were killed in that wretched war that I fear a generation of young women will not find love nor a husband. They do not always go together, of course – but I think they should... Do you love him, my dear?'

'I... I think I might,' Winnie told her shyly. 'I had a stupid crush on Mr Harper when I worked for his wife, as you know – but I feel this is different. Even when I was jealous of Mrs Harper, I knew in my heart it was wrong to envy her her husband, but I was silly and bitter – but that has all gone. You helped me to see how wrong it was and gave me hope, Mary. I've found a new life working with the Women's Movement. Now, I think there may be a chance for me to be truly happy.'

'I am so pleased for you,' Mary said. 'As you know, I am a firm believer in the right of all women to be independent if they choose, to work and live without fear of censure because they choose not to wed – but I wouldn't be without Constable Winston.' She smiled lovingly. 'He is a good man and he supports my ideals – not that we don't argue sometimes, for we do, but if the love is there, it doesn't matter.'

'Sam fought in the war,' Winnie said. 'He told me it is something he did because it was his duty, but he has banished the memories. It isn't something he wants to talk about.'

Mary nodded soberly. 'I don't think any of them do. And this young man is a cobbler you say, with his own little shop?'

'He isn't rich, Mary; it's just him working at his bench.' Winnie smiled. 'He lives in a flat over the top, but he helps to support his widowed mother – and his sister does, too.'

'And when did you learn all this?' Mary asked her, smiling.

'After we'd made our little plan, we went for a walk in the sunshine and just talked,' Winnie replied. 'He is nice, Mary. You will like him.'

'Then you must bring him to dinner one night,' Mary said.

'Yes, I shall, after we've been to the theatre on Saturday…'

Mary nodded thoughtfully, then, 'Have you given any thought to visiting your mother, my dear? I know you were unhappy at home and she didn't give you cause to love her – but perhaps you should just call and see one day, in case she needs anything?'

'My aunt looks in every now and then and helps her,' Winnie said awkwardly. 'I know I should, Mary – but she won't be pleased to see me.'

'Give her the chance,' Mary suggested. 'Just take a little gift – some cakes or fruit and ask how she is, my dear.'

'I will,' Winnie said and kissed her cheek. 'You saved me, Mary, so I'll do anything you ask – but she won't want to see me.'

15

'Sam told me that man has had the cheek to start up again,' Susie reported to Lady Diane after her afternoon off to visit her mother. 'Before I visited Mum, I took your best black leather shoes for Sam to mend, my lady. You find those so comfortable when out at the races with his lordship, and the sole was wearing a little thin. As I was passing Madame Pauline's, I saw a notice that said it was under new management, but Sam told me the same people are running it.'

'That is as Henry expected,' Lady Diane replied, not seeming in the least surprised. 'He said the police would allow it – Mr Barrow, as I believe he is named, is the bait to catch the big fish in all this.'

'The big fish?' Susie smiled at the sporting term. His lordship liked a bit of trout fishing when in the country.

'Yes – the man behind it. Mr Barrow is only a minnow, according to the police's theory. A bit of a bully and not totally innocent – but not the one they need to catch; he can be dealt with later.'

'Have they got men watching the clothing factory?' Susie enquired. 'Sam was most put out that he'd got away with it.'

'Only for the moment,' Lady Diane assured her. 'Someone will be watching, I am sure. The police are quite determined now, according to what the chief constable told Henry.'

'I hope they catch him – but it is those poor girls I am most concerned for. Do you think they are still alive?'

'Henry believes so and, also, I imagine, the police; it is their hope, at least. It is why Mr Sinclair has not been instantly dismissed.'

'How can his lordship tolerate that man now?' Susie asked. 'I am sure I could not bear to look at him.'

'Well, you must not show your dislike if you should meet him,' Lady Diane stated. 'I am told he may call here to see his lordship this afternoon. Henry will have to bite his tongue if he isn't to give the game away, but Molton has strict instructions to take him straight up – but if you should meet him, behave with politeness.'

'Yes, my lady. I shall do as you ask.' Susie knew that she would find it difficult to do so, should their paths cross. Yet as she was the only one of the household staff to have been made aware of Mr Sinclair's perfidy, it was her duty to behave as if nothing had happened.

'You must, for if he realises that his thievery has been discovered, he might suddenly disappear and all hope for those girls will be lost. Now, pay attention, Susie,' Lady Diane said, a sparkle in her eyes. 'I am going to meet some people this morning and I want you to accompany me. Please wear the suit I bought you...'

'My lady!' Susie exclaimed. 'What are you up to?'

'Patience, Susie. You will find out soon enough.' Lady Diane smiled mysteriously. 'It will be both interesting – and amusing.'

* * *

The visit was to a clothing factory. They were a respectable firm that made day dresses and outerwear for ladies, situated just off Clerkenwell, near to where the jewellers' workshops were clustered. On this occasion, the owners were expecting the visit and Lady Diane was welcomed into the smart reception; she and Susie were given a tour of the showrooms, cutting room and the sewing room, also the stockroom.

The contrast between their visit to Madame Pauline's was marked. Nothing could have been friendlier, and although the girls in the sewing room were equally as busy as those at Madame Pauline's, the atmosphere was entirely different. Everyone was smiling and happy, pleased with the interest they were being shown. Lady Diane asked lots of questions, of the seamstresses, the cutters, pattern makers and the reception staff. They were answered in full each time and invited to watch a model display some of their better dresses, after which they were offered tea and biscuits by the manager. This was refused, but they were thanked graciously by Lady Diane for the offer and their hospitality, and the owners invited them to return whenever they wished.

'We might do that,' Lady Diane said with one of her delightful smiles. 'It has been a revelation, Mr Dunstan. I am so grateful that you allowed us to visit your establishment.'

'Harpers Emporium is one of our very best customers,' he said, looking pleased. 'When Mrs Harper said that a friend of hers was interested in looking around the factory I was delighted to agree.'

'Yes, she was kind enough to arrange it for me when I asked her. Thank you so much for accepting her suggestion. It has been very helpful,' Lady Diane said and shook hands.

* * *

Lady Diane and Susie went out into the busy street and his lordship's chauffeur brought the car to the door for them.

Lady Diane thanked him as he opened the door for her and then went round to do the same for Susie. They settled into the back seat and she gave the order, 'We will go to the Savoy, Stirling. It is time for luncheon and I was not sure how long we should be so I told Molton we would be out.'

Susie looked at her as he nodded, returned to his seat and started the engine. 'Who is Mrs Harper?' she asked.

'Oh, didn't I tell you?' Lady Diane smiled. 'She is a new friend of mine. Her husband owns Harpers – the emporium in Oxford Street – the wrong end, actually, but never mind. It is quite a fashionable place these days and growing, in size and importance. I telephoned her about something and we got talking. She is an intelligent lady and we have some interests in common. I've visited her at the store and talked to her in her office a couple of times since. She told me about a charity she runs for men wounded in the war, some of them are still suffering, I fear. She asked if I would attend one of their meetings and I agreed – and then I asked her if she knew of a respectable dress manufacturer that I might visit, and she arranged it all for me.'

Susie eyed her with a hint of humour. 'And does his lordship know about this visit, my lady?'

'Not yet. It is hardly necessary for him to know all the details of my day,' she said airily and then gave a little giggle. 'Naturally, I shall tell him, because Stirling will anyway. It is research, Susie. If you want a man to respect your ideas, you must do your research. When I present his lordship with my business plan, he may not refuse it as a whim.' A look of satisfaction mixed with mischief touched her lips.

'My lady?' Susie was surprised. 'It sounds as if you are really set on this idea of yours?'

'Well, you know, the more I think about it, the more I like the idea,' Lady Diane said. 'Yes, if I wish, I can spend my whole life as the spoiled darling of a wealthy man, but I find too many hours are spent in idle chat with acquaintances – who are not truly friends. I love my husband and I look forward to becoming a mother – but why cannot I have more in my life?'

Susie nodded her understanding. Put that way, it was a very reasonable request. She knew well that her ladyship was bursting with energy and, though her life was filled with plea- surable outings, there were perhaps only so many times one could visit museums or attend card parties and take tea with acquaintances, without it becoming a little tedious.

'Do you need to have your own business?' she asked. 'Could you not design for another firm – like the one we visited this morning?'

'It is possible I might,' Lady Diane replied. 'Mrs Harper suggested something of the sort, when I told her I was exploring the idea of creating my own designs... She is a businesswoman, Susie. I read about her in one of the society columns. The way she kept that store going throughout the war was amazing.'

'I dare say, my lady – but she is not married to Lord Henry Cooper.' Susie sounded and looked doubtful.

'No, her husband is an American,' Lady Diane replied. 'It seems they don't have stuffy notions about wives working the way some English gentleman do.'

'My lady, you ought not...' Susie reproved.

'Oh, Lord Henry isn't one of them; he isn't stuffy at all, just slow to embrace change,' Lady Diane said confidently. 'You will see. Once he has accustomed himself to the idea, he will acknowledge that it makes perfect sense. It will be done discreetly, of course – but the idea that a lady cannot work is truly outdated, Susie. Women of all stations worked hard throughout the war; many ladies of good breeding became nurses and ambulance drivers, women of all classes did so many things they would not have dreamed of before – and my designs are worth seeing on the rails of the better shops, like Harpers,' she concluded defiantly.

'It is still trade, my lady,' Susie reminded her. 'I think your aunt would call it a disgrace.'

'Yes, she would. Indeed, I am counting on her to do so,' Lady Diane said with an impish smile. 'For the moment she forbids me to do anything of the sort, Henry will say that I shall. He cannot abide to remember the way I was treated before our marriage.' A little gurgle of laughter broke from her as Susie's eyebrows rose in disapproval. 'Yes, I know I am very bad, Susie, but I do think it is a splendid idea... don't you?'

'Perhaps,' Susie replied and then smiled. 'Yes, my lady. I do think it is very exciting – but only if his lordship approves.'

'Well, we shall see,' Lady Diane said and her hand rested lightly on her now noticeably rounded stomach. 'There is no hurry, after all. I should not wish to begin the business until after the birth, naturally. That gives me plenty of time to prepare a plan and work on a portfolio of designs.'

Susie nodded her approval. There were a few months to go until the child was born later that year. During that time, her ladyship would either come up with something brilliant that his lordship could not refuse or simply tire of the idea and forget it as she basked in the pleasures of new motherhood.

16

'We've got a rota all worked out,' Winnie told Sam when they met for afternoon tea, before going on to the first house of the Music Hall evening. 'All the girls were keen to help and so there won't be the same person watching more than once a fortnight. Except for me. I'm going to do the first one so that I can take a picture of Mr Barrow. Once we have him on file, everyone will be on the watch for a different man. We don't want to take lots of pictures of Mr Barrow and arouse suspicion.'

'You must take the greatest care,' Sam warned. 'I wish I could offer to help with the official rota, but I have to keep the shop open.'

He led the way inside the pretty teashop in the Haymarket. The tables were set with pristine white cloths and soft music was playing in the background. A waitress came up to them as soon as they sat down and they both decided on a tea, with cucumber sandwiches, scones, jam and cream. It was such a treat to come to a place like this!

'Oh, this is so nice,' Winnie murmured, looking about her with appreciation. Vases of flowers stood on tables at either end of the large room and she saw a square of shiny wood floor, giving a little gasp of surprise as one of the couples got up to dance a waltz. 'Look, Sam, they are dancing.'

'Yes – would you like to?' he asked. 'I'm not very good but I'll try...'

'Oh no, I've never been dancing, though I would love to – but I should trip over your toes.'

'I saw an advertisement for dancing classes,' Sam said. 'We could both go – learn together?'

'Oh, that would be lovely,' she exclaimed and blushed. He was suggesting that they would meet regularly and it made her heart beat a little faster. He was such a caring, gentle man and she was liking him more and more each time they met. 'We could come here again when we've learned a few dances...' she suggested and her blush deepened, but he was smiling and nodding.

'That sounds good to me,' he said. 'Ah, here comes our tea. Those scones look good.'

A stand with tiny sandwiches, fresh warm scones, two kinds of jam and a large pot of Cornish cream was placed neatly on their table and then another girl brought the tray of tea. Winnie poured their tea. She knew how Sam liked it now, with milk and one sugar. He'd told her that before the war he'd heaped sugar in his tea, but in the Army, he'd got used to a strong brew and no sugar.

They watched various couples get up and dance while they ate the delicious food and drank tea, talking about all kinds of things.

'Mum has been a widow for ten years now,' Sam told her. 'She and dad used to like dancing before the war. I think she doesn't get out as much as she should these days. She always says no when I offer to take her somewhere – she says I do enough for her as it is.'

'You are very fond of your mother,' Winnie observed. 'You don't live with her, though?'

'I did for a while when I came back from the Front,' Sam said. 'I was working for someone near where she lives – then I got my own shop and it had rooms over the top so it made sense to live there rather than walk a couple of miles there and back. I visit her as much as I can...'

'I haven't seen my mother for months,' Winnie confessed. 'We had an argument and parted on bad terms – but we didn't really get on for a long time before that.'

'Perhaps you should try visiting her one day,' Sam suggested. 'If you wished, I would go with you.'

'Perhaps,' Winnie sighed; it was what Mary thought she should do. 'I don't know yet. I'm not sure she would want to see me.'

'Well, my mother does,' Sam said and smiled at her. 'I told her that I'd met a girl I like and respect and she was so pleased. She asked me if you would come for tea tomorrow.'

'Oh... Yes, of course, I will. I should love to meet your family.'

'I'm not sure if my sister will be there. I think you and Susie will get on well. Did I tell you that she works for a titled lady?'

'No, I don't think so,' Winnie replied. 'You said she was a lady's maid – but you didn't say who for.'

'Lady Diane Cooper. She is married to Lord Henry Cooper – a very wealthy man – and she is the darling of society,' Sam said and Winnie's breath caught in a little gasp. 'What? Are you all right?'

'Yes. I've heard that name recently...' Winnie said. It was such a coincidence and she didn't know whether his sister knew anything about the scandal of Lord Henry's agent being a thief and perhaps involved with Madame Pauline's. Had Sam's sister told him? What would he think of Winnie for keeping that bit a secret?

Sam's gaze narrowed. 'Something has upset you,' he said, concerned. 'You know something that you don't want to tell me...'

'It isn't that I don't want to,' Winnie replied hastily. 'I was told in confidence and I gave my word I wouldn't tell anyone.'

'Then you must keep it,' he agreed instantly. 'I don't want you to break your word – but it's strange, Susie is keeping something back from me, too, and that isn't like her.' He frowned. 'Did you know that it was Lady Diane's own design that was copied at the factory?'

'Well, sort of, but only after we'd made it, when I saw a picture of her wearing a similar gown in the society columns,' she admitted it since he obviously knew about it.

Sam nodded his head. 'It's something to do with Lady Diane or her husband – the thing you can't tell me. Seems odd you both know something you can't share, but it doesn't matter, as long as it doesn't place you in danger.'

'Oh no, it doesn't do anything like that – it is to do with what went on at Madame Pauline's but...' She shook her head. 'I mustn't say anything more about it, Sam. I am sorry. I trust you but...'

'I shan't tease you,' he said. He glanced at his silver pocket watch. 'I'd best pay the bill or we shall miss the start of the show.'

Winnie got to her feet and followed as he went to the counter and paid for their tea. Sam was being polite, but probably felt that she ought to trust him with whatever she was keeping secret. It wasn't her secret, though. If his own sister hadn't told him that the property in Dressmakers' Alley belonged to Lord Henry Cooper, it wasn't for her to do so.

* * *

The slight tension between them wore off during the performance. Listening to the outrageous jokes of the master of ceremonies, joining in with popular old songs and laughing at the comedians, they both relaxed. When they left, they walked arm-in-arm back to Winnie's lodgings, where they said good-night at the door, back on good terms again.

'Thank you for a lovely evening. It was a real treat,' Winnie told him. 'What time shall I see you tomorrow?'

'I'll call for you at three, if that suits you?'

'Yes, thank you. I will be here waiting – and I'm sorry, Sam. I promise I'll never keep anything from you again, and I'll ask Mary if I can tell you.'

'You don't need to,' he replied. 'My only concern in any of this is to find those girls if we can – and to protect you.'

'I know...' Winnie looked up at him. 'Thank you.'

'You don't have to thank me for caring for you,' Sam said and bent his head to kiss her on the cheek.

Winnie didn't know how it happened, but she turned her head slightly and their lips touched briefly. She felt such a surge of warmth that she almost swayed into his arms and just managed to control the need to nestle against his chest.

'I always shall, Winnie, whatever life brings.'

Then he turned and walked away.

Winnie went into the building and ran up the stairs to the first landing and turned right towards her room. Inside, she leaned against the door and touched a finger to her lips. She had never been kissed by a man before, other than on the cheek by her father, and hadn't known what to expect, but the desire to feel his arms around her had been strong and she felt heat spreading through her. Had she been too forward? No, she was sure she hadn't.

She sat on the bed and then lay down fully dressed. Winnie was a little afraid to trust her own heart. Nothing so wonderful had ever happened to her in her whole life and she was scared it would all just slip through her fingers. Sam hadn't liked it that she'd kept a secret from him, even though he'd accepted it with a good grace. It would be too awful if he changed his mind about her, thinking her secretive and deceitful.

No, no, he wouldn't do that – and she would tell him everything about the operation they had planned to keep watch for Mr Barrow's brother... who might be Mr Sinclair and the agent to Lady Diane Cooper's husband.

* * *

On Sunday morning, Winnie popped round to the flower shop in Dressmakers' Alley. The shop wasn't open to customers, but as she'd hoped, Lilly was there, her door open as she cleaned her shop ready for the next day.

Winnie popped her head in and spoke her name and Lilly stopped sweeping and looked at her. 'Oh, you made me jump,' she said with a laugh. 'I haven't seen you for a while. You don't work at Madame Pauline's now, do you?'

'No, I don't,' Winnie said. 'I just dropped in hoping you might have a few flowers left I could buy.'

'Yes, there are some that are still fit to sell,' Lilly said. 'I usually come in on a Sunday, just for an hour to tidy up and sort out the dead flowers. We'll have lots of fresh tomorrow.'

'I am going to tea with a friend's mother and I want to take them as a little gift,' Winnie told her. 'If you have any that will last a few days?'

'I have these lilies,' Lilly said. 'They are still in tight bud but will come out by tomorrow if they are in a warm room. I keep the shop cold to preserve them for as long as possible.'

'Yes, one or two are just showing pink,' Winnie said. 'I'd like that bunch please.'

'I'll let you have them for a shilling – but you can owe it to me,' Lilly said. 'My mother would kill me if I did trade on a Sunday. She doesn't like me coming in at all, but I like to get things right here before I start to help her and cook Sunday dinner.'

Winnie laughed. 'I'll bring it tomorrow. I'm coming this way in the morning.'

She left the shop and started to walk home, pleased with her purchase. Sam's mother enjoyed flowers and she wanted her to like her.

As she walked past Madame Pauline's, curious to see the change of the sign over the door for herself, the door was flung open and Mr Barrow came storming out, followed by the man she had seen once before. It was obvious that they were having a furious argument and she heard them shouting at one another as she shrank back into a doorway, wishing that she'd brought her borrowed camera with her.

'I won't do it!' Mr Barrow yelled furiously. 'I've done with all that. I've told yer – so you can just clear orf and stay away from me in future.'

'Damn you for a fool!' the other man said, enraged. 'I'm warning you... You'll do as I ask or you will be sorry.' His voice was so threatening that Winnie shivered even though it was not directed at her – he was an evil man; she was certain of it.

They had turned the corner of the alley, and Winnie heard

no more words, though there was some shouting and the sounds of what might have been a fight. She stood as if turned to stone, shivering and shocked.

After a moment or two, she pulled herself together and then realised she had lost a perfect opportunity. She ought to have followed them, to see if she could discover where Mr Barrow's brother went. Running quickly in the direction they had taken, she turned the corner, but they had gone out of sight. Annoyed with herself for being taken off guard and failing at the first opportunity, she decided that next time she saw either one of them leave the building she would follow and see where they went.

Shaking her head over the missed opportunity, she went home to get ready for the afternoon's tea at Sam's mother's house. She wanted to look her best because first impressions were important and she did so hope that Mrs Collins would like her.

17

Curse him! Bert rubbed at his throat where the knife had pricked him and blood trickled. He hadn't seen it coming, but quick as a flash it was at his throat, the point just pricking his skin.

'You will do as I tell you or I'll kill you,' Cyril had threatened even as Bert had forced his arm back, showing him his strength, but Cyril was clever and quick. If he'd wanted to kill Bert, he'd probably had his chance, but he didn't want him dead – he wanted him to do his dirty work for him, again.

Another girl was dead. The red-haired one with the fiery temper. Cyril was demanding that Bert get rid of the body for him – but he'd refused. He'd gone on refusing after he'd wrestled the knife from his brother's hand.

'Do your own dirty work,' Bert had growled at him. 'Try that trick on me again and I'll break your neck.'

'You might be stronger but you're stupid,' Cyril had sneered. 'Don't think I can't have you killed because I can, just like that. I give the order; you're dead.' He'd snapped his fingers contemptuously.

'If you have men who will kill for you, let them get rid of the girl,' Bert had snarled back at him. 'I've told you, once was enough – I don't hold with blokes like you and I won't work for you again.'

'You want your business to continue?' Cyril had leaned closer, the knife in his hand flicking out and narrowly missing Bert's right eye. 'I put your name on the lease and I can take it off.'

'No, you can't. I checked,' Bert had stared him out, calling his bluff. 'I may have been down on my luck when you found me and you gave me a chance – but I paid you back times over. It's my business now and you can't make me do anything.'

'We'll see about that,' Cyril had hissed. 'Where my mother got you from, I'll never know, but it makes no difference. We're done. Watch your back, little brother. You may think you've won, but I gave you a chance – now you're on borrowed time.'

Cyril had walked off then, disappearing down an alley. Bert had taken a moment to get his breath before going into the nearest pub. He needed a drink to calm his nerves. It had taken guts to stand up to his brother – if he even was who he'd claimed to be. Bert had no proof they were half-brothers, just Cyril's word. He'd seemed to know all about Bert's life and the way the mother they shared had died, but how was he to know if one word of it was true? It could have been lies just to get him to do his dirty work.

Cyril would make a bad enemy; Bert had no doubts about that, but he was tired of jumping when he clicked his fingers. For a moment, he felt sick as he thought about the girl Cyril had wanted him to send to a watery grave. Let him do it himself or get one of his bully boys to do it, Bert had made up his mind. He wanted no more to do with him. Cyril's threats to have him killed would hang like a cloud over his head, but he would watch where he went and keep away from dark alleys after sunset.

A pint of bitter and a whisky chaser in front of him, Bert smirked to himself. He'd shown Cyril he was stronger than he was – and that was enough to boost his confidence. If his so-called brother had all these men ready to kill for him, why had he come to find him to get rid of the wretched girl?

Another two beers and he was chuckling to himself. He'd seen Cyril off and now he owned Madame Pauline's and it was all set to go with three new orders on the books. Life was beginning to look up. He congratulated himself as he downed another whisky.

Cyril scowled as he walked to his car and got in. He sat for a moment, his thoughts working fast and furious. It had been a test for the man he knew to be his brother – a man whose very existence was a stench in his nostrils. To think that that whore had sunk so low as to give birth to a fool like Barrow – he was as strong as an ox but dense, no brains to speak of, the son of a docker. If he thought he could take what belonged to Cyril and get away with it... But he would let him try for a while, let him think himself safe.

Cyril liked to make others suffer. He'd been a spiteful boy, so they'd told him at school when he kicked other boys in the ankle and pulled wings from trapped butterflies. He'd killed cats, too, after torturing them – nasty things cats, with claws and sharp teeth. He'd enjoyed killing the one that had scratched his face when he'd teased it.

Now, he enjoyed teasing or tormenting young women. He liked to see them on their knees, where they belonged. The red-haired one had particularly pleased him with her temper and her fighting, her tears made him smile; she'd scratched, too. His cheek was sore where she'd marked him – but she was dead now, the little vixen. One of Cyril's friends had accidentally killed her – or so he said. He was useful to Cyril, had opened doors for him in the past, and helped him to amass the fortune he was now steadily building for the day he retired. Cyril had been apprehensive when he started his illegal dealings, but it had been necessary to pay off his gambling debts. After that, the money had been too tempting for him to go back to merely being the agent of an important man.

He scowled as he thought of his most pressing problem. Cyril had promised his friend, who was a prominent business-man, that he would see to the disposal of the dead girl – what he'd meant was Barrow would, but the fool had turned pious on him and was refusing to carry out orders. He would pay for that when Cyril was ready.

There were others who would do it, for a price. He knew that every favour called in had to be paid for and had hoped he could still dominate his brother. He would ask Barrow again, give him another chance, but if he refused... When the time was right and he was ready, he would kill him, or Dirty Sid would do it for him.

A sneer touched his mouth, making him ugly. Next time Barrow would be bound hands and feet, and on his knees. He wouldn't get a chance to fight back.

18

Winnie popped into Lilly's shop and paid her the shilling she owed her. She was busy making a flower arrangement and didn't have time to chat long, though she asked if tea with her friend's mother had gone well and Winnie nodded.

'Mrs Collins was very nice to me,' she told Lilly happily. 'She approves of... of me, I think...' Winnie had almost mentioned the Women's Movement, because Sam's mother had been very interested, but she'd remembered in time that she was part of a secret investigation, and although she was sure Lilly could be trusted, it was best not to involve her so she just smiled and left the shop.

Walking on, her camera concealed under the jacket she carried over her arm, she saw the door of Madame Pauline's open and two men came out, but neither of them were of interest to her. She walked past and then paused to look in the window of a small grocer's on the corner, lingering for a few moments. When the man she believed was Mr Barrow's half-brother approached, she turned away. He walked past her, paused outside Madame Pauline's and then went in. In that moment, Winnie took a photograph side on. Fortunately, he didn't turn his head towards her and she felt a little thrill of pleasure that this time she'd managed to get the photo – but what next?

As she hesitated, Mr Sinclair – if that was his name – came out. He looked angry and stalked off down the alley and around the corner. She'd heard him quarrel with Mr Barrow the previous day – what could have brought him back so soon after their quarrel?

Winnie hesitated for a second and then ran after him. If she was going to discover anything, the best thing was surely to follow him and see where he went.

He walked briskly and Winnie followed at a slower pace, not wanting to catch him but needing to keep him in sight. After a few minutes walking, he stopped, glanced over his shoulder once and then got into a van that had an advertising slogan written across its sides. It read:

Stanley's fine cakes and bread

Winnie carefully moved her jacket back and took a picture of the van, though she wasn't close enough to get Mr Sinclair in the van.

The driver drew away from the kerb and was soon turning into another lane that led to the busy Commercial Road. Winnie frowned. Why had the van been parked all this way from Dress-makers' Alley? Surely, if Mr Sinclair wanted to visit his half-brother's establishment, he could have parked the van in the alley? It was hardly ever used by traffic, only the occasional delivery to the grocer's shop or one of the other small businesses.

Perhaps the clue was in the slogan written across the van? If he didn't want it to be seen or noticed – might it be that he wanted to keep somewhere secret – a bakery or a shop called Stanley's?

It was an idea that struck her as important and Winnie couldn't wait to tell Constable Winston. She had the photograph she needed of Mr Sinclair entering Madame Pauline's – and she had another of his van. It was all building into a tapestry that she could present to Mary's husband.

'What were you doing there, Winnie?' Constable Winston asked with a frown. 'You shouldn't take such risks, young lady. There's no need for it, we have it all under control.'

'You let them get away,' Winnie retorted and then flushed as he looked annoyed. 'I know it wasn't your fault – but I feel angry that those men got away with their crimes.'

'They haven't got away with it yet,' he told her sternly. 'You don't need to spy on Madame Pauline's. We're ahead of you there…'

'You mean you have someone watching that place?' Winnie said. 'I haven't seen anyone.'

'It's good that you haven't noticed our man,' he said and his smile was a little superior. 'If you didn't, then Sinclair won't have either.'

'You didn't tell us the police were keeping a watch,' Mary said indignantly.

'It isn't for you to know all that goes on down the station,' he replied. 'You must stop this, Winnie. If Sinclair sees you and puts two and two together, he might come after you.'

'I don't think he noticed me,' Winnie said. 'I let him get ahead of me – and I photographed the van he got into. Don't you want to know about that? I am sure it is a clue – it might be where the girls are hidden. Stanley's fine cakes and bread, that's what it said on the van.'

'Why do you think it might be a clue?' he asked with a frown.

'Because why would he have the van parked a long way from Dressmakers' Alley unless it was to hide it?'

Constable Winston looked at her for a moment and then nodded his agreement. 'That is a point. It may be for other reasons – but if he walked that distance to avoid it being seen in the alley, it might mean that he has the girls there. Yes, clever girl.' He frowned at Winnie. 'You are quite sure he didn't see you take those photographs?'

'I had my camera beneath my jacket, which was over my arm,' Winnie told him with a little smile of triumph.

'It remains to be seen if they have taken properly,' he said, but there was a slight nod of approval. 'I'll speak to the chief and we'll put a man on the bakery and see what transpires...'

'So you're not cross with Winnie after all,' Mary said and looked relieved. 'I'll take that film to be developed in the morning, Winnie. We'll see what you got.'

'No, I'll take the film to our man,' her husband said. 'If there is anything that may help when it comes to a court case, we want to make sure it doesn't go astray.'

Mary pouted, but then gave in. 'At least you're taking it seriously,' she said and he chuckled.

'Aye, I am that – Winnie has some bright ideas, but I want you to call off this little game of yours. It is too dangerous. I've told you before – we don't want you harmed, Winnie.'

'Very well.' Winnie sighed. 'I suppose if the police are watching, it is silly for us to be there, too.'

'Good girl. It is so easy for these villains to become suspicious and take flight. If he makes a run for it, we might never find those girls or him.'

'Will your chief listen to you this time?' Mary asked him.

He looked at her for a long moment. 'I reckon he must,' he said at last. 'He got a rocket from someone over what happened last time. In fact, I think I'll go and tell him now.'

'You haven't had your supper yet!' Mary cried.

'Some things are more important,' he told her. 'I might be late back, love. Eat your own supper and I'll have a sandwich when I can.'

* * *

Winnie saw the disappointment in the other girls' faces the next morning, when she told them they had been asked to cease their surveillance of the garment company.

'I don't see why we should do as they say,' Rosalind said with a militant glint in her eye. 'We are just as capable of being discreet as they are.'

'More so,' another of the girls agreed. 'It was all arranged.'

'I know – but I discovered something and...' Winnie shook her head. 'No, I can't tell you yet – but if nothing happens today, then we might go on with our little plan, even though I said we wouldn't.'

'Is something going to happen?' Rosalind asked, annoyance replaced by excitement.

'I am hoping it might already have happened,' Winnie told her. 'We will wait and see, but if it doesn't, then we'll go back to watching ourselves.'

The girls reluctantly agreed, but the normal business of the office seemed slow and boring, enlivened only by a young woman coming in to ask if they could help her find lodgings.

'I came up to London to be a nanny for a good family,' she told them. 'I had to give in my notice – he, her husband, just wouldn't leave me alone. Came into my room at night and tried...' A flush stained her cheeks. 'My father didn't want me to apply for the job. I was working in a factory at home and I thought it would be a better life here. I can't go home so soon or I'll never get away again.'

'We will help you to find work,' Rosalind told her. 'And you can stay at one of our recommended hostels. What can you do? I suppose you don't want to be a nanny again?'

'The girl gave a little shudder. He was horrid... I worked in a factory making corsets at home in Littleport... that's a village in Cambridgeshire.'

'So you are a seamstress...' Rosalind looked at Winnie. 'We do know of a place that is looking for seamstresses at the moment – don't we?'

'Well, yes, we do,' Winnie said. 'It isn't very much money – but you could help us, if you wanted to take it on for a while – and there's a room next to mine at the hostel. If you join us, you can have that for a shilling a week, but you pay for your food.'

'Oh yes, I'd like to do that,' the girl said, her plain face lighting up. 'I read all about the Movement in the papers, even though Dad says you're a daft lot. I think you are heroines.'

'Then I think you might just be able to help us while we help you,' Rosalind told her. 'So what did you say your name was again?'

'It's Sibby – Sibby Thomas,' she said. 'This sounds exciting – what do you want me to do?'

'Come through to the private office and have a cup of tea and a bun and we'll tell you,' Rosalind said and smiled at her. 'If they've banned us from patrolling Dressmakers' Alley, we'll do it another way, won't we, Winnie?'

Winnie stared at her doubtfully for a moment and then nodded. Sibby looked like a sensible girl, and not the kind to get in any trouble. She'd left her last job because of an amorous employer so she would be on her guard for anything untoward – and all she had to do was to tell them if she noticed anything strange happening upstairs at Madame Pauline's.

* * *

Mary was bursting with the news when Winnie arrived that evening. 'I couldn't wait to tell you,' she cried. 'It will be in the papers tomorrow – or some of it will.'

'Did they find those girls?' Winnie asked, her heart jumping as she saw the look in Mary's eyes.

'It's good news and bad,' Mary told her, some of her excitement fading. 'Yes, there were four girls at that bakery in an upstairs room. They have all been rescued and taken to a place of safety, where they will receive care and treatment – but they also found the body of another girl. Constable Winston said that one of the girls told him she'd been beaten for defiance and died of her injuries... but the other girls are too frightened to say anything.'

'Did they name the men that kept them prisoner?'

'Not yet – and unfortunately the main suspect was not there. Two men escaped when the police raided, but another was caught. He is in custody and, unless he gives evidence, he will be charged with murder of the red-haired girl.'

'Oh no! It might be the girl Sam saw struggling that night or one of the others.' Winnie felt sick. 'That poor girl! They killed her because of what happened that night... because she tried to get help.'

'We don't know that,' Mary said. 'Men like that – they kill

easily and for their own reasons. At least some girls have been rescued. We must be thankful for that.'

'Yes – but they will just go out and get more innocent girls,' Winnie objected. 'If he got away – the man behind it all – if there is still no evidence to arrest him...' She clenched her hands to stop herself shaking; her anger at the injustice of what had happened to those girls was so intense. 'He will do it again.'

'The police are looking for him, Winnie. Mr Sinclair was seen going into the bakery by the back entrance just before the raid, although he managed to get away, they can bring him in for questioning when they find him.'

'If they can find him,' Winnie replied, frustrated that yet again this man had escaped the law. 'If he knows the police suspect him, he will just disappear.'

'That is probably true,' Mary agreed. 'His employer has promised that if he goes to work, he will try to keep him there until the police arrive. His days are numbered, Winnie. We must believe that he will be caught quite soon.'

Winnie nodded, but she was burning with indignation that the man had slipped through the net once again. She'd been uncertain when Rosalind had suggested that Sibby should apply for work at Madame Pauline's, but now, she was glad. If Mr Sinclair was nervous, it was likely he might go to his brother for help, even though she'd witnessed a quarrel between them. She would warn Sibby what to look out for and if she saw something suspicious, they might follow him and find out where he was hiding...

Winnie would look elsewhere for help next time. Sam was ready and willing to help. Perhaps they could find some way to imprison the man – to stop him escaping before the police arrived. She didn't tell Mary because she would be sure to say they shouldn't do it – but if they simply reported their findings to the police, their quarry might slip away once more. No, she would talk to Sam about it.

Winnie hadn't liked keeping secrets from him and now she wouldn't. She would tell him how slow and useless the police were and ask him for help. Sam knew everyone in the lanes – good, honest young men like himself.

When Sam knew that another girl had been murdered, he would think the way Winnie did. She smiled grimly. Sam had that quiet confidence and strength of purpose, which made her feel he was a man she could trust. If the local lads were alert, someone would notice Mr Sinclair and, perhaps, he could be followed – or something. Winnie wasn't sure what she thought Sam could do, but she was disappointed in the police for failing yet again to apprehend that wicked man Sinclair, and she felt the need to do something herself to put it right.

19

'It is shocking,' Sam said, nodding his head in agreement as they sat in a corner of the small café near his shop and drank tea. 'That poor girl... I feared the worst the night I saw her banging against that window, if it was her – though I don't think she had red hair.' He looked upset. 'If I'd been able to break that door down, perhaps she would still be alive.'

Winnie reached for his hand across the table and held it. 'It wasn't your fault, Sam. The police should have acted sooner. I told them I thought he was trying to hide his van, which had the bakery slogan painted on its side from anyone who might see him going to Madame Pauline's – and they did raid the bakery, but he got away. If we knew where he was hiding, and we could somehow prevent him getting away... then the police could take him and they might actually do something.'

Sam nodded. 'I know a lot of men who would be up in arms about this – Joe Ross for one. He and his mates went after a predator who had been attacking local girls some months ago, and they gave him a thrashing. They didn't finish him off and he tried it on another girl, but she beat him off and—' He looked at Winnie, seeing her face fiery red. 'What have I said?'

'The girl who beat him off was me – and it was that incident that made me think about telling you about that poor girl, Sam,' she confirmed. 'I was told that monster had been punished by some local men a short time before he attacked me. I think he'd been hiding and drinking a lot – probably scared of getting caught again – and that made it easier for me to fight him. Then Constable Winston turned up and some more policemen and he was arrested. I was lucky to escape with a fright. That girl who was murdered wasn't so lucky. And now one of those girls who was kept prisoner above Madame Pauline's has been murdered, too. It makes me so angry. Women have the right to live their lives without fear of attack or being forced into things they don't want to do, Sam. Four other girls were being held in that bakery. If I hadn't followed that wicked man they might still be there in fear of their lives. I think if the police can't protect them, others should.'

'That was a terrible experience for you,' Sam said. 'I am so sorry that happened to you, Winnie.'

'Oh, it's over and forgotten,' she dismissed it with a smile for him. 'But these things shouldn't be allowed to happen, Sam.'

'The police can only do so much I suppose – but I agree that man must be stopped,' Sam said, looking grim. 'I'll speak to Joe and ask him if they'll help us to find Sinclair. If he collected rents in this area, it is possible some of them will know him.'

'If only I hadn't given that roll of film to the police, I could have had his photograph developed – but *I* did the right thing. They let us down once more...' Winnie said regretfully.

Sam nodded thoughtfully. 'Would you and your girls be prepared to keep watch again?'

'Yes. We would – and we have another girl on the inside... At least we shall have if they give Sibby a job.'

'I've heard they are desperate for workers,' Sam said grimly. 'Some of the girls wouldn't go back after what happened. If Sibby gives us the tip-off, I know Joe and his friends would help – they will be on the lookout, too, and a lot of them work in the lanes around Dressmakers' Alley... If he ventures into the area, one of us will see him.'

Winnie nodded and smiled. 'I should've told you everything before,' she said. 'I am sorry I didn't – will you forgive me?'

'Nothing to forgive,' he said and squeezed her fingers. 'I don't think you should feel uncomfortable about breaking your promise not to tell anyone, Winnie. When we help catch that rogue, you will be vindicated.'

Sam was thoughtful after he returned to work at his shop. Winnie had come to him for help; she was relying on him and that made him feel responsible. He made up his mind to seek out Joe Ross that very evening. The sooner the men of the lanes got together, the better. It wasn't right that men like that fellow Sinclair should be allowed to get away with mistreating young women. In his opinion, men should protect their women, not allow others to harm them. Now that he knew Winnie had been attacked by a man who had already raped more than one young woman, he understood her passionate need to help others. The very idea outraged Sam. What kind of a man did these things? In his opinion, they were not fit to live.

When Sam found his friend having at drink at the Pig & Whistle in Mulberry Lane later that evening, Joe listened to his story and his eyes kindled as the story unfolded.

'You should have come after me instead of the coppers that night,' Joe said fiercely. 'I can't stand buggers that hurt the lasses. I'd have stopped them. I knew of the back entrance to Madame Pauline's, because I used to deliver coal there.' He frowned. 'They stopped using me a year or so back... I asked them how business was when they blocked out the top windows; I thought they must have expanded.'

'And they cancelled their order after that?'

'Yeah – told me they'd changed to coke and had a better supplier.' Joe's expression was grim. 'Probably thought I was too nosy – makes sense if they were keeping girls prisoner up there...' He scowled. 'I'll help you turn the tables on him, Sam. We'll beat him senseless and lock him up tight in my coal store and see how he feels.'

'Be careful, though,' Sam warned. 'He's dangerous and I dare say he has some nasty characters working for him.'

'Yeah, but I reckon a few of us could handle them, eh?'

'Yeah.' Sam laughed. 'Thanks, Joe. I knew I could rely on you. Winnie has given information to the police twice, but he still got away, and even though they are now actively hunting him, I'm not sure I have any faith in them catching him.'

'Got a girlfriend?' Joe asked and Sam hesitated. 'Only asking, mate.'

Sam took a slug of his beer, then, 'I like Winnie a lot – well, it's more than that on my side, and I think she likes me, too – but I'm not sure about the future. She is an independent sort of girl, works with the Women's Movement – and I don't have much to offer.'

'Got your own business, like me,' Joe said. 'Rooms over the top of your shop, too. You shouldn't rate yourself as nothing, Sam.'

Sam nodded. 'I help to keep Mum in her own home,' he said.

'It means sometimes I have to be a bit careful with what I spend. Is it fair to ask Winnie to marry me if I can't give her all the things she deserves?'

'I help out at home too,' Joe agreed. 'My brother Ted does what he can, but he has a wife and kids. It ain't easy – but if I found a girl I loved, I'd just work a bit harder.'

Sam smiled. 'I suppose it would be easier if we lived with Mum in one house and I let the rooms over the shop – but I'm not sure Winnie would be happy like that. She is entitled to her own home.'

'Your mum would love havin' both of you there to fuss over – as for Winnie, you won't know unless you ask,' Joe said and Sam laughed ruefully.

'I reckon you're right,' he agreed. 'First things first, though. Winnie won't settle to anything until this devil Sinclair is sorted.'

'Sinclair?' Joe stared at him. 'I know that name – isn't he some sort of rent collector? I've seen him down on the docks and I know someone he harassed for a rise in rents a while back... threatened to bring in his bully boys to evict him if he didn't pay up.'

'That sounds like him,' Sam said. 'I wonder if his employer knows what he does...'

'Works for some rich bugger, does he?' Joe asked. 'Don't suppose he cares a toss what his agent does as long as he brings in the money.'

'I am not sure about that,' Sam replied thoughtfully.

Susie hadn't told him she knew about Sinclair being involved in the murky stuff at Madame Pauline's, but he had a hunch she did. From what she *had* told him, Sam thought his lordship might be very interested in what his agent had been doing on the docks.

'Are there any more cases of extortion you know of by this man?' he asked Joe.

'I only know about that one because I was there delivering when the rumpus went on over it,' Joe said. 'But I know a lot of blokes run small businesses down there and I'll ask around. Why?'

'It occurred to me that if the police can't prove that he had anything to do with those girls he found, maybe his lor— employer could prosecute him for unlawful dealings on his behalf.'

Joe looked at him hard. 'There's more to this than you're telling,' he said. 'Don't worry, I don't need to know. It sounds to me as if this Sinclair is a right bad 'un and the sooner he's taught a lesson and locked up, the better...'

20

'I sometimes wonder what the devil we have police for,' Lord Henry said, replacing the receiver and turning to his wife, who sat reading *Vogue Paris,* a women's fashion magazine she had sent to her regularly from France. She was in her favourite chair by the bay window overlooking a charming outlook at the rear of the house in Grosvenor Square. It was an elegant Georgian building with high ceilings and three-storied, which had been in the family for many years and had a small but pleasant walled garden at the rear. The Damask roses were in their second blooming and the scent through the open window was heavenly, but it did nothing to soothe his lacerated feelings. 'They have let Sinclair slip through their fingers yet again – this time, the rascal will know they suspect him. He won't come near me, that's for sure. I have taken steps to ensure that he can no longer take advantage of my tenants and he will know that I would be the first to hand him over to the police.'

He was so obviously angry, as he had every right to be. He had trusted Cyril Sinclair, given him a position of responsibility, and felt let down – but the news of Sinclair's other illegal and depraved activities had disgusted him. Now that the police had moved against him, Sinclair would be aware that he no longer held Lord Henry's trust. Many of the tenants had been visited and others would receive letters telling them there would be a new arrangement. It had been decided that Matthew would be his father's business agent in future. As yet, they couldn't know the extent of the damage Sinclair had done to the estate and the family name.

Lady Diane looked up at him and frowned. 'This unpleasant business leaves you in some difficulty, Henry. If he has been charging higher rents unbeknown to you and taking the cream for himself, it means that you are being cheated – and so are the people he is forcing to pay high rents.'

'My real regret is that it didn't come to my notice sooner,' Lord Henry replied, looking annoyed. 'One of my tenants happened to know that I owned his building and he wrote to me directly, asking why his rent had suddenly been doubled. I wasn't sure whether to take it seriously and checked my accounts – or Matthew did for me. There was no record of any increase, so we double-checked and included my farming tenants, and Matthew found several discrepancies. I went to see the tenant who had written to me and told him to pay Sinclair and that I would refund him – I wanted to give the rogue enough rope to hang himself... but now that will stop. All the tenants will be told of the new arrangement. If Sinclair approaches them, they must simply alert the police – and me.'

'Do you believe he has been cheating you for a long time?' she asked, looking at him in concern.

'I cannot be certain, but I think it must have been happening for a number of years. He was well recommended to me when my late agent retired some ten years past, and seemed a decent man. Everything was ordered as I wished. I had no reason to question him.' Lord Henry wrinkled his brow in thought. 'I seem to recall that he raised the question of rents about three years ago and I told him that many of the properties on the docks were only fit to be pulled down. It was in my mind that something ought to be done about them, but for some reason, I let it slide...' He hesitated, then inclined his head as memory came. 'I remember that Sinclair put it to me that if I renovated the properties, it might put the rents beyond the reach of many small businesses.'

Lady Diane's eyes opened wide. 'He didn't want you taking too much interest in them,' she declared. 'The wretch appealed to your better nature to avoid being caught out.'

'I fear you may be right,' he said. 'He took me for a fool – and I have been one.' His eyes glinted with anger and regret once more. 'I blame myself for not taking more note of what was going on.'

'Oh, Henry my dear. You cannot blame yourself – it is Sinclair who has cheated those people, not you.'

'Because I, in my complacency, allowed it to continue,' he said, a glimmer of steel in his eyes. 'I was a rich fool who had more money coming in than he needed, so I let the rogue continue – until Matthew discovered his thieving ways. I have lost money in more ways than I dreamed, but it is the others, men with small businesses who have suffered far more. I am angry for the way they've been treated and I intend to discover just what has been going on. Matthew has a list of all my properties now and we shall visit every one of them, in time, and make what reparation we can – I intend to sort this mess out one way or another. Sinclair will not dare to come near me, but he shall not continue to cheat others if I can help it! I will only be satis-fied when that man is behind bars.'

'Good for you and Matthew!' Lady Diane jumped to her feet and went to embrace him. 'No wonder I adore you. It is marvel-lous that you care so much for others less fortunate.' She smiled up at him lovingly.

He bent his head and kissed her and then sighed. 'I should have been more vigilant sooner,' he said ruefully, but she shook her head.

'You were let down by a man you trusted, dearest. Now that you know, you can do something to put it right.'

'Yes, I can, my darling, and I shall,' he told her and stroked the side of her face gently. 'Thank you for believing in me, Diane – and I haven't forgotten your request. Is it still in your mind that you would like to have your own business?'

'Yes, it is, Henry, but not until after our child is born.'

'Then I shall look for somewhere suitable for you, dearest,' he told her. 'We have a few months yet...'

'Yes, we do,' she agreed. 'I have prepared a business plan, Henry, if you would care to look it over – but there is no rush, my dearest, no rush at all.'

* * *

'I think you should tell your brother the whole story now,' Lady Diane said when Susie came to help her change for the evening before her night off. 'If he happens to see that wicked man, he should inform the police.'

'Yes, my lady, I will tell Sam,' Susie assured her. 'He knows some of it, but I didn't tell him everything, just as you asked me.'

'There is no longer a need to keep Sinclair's identity quiet,' Lady Diane said. 'He will be aware he is being hunted now – so your brother may as well know the whole truth. Sinclair will not dare to come here, but may still try to steal money from his lordship's tenants. Indeed, I dare say he may need money before too long has passed, and until all the tenants have been informed, he may still try to collect money from them.'

'Lord Henry is writing to them all,' Lady Diane informed her. 'He will visit every property and try to discover just what has been happening. I know that he blames himself for not looking into things before this.'

'His lordship trusted his agent as he had every right to do,' Susie said. 'Yet I understand that he may feel some responsibility – as Sam does, because he was unable to prevent that girl from being taken away. And now she is dead...'

'Lord Henry is furious that Sinclair was allowed to escape yet again.'

'Yes, I am sure he is.' Susie nodded in sympathy. 'But these things happen.'

'They do indeed,' Lady Diane sighed and then gave her head a little shake. 'Well, I must not concern myself, for I can do nothing.'

'No, my lady. It must be for others to act,' Susie agreed, and then to change the subject, 'What would you wish to wear this evening, my lady?'

'Ah yes, we have a soirée to attend... I suppose my peach silk, since I know you altered that to fit me beautifully and yet...' She sighed. 'I am a little tired, Susie. I think I shall rest this afternoon. I had planned to go visiting, but I think I will stay in my room. You may bring me my sketchpad – and take a few hours off if you choose.'

'Are you feeling unwell, my lady?' Susie looked at her anxiously, as Lady Diane never rested in the afternoons.

'No, just tired. I dare say it is my condition.' Lady Diane

smiled and placed a hand on her pleasantly rounded navel. 'No reason to worry anyone – and I do *not* want the doctor.'

'I think I shall stay within call,' Susie said. 'Just in case you want me. I'm making a new dress for my mother and will spend my time doing that unless you need me.'

21

Bert glanced over his shoulder as he turned the corner of Dressmakers' Alley. He'd been to the cloth manufacturer he frequently used to order some winter materials. It was summer now, but in the rag trade you had to plan for the seasons ahead. Business was fair, ticking over, but the orders were smaller these days. Cyril had been good at getting large orders, Bert had to give him that, but the thought of his half-brother made him uneasy and he looked back once more. People were going about their business, the barrow-boy on the corner selling fruit, his cheeky cockney voice loud enough for the whole street to hear. A woman was buying some apples from him and two girls were standing talking outside the flower shop. Bert frowned as he thought he recognised one of them... but she didn't hold his interest for long. His fear that he was being shadowed had grown of late – and there was only one reason he could think of as to why he might be being followed.

Cyril had called at the workshop when he was out and had left him a cryptic message. Mrs Jarvis had been puzzled by it, but Bert knew what it meant.

'He said he hadn't forgotten anything,' Mrs Jarvis had said. 'I asked him if there was anything else, but he said you'd understand, Mr Barrow.'

'Nothing for you to worry about,' Bert had told her. She'd been uneasy about returning to the workshop after the police raid, but he'd managed to talk her round. She'd been left penniless when her husband had died and, at her age, she'd never find another job as easy as this one; it was hard labour scrubbing floors rather than sitting at a desk each day, speaking to customers, for twice the money. Her conscience might prick her, but she'd put it aside. She was worried that Cyril would make her leave her little home, which was one of the many properties he collected the rent from, but Bert assured her he wouldn't if the rent was paid.

She hadn't asked him about the top floor or what had gone on there and he understood that she didn't want to know. Both she and Betty had had a good idea, but they'd turned a blind eye – much as Bert had himself. He regretted now that he'd ever got involved with the devil who called himself his brother, but he'd been desperate.

All that was over now. He'd made up his mind that he wouldn't help Cyril with his rotten schemes again. He was going straight and managing, and it felt good. Yet, as he glanced behind him again, and caught sight of a man he'd seen before, a chill went through him. If Cyril was having him followed, he had a good reason – and Bert could only think of one. His half-brother wanted him dead. He knew too much…

Bert grunted to himself. What he knew would hang Cyril if the police ever managed to catch him. He had drugged and kidnapped young working girls, his gentle manner fooling them into thinking he was a kind man to offer them work and a place to stay, only to discover too late what he intended. At least two of the girls had died. There might have been more before Bert got involved. His brother was also a thief, stealing from his employer and guilty of extortion by foul means. The bully boys he used to persuade small business owners to pay up were thugs who would kill if they were paid enough. And he'd done all this while leading a double life as the agent of some toff. Bert didn't know Cyril's employer's name; he'd been careful never to reveal it.

If Bert had known, he might have sent a letter informing the man that he was being taken for a fool. Even now, he could go to the police and inform on Cyril – but would they believe him? He already had a criminal record and, when questioned after the raid on Madame Pauline's, he'd denied everything. To inform on his brother would be to incriminate himself – but prison was better than being dead.

Bert cursed loudly, startling a passer-by. He'd give Cyril up to the law without a blink of the eye, but he wanted to make a success of Madame Pauline's. The name was his invention, based on something he'd heard about the woman who had once employed most of the seamstresses in Dressmakers' Alley. She'd been French, an émigré, and had made a name for herself, and a fortune, but only by using the poor girls who worked for a pittance. Bert reckoned it was his right to run the business he'd set up, not Cyril's. His half-brother had used him because he needed money to repay the hard men he'd owed money to – but Bert hadn't bargained for what came afterwards. That was all down to Cyril. If Bert was sent to prison for several years for his part in his brother's crimes, he'd never get another chance. He was stuck between the devil and the deep blue sea. He couldn't chance informing on his brother – and maybe he was imagining that Cyril was having him followed.

He jutted his chin as he approached the workshop and saw a

girl staring in the window. The girl looked at him as he turned into the shop and he paused with his hand on the door handle. 'Are you lookin' fer a job?' he asked gruffly.

'Yes, if there are any going. I've worked in a corset factory for a time.'

'Not from round 'ere, are yer?'

'I lived in the country but came up for a job... but it didn't suit me.'

'What's yer name then?'

'It's Sibby – Sibby Thomas.'

'Right, come on in and we'll give yer a trial. If yer any good, it's thirty bob a week for a start and Saturday half-day...'

'Oh, thank you.' Her face lit up. 'I really need this job, Mr...'

'Barrow,' he said. 'I'll take yer into the workshop and yer can start straight away.' He glanced round once more as he went inside, but there was no one loitering. It was probably just his imagination that he'd had a shadow that morning.

* * *

'He went to Drakes Woollens,' Dirty Sid said with a sneer. 'Down that alley, I could 'ave took him out wiv a knife in the back any time, boss. Just give me the wink and he won't bother yer no more.'

'He doesn't bother me now,' Cyril replied coldly. 'He's the one that's bothered and that's what I want – but he'll pay when I'm ready, just as that nosy girl will. Have you traced her yet?'

'Yer didn't give us much to go on, boss,' Dirty Sid said, wiping the snot from his nose on his filthy jacket sleeve. Thin, wiry, but immensely strong in the arms and wrists, he had rotten teeth, a crooked nose and furtive eyes that reminded Cyril of a sewer rat. 'Said she were a plain girl wiv dark 'air scraped back orf her mug, and 'er name was Winnie Brown, but I ain't got no idea what she looks like.'

'No one gives me trouble and gets away with it,' Cyril snarled. Wind rippled across the surface of the river, its waters, deep, dark and the keeper of murky secrets. 'I know she followed me. She was the one came storming in when she was dismissed and demanded her wages. I sensed then she was a troublemaker and gave her the money to get rid of her, but she was no ordinary seamstress. Betty told me she'd been snooping around – I know she followed me and she took a photograph of the bakery van. I caught sight of her.' He swore. 'I should've gone after her then and given her a smack or two. She is the one that informed on us to the coppers; I'd swear on it. I intend to teach her a lesson when I get her.'

'Yer said she worked at the place what was raided? How did a girl like that 'ave a camera? They're not cheap ter come by.'

'I don't think she was what she made out to be,' Cyril said. 'She was sent to spy on us. The police raided after she was sacked – and then she followed me. It had to be her.' He'd wondered if his suspicious employer had employed her to spy on him – or rather his ex-employer as Cyril daren't go near Lord Henry now that the cops were after him.

'I did see a girl 'anging around in Dressmakers' Alley...' Dirty Sid coughed a gob of phlegm and spat it out on the riverbank, causing Cyril's lip to curl in disgust, but he made no comment. 'She was there when I followed him to Drakes Woollens and she was there again when I followed 'im back.'

'Then she is the one,' Cyril said, a gleam of malice in his eyes. 'She's still spying on Barrow – the police probably think he will lead them to me.'

'Does he know about this place?' Dirty Sid cocked his head at the pleasant, bay-fronted house that stood at a distance from the river, its lawns leading down to a picket fence separating it from the footpath that ran along the Thames. From the outside, it looked a perfectly ordinary modest house, with its thick lace curtains, heavy oak door and shiny brass knocker. No one would guess that the gentleman who occasionally went in and out was wanted by the police.

'Only those I trust know of this house,' Cyril replied. 'I want that girl, Sid. You know what to do. She knows me so won't trust me; I can't take her for a cup of tea or a drink and drug her, as I've done in the past – you'll have to grab her and bring her here. I want her alive.'

'I'll need 'elp,' he said. 'Can I 'ave Basher?'

'No, he's too rough with the girls. You can take Doug – but be careful. I don't want a public scene that brings the coppers down on us. Follow her, find out where she goes and what she does – and get her at night.'

'Yeah, it will be a pleasure, boss.' Dirty Sid leered at him craftily. 'Do I get a bonus when it's done?'

'It depends,' Cyril said. 'You can have one of the girls for the night – but money is tight for a while.'

'That will suit me, boss.'

Cyril frowned as Sid slouched off. The man stank, his breath worse than a blocked drain. The girls hated him, even those who were happy to service Cyril or his friends, but he was useful. He'd been told to get rid of the red-haired girl's body after she met with a *little accident*, though the police had found her body, when they'd raided the bakery. Sid had been going to dispose of it but had been slow to act, leaving it under some sacks in a shed out the back. Bert should've finished the task; he would have done a quick neat job of it; she would've been in the river far downstream, nothing to connect her to him, no clue where she'd come from, but he'd refused. Sid never refused, whatever the job, so Cyril tolerated him. When he was ready, he would let him have his fun with Barrow. Cyril's half-brother had dared to raise his hand to Cyril, to defy him and for that he would pay with a slow and lingering death. Cyril would enjoy seeing Sid cut him to ribbons with his knife. Sid was an artist with that knife of his. Most of the other men Cyril employed to help him run his dirty little empire were afraid of Sid – strong men who normally feared little – got shivers down their spine when Sid turned up.

Cyril had saved Sid's life. He'd found him on the riverbank one cold night, desperately ill with the sweating sickness, and he'd taken him into the house, nursed him back to health and given him a job. Sid was slavishly devoted to him. Cyril had no fear of him, though he knew him to be a murderer, even before they'd met.

Cyril's brow furrowed. Much of his property empire, as he'd come to think of it, was lost to him now. The money he'd embezzled from his employer, Lord Henry, had gone into his other little schemes; the girls had to be housed and his men had to be paid or they would simply walk away and find another boss to work for.

There were many men like Cyril who made money through the sufferings of others; extortion, gambling, fencing stolen goods and women were profitable. Cyril had dreamed of becoming one of the richest and most feared gangsters in the East End of London, but because of his brother's stupidity in employing a spy – that girl! – his dreams had temporarily hit a brick wall. Bert couldn't have known the girl was a spy, but it was still his fault for not being more careful. Cyril had been almost

ready to finance his own gambling club but the deal had gone
sour now that he was being hunted.

He still had some money stashed away. Cyril had become
quite rich from all his rotten dealings, but his job as a property
agent had gone, and all the money he'd creamed off the top of
rents due to his employer were lost. His lordship had caught on
somehow, probably that clever dick son of his – he'd always
sensed the cocky so-and-so didn't trust him, and nor did her
high-and-mighty ladyship and now he'd been caught with sticky
fingers for embezzlement. They were probably crowing over it
right now. God how Cyril hated people like that! He'd been
lucky to get a position of trust, but he'd envied his employer and
wanted more.

Cyril thought of his former life with bitterness. He'd thought
Lord Henry too careless and comfortable to bother about the
odd discrepancy, but that son of his was clever. Between them,
they'd cut the ground from beneath his feet. After running from
the police, he'd tried to collect some rent from one of his
victims, but the man had laughed in his face and threatened to
call the police. Other men would move in on Cyril's territory
while he was hiding out, even though he still had his own bully
boys. Word soon spread in the underworld. The small shops,
cafés and market traders he'd forced to pay protection money
would be taken over by another trickster while he had to hide
out from the police. Even men he'd thought his friends and
done favours for would spurn him until the heat was off, so he
had no choice but to lie low.

It was a setback, but Cyril didn't believe it was the end. If he
lay low for a while, the police would forget him and go after
someone else. There were bigger fish than him in the under-
world of crime that permeated the huge sprawling city of
London. For the moment, Cyril was on the list of most wanted

criminals, Lord Henry would make certain of that. And he had friends in high places, but soon, another murder, a swindle in the city, or a gang shooting would hit the newspaper headlines and the police would be told to concentrate on whatever was arousing public concern. He only had to bide his time and he could start again.

If things got too hot in London, he might go elsewhere for a year or two – but he liked it here and he would give himself time. Meanwhile, he had a score to settle with his brother and that nosy girl. She'd dared to follow him and take a photograph of him getting into the bakery van he was sure of it. There was only one possible reason she would do that – she was spying on him for someone. He doubted the police had the brains to set a female spy on his tail – so that left only his lordship or that interfering son of his. Maybe when he'd dealt with the girl, Cyril would think about getting even with them…

22

Winnie needed a new dress. Sam had taken her out several times now, to the cinema to watch a motion picture; they'd chosen *Only a Shop Girl*, starring Estelle Taylor and Mae Busch, which had made Winnie cry. They'd been to dancing classes twice so far, to a tea dance, listening to romantic music from a string quartet, and for a supper of fish and chips with mushy peas, and he'd said they would go to another tea dance at a hotel that weekend; it wasn't a posh one up the West End, but it was a nice place, called The Waverly, and just off the Commercial Road. She'd worn her best dress three times already and wanted something special for the visit to the Waverly, but counting the money in her purse, she knew she would be lucky to find anything for what she could afford. The smart suits and dresses priced at more than five guineas in Selfridges or Swan and Edgar were not for her. Winnie hesitated outside Harpers Emporium for several minutes, wondering what she would do if she saw Mr or Mrs Harper, but then decided to brave it.

The young man in the lift had a scarred face but was very pleasant and wished her a good day as she left the elevator. She wandered into the dress department first, immediately inhaling the light delicate perfume that came from some fresh lavender in a vase on a small table. It was such a comfortable atmosphere and she felt more at home there than in some of the other big stores. Looking through the racks, Winnie found three day dresses she liked; all of them could be worn to church or for an afternoon walk and even a tea dance if she wore a spray of artificial flowers on the shoulder. She was hesitating over which one she should ask to try on first when her eye caught sight of a dress on a shop mannequin. It was an emerald green, had a squared neckline and the new loose shape that fell to the hips and short sleeves, trimmed with braid. It looked as if it would show off her legs from about mid-calf; she had nice shapely legs and thought it would suit her.

'May I help you, miss?' a sales girl enquired as Winnie stood with the three dress on their hangers. 'Would you like to try them on?'

'I was going to,' Winnie replied hesitantly. 'Then I saw that gorgeous green dress on the stand.'

The girl smiled. 'Yes, it is beautiful, isn't it? We have it in size 36 and 38 only...'

They had her size!

Winnie took a deep breath. 'I am not sure I can afford it,' she said. 'How much is it?'

'Expensive,' the girl said and her sigh echoed Winnie's. 'It is nine guineas, I'm afraid.'

'Oh... then I'd better try these,' Winnie said and her disappointment showed. 'I thought it would be too much for me.'

'Me too,' the girl sympathised. 'Even with my staff discount, I could never afford it. It is a new range Mrs Harper is trying.'

Winnie nodded and followed the girl to the changing department. She tried on each of the three dresses in turn and a navy blue and white spotted one looked quite good on her, but all she could think about was the green dress. It filled her with longing, but she could afford thirty shillings at most and the dress was beyond her means.

'I might come back for the polka dot,' she told the salesgirl. 'I'm sorry, but I can't think of anything but the green dress.'

'I know how you feel, but the navy and white does suit you.'

Winnie nodded and left, feeling disappointed. She exited the shop and wandered down into Soho. There was a cluster of market stalls at one end and she could see that one of them was selling clothes. People thronged the busy street and the stalls were doing a good trade. She walked towards the one selling clothes and looked at the dresses for sale. They were all meant for summer and there was a green and white flowered dress. Winnie held it up against herself. It had the new dropped waistline and short sleeves, but nothing like the finish or style of the one she'd coveted in Harpers. Sighing with regret for the dress she still wanted, she wandered past stalls selling bric-a-brac, second-hand clothes, handbags and cheap straw hats, to the material stall – and there, right before her eyes was a roll of beautiful, silky, emerald green cloth.

She touched it and the quality was good. On a part of the stall were packets of paper patterns and she saw a similar style to the one in Harpers. Before she'd worked at Madame Pauline's, Winnie would have doubted her ability to make a dress like that, but the design looked easy to follow. She checked the back of the pattern and saw that it needed two yards but thought she might buy a little extra material to allow for mistakes when cutting the sleeves.

'How much is this material a yard?' Winnie asked.

The man behind the stall looked at her for a moment, considering. 'For you is it, love?' he asked and she nodded.

'Right, for you, I'll do a good price – six bob a yard, and I'll throw that pattern in if yer like.'

'Thank you.' She blushed as he winked at her. Winnie hadn't been flirted with like that before and put it down to her newly bobbed hairstyle that waved softly about her face; she'd had it done recently on a sudden whim.

The look in the trader's eyes made her a little shy, but she watched as he expertly measured and then cut her the three yards she ordered. It would allow for mistakes and if she had enough extra, she might make herself a small bolero to wear with her dress sometimes. The sleeves were just little caps and on chilly days it would be nice to have something to slip over.

'It was kind of you to give me the pattern.'

'That's all right, love,' the cheeky stallholder said. 'I'd like to see that when it's made up.'

'If it is successful, I might make some more dresses,' she told him and took her brown paper parcel, smiling as she carried it home by the string loop. Winnie didn't have a sewing machine, but Mary did and she would help her pin it to the right length, and they would cut out the pattern together.

* * *

Mary loved the colour of the material when Winnie showed it to her later that day, and they spent that evening cutting out the pieces and tacking them together. Winnie arranged to go back the next evening for Mary to help her pin the hem to the right length when she had sewn the pieces together.

She was about to say goodnight when Constable Winston came in. He smiled at Winnie and asked her how she was getting on.

'I'm fine, thank you,' she told him. 'We've been making me a new dress. Sam is taking me to a tea dance this weekend.'

'That's nice,' he said. 'I like your young man, Winnie. Proper upright citizen.'

'Yes, Sam is a lovely person,' Winnie agreed. 'Well, I must go. I'll see you tomorrow, Mary.'

'I'll walk you home, Winnie,' Constable Winston said, insisting when she said it wasn't far and that she would be all right.

'I'd rather take you,' he told her. 'It won't be any trouble and Mary will have my supper ready when I get back.'

'Thank you,' Winnie gave in gracefully. 'It is very kind.'

'I know you're a capable girl,' he said as they went out into the street together. It was a light night and warm enough for Winnie to need only a thin jacket over her skirt and blouse. 'And I know you've only a few streets to go – but that man hasn't been caught yet and—'

'I was going to ask about that,' Winnie said. 'Hasn't he been seen at all?' She knew that the efforts of the local men had, so far, been unsuccessful. Mr Sinclair was keeping his head down or simply staying away from the area.

'We're working on something,' Constable Winston told her. 'I can't tell you anything more – but there has been one brief sighting.'

Winnie stopped and stared at him. 'I'm glad and I hope you get him soon.'

'It isn't always just nabbing him,' her friend told her heavily. 'We have circumstantial evidence, but what we need is to catch him red-handed. The bugger – I beg your pardon, Winnie – but it makes me so angry that men like him slip through the net time and time again. Unless we have enough evidence, he might wriggle out of the serious charges. His previous employer will charge him with embezzlement so we can put him away for a while – but he should hang.'

'Yes, I agree,' Winnie said. 'Isn't it enough that we know he was involved with those girls they found – and the poor young woman who was murdered?'

'He has men to do his dirty work,' Constable Winston said, lowering his voice. 'I'd like to tell you more, Winnie – but there's another filthy little criminal we've been after for a while and he's been seen in the vicinity of Dressmakers' Alley recently. We suspect... But, no, I've already said too much. It might be dangerous for you to know it all.' He stopped and looked at her as they reached the hostel. 'I don't want you going to Dressmak-ers' Alley, Winnie. Things might turn nasty soon and if you were caught up in it all, Mary would never forgive me.'

'I think I've misjudged you,' Winnie said, looking up at him. 'I thought you – or your colleagues – had just shrugged your shoulders and stopped bothering.'

'We'll never give up,' he told her and his chin jutted in deter-mination. 'There are men down the Yard that are working twenty-four hours a day trying to outwit the rotten so-and-sos that make this city a cesspit of crime. It might look as if we're careless or not bothered to the outsider, but we're like terriers – we never let go once we scent blood.'

Winnie felt a new respect for him and shame that she hadn't trusted him more. She said goodnight, after thanking him for walking her home and went inside the hostel. Her thoughts were confused as she ran up to her room. If it wasn't just a simple matter of grabbing that man and holding him until the police took him into custody, it might be that Sam and his friends could do more harm than good. She would have to tell Sam what Constable Winston had confided to her when they met that weekend.

23

'It's my turn to patrol today,' Rosalind announced as Winnie entered the office the next morning. 'You've done it two days on the run, Winnie. I'll take your place – someone might notice you if you go again.'

'I'm not sure we ought to continue,' Winnie said hesitantly. 'I've wondered if we might be in the way if the police are still watching. Perhaps we should leave it for a while.'

'I need to get my shoes mended,' Rosalind replied, looking annoyed. 'I'll just walk up and down once and see if anything different is happening. Honestly, Winnie, you think no one else can do anything. I shan't be noticed. I wear something different every time I go.'

'Well, just be careful,' Winnie warned. 'Do you want the camera?'

'Yes, of course. I might see something interesting – and most of us still don't know what this Mr Sinclair looks like. None of the pictures we've taken have been him.'

'He might be keeping clear of the place,' Winnie suggested. It would be useful to have a photograph of Mr Sinclair – and there might still be a part for them to play in this long-running saga. Constable Winston had warned her to stay clear – but no one would be looking for Rosalind. 'Go on then, if you want to, but if there is any trouble, stay out of the way and don't get involved.'

'What do you know that you aren't telling me?' Rosalind's eyes flashed with excitement.

'Nothing – but there might be trouble if Mr Sinclair does show up, so remember what I've said.'

'Oh yes, I shall,' Rosalind promised. 'I thought we were never going to have any fun, but I'll be careful, I promise.'

Winnie watched her leave, her head up and her pretty face alight with excitement. Rosalind led a very sheltered life at home with her invalid mother and younger sister, and her little job in the office was her only escape from the tedium of the sickroom. She had embraced the Women's Movement with all her heart and clearly enjoyed getting involved in the more dangerous assignments. She had already been arrested once for causing a riot when the women had demonstrated outside Selfridges and one of them had broken the windows with a hammer. Rosalind had been let off with a caution, but some of the girls had been detained in the cells.

Winnie looked at the clock. It was a quarter past nine. She felt a shiver at the nape of her neck and wondered if she ought to have told her friend not to go – but she could hardly prevent Rosalind from walking down the alley to get her shoes repaired at Sam's shop.

*   *   *

Bert saw the girl loitering outside his premises. He frowned, certain that he'd seen her there on at least three occasions over the last month. He'd been out to order a stock of leather buttons for the new autumn suits they had begun to make that week and she'd been on the opposite side of the road. Now she was looking at his premises, trying to peer in through the glass door, which had a faded brown blind pulled down its length but gaped at the side so that she could probably glimpse the reception area.

She started as he came up to her, her eyes wide with guilt and her reaction convinced him.

'What do you want?' he barked at her, grabbing her arm, and turning her to look at him. 'You're not after a job – you don't look as if you need one to me.'

'I was looking for a friend of mine,' the girl replied. 'I think she works here...'

'What's her name?' Bert said and glared at her. 'If you're spying on me, I'll make yer sorry. Who sent yer here?'

'No one sent me,' the girl replied, raising her head proudly. 'My friend promised to meet me yesterday, but she didn't, so I came looking for her...'

Bert hesitated. It was possible she was telling the truth, though his instincts told him something wasn't right. 'What's her name then?'

'Winnie – Winnie Brown,' she blurted, sounding scared. 'I know she works here.'

Bert frowned; the name rang a bell, but he couldn't quite place it for a moment and then it clicked. The girl who had dared to demand her wages when Betty sacked her. 'Not any more,' he muttered. 'She left a couple of months back.'

'Oh...' the girl said, looking puzzled. 'She didn't tell me.'

'Clear orf,' Bert told her, releasing her arm. She was probably lying, but he didn't want any trouble. She rubbed at her arm, hesitating. 'You may be tellin' the truth – but if I see yer 'angin' around again, you'll be for it.'

'I was only going to the cobblers and decided to see if Winnie was all right.'

'Go on then.' Bert let her go and turned towards the workshop. He didn't think he'd been followed that morning, but he was getting jumpy.

As he was about to enter his premises, he heard someone cry out and turned to see the girl he'd just spoken to being accosted by two ruffians – one of whom he recognised as being Cyril's man. Without thinking what he was doing, Bert went after them and grabbed the larger of the men by the arm, dragging him off the girl. He turned him around and headbutted him, then punched him in the stomach, sending him to his knees where he kicked him full in the face. The girl had rounded on the skinny man and was fighting hard, her long nails scoring his cheek; she kicked him in the shins as Bert grabbed him around the throat from behind, his arm pressing so hard that he gasped for air. Bert chopped at the back of his neck with his right hand and sent him to the ground; he then kicked him in the head for good measure, breathing hard as he looked at the girl.

'Are you hurt?' he asked harshly and she shook her head. 'Get away now, while you can and find yourself another shoe mender. I might not be here next time.'

'Thank you, Mr Barrow,' she whispered, her face white. 'I... Thank you...' She walked off quickly, past the flower shop and around the corner out of sight.

Bert stood over the two men on the ground, both eyeing him warily as they fought to recover their breath. He'd taken them by surprise, but given a chance, they would come at him again. He was preparing for the onslaught, when a couple of local men appeared from nowhere and stood next to him.

'Havin' a bit of bother?' one of them asked.

Bert nodded, vaguely recognising him as the coal merchant who'd been too nosy.

'Want any help with this filth? We saw what they did – tryin' to rob that young woman.'

'I'm not sure it was robbery,' Bert replied gruffly. 'I doubt they'll give us much trouble now.'

The two men got to their feet, glaring at Bert. The thin one muttered something as the heavyweight took a step forward. 'Leave it, Doug,' he muttered. 'We'll get the bugger another time…'

They slunk off down the alley, not looking back but clearly at odds with one another as they got into a filthy old van and drove off, in a small cloud of exhaust fumes and a loud bang. Bert was unable to hear their words, but he thought the smelly one was blaming his companion for what had just happened.

'Surely they weren't trying to abduct that girl in broad daylight?' Joe Ross, the coalman, asked when the men disappeared around the corner. 'They couldn't have thought they'd get away with it!'

'They might if Mr Barrow hadn't stopped them,' his companion said. 'We weren't near enough to grab them, Joe. They had only to hustle her into that van and we'd have lost them.'

'It's been done before,' Bert said. 'Most folk are too busy to notice – and if they do, they just say the girl fainted.' He picked up a rag and held it away from his face and sniffed. 'I reckon that's strong enough to knock a girl out.'

Joe sniffed, jerking back as the sharp odour stung his nose. It smelled of the stuff they used in dentists – chloroform. 'Lethal! Shouldn't be allowed… if a decent girl can't walk the street safely...' He looked over his shoulder. 'I think I'll run and catch her up – see if she is all right.'

'She'll be gone by now,' his companion said. 'We've got other things to do, Joe.'

'Yeah, all right,' Joe said but looked regretful.

Bert watched as they walked off. His knuckles felt sore where he'd punched the bugger the smelly one had called Doug. It was the stinky one that had been following him right enough; he'd been in the van the night Cyril had taken the girls away. Bert would never forget his evil face.

An icy shiver touched his nape. He'd stopped that girl being abducted – and Cyril wasn't going to like that one bit...

* * *

It was half-past eleven when Rosalind returned to the office looking pale and shaken. Winnie knew instinctively that something had happened and she told her to sit down and asked the other girl in the office to make a pot of tea.

'What happened?' she asked.

'Oh, Winnie – it was so strange,' Rosalind cried. 'I was frightened for a while, but on the bus here I started thinking. I'd taken my shoes in, spent some time looking in the windows and walked right around the block. I saw Mr Barrow go out earlier – and he must have seen me for he returned when I was standing outside his window and he grabbed my arm. He demanded to know what I was doing, so I told him I was looking for a friend – and he made me name her, so I told him it was you. He gave me a little shake and told me to clear off and not come back... but then...' She gave a little gasp. 'Two awful men grabbed me as I was walking away,' Rosalind told her, shuddering at the memory. 'One of them smelled foul and the other one had a face like a pugilist… and they were arguing. They were going to abduct me, but then the most surprising thing happened—'

'Oh, Rosalind!' Winnie stared at her in horror. 'How terrible for you. What happened – did the police come?'

'Mr Barrow saved me,' Rosalind said, sounding as though she couldn't believe it. 'He grabbed one of them by the throat and punched him and kicked him. I was struggling against the one who smelled like a drain; I scratched his face, but he was stronger than he looked, for he was much smaller – but then Mr Barrow set on him and told me to run away. I walked very fast and caught a bus just as it was passing the end of the alley.' She looked shocked and frightened, as well she might, for had she been taken, she might even now be dead or imprisoned with other unfortunate girls.

'Mr Barrow did that?' Winnie was stunned. 'I thought he was as evil as his brother… if that man was his brother.'

'Well, that's what he did,' Rosalind replied. 'It doesn't change that he was a part of all those horrid things that went on there, Winnie.'

'No – but…' Winnie shook her head. 'What did he say to you?'

'Told me to find another shoe mender because he might not be there next time.'

'It was lucky for you he was… but why would those men try to abduct you in broad daylight?'

Rosalind was silent for a moment. 'I'm not sure – but I think the big one made a mistake. The other one swore at him, told him he'd grabbed the wrong girl.' She looked at Winnie. 'I think that he believed I was you… I think he heard Mr Barrow repeat your name and thought it was my name…'

'Me?' Winnie stared at her. 'Why… I don't understand. Were they going to let you go then?'

'No, because the one called Doug said I'd be useful and they'd take me anyway. The other one said it was a mess and he wasn't taking the blame. I just don't see why it was you they wanted – unless you'd been noticed following someone?'

'I don't think...' Winnie's words trailed away, because of course she had followed Mr Sinclair and taken a photograph of the bakery van. He might have noticed her, though she'd been very careful. 'Well, I suppose that might be it. I'm sorry they frightened you, Rosalind.' She felt sick as she realised what might have happened if Mr Barrow hadn't stopped them from taking Rosalind. They would either have killed her or used her as they did other innocent girls. 'You mustn't go there again. If you have to fetch your shoes, get someone else to get them... or I'll ask Sam to bring them with him...'

'Nor must you go there,' Rosalind said firmly. 'I think we should call our operation over, Winnie. If they are looking for you, it could be too much of a risk. I only realised the extent of the danger I was in when I was almost abducted.'

'I did suggest that we did so this morning,' Winnie reminded her and then frowned. 'Were there no police around?'

'Well, if there were, they did nothing to help me,' she said tartly. 'Useless as always. All they are good for is arresting us for demonstrating.'

'Yes, I sometimes think the same...' Winnie looked thoughtful. She would speak to Constable Winston that evening and hear what he had to say.

24

'Well, that was a nasty experience for your friend,' Mary said when Winnie had finished her story. 'I thought you'd stopped all that amateur spying?'

'I think Winnie wasn't happy with our performance,' Constable Winston said, looking stern. 'Don't think it hasn't been noticed, Winnie. We've been aware of your little band of sleuths, walking up and down the alley. But you've a perfect right to do it and we couldn't stop you without giving ourselves away.'

'Did your colleagues see what happened to Rosalind?'

'Not to my knowledge,' he replied. 'We're keeping a watch, Winnie, but we don't have enough resources to make it twenty-four hours. Our beat police walk the area and keep a sharp eye for the man we're after, but our special men can only spare so many hours, mostly at night, as we believe that's when something is likely to happen.' He frowned at her. 'I never dreamed they would try anything so audacious in broad daylight – but why snatch her?'

'One of them heard Mr Barrow say my name.' Winnie

explained that Rosalind had given it as an excuse for spying. 'They were arguing about it. The one Rosalind said smelled awful must have seen me at some time and told the one called Doug he'd grabbed the wrong girl.' A chill went down her spine.

'Why would they want you, Winnie?' Mary asked, looking anxious.

'I can only think I was seen when I followed Mr Sinclair. He may have seen me take his photograph – or perhaps they just connected the police raid with me somehow...'

'So our Mr Sinclair is a clever bugger then.' Constable Winston shook his head as Mary looked at him reproachfully. 'Sorry – but it makes me angry to think he is sitting somewhere laughing at us. If his men dared to try to snatch her in the middle of the morning, he is a cocky so-and-so and I'll be glad when he is behind bars for good.'

'But when will that be?' Mary said in a cross tone. 'All you've done so far is to swear and talk about what you'll do and nothing happens.'

'Oh, it will,' he said confidently. 'In fact...' He glanced at the black marble clock on the mantelpiece. 'It might be happening even now.'

Winnie and Mary both looked at him.

He smiled and nodded. 'I couldn't tell you before, but we've traced Sinclair to a house by the river...' He laughed as they both looked astonished. 'The smelly one as your friend called him is well known to us, Winnie. He is called Dirty Sid – and he's an evil little b— devil. We've been after him for a while. He's suspected of a couple of murders to do with gangland activities, extortion and other things. When he was noticed in the area of Dressmakers' Alley and seen to follow Mr Barrow, our man followed him. We've got a photograph of him talking to his boss – who is none other than our Mr Sinclair – on the riverbank.'

'Oh, Winston!' Mary cried, laughing. 'That is so clever – to follow him because he followed Mr Barrow.'

'We're not as daft in the police force as some folk think,' Constable Winston said with a glance at Winnie.

She blushed and looked down for a moment. She'd thought she was being clever spying on the evil men who had harmed those poor girls, but now she realised that she was out of her depth – and perhaps the police were more aware of what was going on than she'd believed. 'It was clever,' she said. 'I hope you get your Mr Sinclair this time.'

'I hope to God we do, too,' he replied fervently. 'If he gets away again, I doubt the chief will spend any more money on trying to track him. There is too much crime for us ever to catch all the criminals. He wouldn't have been a priority if it hadn't been for his lordship's insistence he be apprehended.'

'He is a murderer,' Winnie cried indignantly.

'That has yet to be proved,' Constable Winston said heavily. 'We have proof he's a thief – and we have good reason to believe he is involved with the abduction and unlawful imprisonment of young women, but we do not yet have evidence that ties him to the murder, or murders.' He sighed. 'What we really need is solid evidence.'

'Surely what you already know is enough to arrest him?' Mary argued.

'Yes, we can arrest him – but a man like that, who must have money stashed away, can afford the best legal advisors and they will help him wriggle out of it, unless we have the evidence.'

Winnie glanced at the clock. 'I suppose I'd better go – thank you for helping me finish my dress, Mary.'

'It suits you,' Mary told her. 'I hope your young man likes it, too.'

'I'll walk you home,' Constable Winston told her and Winnie

didn't object. If she was a target, there was no sense in making it easy for the men who were after her.

'Thank you,' she said and kissed Mary on the cheek.

* * *

Despite it being summer now, the air was chilly that evening; it had turned colder after a period of lovely settled weather, and Winnie had come out with just a knitted jacket over her dress. She shivered, looking over her shoulder twice as they walked the short distance to her home in the hostel.

'You are safe enough with me, lass,' her escort told her. 'But make sure you don't walk alone at night until we're sure we have that devil locked up tight.'

They paused outside the hostel and that was when it happened. A man rushed at them out of the darkness, making Winnie give a shout of fear, but instead of attacking her, he pressed a package into her hands. She looked at him in surprise as she recognised his face in the light of the gas lamps.

'Mr Barrow?' she said cried. 'What is this?'

'It is what you've been looking for,' he said and nodded at Constable Winston. 'Just don't let him know where it came from or I'm a dead man...'

'But how did you know where to find me?' Winnie asked him.

'My brother isn't the only one who knows how to find some-one.' He smiled oddly. 'I knew that girl – Sibby, she calls herself – was up to something, snooping around. Saw her peering round the bend in the stairs twice; she looked guilty when she knew I'd seen her. So I followed her home one night and saw her talking to you. She won't find anything wrong at my place now. That was all Cyril...'

'Why didn't you give us this evidence before?' Constable Winston said, taking it from Winnie and pushing it inside his uniform coat.

'Because he rescued me from the brink of hell. I didn't know then what a devil he was. Besides, I knew you would arrest me for what *he* made me do.'

'Not necessarily,' Constable Winston said. 'If you will stand up in court and help us convict him, I think my chief would see you didn't suffer for it. We know he's the one we want.'

'Put him behind bars and I will,' Bert said. 'That's if I'm still alive. My days are numbered unless you do.' And with that, he turned and walked away.

For a moment, Winnie and Constable Winston just stared at each other in silence and disbelief, then, 'I thought he must have some decency when he rescued Rosalind,' she said. 'I would never have thought it. He seemed such a harsh man.'

'He's been to prison and that makes a man harsh.'

'Yes, I suppose so. What do you think is in that package? Evidence of his brother's guilt?'

'If it's details, dates, names,' Constable Winston tapped his jacket. 'We've got Sinclair bang to rights. He'll hang if the evidence is here.'

'Good.' Winnie peered into the gathering gloom and shivered. 'If I'm so easy to find, I might have to move.'

'You can come and stay with us for a while,' Constable Winston suggested. 'Bring your things round in the morning, Winnie. It shouldn't be long now before this little nest of vipers is stamped out.'

'Thank you, I will,' she said. 'I'll lock my door tonight, as soon as I get in.' She said goodnight and went in and Constable Winston watched until she was safely inside and then walked away. Barrow must be desperate to come here this evening to deliver incriminating evidence against his brother.

It was to be hoped that, Barrow, their prime witness survived because despite the bulky package of what Constable Winston hoped was damning evidence, Sinclair might still get away with it. If the witness was dead, it would only be his written word – not an oath sworn in court. It could be enough, but until the package was examined, they wouldn't know...

Lost in his musings, Constable Winston was taken off guard when a man jostled him from his left side. He felt the hand at his coat, reaching for what was inside, but he caught the man's wrist, twisting it as he brought up his truncheon and struck him in the face. As the would-be thief staggered back, the stench of him almost made Constable Winston gag. He struck again and then pulled his whistle and blew twice.

Another whistle answered it and his attacker ran off, but not before Constable Winston received a sharp, stinging blow to his hand. He felt the warm trickle of blood and knew that, had he not been still carrying his truncheon and whistle, he would probably be lying dead on the ground of knife wounds.

Pounding feet heralded the arrival of another police constable. He saw Constable Winston stagger to the wall and then the blood.

'Winston...' he said. 'Did you see who attacked you?'

'I know who it was,' he replied through gritted teeth. 'We've been after Dirty Sid for a while.'

'And I just missed him...' The constable looked round as if considering where he might find their quarry, but a gasp from Constable Winston brought his attention back to him.

'I think you'd better get me to the station. I need this tended before I go home – and I need to talk to the sergeant!'

25

Bert let himself into the cottage Cyril had rented to him; it wasn't much of a place, no modern lighting or plumbing, and only a basic toilet in the back yard, but he'd made it home and it was comfortable enough. It belonged to his brother's employer and he expected to be evicted for non-payment of rent at any time, as he hadn't paid since the breach with Cyril.

He stiffened as his hand reached for the matches he kept by his oil lamp, sensing that he wasn't alone.

Striking the match, he lit the lamp, managing to keep his hands from shaking. He already knew who it would be.

'I suppose you always had the key,' Bert said, outwardly calm and looking at his brother. 'Are you here to kill me?'

'Perhaps,' Cyril replied with a shrug. 'You might still be of use to me, Bert – if you wish to be.'

'What do you want?'

'That isn't a nice way to greet your brother,' Cyril sneered. 'Because of you, and that wretched girl you employed, the police raided my house tonight. I was lucky that I'd gone to meet someone, but they ransacked the place, caught two of my men and took two girls away. I need a place to stay for a while, lie low.'

'The coppers will come here for sure,' Bert told him. 'I've been watched and followed ever since the night they raided the workshop.'

Cyril swore.

'No good blaming me. You were the one that brought the girls in. We were doin' fine until you got greedy. You can't stay here.'

'I've got nowhere else to go. It's just for a few nights, until I work out how to get the money I had hidden at the house. They will maybe watch it for a few nights, but then they'll leave it locked up.'

'I can't risk yer being found here,' Bert objected. 'I've got a few quid – I'll give it to yer and you can clear orf.'

'That isn't very friendly, after all I've done to help you, brother.'

'You used me – but I'm not the dumb ox you thought me,' Bert said sourly. 'I doubt we're even related.'

'Get the money then,' Cyril snarled. 'You are an ungrateful turd, Bert Barrow, but we did have the same slut for a mother...'

Bert turned away to the dresser drawer, his hand searching for the secret compartment where his money was hidden. As he reached inside, he heard a slight noise behind him and started to turn as a sour smell assailed his nostrils. Not fast enough. The knife struck him deeply between the shoulder blades three times and he went down to his knees. He knew in that moment he was done for. Cyril's henchman had been hidden somewhere and he'd been too confident of handling his brother.

'Don't kill him. I want him to suffer,' Cyril said, but it was already too late.

Bert fell face forward to the ground, his lifeblood draining from the knife wounds that had gone deep into his heart. He vaguely heard Cyril cursing his assassin, but then everything went black.

Cyril took the money, his eyes sweeping the small room for anything of value, but there was nothing, not even a decent pair of candlesticks he might sell. Bert had lived with the basics, putting everything he had into making a success of the business he'd so wanted to own. Stupid fool. He could have earned more if he'd gone along with Cyril, done what he'd wanted. He'd thought he was a hard man, but inside it turned out he had a soft spot. Cyril despised that – he spat on the body.

The cash in the secret drawer amounted to two hundred pounds; a pittance, but it would do for now. Cyril stuffed it inside his jacket and then looked down at the lifeless body of his half-brother. He felt nothing but annoyance that Bert had got off so lightly. Sid had been too enthusiastic with his first strikes, more's the pity.

'Do yer want me to get rid of 'im, boss?' Dirty Sid asked, wiping his knife clean on Bert's trouser leg before putting it back up his sleeve, where it habitually lived, always ready to strike.

'Just drag him into the corner and we'll leave him here,' Cyril said with a shrug of contempt. 'Can't risk you getting caught, too, Sid. They got Basher and Doug. We can stay here tonight, but we'll leave before it's light. This money will help us find somewhere to stay until the heat dies down.'

'Right,' Sid said. 'Do yer reckon 'e's got anythin' to eat in this dump?'

'Have a look in the kitchen,' Cyril ordered. 'He didn't bring anything with him, so he must have some food here.'

Dirty Sid went off and came back a few minutes later to report that there were bacon, eggs and bread in the kitchen cupboard.

'Can you cook?' Cyril asked and nodded as his henchman shook his head. 'I'll do it then.'

He went into the tiny kitchen and lit the gas lamp and then the gas ring that Bert had used to cook his food. It was clean enough but bare of all but the essentials. Cyril was used to the good things in life and he turned up his nose. It wasn't much of a hideaway, but if hadn't been sure that someone would come looking when Bert didn't turn up at work, he would have used it for longer. At least he had some extra money to buy his safety for a while. It was nothing compared with the thousands he'd had stashed away, but for the moment that was out of his reach.

As he cooked the food in the way he'd been taught in the kitchens his mother had once reigned over up at the big house where she'd been employed, Cyril felt mounting fury. His brother was dead, but that had done little to assuage the frustration of losing so much. His small but growing empire was gone. He had little chance of regaining it for the foreseeable future. Maybe it *was* time to cut his losses and move on. In one of the other big cities, he might find another job as an agent that would enable him to begin again; he could change his name, and his way of speaking would always gain him respect. He'd learned to speak as they did – the county family that had employed his parents – until his father was killed during a fox hunt from a terrible fall and his mother had gone off, leaving him to the mercy of her erstwhile employers.

Cyril had been the son of a hunt master, the keeper of horses and hounds, always the first to take a fence, but this time the fox had run out and spooked his horse, resulting in a tumble that led to a broken neck. Sir John, a blunt hearty man, had been fond of his faithful huntsman in his way, and out of pity had taken Cyril in, treating him almost as a son. It was he who had shown him how an estate worked, his own son off to college and interested only in becoming an Army officer. When the chance arose, he'd recommended Cyril to Lord Henry as his agent.

Now, all that was in the past. Cyril needed to disappear, become someone different, take another name.

As the bacon crisped to a nicety, Cyril made his plans. Even when he had the money he'd hidden, he would need to start small and build up. He wasn't sure that he would have any need for Sid, perhaps better to ditch him before he left London – but he wasn't quite finished yet.

'We're going away soon,' he told his henchman as he carried two plates piled with food to the table. 'Eat up, Sid. I've still got a score to settle. This time, I don't want any mistakes. Get the girl and you can have your fun with her before we kill her.'

'Yeah, boss, right,' Sid muttered, spitting through a mouthful of hot food. 'Where we goin' then?'

'Glasgow perhaps.'

'Cor blimey,' Sid muttered and nearly choked. 'I don't know as I fancy foreign parts...'

'Want me to leave you behind?' Cyril asked coldly and Sid blinked.

'Yer'd never do that, boss. Who would look out for yer?'

'Glasgow for a start,' Cyril said, ignoring his protest. 'Once the heat has died down, we'll come back to London.'

'Yeah, suits me,' Sid agreed, having thought it over. 'What about this girl then? How do I get 'er and when?'

'After this evening, I dare say she will stay clear of Dressmakers' Alley, but I imagine she lives at that hostel. Be there when she leaves in the morning,' Cyril said. 'When you get her, bring her to the warehouse we've used for the girls before.'

'In daylight, boss?' Sid looked nervous. 'You know what 'appened the last time we tried that – and I ain't got anyone ter 'elp me neither.'

Cyril nodded thoughtfully. 'I'll write a letter for her, asking her to visit Bert here. After he betrayed me last night, she'll trust him. Just give it to her and scarper, but follow from a distance. If we can lure her here, so much the better.'

'Yeah, that's clever, boss,' Sid said and then frowned. 'What 'appens when she gets 'ere?'

'I'll be waiting for her. You will follow and then we'll grab her. I want to teach that bitch a lesson she won't forget – not that she'll be alive by the time you've done with her.'

Sid's smile was enough to send icy shivers down the spine. 'Do you think she will fall for it, boss?'

'If she doesn't, we'll need to think again. If she takes notice of her copper friend, she will go straight to him – but she is too nosy for her own good and I think she will fall for it.'

26

Winnie packed her smaller suitcase, deciding to leave her winter clothes in the closet at her room in the hostel. She would only be staying with Mary and Constable Winston for as long as it took the police to catch the elusive Mr Sinclair. Hopefully, that would not be long now that Mr Barrow had given them some evidence against him, though they still had to catch him – and he would be lying low somewhere.

She left her lodgings, feeling the warmth of the sunshine on her face as she set out to walk the short distance from the hostel to Mary's house. In the light of morning, some of her fear had gone and she wondered whether it was truly necessary for her to impose on her friends. Surely, now that he knew he was being hunted, Mr Sinclair would not risk trying to harm Winnie. She couldn't be sure it was the reason behind the attempt to abduct Rosalind. It might just have been a random attack... and yet, she didn't think so.

Winnie was startled as a small, very dirty little boy suddenly rushed up to her and pushed a piece of paper into her hand. It was just a scrap really and slightly soiled. She stared after the child, who had dashed straight off again, then opened the piece of paper. A few words were written there.

I need to talk to you urgently. Something important has come to my notice. Come to this address if you want to see my brother behind bars.
    Bert Barrow

Winnie felt a cold tingling at the nape of her neck as she read the cryptic note. She wished she'd asked the boy who had given him the note, but he'd disappeared. A street urchin, he'd have taken sixpence from anyone to deliver it. Was it a trap? Winnie was an intelligent girl and understood that if Mr Barrow's brother had somehow discovered that he'd betrayed him and given her incriminating evidence, he might try to harm her.

The address was not far from Dressmakers' Alley and to reach it she would need to pass Sam's shop. Making up her mind, she went back into the hostel and deposited her suitcase in her room. She would walk to Sam's and tell him what had happened and she didn't want to be hampered by a heavy suitcase.

When she returned to the street, carrying a basket that contained a pair of shoes, Winnie looked about her but was unable to spot anyone who might be watching her. She set out at a determined pace, her nerves tingling with a mixture of excitement and fear. A plan had begun to form in her head and she thought it might work, if she could only persuade Sam to accept her part in it, because he wouldn't be happy at her taking any risks...

* * *

'Well, I don't know where he is,' Betty said to Mrs Jarvis as they stood outside the workshop in Dressmakers' Alley, waiting for their employer to open the door. 'It isn't like him to be late. I don't know why he didn't give me a key when he changed the lock. He said he was going to, but he hasn't.'

'What are we supposed to do then?' Mrs Jarvis muttered. 'I need to take the weight off my feet. Standin' here for nearly an hour we've been, Betty. You'd think he would at least send a message.'

'Should I go round and see if he's ill?' Betty asked doubtfully. 'We've got that order to get out today and we can't afford to lose it. It isn't easy to find the work after that raid, and, if we mess up, we'll all be out of a job.'

'You'd best go round and see if he's there.' Mrs Jarvis told her. 'If he is ill, you can bring the key. I'm going to wait here with the girls or they won't know what to do.'

Two of the girls were sitting on the doorstep, three others had gone to a café around the corner and several others were outside the flower shop, chatting and laughing with Lilly who ran it with her husband. Carl, who had come back to them as their sole cutter, had gone to the café, telling them to let him know when he was wanted.

'Tell them to wait until I get back,' Betty muttered crossly.

* * *

Betty set off for Bert's home, grumbling to herself. Sometimes she wondered why she still worked for him. She had the skill to work for any clothing manufacturer, but she'd stopped with him through thick and thin. Betty had a soft spot for the man, despite his temper and his harsh words. She knew he'd had a hard life and suspected that he wasn't as bad as he made out.

Bert had had to fight for everything he'd ever got and she'd done much the same, so they had something in common. He would never let anyone see there was a softer side to him if he could help it, but she'd seen it a few times, though she had more sense than to get on his wrong side, because in a temper he could lash out violently.

It wasn't like Bert not to make sure that the workshop was open and running, though. Even if he needed to buy materials, he would get things going before leaving to do his errands. Betty felt a prickle of unease at the nape of her neck. She knew more about the quarrel with Bert's brother than most of the others. He'd told her Cyril wouldn't be around in future – and warned her not to tell him anything if he did come to the workshop.

'He's out of things now,' he'd told Betty. 'I was a fool to let him push me into that other stuff. It won't happen again. I'm going to run things proper in future.'

It was the reason she'd returned. She'd had enough of looking over her shoulder and trying not to think about what was going on upstairs. Bert had promised her more money and a share in the profits once the business picked up.

As she passed the cobblers, she glanced in and saw a girl she recognised. Her brow creased in a scowl. That Winnie Brown – if that was her name – she was the one that had caused all the trouble. Bert had questioned her about the girl and she knew he suspected her of ratting to the police. She agreed that they should never have employed that wretched girl in the first place.

Turning the corner, Betty walked swiftly. She was in a hurry to get on with the day and annoyed that Bert hadn't sent word, telling her what to do. It just wasn't like him.

She reached Bert's cottage and paused outside, glancing over her shoulder. Tapping on the door, she waited impatiently, but there was no answer. Surely, he was there? He had to be. Betty was really annoyed now. Had she walked here for nothing? Where the hell was he?

Frustrated, she rattled the door handle and to her surprise it opened. She pushed it wide and called Bert's name but there was silence. Betty hesitated for a moment and then went inside. She was puzzled because Bert always locked up. Could he have had an accident?

She walked through the tiny hall into the small sitting room. The curtains were drawn and it was not light enough to see much, so she walked to the window and pulled them back, letting the sunlight in. As she turned, she saw Bert's body slumped near the dresser. He was lying in a pool of something dark that looked like – blood!

'Bert!' Betty screamed and rushed towards him. He'd been stabbed in the back by the looks of the dark stain on his jacket. She sank to her knees by his side, trying to turn him, hoping that he might by some chance still live, but as she saw the blue-marbled white of his face, she knew he was dead. 'Oh, Bert,' she sobbed. 'Who could...? It was that bugger what done it!' Betty jumped to her feet. She was wild with anger and a grief she would never have expected to feel for Bert.

At that moment, she heard a sound behind her and half-turned to see the face of a man that stood so close that she could smell his stale breath.

'It was you,' she accused. 'You killed him! You killed Bert...'

'I just found him here,' Cyril said. 'I came to find him and he was dead when I got here.'

'No!' Betty looked at him in horror. He hadn't shaved and she knew he'd been here all night – and Bert had been dead for a while. 'You murdered him. You're an evil devil and he told me it was all you – the girls, the men... that was all you.' Rage had overtaken her and she spoke without thinking. 'I'm going to the

police and I'm going to tell them everything I know about
you—'

'Then I can't let you leave here alive,' Cyril said and moved
towards her threateningly. 'Don't think I can't kill. I've killed
before. Your precious Bert was just my dogsbody – to clear up
when I needed him, but he refused me. Said if I didn't leave him
alone, he'd go to the coppers. So he's dead now. I had him
killed...' He smiled unpleasantly. 'But I'll deal with you myself,
you interfering bitch.'

Betty took a step back and screamed as Cyril lunged at her.
He grabbed her right wrist, twisting it and trying to subdue her
as she continued to scream and then call for help. Betty
scratched his face and kicked, fighting for all she was worth.
Cyril was wiry and stronger than he looked and his hands went
for her throat. She tried to poke her thumb in his eyes, but he
jerked back and his fingers closed around her throat, cutting off
her scream. She fought for breath as the room seemed to go
black around her and she knew she was dying.

Just as she was losing consciousness, shouting and voices
penetrated the blackness, telling her that other people had
arrived. Something or someone had caused Cyril to let go of her
throat and she slumped to the floor. A fight was going on in the
room and Betty knew that there was another woman and a
man... No, there was more than one man. A little smile touched
Betty's mouth before she slipped into the blackness... It served
the bugger right for what he'd done!

* * *

Moments earlier, Winnie had heard the screaming as she
approached the house she'd been told to meet Mr Barrow at.
Sam had agreed that he would follow her and he'd also

managed to bring Joe Ross, hailing him as he passed his shop with a bag of coal on his shoulder. At the first scream, Winnie had broken into a run and she knew that Sam and Joe were behind her. The front door was slightly ajar and she rushed in, towards the sounds of the desperate screaming.

For a moment, Winnie paused on the threshold of the small room, but then, seeing Betty struggling with a man, she acted on impulse, bending to pick up a pair of heavy fire tongs. Without pausing, she rushed at the man's back, which was towards her and started beating at his shoulders and the side of his head. He swore and tried to avoid her while continuing to strangle Betty, but she was relentless and kept on hitting him as hard as she could and, in the end, he gave a muffled curse and let go of Betty, turning to face her.

'I might have known it would be you,' he mumbled and made a grab for her.

Winnie yelled in defiance and struck him full in the face with her iron tongs, making blood spurt and him groan and jerk away. He swore and came at her again, trying to grab her, but Winnie whirled around and he caught at air. She pushed a chair in front of her and before he could tear it away, Joe and Sam burst into the room.

With a cry of rage, Sam went for Cyril, grabbing him by the shoulder and turning him to punch his nose. Cyril reeled but fought back, his signet ring catching Sam above his left eyebrow as he struck him; he headbutted Sam, making him stagger back, but that was his last hit. Sam's fists went into Cyril's face again and again, then into his stomach, and he sank to his knees, doubling over, blood trickling from the side of his mouth, as Sam kicked him in the side for good measure.

Joe had picked up a poker and stood over him threateningly. Sam was breathing hard, blood smeared on his eyebrow where

Cyril had caught him. Winnie had run to Betty as soon as the men took over the fight, kneeling by her side and stroking her face gently as her eyelids fluttered.

'Oh, Betty, thank goodness,' she cried as Betty looked at her. 'I thought he might have killed you.'

'You saved me,' Betty croaked and managed to sit up, Winnie supporting her. 'Thank you... he murdered Bert. He pretended he'd just found him, but I know it was him...'

Cyril looked at her with hatred. 'It wasn't me – it was Sid. I told him to frighten him, but he killed him. He is the one they'll hang, not me—'

'Boss, no!' The cry was shrill, like that of a wounded animal, and came from the doorway. They all looked as one towards the sound and saw the filthy little figure of a man that stood there, horror and grief on his ugly face at Cyril's betrayal. Despite what he was and what he'd done, he was almost pitiful, let down by the one person he'd trusted. For one instant, he hovered, as if stunned by the betrayal, and then he was gone.

'*He's* your murderer,' Cyril said. 'Try proving otherwise.'

'You'll be going to prison for a long time at any rate,' Joe told him and bent down, hauling him to his feet. He twisted Cyril's arm up his back and held it. 'Tie his wrists with the string in my pocket, Sam. This one isn't getting away.'

'You can't prove anything,' Cyril snarled, but the look in his eyes was apprehensive, furtive. 'Let me go and I'll make it worth your while... all of you.'

'You don't have enough money,' Sam told him.

'We'll tie him to this chair,' Joe said, pushing a single chair forward. 'Winnie, go and look for a policeman. There must be one about somewhere.'

Winnie went out into the street. A small crowd had gathered, attracted by the commotion and the sound of screaming. 'We need a policeman,' she said and then sighed with relief as a familiar face pushed his way through the crowd. 'Constable Winston. We've got him. I caught him trying to murder Betty from the workshop – and Mr Barrow has been stabbed to death, even though he's saying it wasn't him but one of his henchmen...'

'I thought I told you to stay out of it,' her friend said and went past her into the terraced house. Winnie noticed that one hand was heavily bandaged and followed him back into the house. She, in turn, was followed by another, younger police officer.

Constable Winston stood for a moment taking in the scene before him. He nodded but looked grim. 'Make sure he doesn't escape,' he told the other officer and bent down to look at Bert's face. 'Been dead for some hours by the looks of him.' Getting up, he looked at Betty, who was gingerly sipping a glass of water Sam had given her. 'Attacked you, did he?'

'Tried to strangle me,' Betty replied in a croaking voice. 'When Bert didn't turn up this morning, I came looking for him – found his body lying there and then he attacked me. He killed Bert and he was going to kill me, too.'

'How do you know he killed Bert?' Constable Winston asked her.

'Because he boasted about it before he tried to strangle me,' Betty said and met his gaze coolly. 'He told me Bert was a fool and that he'd got what he deserved – and he said he'd murdered him.'

'She's lying,' Cyril blurted. 'It was Dirty Sid. I only told him to teach him a lesson...' His eyes held uncertainty now, perhaps a little fear.

'He told you he'd killed and he tried to kill you – and we've got a body.' Constable Winston nodded, looking satisfied. 'Right, we'll take over now... Do you need to go to hospital?' His eyes met Betty's.

'No – but I need the key to the workshop.' She looked down at Bert. 'It will be in his coat pocket.'

'No need for that today,' Constable Winston said. 'That place will remain closed until we've finished our investigations.' He looked round at Winnie and the two young men and nodded. 'Thank you for what you've done, though it isn't what I would recommend – but you have my thanks. We're in charge now.' He nodded to his younger colleague. 'Cuff him, Jones. We'll take him down the station and charge him.'

'We'd best call for reinforcements – can't leave this.' Constable Jones nodded to Bert's body lying on the floor.

'No, we need to protect the evidence,' he agreed. 'Nip off and telephone the station and I'll stay here until you get back.'

'One of his bully boys was here earlier,' Sam told him. 'You'd best stay together in case he returns. I'll ring the station for you.'

Constable Winston agreed to it and Sam took Winnie's arm.

Betty stared at them and then followed them into the street. She was hesitating, looking back at the house.

'He won't give you the key,' Joe said, guessing why she was reluctant to leave. 'I know a way in to your place, though, if you want?'

'How?' Betty demanded, looking at him with sudden hope.

'I'll show you,' Joe said, glancing back over his shoulder. 'Nothing happened there. They've got all the evidence they need here. I'll get you in to the workshop if you want.'

'Yes, I do,' she said and turned to Winnie. 'Thanks for savin' me life. I shan't forget...' She walked off with Joe.

Sam had run to the end of the road to the red phone box. Winnie looked back at the house and then walked up the road, meeting Sam as he came out of the box.

'They are sending some officers,' he told her. 'They will go through the house for evidence and seal it. Where did Joe go?'

'He was going to get Betty into the workshop. She has an order she wants to get out today.'

'Why? It isn't her responsibility. Unless Bert left a will, his only relative is his half-brother... and I doubt he'd want him to benefit from her efforts.'

'I expect she is thinking of the girls and herself,' Winnie said and took his arm. 'They will all be out of a job if no one takes over.'

Sam nodded. 'Are you all right?' he asked her. 'You should've let me and Joe tackle him.'

'I heard a scream and knew something bad was happening. When I got inside, I saw he was trying to kill Betty – and you weren't far behind, so I went for him.' She smiled at him. 'I knew you wouldn't let me down, Sam.'

He chuckled softly. 'You're a brave girl, Winnie. Are you brave enough to wed me, even though it might mean living with my mother?'

Winnie stopped dead in the street, her eyes on his face. 'I like your mum,' she said and smiled. 'Was that a proposal, Sam Collins?'

'Yes.' He bent his head and kissed her, right there in the middle of the street ignoring an urchin's loud wolf whistle. 'I love you, Winnie Brown – will you marry me?'

27

Winnie stared at him for a moment, her heart catching, and then she smiled and held out her hands to him. 'Yes, I will marry you, Sam,' she said a little breathlessly. 'I'll be happy to live with your mum – and to look after her when she needs it.'

Sam gave a whoop of joy, picked her up and swung her around in delight as she squealed and held on to him. She laughed as he set her down again, still only half-believing what had just happened. Sam loved her and he'd asked her to be his wife! And she'd said yes!!!

'Mum likes you,' he told her as his hands tightened around hers, their fingers entwining. His eyes were glowing with love, making her tingle all over. 'Susie does, too, though I would have wed you anyway, whatever they thought. When I saw you battling that monster earlier, I knew that I couldn't live without you, Winnie. Had you been the one to be strangled, I'd have killed him!'

'I thought you might anyway,' Winnie said and looked at him admiringly. 'I didn't know you could fight like that, Sam.'

'You learn a lot of stuff in the Army. I don't make a habit of it,' he told her with a chuckle. 'But he deserved it – I hope they hang him.'

'He certainly ought to,' Winnie agreed. 'If I hadn't gone for him, I think he would have succeeded in murdering Betty. Thank goodness she seems all right.'

'Tough as old boots, that one,' Sam said grimly. 'She seemed determined to keep that business going. Maybe it was just reaction to the shock. I don't see how she will be able to, though. Even if she manages to get the order she's so anxious about out, she won't be paid immediately – and it takes money to run a place like that.'

'Yes, it does,' Winnie agreed, her hand on his arm now as they walked back to his shop. A sudden thought occurred to her, 'I'll have to go and see my mother, Sam. I left on bad terms with her and she might not want to see me, but I must tell her we're to be married – even though I don't need her permission.' Mary had wanted her to go sooner, but she had resisted, even though she knew she ought, but now it had to be done.

'Of course you must, my love,' Sam said and looked at her. 'I want to kiss you, Winnie. Can I when we get back to the shop? I'll put the closed sign up for a moment…'

'I should like that,' Winnie told him as he unlocked the door and went in. She followed him inside, enjoying the smell of fresh leather and glue that always permeated the little shop. 'Sam—' But her words were lost as he gathered her into his arms and kissed her, softly at first so that she responded and then with increasing passion. When at last he let her go, she sighed with content. 'I didn't know kissing could be like that!'

Sam grinned at her. 'Nor did I.' he confessed, a warm chuckle in his throat. 'I've never met another girl I wanted to kiss as much as you, Winnie. In fact, you're the only girl for me…'

Winnie was about to tell him what she thought of that when an impatient rattle at the door made them look round.

'I'd best open up,' he told her. 'Go through into the back room, love, and put the kettle on. I'll come in a minute and we'll talk.'

* * *

It was mid-afternoon when Winnie finally reached Mary's home. She hadn't brought her suitcase and her friend raised her eyebrows. 'I thought you were coming to stay,' she said. 'Bill said you were a bit upset last night.'

Winnie launched into her story. She told Mary how she'd been given the note and gone to Mr Barrow's house and what had happened. 'You haven't seen Constable Winston then?'

'No, not since he left home this morning. He was stabbed in the hand last night, just after you went into the hostel, but the foolish man insisted on reporting for work this morning.'

'Oh, I'm so sorry! I saw the bandage this morning, but he didn't say anything and there was so much going on...' She gave a little shudder, remembering the frightening moment when she'd seen Betty attacked and had done what she could to save her.

'You know what he is – stubborn.' Mary looked at her appraisingly. 'Fancy you standing up to that man like that, Winnie – and you saved Betty's life, too.' She nodded her appreciation. 'You were so brave – but it was dangerous.'

'Well, I managed it because I had to, though I couldn't have done it alone,' Winnie agreed. 'If I'd ignored the note or taken it to the police, Betty would have been murdered. I think it was me he was planning to kill, but she got there first. He hadn't reckoned with her going to investigate when Mr Barrow didn't turn up for work – but she was worried about getting an order out. So worried that she asked Sam's friend to let her into the workshop afterwards – he reckons he knows a way to get inside, at the back, I suppose. I'm not sure why she still thinks it is important – but perhaps she is hoping to take Madam Pauline's over now...'

'She might be, but it might be that she doesn't know what else to do.' Mary nodded. 'I don't know who will take over, unless Mr Barrow had a family?'

'Just his half-brother, as far as I know – and he will be in prison for a long time, if he doesn't hang.'

'He should hang,' Mary said with a little shudder. 'I don't like to think of anyone dying like that – but what do you do with monsters like that man?' It was the age-old question that could never be answered – was it right to take a life, even when it was an evil murderer's?

'You hang them,' Winnie replied, certain of the rightness of it after what she'd witnessed that morning. 'He isn't worth wasting your pity on, Mary. I shan't give him another thought. I'm just glad he's been caught at last.' She hesitated for a moment and then smiled. 'Besides, I've got some exciting news—'

'He's never gone and asked you?' Mary said as she looked at Winnie's face. As Winnie nodded, she gave a little scream of pleasure and hugged her. 'That's wonderful, love! I am so pleased for you – and you deserve it.'

'Sam says I'm the only girl he's ever loved, Mary – and I love him. I've known for a while he was a man I could marry. I wasn't sure he would ask me, but he said he couldn't bear to lose me...' Winnie clasped her hand. 'He wasn't sure he ought to ask me, because he must look after his mum and thought I might object to living with her, but I don't. I like her and it means I can carry on working for a while if I want.'

'You can help us and still be married,' Mary agreed. 'We don't have any silly rules about our girls being single. We might be struggling for equality, but that doesn't mean we don't appreciate a loving husband and family.'

'I might help Sam by serving in the shop while he gets on with his work,' Winnie said. 'We haven't really talked about it yet, but there's no reason why I can't continue to work until we have children, is there?'

'None at all,' Mary confirmed. 'There are men who won't hear of their wives working. You know that, Winnie, but it is old-fashioned. Some women are forced to go scrubbing to hold the family together, because their husbands either can't or won't work – and there are war widows who have no choice but to work.' She was thoughtful for a moment, then, 'Have you considered finding another job as a seamstress, love? You made that beautiful dress for yourself – and it seems a waste not to use what you've learned. And you'd earn more at a decent workshop, too.'

'I do enjoy dressmaking, especially nice things,' Winnie told her. 'But I don't like the way we were forced to work at Madame Pauline's. There was no time to take pride in your work or look at the finished article. Besides, I expect that place will close soon. Sam says they can't continue without someone to get the orders and look after the money.'

'No, I don't suppose they can,' Mary replied. 'Perhaps someone else will take it over. If they did, would you consider working there?'

'I might think of it,' Winnie considered aloud. 'But only if they were a decent firm that made nice things and treated the girls properly.'

'Well, it is something to think about.' Mary smiled at her. 'So when is the wedding then?'

'We need to save a little first,' Winnie said. 'We'll both save as much as we can for the wedding. If I move in with Sam's mum, I'll save my rent, and he can let the flat over the shop and that will help. It means he has further to walk to work, but he might buy a second-hand bicycle.' She smiled. 'I really like Sam's mum and I think it is a good idea to live with her. She can't manage very well alone and he's been worried about her. Now he doesn't have to be, because I can do the chores she can't manage – and she will have a meal ready for us both in the evening.'

'That's a good idea,' Mary agreed with a laugh. 'Save on bus fares – he can mend his own shoes.'

'I doubt Sam uses a bus except if it's pouring down.' Winnie laughed with her. 'Yes, we'll never have to take our shoes to the menders. It gets quite expensive when you have three or four children.'

Mary nodded, smiling as she saw the excitement in her eyes. 'So you're happy at last, Winnie. Don't you think it is time you visited your mother, dear?'

'Yes, I do. I know I should have done so before, Mary. You've told me enough times – but she always makes me feel... well, miserable.'

'I know. You've told me how she went on at you for hours, complaining, blaming you for every little thing – but she is your mum and she's had a hard life.'

'I know and I will – Sam is coming with me. He says we'll go on Sunday morning and then go back to his home for lunch.'

* * *

It was past six when Constable Winston arrived home. Winnie was just about to leave when he came in, but he asked her to stay.

'You'll want to know we have our Mr Sinclair safely locked in the cells,' he told her. 'He has been charged with various counts, from embezzlement to murder – the murder of his brother and the attempted murder of Mrs Betty Ford.'

'Oh, is that her name?' Winnie said. 'I never knew it...'

'She doesn't use it as a rule,' he told her. 'She was married to a man for five years, but then he cleared off and left her. She had two children to support – both died of diphtheria in their early years, and she moved in with another man, who beat her and then deserted her. Seems she had a rotten life, working in bars and greasy cafés washing up, though she'd been a seamstress in her youth – and then Barrow gave her chance to run that place for him. She is quite cut up over his death. Found her working late to get the last order out for him...' Constable Winston cleared his throat. 'She was in tears. Said it was all she could do for him.'

'Oh, poor Betty,' Winnie said. 'I didn't know she'd had such a rotten life.'

'She may seem hard on the outside, but I daresay there is a heart there somewhere,' Constable Winston replied. 'I told her it was best to close the place down, because the landlord will likely want to let it again. She says she'll try to carry on as long as she can. Apparently, she has a bit of money put by and she will use it to buy materials and pay wages.'

'She could lose all her savings,' Mary objected. 'And for what? I can't see this Mr Barrow did her any favours – apart from giving her a job...'

'Well, it won't last long,' he said. 'The landlord is sure to want them out unless they pay the rent.'

'I doubt if she has enough savings to pay the girls for long,' Winnie agreed. 'Even though the wages are low, it will cost quite a bit – unless some money is owed them or Mr Barrow had some put aside.'

'There was none at the house – at least none we found when we searched it,' he said. 'If there had been, we should have confiscated it. Besides, even though Sinclair can't benefit from his brother's estate due to the circumstances of having murdered him, she can't either.'

'I pity all those girls,' Winnie said. 'Perhaps someone else will start up there if the landlord lets it again.'

'Let's hope so,' Mary agreed. 'You won't stay to supper, Winnie?'

'No. I am meeting Sam later,' she said and glanced at the clock, 'We might buy some pies and chips to celebrate with his mum.' She kissed Mary and flashed a smile at Constable Winston. 'Mary will tell you all about it,' she called as she left with a wave.

28

'So, you've decided to come at last, have you?' Winnie's mother gave her a spiteful glare when she and Sam walked into the kitchen of her former home. Mrs Brown was sitting in her chair by the range, which was lit even on this warm summer day, and a stale smell of boiled cabbage hung in the air. She didn't get up but just glared at them belligerently. 'And who is this you've seen fit to bring with you then?'

'This is Sam Collins, Mum,' Winnie said and Sam advanced into the tiny kitchen and offered his hand, which was ignored. 'Sam is the man I am going to marry.'

'Are you indeed?' Mrs Brown stared at them both with dislike. 'And what about me? What if I say you shan't marry him without my consent?'

'I'm twenty-one; I don't need your consent,' Winnie replied, her cheeks flushing. She felt the familiar sinking inside. Why did her mother always have to be this way? 'I know I should have come to see you before but... I was upset.'

'And so you should be,' her mother said tartly. 'You had a good job with Mrs Harper and what must you do but shame me?

Running off like that without so much as a word. I could have died for all you cared. And now you turn up to tell me that you're getting married to a person I don't even know. Well, I don't want to know, miss.' An oddly triumphant look came to her face then. 'As it happens, you're lucky you found me. If you'd come next week, I'd have been gone. I'm getting married myself and moving to the country.'

Winnie stared at her for a moment, shocked beyond words, and then she smiled in relief. 'That is wonderful, Mum. I am so glad for you.' She wouldn't have to feel guilty any longer if she didn't visit, because she'd know her mother was comfortable in her own home.

'Well, so you may be,' her mother said with a look of satisfaction. 'Mr Robinson has a nice little farm and two small boys. He took me down and showed me his home and very comfortable it is too. Besides, I always wanted a son – they know how to treat their mothers, not like some ungrateful daughters...' She sniffed. 'Well, I washed my hands of you when you ran off, as I told my sister – she was all for making excuses for you, saying you'd come round when you were ready, and you weren't a bad girl – but I would hear none of it, miss. You need not have bothered to visit. I'm going where I'll be appreciated and I don't mind if I never hear from you again. Like your father, you're an uncaring wretch.'

'In that case, I am wasting my time here,' Winnie said and took the hand Sam had offered to her. He'd remained silent, but she knew from his rigid stance that he was holding back with difficulty. Her own face was tight as she fought her tears. 'Let's go. I might have known she wouldn't want to know I was happy.'

Winnie's mother gave a snort of disgust. 'As for you, Sam Collins – or whatever your name was – you watch out she doesn't leave you in the lurch.'

Sam turned to look at her. For a moment, he regarded her in silence and her face turned pink as she read the contempt in his eyes. Then he nodded. 'I know my Winnie,' he said. 'She is a brave girl and whatever you think she did wrong in the past, that is over. I'm sorry you are so bitter, Mrs Brown. I hope you find happiness in your new life.' He held Winnie's hand to his mouth and kissed it. 'Come, my love,' he said. 'I believe my mother and sister are waiting for us at home. They both love and appreciate you, as I do.'

Winnie smiled at him but said nothing. She didn't look back as they exited the kitchen door. Once outside, she turned to him, her eyes wide with hurt. 'What Mum said... I told you of the stupid things I did that time at Mrs Harper's... but it was so hard living with Mum's bitterness and seeing another way of life, a life such as I had never dreamed of, it made me jealous and I did something wrong. I've wished since it had never happened but—'

Sam placed a finger against her mouth. 'Everyone makes mistakes in their lives, Winnie. You must have had a rotten time for years. It was no wonder you had a fit of envy when you saw how it could be... but you don't envy Mrs Harper now?' He looked at her searchingly.

'No, not one bit,' Winnie said and her fingers tightened around his. 'I was a silly girl then, Sam, jealous of the lovely things I'd never had, but I've grown up now – and I've seen there are girls and folks much worse off than we were. Mum always had enough to get by on; her sister saw to that, giving her a few bob when she needed it, but she never stopped complaining. It was usually me that was wrong – or my dad. I loved him, even if he did drink a bit too much at times. After he died, there was nothing left but misery.'

'Forget about it now,' Sam told her and squeezed her hand.

'Maybe one day your mum will regret what she said to you, but unless she makes the effort to tell you so, you are to forget her, right?'

'Yes, I will,' Winnie said and sighed. She knew her mother's spite would linger in the back of her mind. Perhaps it was her fault for putting off the long-overdue visit, but it might have been the same even if she'd gone as soon as she was settled. Her mother had no love for her. She'd never been a kind or caring woman and the years had made her sour. Perhaps now that she was to marry a prosperous farmer and look after his boys, she would be happier. Winnie hoped so, but somehow, she doubted that anything would change her mother.

'Susie will be at Mum's this afternoon,' Sam told her. 'I know she will be excited to hear our news. I'm sure you will love each other, Winnie. She's told me enough times she wants to be an auntie before she is too old to play games with the children.'

'Won't she marry herself then?' Winnie asked, her thoughts taking a new turn at this.

'Susie?' Sam frowned and looked thoughtful. 'I can't see it happening. She is devoted to her lady – and from what I've heard, she has a good job and enjoys her life.'

Winnie nodded; it was true that many women in service never married, though some employers were happy to take on a married couple. 'It seems a shame though, if she likes children.'

'Her ladyship is expecting later this year, so Susie told Mum. I dare say she will help with the child sometimes – though there will be a nanny, of course.'

'Strange ways the aristocracy has,' Winnie remarked. 'I shouldn't want to hand my baby over to a nanny.'

'We couldn't afford it,' Sam said with a chuckle. 'Might be nice when they cry all night long, I suppose – but no, I wouldn't want it either. They have some odd customs, the toffs, but Susie says her lady is different, so maybe she'll change things.'

'Well, it's so nice to meet you,' Susie said and came to kiss her cheek as Sam took Winnie into his mother's kitchen, where the two women were talking over a pot of tea. The smell of herbs and baking welcomed them as much as the happy faces. Here, everything was as neat as a new pin, the only clutter a row of pot plants growing on the windowsill. 'Sam has talked about you a bit, but it came as a surprise when he told us he was going to get married.'

'A nice surprise,' Sam's mother said, smiling at Winnie as she beckoned her to her chair. 'Come and kiss me, Winnie. I couldn't be more delighted and nor could Susie. We've both hoped Sam would find a lovely girl and now he has.'

Winnie blushed and then kissed her cheek. 'Thank you, Mrs Collins. I think I am the lucky one to have found Sam and have him love me.'

'Well, you are both lucky,' Susie said. 'Did you have a nice visit with your mum, Winnie?'

'Mum... told us she was getting married too, didn't she, Sam? She'll be going to live in the country soon...' Winnie avoided Susie's bright gaze, not wanting her to guess how awful it had been.

Susie nodded. 'And when is your wedding to be?'

'Not just yet,' Sam told her. 'We'll get engaged, but we need to save a bit before we're wed. Winnie doesn't earn much where she is and she might try for a job as a seamstress again, if she can find a decent place.'

'Oh... I might,' Winnie agreed. 'We do need to save a bit of money before we marry.'

Susie nodded. 'Yes, because there will be none to spare once the children start coming.'

'Susie, give them a chance,' her mother remonstrated and Susie laughed.

'You know me, Mum. I say things as they are – my lady says it's what she likes about me.'

'How is your lady?' Mrs Collins asked.

Susie frowned for a moment, then, 'She is frustrated and getting a bit tired,' she said. 'Now that she is six months gone and showing a lot, she can't go to the social events she enjoys – at least she enjoys some of them. She likes to go to the races with his lordship or a regatta or a cricket match, as well as theatres and parties, but it isn't done to go out much when you are in a delicate condition, as they call it in her circles. So she often spends her time...' She paused, then, 'Well, she likes to sketch.'

'I suppose she will have a nanny for the baby,' Mrs Collins said. 'I worked in a big house when I was young – before I married your father – and they had two nannies and a nursery maid. The head nanny was far too old to do much, but her word was law. There were some ructions in that nursery, I can tell you.'

'Oh, it won't be like that with Lady Diane. She does have Nanny, of course – she has been with the family for years. Lord Henry is fond of her and she will have a maid to help her, but Lady Diane says that she will look after her baby herself as much as she can.'

'A modern young woman.' Mrs Collins nodded her approval. 'I think you were lucky when she took you on, Susie.'

'Yes, I was. She gave me another bonus this week, Mum.' Susie opened her purse and put two pounds and ten shillings on the table. 'She gave me five pounds and told me to have a holiday. I was very grateful for the money, but I refused the time off. I'll look after her as usual this evening, though she has told me to train up one of the younger maids to help me. She has plans for the future...'

'You shouldn't give me all that,' Mrs Collins said. 'Keep some for yourself, Susie.'

'I shall buy myself a new dress with the rest of it,' Susie said. 'Or I might make one...' She looked at the green dress Winnie was wearing. 'That is a lovely dress, Winnie. Do you mind if I ask where you bought it?'

'I made it myself,' Winnie told her. 'I saw a similar one in Harpers but it was far too expensive for me – so I bought a pattern and the material and made it for a fraction of the price.'

'It suits you well,' Susie said, looking thoughtful. 'Which reminds me...' She turned to her brother. 'What has happened about that place – Madame Pauline's. You told Mum it might be closing down soon...?'

'I'm not sure,' Sam replied. 'I know the woman in charge – Betty – she is trying to keep it going for the sake of the girls, and herself, I suppose – but I doubt she has enough money to pay wages and the rent.'

'No, that would be quite a lot,' Susie agreed. 'It was all very shocking – and Sam tells us you saved Betty's life, Winnie?'

'Well, I suppose I did,' Winnie said. 'At least I kept her attacker busy until Sam and his friend, Joe Ross, arrived. I doubt I could have stopped him if they hadn't followed me.'

'It took courage to go for him, but then you've been doing several dangerous things, I hear,' Susie said, looking at her with approval. 'I like you, Winnie. It's just what I would have tried to do myself in that situation.'

'Now don't you talk silly, either of you,' Mrs Collins

instructed with a little shiver. 'I'm just glad they've put that awful man away. It isn't safe for decent girls to walk the streets when the likes of him is let loose.'

'Well, he won't be now,' Sam said. 'So let's forget him. What's for dinner, Mum?'

'I made a lovely cottage pie and there's apple crumble for afters,' Mrs Collins said. 'Susie, you and Winnie can set the table while I put the vegetables on and then we'll be ready to eat in a jiffy.'

'Come on,' Susie invited. 'I'll show you where we keep the cloth...'

She led the way to the dresser and opened a drawer, taking out a pristine white linen tablecloth. 'So you're a seamstress,' she said to Winnie. 'I might have some news for you one day, if you're interested in a good job...?'

'Oh, what sort of a job?' Winnie asked, but Susie only shook her head and smiled mysteriously.

'I can't say for certain yet, but I will soon...'

Winnie nodded. Susie liked to tease. She wouldn't ask questions – but she might start looking for a new job in the next week. Sam was right. Her job with the Women's Movement was pleasant but she didn't earn much above her food and lodgings. She wouldn't mind working for Madame Pauline's if they paid her properly and weren't quite as strict as before – but it would probably have to close very soon. It couldn't stay open much longer now that Mr Barrow was dead and his brother in prison.

29

'Did you have a good evening?' Lady Diane asked when Susie took her tea tray into her bedroom the next morning. 'You really should have taken a little holiday, Susie. Meg could have looked after me for a few days.' Meg was a new parlourmaid who had some talent for dressing hair and had been taken on as a helper for Susie.

'Perhaps I shall when she is more confident, my lady,' Susie told her. 'But a day off now and then is sufficient. Apart from visiting my mother, I don't have many interests outside my work.'

'That worries me a little,' Lady Diane said. 'I feel that I take up too much of your life. You should have fun sometimes – perhaps go dancing with a gentleman friend.'

'I don't know any gentlemen who would like to take me dancing,' Susie said and laughed as she moved around the room, tidying the bedcovers and laying out a satin dressing gown. 'Should I ask Mr Fox if he will take me – or Mr Molton?' The mischief in her eyes made her mistress laugh.

'I think he would be shocked,' Lady Diane replied, but

looked at her enquiringly. 'Surely there must be someone – perhaps a visit to the theatre or the seaside with your brother?'

'I did visit the sea with my brother once some years ago,' Susie remarked as she opened the curtains to let in a little sunlight. Outside, the doves were cooing from chestnut trees in the square and a cat was sitting in a patch of sun licking its paws. 'Cold and wet and windy it was. We walked about and got frozen and then dived into a café and sat drinking coffee most of the day.'

Lady Diane looked at her curiously. 'Is there nothing you like to do for fun?'

'When we visit the country, I like to walk,' Susie said. 'Sometimes on my afternoons off in London, I visit the park and talk to the nannies out with their charges – or I go to a nice tea shop. At other times, I visit the big stores and sometimes I try on the smart clothes. When I have time, I read books – history mostly.' She laughed. 'I am a woman of simple tastes, my lady. I enjoy caring for you, looking after your clothes – and I chat to the other servants in the evenings. Now and then we have a game of cards – and if Mr Molton is in a good mood, he gives us a glass of sherry.'

'Have you never wished to marry?' Lady Diane looked at her searchingly.

'I've never met anyone that I thought I liked enough to marry,' Susie replied. 'However, I am delighted to say that my brother has decided to marry and that is something both my mother and I have wished for. Winnie is a lovely girl and I think they will be happy.'

'You must tell me when they get married and take some time off then.'

'Yes, I shall,' Susie promised, nodding happily. 'Winnie is a seamstress – quite good, actually. She has an eye for style –

made herself a pretty dress. She told me she'd copied it from something she'd seen in Harpers.'

Lady Diane looked at her with interest. 'Where does she work?'

'She is a member of the Women's Movement and a sort of volunteer. I think she gets her board and lodging and a small remuneration, but not enough – she is looking for a job, probably as a seamstress. She worked at Madame Pauline's for a while.' Susie smiled as she saw the gleam in Lady Diane's eyes. 'She was the young woman who helped them catch Mr Sinclair. Sam told my mother that she attacked Sinclair when he was trying to strangle that unfortunate woman.'

'Lord Henry told me some of it,' Lady Diane confirmed. 'His friend, the chief constable, telephoned after Sinclair was arrested to tell him that the man had been caught and would probably hang. Henry was so relieved the rogue was behind bars. I didn't know the young woman involved was engaged to your brother.'

'I don't think she was until after the event. I believe they had been courting in their way – I understand she has been deeply involved in some investigation the Women's Movement was making into Madame Pauline's... but it seems seeing her in danger affected my brother powerfully. He asked her for her hand, even though they still have to wait for a while before they can wed. They neither of them have much money.'

'Oh, how difficult for them. I should not have liked to wait too long after Lord Henry asked me to marry him,' Lady Diane said and sipped her tea, thoughtfully. 'I think I should like to meet this Winnie – could you arrange for her to come to tea with me?'

'Bring Winnie here?' Susie was startled. 'Are you sure you wish for it, my lady?'

'Oh, don't be stuffy, Susie,' Lady Diane said. 'You know I don't go out much at the moment. I am bored and there cannot possibly be anything wrong if you bring your friend and both of you have tea with me in my private parlour, now can there? She must be a presentable young woman or you wouldn't approve of her.'

'What would his lordship say?' What would the servants say? Susie knew there would be some raised eyebrows and not a few comments below stairs if it was known that her ladyship was entertaining a girl not of her class in her private parlour.

'Lord Henry is so busy with all this nonsense over his property that he will not even notice, and he never interferes with my friends, you must know that, Susie.' Lady Diane frowned at her. 'Now, say you will ask her.'

'My lady—'

'How do you imagine I am to run a business if I never meet the people I wish to employ?' Lady Diane demanded. 'I thought I might start by asking Winnie if she will make me some maternity clothes and also some baby things, just to keep her busy until I am ready to employ her full time. I have designed my own christening gown...' She reached for her sketch pad. 'Look – do you not think that remarkably pretty?' She showed her a long gown of white silk with an overdress of lace and ribbons.

'Yes, my lady – but I could do that...'

'You have enough to do as it is, training Meg and looking after me – and you will soon have far more—'

'What do you mean?' Susie stared at her in wonder. She saw the sparkle of excitement in Lady Diane's eyes and gasped. 'His lordship has never agreed to let you open your own business?' Surely, he hadn't given in? Susie never would have thought it.

'Well, he has my business plan and last night over dinner he looked at me oddly and said he had never realised that I had devoted so much time to my dream.' She smiled. 'He thought the sketches I showed him beautiful and my ideas for the running of such a place sound. So I really do not see why I should not have my way. We have discussed the practical side and he was impressed by my ideas.'

'My lady...' Susie was speechless for a moment, then, 'You really intend to go through with it?' She'd known her ladyship would not be satisfied unless she had some kind of business but had expected it to be limited to something small and discreet – perhaps designing for another firm.

'Yes, of course.' Lady Diane smiled. 'Much of the burden will fall on your shoulders, Susie. You will still be my personal dresser – no, my personal assistant. You will oversee all my affairs, my clothes, as you do now, discuss my social engagements, but also my business. I shall have Meg to look after me. She will dress my hair and wait on me, but I shall still want to have time with you each day. The actual running of the day-to-day work will be done by someone you and I will choose – and we shall discuss everything, but you will be my right hand. You will, of course, receive a much higher wage than you do now – and you are entitled to holidays, even if you do not want them.'

'Me...?' Susie stared at her in astonishment. 'I have never thought of such a thing. Do you believe me capable of it, my lady?'

'I am very sure of it,' Lady Diane told her in a decided tone. 'Matthew has told me he will handle the accounts for us and he is checking my costings. I shall be in charge of design and we will discuss anything that becomes necessary, but you will hire the workers and source the materials – and our salesperson will see to the orders. Oh, I dare say there are many factors I have not yet thought of, but together I am certain we can do it.' She smiled. 'I have asked my new friend, Sally Harper, to tea this afternoon – and I believe she can help me source various firms I may need to contact to arrange favourable terms, for materials and other things. If we succeed, she will be one of our customers, too.'

Susie hardly knew what to say. Never in her whole life had she looked for anything above her station. It was a new world that was being offered her and she wasn't sure yet if she actually wanted the life that she could see ahead of her. 'I don't know if I can do it, my lady.'

'Please do not say no yet,' Lady Diane said, giving her one of her irresistible smiles. 'I dare say I could find someone else – I am sure there are other women who might enjoy the chance, but I want you. You are my friend, Susie. In time, when Lord Henry has got used to the idea, I hope to do more myself. Yes, I could employ a full-time manager and all the seamstresses and cutters and everyone else I may need – but it wouldn't be half as amusing if you were not a part of it.' She raised her beautiful eyes to Susie's. 'Don't you see how much fun we could have?'

Susie looked at her, saw the appeal in her face, and knew she could not refuse. 'I suppose it would be fun, my lady,' she said. 'If it is really what you want – and you are happy with Meg to look after you...'

'She is not yet as good at dressing my hair as you,' Lady Diane replied. 'I believe she may do very well in time – she loves caring for my clothes, but she is not you, and never could be. As I've tried to tell you before, Susie, I do not see you as a servant – you are my friend and I want you to share my adventure. We shall be partners – and, if we are successful, you shall share in the benefits of our endeavour.'

'Are you perfectly sure you want to go ahead with this, my lady? Even if I do as you ask, you will need to be involved and to supply new designs regularly.'

'Yes, I know, but Henry says I must promise not to tire myself too much, and I won't.' She smiled winningly.

'And you want to start almost immediately?'

'Yes, once it can be arranged,' Lady Diane confirmed.

'Are you certain his lordship will agree?'

Lady Diane nodded, a sparkle in her eyes. 'Yes, he has already said it sounds feasible, and that means he likes it.' She laughed delightfully. 'You know he never denies me anything, Susie. I just had to give him time to accept the idea.'

'Where is this workshop to be... in Madame Pauline's?' His lordship owned the building and it made sense to take it over.

'It is perfect for my needs once I have it renovated. I shall have bigger windows that open to let in air. I intend to purchase more modern sewing machines for the seamstresses, and the upper floor will become a showroom and store and there will also be a restroom for the girls to have their breaks...' She nodded as she saw Susie's surprised expression. 'Yes, I have thought it all through. That is what impressed Henry. I intend it to be a high-class establishment – a bit like Harpers Emporium, only at the wholesale end rather than the retail and our clothes will be quality items. I hope within the price range of women of moderate means. Not yet for working women, but perhaps one day... it is my dream that young women of all classes should be able to buy pretty clothes straight off the rail.'

Most young women either made their own dresses or bought cheap, often faulty goods from the market – and some women felt themselves fortunate if they could purchase even a second-hand dress. Susie thought that many things would have to change before Lady Diane's dream could happen – if it ever could.

'What of Betty and the girls who work there?' Susie asked. 'I believe there is a cutter, too, though I know nothing of him.'

'We shall hope to employ them, providing they can meet your exacting standards, and we'll give them enough time to work on a garment, rather than being forced into slave labour,' Lady Diane replied, a serious note in her voice now. 'Henry must sort out the lease. It was in Mr Barrow's name, of course, and there can be no legal objection to my taking it over as he is deceased and his only relative a criminal accused of murder as well as embezzlement. Mr Sinclair would not be entitled to take it over without Henry's agreement, which he would never have – or so Henry's lawyers have told him – even if he were to avoid the penalty for his crimes.'

'I should think not,' Susie said. 'That man must not be allowed to go free after all he has done.'

'I am sure he will not,' Lady Diane said. 'So I want you to visit the workshop and if it is still trying to struggle on, inform whoever works there that we shall be hiring quite soon. I hope the renovations will start in the next week or so.'

'When did you wish me to tell them?' Susie asked. 'I could speak to my brother about Winnie too.'

'Go this afternoon, when I am having tea with Sally Harper,' Lady Diane said and smiled. 'Meg will look after me. You need not hurry back.'

'Very well, my lady – what would you like me to put out for you to wear this afternoon?'

'I think the pink cotton for this morning, and my lilac tea-gown for this afternoon. You may tell Meg to bring me some breakfast up – just toast and marmalade. I think I shall stay in bed and work on my sketches. Henry will not be in for lunch, so I may as well rest this morning and be refreshed for my little tea party this afternoon.'

'You are not feeling ill?' Susie asked, a little anxious.

'No, just tired,' Lady Diane said. 'I do very much want to

hold my little girl in my arms, Susie – I do hope it will be a girl...'
She sighed. 'Of course, I will love a boy if that's what I have, but
Nanny says it will be a girl, and she knows these things. Some-
thing to do with the way I am carrying the babe – but I must
confess I shall be very much happier when she or he is here.'

* * *

Susie nodded and left Lady Diane and went away to inform Meg
of her duties for the day. She spent some time in the kitchen
talking to Cook, and then an hour in the ironing room, pressing
some of her ladyship's clothes. Once that was finished, she went
up to her own room and looked through her wardrobe. The role
her ladyship had offered her was very different from the one
she'd been accustomed to and her clothes for when she was off-
duty were simple. Susie rarely spent much money on herself,
preferring to make sure her mother had small treats and was
never in a worry about how to pay her bills. The only thing she
had suitable for a hot day was a pale blue dress with a dropped
waistline and three-quarter length sleeves, which she had made
for herself. It hardly fitted her new position, but the smart suit
Lady Diane had given her was too warm for such weather as
they were having just now.

Frowning, she glanced through her wardrobe again and
discovered, right at the back, a dress Lady Diane had worn only
once and given to Susie because it did not suit her. It was a pale
grey with long sleeves that buttoned at the wrist and a slanted
neckline, made of a soft silk that rustled slightly as the wearer
moved. It would be cool and smart, but reached only a few
inches below her knees. Shorter than she normally wore, Susie
had hesitated to wear it as a servant, even an upper-class one,
and thought it not fitting. In future, she would be something

more – though as yet she wasn't quite sure what her new status meant – and she would need to dress appropriately.

Susie tried the dress on. It looked neat and elegant, as it ought, for it had been expensive. With a few adjustments, it would fit her. It was not the first dress passed on by a generous mistress, though Susie seldom wore one of Lady Diane's gowns, for she had no occasion to do so. Two others had been sold and the money given to Susie's mother. This time, Susie knew she had no alternative if she was to make the right impression. She could not do what Lady Diane had asked of her unless she looked the part. If she was to become the manager of a clothing workshop, she must be suitably dressed.

Nodding to herself, she took the dress down to the sewing room. There was a modern machine there, replacing the old treadle model Nanny had once used for Master Henry's clothes, and it would not take her long to make the adjustments.

30

Susie stood outside the shopfront and looked critically at the window. It had not been washed for a while and was smeared with dust from the street. The alley itself had recently been cleaned by the street sweeper with his broom and little cart, but some of the properties had peeling paint and looked in need of renovation, including this one. It was high time some attention was paid to what was otherwise a substantial property.

The faded window blinds were still in place, which meant when she entered, she would hardly be able to see after the bright sunshine. She knew she must be firm and confident, otherwise she would fail at the onset. Taking a deep breath, Susie opened the door and went in, blinking in the sudden dimness as a bell clanged noisily.

Nothing had changed since her last visit and the woman behind the desk looked up at her, frowning in puzzlement. As she belatedly recognised Susie, her expression changed to one of apprehension.

'What do you want?' she asked, her tone hostile. 'You came here before...'

'Yes, I did, when Mr Barrow was in charge.' Susie gave her a haughty stare. 'You are Mrs Jarvis, I seem to recall...'

'What's it to you?'

'As the new manager of this establishment, I am here to speak to those who may be future employees. I am Miss Susie Collins and my business associate and I have secured the lease of these premises.'

'I told Betty you was spying for another firm!' Mrs Jarvis exclaimed indignantly. 'You can't just walk in 'ere and take over...'

Susie gave her a quelling look. 'I have come to inform you of certain things – but I need to speak to all the staff. Would you please accompany me into the sewing room?' She had not held the position of Lady Diane's dresser for nothing and her voice carried authority.

'You can't go in there,' Mrs Jarvis said weakly, but Susie ignored her and went past the desk and through the connecting door. 'Betty... it's that woman again...' she squawked in protest.

The sewing room was not as busy as the first time Susie had entered it; only half of the stations were occupied by seamstresses and they all stopped work and looked up. Betty stood up and then walked towards her.

'She says she's the new owner,' Mrs Jarvis screeched. 'Says she wants to inform us what's going on...'

Betty nodded and then let out a sigh. 'We knew it would happen,' she said. 'The rent was due more than a month ago and Barrow hadn't paid it. I've done what I could but...' She shook her head and looked at Susie resentfully. 'Go on then, Miss... whatever yer name is. When do we have to be out?'

'Miss Collins. The renovations are to begin in the next week or so. My associate and I intend to reopen as a clothing manufacturer when this building is fit for purpose, which it is not at present. You need more light and air in here – and the machines you use could be better...' Susie was aware that a door had opened behind her and a man had entered the room. He nodded to her as she turned to look at him but didn't speak.

'What about the girls and me? Carl, he's the cutter – and Mrs Jarvis, too?' Betty asked. 'Are yer throwing us out too?'

'We hope to employ those who meet our exacting standards,' Susie informed her. She raised her head and her gaze swept over the watching faces, seeing how intent and strained some of the girls were. 'When I last visited, I saw that the seamstresses were put under intolerable pressure, which resulted in shoddy work from some. That is all very well if you are selling cheap clothing, but we intend to look for a higher class of customer. Our designs will be original to us and intended for women of moderate means. We shall expect careful work, seams turned instead of rough edges, and straight.' Her gaze lingered on a guilty face. 'We shall not be selling spoiled garments to market traders. A woman who has paid several guineas for a dress does not want to see an exact copy of it hanging on a market stall. It also means that each seamstress will be responsible for the garments she completes. Careless, shoddy performance will not be acceptable. However, the wages will be fair and those of you who care to return to us will be given ten-minute comfort breaks when needed, a tea break of ten minutes three times a day, and half an hour for lunch each day. Also, a day off on Saturdays. If we should need to work late or come in on a Saturday, you would be paid double time, though I do not anticipate the need.'

'You'll not make a penny profit,' Betty said scornfully. 'Have you any idea how cut-throat this business can be? You with yer expensive dress and yer hoity-toity ways.'

'If I was catering for the market you've known, I dare say I would not,' Susie answered fairly. 'But women with money to spend want quality and design. Not all can afford to go to the top fashion houses in Paris and have their wardrobe bespoke, but they still want style and originality. I believe my— associate has done her costings. I am speaking of the kind of clothes you might find in the top range at Harpers or Selfridges or other exclusive stores. Simple-looking dresses may cost as much as nine guineas there and some evening gowns will be much higher priced. Of course they also have their cheaper ranges but still demand quality.'

'We can do quality,' Betty said truculently. 'With Barrow, it was always get them out cheap...' She shook her head as a look of grief entered her eyes. 'He promised it would be better in future, but that devil done for him.' A sniff issued from her, but she tossed her head. 'What else did you have to say then, Miss—?'

'Miss Collins,' Susie told her. 'I think I have probably said enough for the moment, Mrs...?'

'Ford, but everyone calls me Betty. Mr Ford is long gone... cleared orf with never a thought for me.'

'Perhaps you were better off without him then, Mrs Ford,' Susie said. 'When we are ready to hire, there will be a notice in the window – also in the daily papers.'

'What are we supposed ter do in the meantime?' Betty demanded. 'I've used up all the money Bert left and we'll not be paid yet for the orders we got out. How are they supposed ter live?' She jerked her head towards the listening girls.

'What are you owed?' Susie asked. 'If you give me the particulars, I will see if I can get at least some of the money for you...' She glanced at the old-fashioned sewing machines. 'We shall not be requiring these and I daresay they will be sent to the scrap yard. If you could help us by having them disposed of, I am sure we would be happy to pay for the service.' It was the most Susie could offer them. She could not pledge Lady Diane's money to keep several seamstresses sitting idle – especially when she was not yet certain of their skill. However, as she saw a gleam in Betty's eyes, she knew that it was sufficient.

'Well, we could do that,' Betty replied with a glance at Carl, who nodded silently. 'What will you pay?'

As she'd expected, Betty probably knew of someone who would buy them. Even a few pounds might be enough to help these young women over the period needed for refurbishment here.

Susie opened her purse and took out five pounds, which Lady Diane had given her for expenses. She'd told her to take a cab and buy herself a nice tea after she'd visited the workshop, but Susie had travelled by bus and she could well afford to purchase a pot of tea if she desired it. 'I think this should cover it,' she said, handing the notes to Betty. 'I imagine the builders would clear them away to the scrap yard for a few pounds.'

'I can do better than that,' Betty replied. 'Not everyone can afford everything modern. I know someone who will use them...'

'The furniture upstairs has to be cleared too – I believe we understand each other, Mrs Ford?'

'Yes.' Betty looked at her hard for a moment. 'If yer deeds are as true as yer words, I'll be the first to sign on – if yer want me?'

'I think you may be sure of a fair trial,' Susie replied. 'You know what I expect and no one who gives me the 100 per cent I ask for need fear unfair treatment.'

Betty was thoughtful for a moment, then nodded her head.

'Yer might do it,' she said, giving judgement. 'I'll give yer a fifty-fifty chance of success.'

'Thank you – and now I'll leave you to it.' Susie glanced around at the silent seamstresses. 'Perhaps I shall see you when the renovations are finished?'

Silence greeted her words and then one woman, not a young girl, spoke, 'I'm Yvonne, Miss Collins, and I'll be applying for a job when you start. I might have to find a temporary job in a café washing up until then – but I'll be first in the queue to sign on.'

'Thank you, Yvonne. I shall look forward to that day,' Susie said.

One or two others murmured something, clearly uncertain, and Susie took her leave, nodding to Mrs Jarvis as she passed her. From the look on her face, she was still resisting the change, but Susie had already decided she would not do for their receptionist and must be relegated to some other job if she applied.

* * *

After leaving the workshop to an anticipated buzz behind her, Susie walked the short distance to her brother's small shop. He looked up as she entered, surprise and then a smile in his eyes. Susie greeted him with a look filled with affection; she had always felt a special kinship with her brother and was eager to tell him her news. He listened as she explained what she had been doing and then nodded, grinning from ear to ear.

'That's grand news, Susie,' he congratulated her warmly. 'You deserve it and I know you'll make a success of it.'

'I hope I shall,' Susie confided, 'but I'm quaking inside, Sam. Betty declares we'll never make a penny, but I hope she is wrong. My lady is relying on me.'

'As to that, I suppose her husband can afford to lose a few thousand and never know the difference, but,' he added swiftly as a protest rose to her lips, 'I know you, Susie. You'd hate the business to fail and you'll do everything in your power to make it work.'

'Do you think I did right, telling them to clear the old stuff out – they will keep the money they get for selling it, of course.'

'Well, who is going to claim it?' Sam asked. 'Bert Barrow wasn't one to make a will. Sinclair was his only relative and a convicted murderer can't inherit his victim's property – so I can't see any problem. I know unclaimed money goes to the Crown, but no one is going to bother about some old-fashioned sewing machines. I dare say his lordship had as much right to them as any for his unpaid rent.'

'Yes, I suppose so,' Susie said. 'I thought we had more chance of getting those girls back if we paid something towards their wages until we can start hiring.'

'You'll get plenty of girls wanting a job when they see the changes you intend making,' Sam said. 'I've every confidence you'll make a go of it, Susie – and what a feather in your cap, love. You will be earning more money too and you'll find life very different, have more time to yourself, I shouldn't wonder.'

'Oh, I still need to oversee Meg,' Susie said. 'I shall not abandon my lady to her – but it will be different. I've spent most of my life in service and the hours are often very long. I please myself with what I do in the evenings, when my lady and his lordship are out – but I normally have just the one free afternoon a week and a night off if I ask for it.'

'It would never have suited me. I like to be my own boss,' Sam told her. 'I might get to see you now and then if you're this way more often. You can go out with Winnie sometimes – she likes dancing and the theatre and I sometimes work late to catch up when I'm busy.'

'It was about Winnie I came to see you,' Susie said. 'I told Lady Diane about the dress Winnie made and she wants her to come to tea and talk about some maternity clothes for her, as most of her clothes are too small now – and to alter them would spoil them. So she wants some comfortable day wear – and perhaps a christening gown.'

'Go to tea with your lady?' Sam stared at her, taken aback. 'I'm not sure how Winnie would feel about that...'

'It might lead to a really good job for her,' Susie advised. 'My lady is most insistent we should both have tea in her private parlour. I've told you before, she treats me like a friend, Sam – and I suppose now I shall be on even closer terms with her.'

'Well... I'll ask Winnie and see what she says,' Sam agreed a little reluctantly. Susie could see he didn't quite approve. Like most folk, he was conscious of place and class and would himself feel awkward in the company of a lady of quality.

'I think Winnie will love it,' Susie said, 'and I also think she might like the position of receptionist at "Miss Susie" – don't you?'

'"Miss Susie", is it?' Sam chuckled softly. 'It will be sixpence to know you soon.'

'Oh, it already is,' Susie returned with a flash of humour. 'You're privileged personnel...'

Sam laughed out loud at that. 'Get on with you, Miss Collins,' he teased. 'I'll tell Mum and Winnie this evening – she is coming for supper after she visits Mary Winston this afternoon. We're considering Winnie moving in with Mum.' He hesitated, then, 'I'm not sure about the job. Winnie is passionate about the Women's Movement.'

'She doesn't need to leave the Movement, but the job in the

office there can't pay much? She could work elsewhere and still support them.'

'Well, I'll speak to her about it – she might like the idea.'

'Why not – and why not get married sooner?' Susie replied. 'If I have a better job and earn a lot more – you won't need to do so much for Mum.'

'That wouldn't be fair on you,' Sam replied with a frown. 'It's time you had a bit of life, Susie. You supported Mum the whole time I was serving in the Army during the war.'

'Well, they didn't pay you much, did they? You were only nineteen when it started. I'd been in service a few years and Lady Diane was very generous when I became her personal maid. I'm paid two hundred guineas a year, Sam, and that's not much less than Molton, and more than Mrs Beavis, the house-keeper. Only Cook gets as much as I do amongst the female servants... and I'll be getting more now, especially if we succeed.'

'Mrs Beavis puts in less hours than you do,' Sam retorted, but he knew it was a generous wage for a lady's maid. 'If you weren't so happy there, I'd have told you to leave and look for a better position years ago.'

'I doubt I'd find one,' Susie said with perfect truth. 'It is far more money than those seamstresses get, Sam. Most girls in service earn thirty shillings a week if they are lucky – and I live in. It might be possible to earn more as a department supervisor at Selfridges or Harpers, perhaps, but then I'd have to pay for my lodgings, which would take at least half... and I'd be lucky to get such a position.'

'You give half your money to Mum,' Sam put in. 'But I must admit Lady Diane is generous to you – Mum loved that silk shawl you passed on to her for her birthday.'

'It was brand-new, never worn,' Susie told him. 'My lady buys things and if she doesn't like them, she offers them to me.

She gave Meg a silk scarf the other day...' She directed his gaze to the dress she was wearing. 'This dress probably cost fifty guineas. It came from Paris but didn't suit my lady's colouring so she gave it to me.'

'Well, you will need to look the part for your new job,' Sam agreed. 'Winnie might make you a couple of dresses if you bought the material.'

'I could do it myself,' Susie replied thoughtfully. 'But I'll see how she feels about making Lady Diane's things first.' She glanced at the clock on his wall. 'I should get back. I was told not to hurry, but I want to make sure Meg has done all I told her.'

'When are you going to take time for yourself?' Sam asked her as she prepared to leave. 'I can't remember the last time you went anywhere or did anything for fun.'

'Perhaps I'll do as you say and suggest a night out with Winnie,' Susie said. 'We might go to the picture house...'

'Well, be careful which one you choose,' Sam said. 'Some of them can be rowdy. The men whistle whenever a pretty woman is on screen – and some of the girls scream when they see Douglas Fairbanks!'

'I did see him in *Robin Hood*,' Susie told him. 'Meg and Mr Fox were raving over the film, so I went on my afternoon off to the matinée.'

'And what did you think?'

'He is romantic, I suppose,' Susie admitted. 'I like Mary Pickford and they are good together – but I wouldn't want to go often; it's too stuffy and I don't like the smell of cigarette smoke.'

'No, that is the problem. People will smoke and it's not pleasant if you don't,' Sam agreed. 'You'll take Winnie one night then?'

'I'll arrange it next time I see her,' Susie promised. 'I'd best go – give my love to Mum and Winnie. I'll visit on my evening off.'

Sam let her go and returned to his work as she closed the door.

* * *

The sky had clouded over, but it was still warm – thunderstorm weather, Susie thought as she walked towards her bus stop. She wanted to get back now, eager to tell Lady Diane what had happened at the workshop and, hurrying, accidentally knocked into a gentleman walking out of a shop. He was turning round, talking to someone, so neither of them saw the other. He swung about at once, took his hat off and apologised profusely.

'Forgive me, madam,' he said. 'I was distracted, but that does not excuse my bad manners. I hope I did not tread on your toes?'

'Not at all,' Susie replied. He was a well-spoken, pleasant-looking man with dark hair and blue eyes. 'I'm afraid I was in a hurry to catch my bus and didn't look where I was going.' She made a little sound of annoyance as a bus went sailing past the end of the alley. 'Oh, what a nuisance. I've missed it – and the next one may be twenty minutes or so...'

'I made you miss your bus?' the man said, looking concerned. 'Allow me to give you a lift in my car, madam.'

'It is *Miss* Collins and it was my own fault. I spent too long talking to my brother.'

'But I have delayed you – where did you wish to be taken, Miss Collins?'

'It would be too far out of your way,' Susie prevaricated. 'Do not concern yourself, sir. I shall take a cab.'

Susie walked quickly away, knowing that he was staring after her and probably thought her rude – but how could she just accept a lift from a stranger? It wouldn't do. It wouldn't do at all.

The cab fare would cost her several shillings and she'd given Lady Diane's money to Betty at the workshop, but she had enough in her purse to cover it and she really didn't want to stand around waiting, because the summer was drifting towards autumn and there was a storm coming from what she could see.

31

Winnie entered Mary's house at about the time Susie was leaving Sam's shop. She stopped on the threshold of the kitchen, seeing that Constable Winston was there and that they appeared to be in the middle of a serious conversation. Mary had been peeling vegetables and all the detritus was still strewn on the pine table as she stared at her husband, an odd, frightened, look in her eyes.

'I'm sorry. I didn't knock,' Winnie said. 'Shall I come back later, Mary?'

'No, come in, my dear,' Mary told her and the look she gave her sent shivers down Winnie's spine. 'Oh, this is terrible. I don't like to worry you, love – but that wicked man has got loose...'

Winnie felt coldness at her nape and shivered. 'You don't mean they let him go?' she cried, for she had no doubt of whom they were talking. 'How could they?'

'He wasn't let go,' Constable Winston told her heavily. 'He was being transferred from the cells to a remand prison and there was an accident on the road. I'm not perfectly certain how it happened, but a bus ran into the Black Maria and the back door burst open. Afore the guards could stop him, he was out and running for his life... and in all the confusion and noise of the accident, they couldn't catch up with him.'

'Oh no!' Winnie sat down on the nearest chair as her legs went weak. Mr Sinclair had got away and she knew he would come looking for her. 'If he comes here – and where else would he go? He blames me for what happened—'

'There's no saying he will harm you,' Constable Winston tried to reassure her. 'I think he'll lie low – and if he can get hold of some money, he will be off to another city where he can lose himself for a while, mebbe Birmingham or somewhere like that...'

'He will want revenge on me,' Winnie said, knowing it in her heart. 'I stopped him when he would've killed Betty. I'm sure that note was meant to lure me to his hiding place and if I'd been there before Betty, he would've killed me. It was only because I stopped to warn Sam of what I was doing, that I was there after her...'

'That's as maybe,' Constable Winston replied. 'Now he knows there is a murder charge hanging over his head, I doubt he'll be worrying about you, Winnie. He will want to get as far away as he can.'

'If he has any money hidden, will it not be in that house you raided?' Mary asked suddenly. 'He's bound to come after it... Are they still watching it?'

They both stared at her as her suggestion made perfect sense.

'No. We thought we'd got him – and so we had until that damned idiot drove straight into the Black Maria. It was an accident and there's no sure way of preventing them.'

'*If* it was an accident,' Winnie objected. 'Might not a man like that have others who work for him to help him escape?'

'In some cases I'd agree with you,' Constable Winston nodded thoughtfully. 'But I don't think he had a lot of men and we've got most of them safely locked up.'

'But what about the one who saw Joe and Sam overcome him?' Winnie asked. 'Mr Sinclair told you he was the one that killed Mr Barrow...'

'Dirty Sid?' Constable Winston looked at her for a moment. 'He is still at large, but I can't see him driving an omnibus – and that was what caused the accident – that and an urchin what run across in front of it.'

'It was an accident,' Mary nodded her agreement. 'An unfortunate one – but I don't think you need worry too much, Winnie. You can stay here tonight, love. No need to return to your lodgings.'

'I'm meeting Sam at his mother's later,' Winnie told her. 'I'll make certain Sam walks me home, Mary. I shall be very careful until he is caught again.'

'It is such a worry,' Mary said. 'I'd be most upset if you were hurt, Winnie love. I'm looking forward to your wedding...'

'So am I,' Winnie agreed. 'I shan't let it upset me, Mary. Constable Winston is probably right and all Mr Sinclair wants is to get away from here as fast as he can.'

Cyril watched the house that had been his hideaway until the police had raided it for some minutes before he approached. The police had nailed wooden slats over the doors and downstairs windows, clearly meant to keep folk out – but he knew a way in. He doubted the steps to the coal cellar had been boarded up, and it would be easy enough to crawl in over the coal and up through the hatch into the scullery. Dirty work, but he wanted to wash the stink of the cells off as soon as he was able and he could once he got into the building.

Deciding that no one was watching, Cyril walked casually across the green to the house. He did nothing to arouse suspicion, even though he knew most of his neighbours were out at work in daylight hours. He'd chosen it because of its secluded locality.

As he'd suspected, the steps down to the coal hatch had been ignored. He wrenched open the small door with a piece of iron he'd picked up from the gutter after getting well away from the accident. It was a weapon of sorts if anyone tried to grab him. Bit of luck that accident, Cyril thought. He'd been quick off the mark to take advantage of the door flying open, quicker than the guards who had reacted slowly with curses but no action. Perhaps they'd thought the lock secure, but it had given under the impact, luckily for him.

The coal house was dark and smelled strongly of tar. Cyril squeezed his way through the small door, stooping to enter the cramped space inside the cellar, and crawled over the heap of coal. Fortunately, it was low as he hadn't restocked it while the weather was so warm; had it been high he might have found it impossible to reach the hatch.

He reached the square of slatted wood that opened into the house and let down the wooden ladder attached to it, then stood beneath it, pushing both hands against its roughness. He'd wondered if something might have fallen over it during the police search, but, to his relief, it opened easily and he climbed up the ladder to enter the big scullery. It was cold and dark; the windows having been boarded over. He could see that it had been searched, because barrels and washing baskets had been overturned.

A smile touched his mouth. They could search all they liked

and they would never find his stash of money. None of them had a brain between them. They hadn't even put him in irons. Had he been chained, he could never have escaped so easily.

Leaving the scullery, he went into the main kitchen. It was a similar scene of furniture tipped over and some broken crockery. His mouth lifted in a sneer of disgust. Pigs that's what the coppers were. One or two of them would be remembered when things cooled down. He'd noted their names and he would get even – just as he would with that girl. If she hadn't interfered, he'd have dealt with that squawking Betty and been on his way before anyone was the wiser. Bitches the lot of them. How he hated women. His mother had been a slut and he believed they were all the same. The only place a woman belonged was on her knees in Cyril's opinion. They were all whores – just like his mother...

The rest of the house had been thoroughly turned over, cushions slit and upholstery slashed. Cyril frowned. What were they looking for? He hadn't expected to find quite so much mess.

He walked upstairs to his bedroom and stared as he saw the mattress had been cut in several places. His frown deepened. These police had been ruthless in their search. It was more like wanton destruction. As if someone had a score to settle. The coppers didn't normally make quite so much mess, or he wouldn't have thought so.

Cyril shivered suddenly. He pushed the bed across the floor and knelt down, staring in disbelief as he saw the floorboards had been wrenched up. Falling to his knees, he searched frantically in the hole, but it was empty – the strongbox he'd hidden had gone, also the handgun he'd kept for emergencies. A string of oaths burst from him as he stared in disbelief. It couldn't have gone. No one knew it was there – no one! Yet this wasn't the work of the police. He was sure of it now.

Cyril sat for a moment and then made a movement to get up. It was then that he felt the cold steel at his nape and in that instant he knew who had taken the money. Only one person knew he had money hidden in the house because he'd told him. 'Think about what you're doing, Sid,' he warned, remaining on his knees. 'Remember it was me that saved your wretched life.' He made a small movement to get up, but the knife dug into his flesh; he could feel the sting as blood spurted and for the first time knew real fear.

'Stay where yer are,' Sid's voice commanded. 'Yer give me up to the coppers. Yer told 'em it was me wot killed Barrow – yer let me down, boss.'

'I knew they'd never get you, Sid. You're too clever,' Cyril said, his mind working furiously. 'I'm glad you took the money. We can use it to go to Glasgow...'

'It's mine now,' Sid said and his tone sent a chill through Cyril. 'It ain't 'ere. I've 'ad it 'id fer days. It took some finding – them coppers never done more than a brief search once they got yer. I knew yer 'ad money 'ere.'

Cyril's brow prickled with sweat beads as fear crawled through him. He knew this man, knew what he was capable of. Sid had always been so slavishly devoted to him. He just needed to make him think he was still his friend. 'We can use it to get started again – be partners this time...'

'I thought you were different... I thought we were friends.'

He sounded eager, more like the old Sid. Cyril's hopes rose. 'Let me stand up and we'll make plans...'

Sid eyed him for a moment or two, considering.

Cyril moved to stand, lulled by Sid's apparent wish to please, but it was mockery. He was taunting him.

'Boot's on the other foot now, boss. I ain't your little dog you can kick no more.'

'I didn't mean it when the cops came,' Cyril said. 'If they'd arrested you, I'd have got you out. Come on, Sid, let me up. You know I'm your friend.'

'No!' The knife jabbed at his nape; he felt sharp pain as the point cut deeper into his flesh. Sid was a monster with that knife and fear of what he may do lent him courage.

With a growl of anger, Cyril thrust upwards and swung round, trying to catch Sid's leg and bring him down. Sid kicked him in the face. Cyril recoiled, but then flung himself at Sid and managed to get hold of his ankle. He pulled as hard as he could and Sid toppled over. In a flash, Cyril was on his feet, but Sid pulled something from inside his jacket.

'You didn't ought ter 'ave betrayed me...' he muttered and then there was a bang and a loud flash as he fired.

Cyril jerked as the bullet went through his thigh. The pain was searing and he stumbled, down on his knees. Sid had clawed up and he sneered down at Cyril clutching at himself, the blood gushing between his fingers.

'You've damaged an artery,' he mumbled. 'Help me before I bleed to death.'

'Sorry, boss,' Sid said. 'I thought you was all right. All me life I've been kicked and spat on and treated like dirt – but you was different. Now I see you used me same as all the rest. You let me down and I didn't like that.' He pointed the pistol at Cyril's head, his finger resting on the trigger.

'No – we can be partners. I'll make you rich...' Cyril's face was wild with terror. 'Sid, please...'

The shot and the blinding flash were the last things Cyril knew before the darkness descended.

* * *

Sid stood staring down at him for a few minutes. Then he took a rag from his pocket, wiped the gun thoroughly and dropped it by Cyril's slumped body. It was Cyril's gun. No one would know who had fired the shot.

'Yer never ought ter 'ave done it,' Sid said mournfully. 'I thought yer was me friend...' He'd been ill used, spat on and despised all his life and when Cyril had saved his life, he'd devoted himself to him – but betrayal deserved no less.

He spat on the floor and then turned and walked away. Sid had got in to the house the same way as Cyril had. Emerging into the sultry night air, he walked away without a backward glance. Cyril had had more cash in that box than Sid knew how to count. He reckoned he'd make a new start somewhere – maybe at the seaside. Sid had only ever been to Southend once but he'd liked it. Yeah, maybe he'd get himself a little pub at the coast. The idea appealed and he smiled to himself. He didn't need Cyril, though he would have gone with him anywhere had he not betrayed him.

Sid felt very clever as he walked away from the scene of carnage he'd created. He'd heard of Cyril's escape with glee. It meant he could get his revenge because no one betrayed Sid and got away with it.

He'd known where the boss would go. They'd discussed the money the night Sid killed Barrow. He'd searched for it as soon as he'd heard that the boss was safely in the cells at Scotland Yard, and he'd found it. Sid knew the places folk hid their valuables; he'd been a housebreaker for years before too many trips to prison had left him unable to fend for himself. He would have died had it not been for the boss. A scowl touched his brow as he knew a moment of loss and a kind of grief.

'You shouldn't 'ave grassed on me,' he muttered to the night air... just as a hand came out and grabbed the back of his collar.

Sid jerked out of his reverie, startled to discover he was staring up into the face of a police officer. As he struggled and tried to break free, three more loomed up out of the darkness and before he could slip his knife into his hand, he was cuffed.

'Wot's this fer?' he snarled like a cornered rat. 'I ain't done nuthin'; yer can't prove nuthin'—'

'I think we can,' Constable Winston said. 'It might interest you to know that you've been followed and watched for the past few weeks, Mr Sidney Smith – if that's your name. I doubt it, but it's the name on our records.'

'I don't care if yer bin spyin' on me,' Sid muttered. 'I ain't done nuthin'.'

'Make sure he doesn't get away...' Another police officer came puffing up to them. 'I got into the house and it was shots we heard – Sinclair is dead, shot through the leg and then the head.'

'It weren't nothin' ter do wiv me...' Sid protested.

'We'll leave that to a court to decide,' Constable Winston told him. 'You are going to prison, Sid. Make no mistake about it. You were seen entering the house earlier this evening – and you are a known associate of Mr Sinclair. We also have a witness who says you murdered a young woman at the establishment of one bakery...'

'Nah, that were Sinclair or one of his posh friends,' Sid denied, furiously struggling, but hemmed in by two burly policemen. 'I only got rid of the body 'cos his bleedin' brother wouldn't...'

'What happened this evening then, Sid? Did you two thieves fall out over the money your boss had stashed away in there? We know he had some, probably hidden in the cellar... or maybe a secret safe? Was that it, Sid? An argument over money?'

Sid spat in the police officer's face. 'That's all yer know,' he jeered. 'He died because he betrayed me. Made out he were me friend and then ditched me…'

'Did he now?' Constable Winston said cheerfully. 'Well, that's helpful, Sid. You've saved us a bit of work by confessing.'

Sid shot off a string of expletives that would have shocked anyone but a hardened copper, who had heard them all before.

Constable Winston smiled in a satisfied way. 'In fact, I'm grateful to you for this night's work. We were having a problem proving our case and Mr Sinclair might have got away with no more than prison for attempted murder if it had come to court – probably a five-year stretch at most. You've done us all a service, whether you meant to or not.'

Sid's savage mutterings brought a smile to the faces of all the police officers present. It wasn't often things got wrapped up so neatly and Sid's intervention was a gift from the gods. Justice moved slowly and was not always able to mete out the right punishment. Every single one of the officers involved in the case felt a sense of deep satisfaction. There would be no more escapes for the murderer named Cyril Sinclair.

* * *

'So it truly is over at last?' Mary gave a sigh of relief as her husband related the story – or the part of it he thought fit for her ears – later that night. 'That man is dead?'

'Yes, my dear, he is,' Constable Winston confirmed, 'and we have our murderer in custody. He won't be given the chance to escape – we'll have him in irons when we transport him. Not that I think anyone would try to free Dirty Sid. Sinclair used him, but I doubt he has friends, even in the criminal world.'

Mary gave a little shiver. 'What terrible lives some folk live,' she said. 'What will happen to him?'

'I expect he will hang,' her husband said. 'Now don't you go feeling sorry for him, love. Men like that don't deserve pity. He's murdered more than one person.'

'No, I know you're right – but it was all so horrid, Bill. I am just glad it is over.'

Constable Winston nodded and gave her a little squeeze. He too was glad this particular case was over, but he knew all too well that it was just one down. Sid was a nasty character but there were many more just like him in the slimy underworld that made up London's criminal element. His job never let up; one day it would be catching a housebreaker, the next chasing a bag-snatcher down murky alleys, and then he might be talking a suicidal suspect down from London Bridge, or keeping watch on a known gangster. There were all sorts and it never stopped.

'At least you can stop worrying about young Winnie,' he said and Mary smiled.

'Yes. I think she is settled now and in a fair way to be happy.'

He nodded and yawned. 'What's for supper, Mary? I fancy a nice bit of cheese on toast.'

32

'Well, that unpleasant business is over and done,' Lord Henry told his wife at breakfast the next morning. 'Sinclair is dead – shot through the head by one of his henchmen.'

'How dreadful!' Lady Diane exclaimed, her hand flying to her face. 'I am glad he is dead – but such a violent end to a most distressing affair.'

'You must not upset yourself over it, my love,' her husband said, looking at her anxiously. 'I imagined you would be pleased he is no longer a danger to anyone.'

'I am...' She suppressed a shiver and then looked at him anxiously. 'I fear you have had a great deal of trouble over this affair, Henry. It has kept you busy for weeks.'

'It was important that we got to the bottom of things,' he replied. 'Matthew has done most of the work, but there was some injustice to sort out. It would be wrong if those people Sinclair cheated were not compensated in some way – and our inspection of the properties has led to many necessary decisions. Some of them are in urgent need of repair.'

'Will that affect the renovations to my workshop?' she asked.

'No, I have given that priority – but yours is only a small job, dearest. I have to decide whether to restore or, in some cases, demolish and rebuild some of the properties.'

'That will cost a great deal, I imagine?'

'Yes, I dare say, but it is not just the money, for to rebuild would cause disruption to several small businesses,' he replied. 'Deciding what to do for the best is what has kept us so many hours over our work and caused me to neglect you. I am sorry for it, Diane. I hope to have more free time soon. We have not been anywhere for an age.'

'I truly do not mind,' she told him with her sweet smile. 'At the moment, I have no wish for lots of parties or even the theatre. I think I should enjoy a drive into the country – perhaps take a picnic to Richmond Park once the weather recovers.' There had been a summer storm overnight and the sky was still overcast.

'Then we shall certainly do so as soon as I have a free day and the sun shines on us.' He smiled and got up, coming to kiss her cheek. 'And now I must work. Will you forgive me?'

She looked up at him, her eyes warm with love. 'You know well there is nothing to forgive. I have every comfort and Susie looks after me. She is such a good friend to me, Henry. I am very fond of her.'

'Yes, I understand that,' he said, smiling down at her. 'You are happy, Diane? I sometimes feel that you needed a younger man – a man who could take you dancing at all hours and make love to you all night...' There was a quizzical look in his eyes that made her laugh out loud.

'My wonderful, ridiculous Henry,' she cried, eyes dancing with mischief. 'You are the perfect man for me. I adore you – and I do not think I could manage to dance all night just at the moment...'

'As long as you are content.' He stroked her hair gently for a moment, bent to kiss her and then walked away.

Lady Diane watched him leave. She did miss his company when he was so busy but perfectly understood the need for his attention to work. That wretched Mr Sinclair had caused so much trouble. She was glad he was dead, though the thought of how he'd died was unpleasant.

She finished her breakfast and got up, then gave a little cry as her head swam for a second. Holding on to the back of a chair, she waited for it to clear. In a moment or so, she felt better. Patting her swollen belly, she smiled. The various aches and pains and occasional dizziness would pass once her child was born and she was counting the weeks. Only another few months.

She had no engagements that day and decided she would spend the morning going through some of her ideas for her future business with Susie. A little sigh escaped her, for she would have so much liked to have been more involved with the venture.

Walking slowly up to her private parlour, Lady Diane thought about the business she was planning. She had created hundreds of designs for dresses, suits and evening clothes, which would last for some years if truth be told. What she really wanted was to see her designs being brought to life – and to take an active part in the creation of the business she'd dreamed of, but she knew Henry would be reluctant to have her do more than hand the designs over to Susie, at least until her child was some months old and she'd recovered from the birth. He'd made that proviso when he'd agreed to help her with the workshop.

'You can conduct all your affairs from home, Diane,' he'd told her. 'I really could not acquiesce to your working at this place yourself. Miss Collins may act on your instructions – and you will have someone to look after the day-to-day running. You cannot possibly wish to spend your days in such an occupation, my love?'

Lady Diane had agreed to the restriction. She supposed it was not strictly necessary for her to oversee it all. With Susie's help, she could create the garments she wanted her employees to make so that they had examples to copy. They had chosen six of her designs to begin with and were in the process of cutting and sewing three stylish day dresses, two suits and one elegant evening dress. Many more would be necessary for their winter collection, of course, but Lady Diane hoped that Winnie Brown would be able to help with the making up of the first examples. Although it was still summer, they would have to begin with the winter into spring range, as orders for autumn wear would have already been placed by retailers and would soon appear in the shops.

* * *

'Ah, Susie,' Lady Diane said as she entered her bedchamber and found her dresser hanging up a gown she had pressed. It was one of the dresses she had designed. 'Oh that velvet evening gown hangs beautifully. Was I not in an interesting condition, as one says, I think I should be happy to wear it.'

'I know I should for the right occasion,' Susie said, smiling. 'I finished it last night and pressed it this morning. I knew you would wish to see it.'

'I believe we made it in your size?' Lady Diane said, stroking the midnight-blue velvet. 'Will you try it on for me, please?' She nodded towards the dressing screen.

Susie hesitated and then agreed, going behind the painted screen to take off the plain, dark dress she wore and slip into the evening gown. She reappeared wearing the evening gown, which was cut to fit smoothly over her hips into a flowing skirt that moved sensuously about her legs as she walked. The sleeves were softly puffed at the shoulders and the cuffs long and narrow with little buttons. The neckline was slightly dipped at both the front and the back, with a thin line of embroidered silk to define the edges. It was simple, elegant and suited its wearer well.

'Oh, that looks exactly as I imagined,' Lady Diane cried with a little clap of her hands as she saw Susie. 'It is very stylish on you, Susie. Yes, I believe it will sell for fifteen guineas, or perhaps a little more at Harpers or Selfridges – expensive but not beyond the wife of a professional man.'

'The material is good,' Susie agreed. 'It is a dress discerning ladies would wear again and again and will last for a long time.' A society lady would not wear a dress more than two or three times, but country gentlewomen might wear a dress like this many times over a few years, for it had quality as well as a timeless style.

'Do you think it needs a spray of artificial flowers on the shoulder?' Lady Diane asked. 'Or shall we leave that to individual taste?'

Susie looked at herself critically. The dress suited her very well. She might have placed a silk flower just near the left shoulder, but the gown was so elegant it hardly needed it. 'Perhaps some ladies would prefer a necklace or a special brooch?' she suggested.

Lady Diane took a large diamond sunburst pin from her jewellery box on the dressing table and pinned it to the front shoulder. She stood back and looked at it and then smiled. 'You always know what one should wear, Susie. It is why I ask your opinion when you dress me.'

'Be careful as you unpin the brooch,' Susie cautioned. 'We do not want a hole to show.' She paused for Lady Diane to remove the brooch, then, 'We shall need more help to get the collection you hope to begin with ready in time.'

'Yes, I was thinking the same. Did you manage to speak to Winnie when you visited your brother yesterday?'

'He was going to see her last evening,' Susie replied. 'I am almost sure she will be happy to help with your maternity gowns as well as the collection, my lady – if her work is good enough. As I told you, I saw her wearing a very attractive dress she made herself, but we shall see.'

Lady Diane nodded, feeling a little spurt of pleasure as she watched Susie go behind the screen to take off the gown. It really seemed as if her dream was beginning to come to life. 'Perhaps there is someone else who might help get the collection ready,' she suggested. 'Someone on whose work we can rely?'

Susie reappeared, wearing her own gown. 'I think there may be,' she said, frowning slightly. 'There was a young woman called Yvonne. She told me she would definitely be applying for a job when the advert went up. Do you wish me to see if there is anyone at the workshop and enquire for her.'

'Yes, please. I ought to have thought of it yesterday, but we only began sewing that dress after you returned yesterday afternoon. Indeed, I did little but help you cut out the pattern.'

'You had made the pattern,' Susie said smiling. 'I am used to sewing, my lady.'

'You must have sat up long into the night to finish it?'

'That is why I said we shall need help,' Susie confirmed. 'If I have your permission, I shall go this afternoon.'

'Of course.' Lady Diane nodded. 'I think we should turn one of the bedrooms into a cutting and fitting room. We must use the back wing of the house so that Lord Henry is not disturbed by comings and goings.'

Susie laughed. 'Oh, certainly, my lady – though he may relent and allow you to visit the workshop from time to time if he finds it inconvenient to have a stream of young women entering his house, even by the back door.'

'He will not know them from the maids,' Lady Diane said, an affectionately mocking sparkle in her eyes. 'He hardly ever notices when we have a new maid – so my sewing girls will not disturb him.'

Susie nodded, but looked uncertain. 'Does his lordship know that you intend to make up your collection at home?'

'Well, I must do it somewhere,' Lady Diane replied. 'I must translate the garment from the drawing to something the girls can see and copy. How can I expect them to know exactly what I want otherwise? In time, if we find enough truly skilled seamstresses it may not be necessary to create an example of every garment, but for a start, I do think it necessary.' She frowned. 'Remember my dress that was copied – that was taken so that someone could see how it was made.'

'Yes, it was,' Susie agreed. 'As long as his lordship does not think it seems too much like trade going on in his house?'

'We are not selling anything here,' Lady Diane said. 'Besides, who will know?'

'The servants – and I dare say someone will discover it before long,' Susie replied. 'However, should his lordship dislike it, we can always remove to the upper floor of the workshop.'

'Yes, we can. But I must admit I feel more comfortable here – for the time being at least.' She touched her belly and then laughed as she felt the kick. 'She lets me know she is there!'

Susie smiled and picked up the midnight-blue evening dress. 'If you are satisfied with this, I will take it and hang it in my room. Just until you decide which room will be best for us to use, my lady.'

'I will consult with Mrs Beavis.'

Susie nodded and took the dress away. As soon as the house-keeper knew so would Molton and then his lordship was bound to hear of it. Whether or not he would be pleased remained to be seen.

* * *

Susie saw that the furniture from upstairs was being removed when she arrived at the workshop that afternoon. The down-stairs had already been cleared of the old-fashioned sewing machines and much of the clutter. As she entered, she found Betty sorting out some rolls of materials. She looked at Susie with quick suspicion, as if she feared some trap.

'Ah, Betty, excellent work,' Susie greeted her with a smile. 'We shall be able to start the renovations on Monday as we hoped.'

'Will you want any of this material?' Betty asked. 'You didn't say and... I thought I'd sell it on the market.'

'Those rolls of lining silk might possibly be useful one day,' Susie said, casting an eye over the shelves. 'I think most of it is end of roll and remnants, which wouldn't be of much use – though I should like that blue wool cloth. I have an idea for that. The rest you may dispose of as you wish. Perhaps some of the girls would like to use it to make themselves skirts or blouses?'

'Most of them would rather have a share of the money,' Betty told her. 'It's a struggle to pay rent and food for those with fami-lies to keep.'

'Yes, I know,' Susie agreed. 'I need some help and I wondered if I should find Yvonne here?'

'She was here earlier, but she went home – do you want me to give her a message?'

'I wanted to ask if she was available for some sewing work while the work was being done here.'

'Why Yvonne?' Betty asked, a glint of belligerence in her eyes. 'I've as much experience as she has...'

'I have my reasons,' Susie said, quelling her with a look. 'I believe Yvonne was one of your most skilled seamstresses?'

'Who told yer that?' Betty asked, then, reluctantly, 'Well, she is – and if you've set yer mind to it, you'll find her at number fifteen Mulberry Lane. That's a few streets away.'

'Yes, I know,' Susie agreed. 'My mother lives that way, though not in Mulberry Lane itself.'

Betty nodded, looking thoughtful. 'Someone told me Sam Collins is your brother. I didn't think it was true, but his mother lives that way; twenty minutes' walk or so further.'

'Yes, Sam is my brother,' Susie told her. She paused, then, 'Will you be applying for work when we start interviewing, Betty?'

'Depends,' she said with a slight sniff. 'I haven't made up my mind yet.'

'Well, you have a couple of weeks to think about it,' Susie told her.

'What do you want left here then?' Betty said. 'Them bins is useful. You'll need to replace 'em if you throw 'em out.'

'Yes, I think we'll save them for now – and the cutting tables. There is no sense in replacing them. It was just the sewing machines L— my associate felt could be better.'

'That's what Carl said.' Betty gave another audible sniff. 'You'll need the rails in the stockroom too.'

'I haven't seen in there – perhaps you'd better show me what else I may need, Betty?'

'You'd best come this way then,' Betty said, abandoning her task. 'I'll show yer where we store and pack the stock before it goes off to the customers.'

'Thank you,' Susie replied and followed her through the cutting room and into the stockroom. Some of the metal rails, which were on wheels and movable, still had garments hanging on them. There were cardboard boxes stacked to one side and more fixed rails lined the walls; in the middle were two long tables and a ream of tissue paper. 'So what is your routine?' she asked Betty. 'After the clothes are finished?'

'We press them if needed,' Betty said with a shrug. 'Then one of the girls helps me pack the garments in tissue, usually about five to a box, and then we stick the labels on the lids. Mr Barrow used to load them into the van – he had an arrangement with someone to deliver them.' She hesitated, then, 'I know you don't approve – but *cabbage* – that's faulty or damaged stock – just goes straight off the rails to the market traders. Some small shops buy a few to sell in their sales, too – and if a line didn't sell for some reason, they were let go cheap.'

Susie nodded. 'We hope that won't happen. End of lines might be sold cheaply after a decent period of time – but definitely no *cabbage* to market traders.'

'What will you do with stuff that's not up to scratch then?'

'It shouldn't happen often enough to matter,' Susie told her with a hard look. 'I warned you; I am not prepared to accept shoddy work.'

Betty shrugged. 'Even the best of them makes a mistake sometimes.'

'An occasional slip may be acceptable – but if it happens often, that girl would not be suitable for my workshop.'

Betty looked at her studiedly for a moment and then nodded.

'If you are given the position, you held previously, you would need to make that plain, Betty.'

Betty made no comment but looked thoughtful.

The boxes were plain brown cardboard. Susie knew that Lady Diane wanted printed lids with their logo and name, but they would still need an address label. It was a job that she might offer Mrs Jarvis if she applied.

* * *

Having seen enough of the layout to discuss various changes Susie thought they might make to working practices with Lady Diane, she made a note of Yvonne's address and took her leave. As she exited the building, she saw a lot of activity in the property across the alley. It had been closed up previously, but now the door was open and it seemed that it was being cleared out, as if in preparation for a new business.

Susie stood looking for a moment and then a man came out. She thought she recognised him but wasn't sure where she'd seen him before. He saw her and put up his hand to acknowledge her. The next moment, he'd crossed the road to speak to her.

'I think you're the young woman I almost knocked over yesterday,' he said, smiling at her. 'Are you taking over the workshop opposite? I've heard it is being renovated.'

'Yes – my associate and I intend to make good-quality clothing for women,' Susie said and he nodded.

'I'm opening a workshop too – we'll be producing children's wear,' he told her. 'I've been a salesman all my life and now I want to make the stuff I've been selling.'

'You'll be looking for seamstresses then?' Susie asked.

'No, that's all taken care of,' he told her cheerfully. 'I hired most of the girls you turned off. Gave them a week's holiday money. I'll be open within a week at most.'

'You did what?' Susie stared at him, feeling annoyed. He'd snapped up her workforce. 'Did they all apply?'

'I only wanted eight for a start,' he replied. 'I mean to start slowly. I'll be hiring more when I get into my stride.'

Susie bit back the angry words. He'd taken half the girls on and she didn't know if it would be easy to secure a new workforce. Feeling frustrated and angry, she bid him good morning and set off in the direction of Mulberry Lane. It was her own fault, of course. Susie recalled that she'd stressed her need for skilled workers but perhaps hadn't given enough reassurances. It would be too annoying if Yvonne had already been snapped up! She hadn't asked him because she didn't want that man to know she considered Yvonne to be important to her plans.

Susie hadn't even asked his name. She'd felt too angry with him for being astute enough to grab her workforce and herself for not telling them they would be paid. She ought to have hired them immediately and given them two weeks' holiday.

* * *

Reaching Mulberry Lane, Susie passed the Pig & Whistle public house, which was shut for the afternoon, crossed the street, and looked for number fifteen. It would just be her luck to find Yvonne had gone out, she thought, but the door opened at her knock and she smiled as she saw the young woman.

Yvonne stared at her in surprise. 'Miss Collins – won't you come in?' she invited. 'I was just about to make a cup of tea. I've been cleaning all day. It isn't often I get the chance to go right through the house.'

She led the way into a small, neat parlour that smelled of

lavender polish. Fresh curtains hung crisply at the windows and bright cushions softened old upholstery, making a shabby room look comfortable. Yvonne's industry at the sewing machine was evidently not reserved for her work.

'Thank you, I will have a cup of tea,' Susie said and sat down, her gaze travelling around the room, resting on the mantelpiece with its friendly clutter and then a toy rocking horse in the corner. It was much used and obviously old, but it made her wonder.

Yvonne returned with a tea tray in a short time, her kettle having obviously previously boiled. She set it down and after asking whether Susie took milk, poured the tea. Susie was offered the sugar bowl and took one lump, stirring her drink. Yvonne sat opposite her and sipped her tea.

'You must wonder why I came?' Susie asked.

'I thought you might,' Yvonne replied. 'I didn't apply for work at the new place, Miss Collins. I think it will be much the same as it was at Madame Pauline's – get it out as quick as you can... and you promised something better.'

'Yes, I did.' Susie felt a surge of relief. 'I came today to offer you work until we are ready to open – we are making a collection, you see. My associate wishes to provide examples that the girls can see so that they have an idea of the standard required. Also, we may need to show our work to the various retail outlets. As a new firm, it will take time to find our customers...'

'A collection? That sounds very different,' Yvonne said, a gleam in her eyes. 'And you want me to help?'

'I have some experience of fine sewing myself, but I shall need skilled workers. My associate wants us to be known for quality and style.'

Yvonne nodded. 'It frustrated me at times because although most of the material we used was good, the workmanship was shoddy, Miss Collins. Some of the girls didn't care what they did as long as they got their wages. Betty should have pulled them up more, but she just wanted to get the garments out – but I've always taken pride in my work.'

'Yes, I rather thought so,' Susie said. 'I'll be hiring girls soon, Yvonne, but in the meantime, I want you to help me prepare the collection – and I must ask you if you can be discreet?'

Yvonne looked at her for a moment, then, 'I know who you work for, Miss Collins. Betty was curious and kept asking questions. Someone thought you were Sam Collins' sister – but no one knew where you worked, except me, and I didn't tell them.' She smiled. 'I know your mother, you see.'

'She has never mentioned you,' Susie said, surprised.

'I have a son of seven years, Miss Collins. I was just fifteen when he was born. Your mother used to work at the Pig & Whistle until she became ill, didn't she?'

'Yes, I believe she did for a short while – so you met then?'

'Mrs Collins was very kind to me,' Yvonne said. 'My mother was poorly and I had to look after her and my son. I earned what I could making clothes – and I made some dresses for Mrs Collins.'

'Oh, I do recall something.' Susie nodded. 'It was before she had that stroke that made her so unsteady that she no longer felt able to work. She is better now, but neither I nor Sam will allow her to go out to work, though she does her own shopping and keeps house.'

'I've seen her at the market once or twice,' Yvonne replied, looking hesitant. 'You still wish to employ me now that you know I am an unmarried mother?'

'Of course,' Susie replied in a matter-of-fact tone. 'Your private life is your own. At work, I am sure you are discreet.'

'Always. Betty is the only one who knows.'

Susie nodded. 'Where is your son now?'

'At school. A good friend of mine gives him his tea. We manage very well and he never interferes with my work.'

'Good – then I shall ask if you would come to Grosvenor Square tomorrow at ten in the morning. I shall be waiting outside for you and I will show you the entrance we use. I will take you to meet my lady – and then we will work together. The work must be done in complete secrecy, because the designs you will see are exclusive to Miss Susie.'

'Is that what you are going to call it?' Yvonne nodded. 'I suppose you could hardly call it Lady Diane.'

'No – and that part of it must remain private for now,' Susie warned her.

'Yes, I understand.' Yvonne made a little gurgle of pleasure. 'It is so exciting! I am really looking forward to it.'

'Unfortunately, it seems we have lost half of our girls to the person who has opened a workshop across the road!'

'Mr Stevens?' Yvonne said and made a face. 'He took the first-comers – and most of them are no loss, Miss Collins. You'll get seamstresses queuing outside the door when they know you're open, don't you worry.'

33

Susie called to see her mother before she returned to Grosvenor Square that evening. Sam came in from work just as she was about to leave and she asked him if he'd spoken to Winnie.

'Yes, I did, and she is excited about being invited to tea,' he told her with a grin. 'She said she'd be happy to make anything her ladyship wanted – if she thought she was good enough. She's always made her own clothes but can make them better since she worked at Madame Pauline's.'

'Well, that green dress she made looked very well on her,' Susie said. 'I've also secured the services of another fine seamstress – though it seems half our girls have found work elsewhere—'

'You mean with the children's outlet across the road from you?' Sam nodded. 'I met the boss. His name is Eddie Stevens and he seems a decent bloke. I doubt you'll find him much competition, Susie. He is paying the girls the basic wage, which works out at just over a pound a week if they're over eighteen.'

'For a skilled seamstress?' Susie raised her brows. 'That is hardly enough to live on, Sam. I think most of those girls were earning as much under the previous owners.'

'I dare say they were,' Sam nodded. 'He says they get generous tea breaks, a lunch break and a whole day off a week, and that he has plenty of girls ready to work for him.'

'Winnie will be up in arms over it,' Susie said. 'She thought they paid poorly at Madame Pauline's when she worked there, didn't she?'

'Some of the girls got fifteen bob,' Sam said with a shrug. 'The older ones were paid more, but they often got fined for the slightest thing. Winnie thought the conditions harsh. Anyway, that's not your intention, is it?'

'No. We want quality work and intend to pay fairly for it,' Susie confirmed. 'My lady wouldn't dream of underpaying the girls who work for her.'

'I hope it goes well for you, Susie. So I'll tell Winnie to come along next week – on Monday, you said?'

'Yes, at three for three-thirty. I shall meet her and show her where she will be working and then take her to meet my lady.' Susie nodded and glanced up at the clock. 'I'd best get back, though Meg is looking after Lady Diane this evening. She is going to the opera with Lord Henry – in their private box…' She hesitated, then, 'Have you and Winnie made any decision about when the wedding will be?'

'We've talked about it, but we're thinking of waiting until next spring,' Sam said. 'I know what you said, Susie – but we both want to save a bit.'

'Well, that's your choice,' she agreed. Turning to her mother, she said, 'I'm off then, Mum. Is there anything you need?'

'Nothing at all,' Mrs Collins assured her cheerfully. 'The pair of you spoil me so what should I need?'

Susie smiled, kissed her cheek and left. She was thoughtful

as she walked to her bus stop. The loss of her potential work-force had troubled Susie, but both Sam and Yvonne seemed to believe she would find replacements easily enough. She decided she would place an advert for more skilled staff in the next week's newspaper. She would need to interview them some-where and the workshop would be invaded with builders by then. Perhaps she would ask Sam if she could use the rooms over his shop for a couple of days. There was a convenient side entrance and it would be better than meeting in a café or trying to use the workshop, with all the noise that would be going on.

Yvonne had been excited to be a part of the new venture. Susie was torn between a certain thrill at the new life opening up to her and anxiety that she would not be able to mould Lady Diane's business into a thriving concern.

* * *

'What do you think of this new venture of Susie's?' Mrs Collins asked Sam after her daughter had left. 'Do you think her lady-ship has any idea of all the work involved?'

'I don't know, Mum,' Sam replied with a frown. 'I sense that Susie understands and is anxious over it – but she thinks the world of her lady and would do anything she asked of her.'

'Yes, I know she does – and that's what worries me,' Mrs Collins said. 'I know these rich folk can be changeable – I don't want my girl to be blamed or set off because it didn't work out.'

'I shouldn't think that's likely,' Sam reassured her. 'It was all Lady Diane's idea. She costed it and Susie said she's done her research. Even his lordship was impressed. Stands to reason he wouldn't have permitted it if he didn't think they stood a chance of success.'

'And that's another thing,' his mother argued. 'When I was in service, the gentry wouldn't have dreamed of anything that smelled of trade. I know a good many of them had to marry down into wealthy merchant families to save their ancestral homes, but for a lady to be setting up in business...'

'Things have changed since the war,' Sam told her. 'A lot of young women weren't given the opportunity to work before then, but they were needed and it gave them freedom. I think quite a few women felt aggrieved when they lost their jobs at the end of the war when the men needed them back.'

'All very well for shop girls and factory workers,' Mrs Collins said with a shake of her head. 'But a lady? No, Sam. I think it may cause a scandal when it becomes known.'

'Why should it?' he asked. 'Susie is handling the business side of it – Lady Diane is just the designer. Can't see anything so very wrong in that. Lots of young ladies draw.'

'But now she wants a hand in making up the collection,' Mrs Collins informed him. 'Susie has found a seamstress to go to the house and help them get it ready. I think his lordship may have something to say about that – using his home for trade...'

'It isn't as bad as that, Mum,' Sam laughed at her worried look. 'A lady can have a seamstress call without arousing censure, I should think – and no sales will be done from Grosvenor Square. You can be sure of that.'

'Well, sit down and eat your supper before you go,' his mother said, clearly unconvinced by his argument. 'Are you seeing Winnie this evening?'

'No. She is attending a meeting of the Women's Movement. Even though she is looking for a job that pays better, she still intends to support them as a volunteer,' he replied. 'I'll go back to the shop and work for a couple of hours before I go to bed.'

'Don't work too hard, love,' his mother begged. 'I know you want to save money, but you need your rest.'

'Yes, Mum,' he replied with a cheeky grin and sat down as she served up a tasty chicken pie with mashed potato and spring cabbage. 'That smells delicious. Winnie wants you to teach her to cook. She's never done very much and she likes your pastry. Says it is the best she has ever tasted.'

'I learned from the cook when I was in service,' Mrs Collins replied, looking pleased. 'She was a marvellous cook, she was, and I'm not bad – but the sauces she conjured up made your mouth water.' A little sigh escaped her. 'I worked long hours those days, I can tell you. When I got married it was like being on holiday with just my own little home to keep nice and you children…'

Sam nodded. He knew his parents had been happy until his father's unfortunate death. After that, his mother had gone back to work to keep her children. Now they looked after her and that was how it should be.

'Susie says they eat well in Grosvenor Square,' he murmured, licking a spot of gravy from the corner of his mouth. 'I doubt it is any better than this pie, Mum, no matter how fancy a cook they've got.'

34

Winnie walked home with Mary after the meeting. They'd enjoyed themselves listening to the speakers, one of whom had come to London recently from America, where the Women's Movement was even stronger than in Britain. Feeling hungry, they stopped to buy hot pies and chips on the way back.

'I'm blowed if I'm going to cook tonight,' Mary said. 'I'll keep these warm in the oven for Bill when he gets home. You'll eat yours with me, won't you?'

'Yes, I shall,' Winnie replied. 'Will you let me use your sewing machine again, Mary? I bought myself some more material this morning. I am going to make myself a dress for the winter. It is cheaper than buying and if it turns out as well as my green dress, I shall be happy.'

'You know I'm only too pleased to help you, love.'

They smiled at each other as they reached Mary's home and went inside. Mary busied herself with warming the plates while Winnie set the table.

'I shall miss this when you go and live with Sam's mother...'

'I'll still come round and visit,' Winnie assured her. 'Even though I may be leaving my job with the Women's Movement once I get a job that pays more, I shan't desert you, Mary, or the cause. We'll still go to the meetings together and I'll pop in when I can.' Winnie might be leaving her office job but she had no intention of giving up her allegiance to the Movement and would volunteer to help whenever she could. They'd provided her with accommodation and given her a job when she had nothing, and she believed with all her heart in the work they did.

'Do you think you'll enjoy working for this Lady Diane?'

'I expect so...' Winnie was thoughtful. 'It is only temporary, though. Sam's sister says there might be another job later, but I'm to go to tea to talk about it all.'

'Well, you'll soon find a job elsewhere, a bright girl like you,' Mary said. 'I dare say we would find you something if need be – though I don't think it necessary. You've come a long way since Bill brought you to me that night.'

'Yes, I have,' Winnie agreed. 'I felt pretty desperate then, Mary, the lowest I'd ever been, but you and Constable Winston have helped me so much. I don't think I've ever thanked you enough.'

'Good grief, you don't have to feel grateful,' Mary chided. 'I just want you to be happy. I am very fond of you, love.'

'Yes, I know,' Winnie said and smiled. 'I am grateful, Mary, and I'm fond of you, too. You showed me that there was a way to be happy, even if I could never have the things I thought I wanted.'

Mary looked at her seriously. 'You don't envy what Mrs Harper has now?'

'You know I don't, Mary. Things are nice but not important. I've discovered what really matters – and that's love. I'm a working girl, what's more, I'm proud of it.'

'Good...' Mary smiled her approval. 'Come and eat your supper, Winnie, and then you'd best get home before it's dark.'

'I'm not scared of the dark,' Winnie told her. 'Not now that awful man is no longer around. Oh, I know he isn't the only criminal. Constable Winston says that there's a whole underworld we don't even know about in this great city, terrible things happen – but if you don't get involved, why should it bother us?'

'I think I was wrong to ask you to work at that place,' Mary said as they sat down to their supper. 'Bill told me it was foolish. He says they would have got on to what was going on there sooner or later.'

'Much later,' Winnie retorted.

'Yes.' She frowned. 'From what Sam told you about that new place, making children's clothes, it sounds as if the owner intends to get his money's worth out of the girls he's taken on.'

'Well, they don't have to work there,' Winnie said and took a bite of hot, delicious pie, swallowing it quickly. She paused and then, 'I've asked Mrs Collins to teach me to cook. Mum would never let me do anything but peel the vegetables or wash the dishes. She said I burned things and it's true I did...'

Mary laughed. 'It's just as well you're moving in there before you're wed then, Winnie. You'll need to know how to cook your husband a decent dinner.'

'Yes, I must,' Winnie said with a smile.

Mary frowned. 'Have you seen your mother since you went there with Sam?'

Winnie shook her head. 'No. She doesn't want to see me. She made it plain enough.'

'I don't like to think of you at odds with her, love. You should try to see her before she leaves London – or you may never do so again.'

'Perhaps I will,' Winnie replied. 'Maybe next week after I

know what I'll be doing for Lady Diane. I might call and take her some sweets – she likes fudge.'

'You do that,' Mary advised. 'I just think if you don't, you might regret it...'

'All right, to please you, I will,' Winnie said. 'Shall I make the tea? The kettle has boiled.'

'There's a good girl,' Mary said as Winnie got up to pour water into the big brown pot. 'I wonder—' She broke off as Constable Winston entered the kitchen. 'Hello, love. There's a pie and chips from the shop in the oven keeping warm for you.'

He didn't answer her, his gaze seeking Winnie as she brought the tea tray to the table. 'Winnie,' he said, his tone warning them that something was amiss. 'Sit down, love. I have some news that will distress you.'

'Sam?' she cried, looking alarmed. 'Has something happened to him?'

'No, it's not Sam,' he said heavily and took a deep breath. 'I hardly know how to tell you – your mother has been killed...'

Winnie sank down onto a chair, her knees suddenly giving way with the shock. 'Mum – dead?' she asked, breathing hard. It was too awful to take in, and it hurt – more than she could ever have thought it would. Yes, they'd quarrelled, but she was still her mother and deep down Winnie loved her. 'What happened? Was it an accident? She wasn't ill – she was getting married again...' She stared at him in bewilderment as the pain made her tremble and tears start to her eyes.

'It looks like murder,' he replied grimly. 'She was found in the kitchen of her home. She'd been attacked – hit over the head with a heavy object.'

'No! No, it can't be...' Winnie felt sick, her stomach lurching. 'Who would do such a thing?' she asked, stunned and horrified. It couldn't be happening! It was like a nightmare. 'Mum wasn't rich; she didn't have any money hidden away, just some small savings my father left her, only a few pounds in a teapot.'

'We don't know what the motive was,' he said and looked at her strangely. 'The neighbour said she heard some shouting the other day – the day you visited her, Winnie. This woman says you quarrelled with your mother and I'm sorry, Winnie, but I've been asked to take you down the station for questioning—'

'Bill, no!' Mary cried. 'You can't possibly think Winnie would kill her own mother?'

'I don't think it,' he replied and shook his head. 'It's just to hear her side of the story and eliminate her from our investigation...'

Winnie looked at him. Her hands were trembling and she felt sick, but she lifted her head and met his penetrating gaze. 'When do you want me to come?' she asked.

'We might as well get it over with,' he said. 'All you have to do is tell the sergeant where you were between eleven this morning and three this afternoon.'

'She was at the office, of course,' Mary said and then stared as Winnie shook her head. 'Winnie...?'

'I went out for two hours, from eleven-thirty until one-thirty,' Winnie replied. 'I walked to the market and bought the material I told you about, Mary. After that, I went window shopping and had a cup of tea before returning to the office.'

'Well, there you are then,' Mary said but looked troubled. 'You must believe her, Bill?'

'I do,' Constable Winston replied. He looked uncomfortable and cleared his throat. 'Yes, of course I believe you, Winnie – but that doesn't mean you're not a suspect. We have to explore every angle. You won't deny you quarrelled with your mother?'

'No. I told you both what she said to me – but she was the one shouting, not me nor Sam. He was so polite to her—' She broke off as she saw Constable Winston's expression. 'You can't think either of us...'

'Your mother didn't have a lot of visitors, Winnie. She told her neighbour you were a bad girl – and the neighbour hasn't seen anyone else go in or out, but she says your mother was alive at eleven when she hung out her washing in the yard they share. She went shopping then and when she got back at three o'clock, she took round something she'd been asked to buy for her and discovered the crime...'

'So whoever did it called between eleven and three...' Mary nodded. 'That's a bit odd, isn't it? Noting the times like that? I'm sure I wouldn't know what time my neighbour puts her washing out...'

'We don't have a communal yard,' her husband said gruffly. 'Besides, as yet we're only asking Winnie to tell us her side of things.'

Winnie stood up. 'I'll come with you,' she said and glanced at Mary. 'If... if they don't believe me, please tell Sam what happened...'

'Of course they will,' Mary said instantly. 'Why shouldn't they?'

35

'I can't believe they kept her in the cells overnight and still haven't released her,' Mary said as she stood in Sam's shop the next morning. 'My Bill is upset over it, I can tell you; but Winnie's story didn't convince them and they seem to think she might have got in a temper and struck her mother without thinking.'

'I never heard anything so outrageous in my life,' Sam said, flaring up in his anxiety. 'I was there when her mother was so rude to her and all Winnie did was answer her. She never got in a temper at all...'

'I know... but she smashed Harpers' window that time and took some jewellery from Mrs Harper, and even though she returned it and apologised for the trouble she'd caused with those silly letters – well, that goes on her record. At least the window smashing does. I'm not sure anyone but me and my husband knows the rest – but she has been involved in a couple of small incidents with the Movement, demonstrations, and the like. They know she works for us and... Oh, it is all nonsense, but Bill says there's a new sergeant down the station and he's very officious.'

Sam took off the leather apron he used for his work and stood up. 'I'm going down there now to see if I can sort this out,' he told Mary. 'I know Winnie. She might have done a few silly things once, but – murder! No, she just isn't capable of it.'

'She wanted me to tell you,' Mary said as he turned the sign on his door to 'closed' and followed him out. 'I wish I knew what to do, Sam. I am very fond of Winnie and I can't bear to think of her in that cell... not for something like this...'

'She won't be there long if I can help it,' Sam replied, setting his jaw. 'If they won't let me see her and they won't release her, I'll get her a lawyer. They've got no evidence; they can't have, because she didn't do it.'

Mary nodded. 'That's it, Sam. You stand by her, lad. I'll do whatever I can – and... well, I'll never believe her capable of killing her own mother, even though they didn't get on.'

'I'll let you know as soon as I can,' Sam promised and they parted company.

* * *

An hour or so later, Sam emerged from the police station, frowning and furious. He hadn't been allowed to see Winnie and for all his arguing and the statement he gave about Winnie being happy her mother was to remarry, despite her mother shouting at her, they didn't budge an inch.

Winnie had seen the standby lawyer the police brought in to all cases for those thought not to be able to pay for their own defence, but they were still detaining her for another day for questioning.

Baffled by the brick wall that had been presented to him, Sam realised that certain officers did believe that Winnie was the most likely suspect for her mother's murder. He shook his head over it. It seemed sheer madness to him. For a few minutes, he was stunned, unable to think clearly about what he could do to help the girl he loved and admired. The future had seemed so bright for her, being asked to tea with... It came to him then. He would go to Grosvenor Square and ask to speak to Susie. Lady Diane was a generous woman and had taken an interest in Winnie, even though they hadn't yet met. Perhaps she might know of a lawyer who could help. It would, Sam knew, take every penny of his hard-earned savings to pay for that kind of legal help, but he didn't falter for a moment.

Walking swiftly towards a bus that would take him in the direction he needed, Sam's face set in grim determination. If it came to it, he would sell everything he had to fight for his Winnie – because he loved her and if she were charged with a crime he knew she could never have committed, it would break him.

Susie looked at him in disbelief when he poured out his story to her. Shocked and disbelieving, she agreed to speak to Lady Diane, for she knew she must tell her it all anyway. Her ladyship was resting in her private sitting room, toying with a new sketch she felt dissatisfied with, but laid it aside immediately when she saw the concern in Susie's face. She listened in silence and then asked Susie to pass her her address book. Red leather and tooled with gold, it lay on the satinwood desk that Lady Diane used for her correspondence.

She flicked through the pages and then got up from her sofa and walked over to the desk, picking up the telephone receiver and asking for the number she required. She was put through immediately by a receptionist on giving her name and explained to her husband's lawyer what had occurred.

After listening for a moment, she nodded to herself, thanked him, replaced the receiver and turned to Susie with a smile. 'I know Hugo Montford well and he will do all he can to help your brother and Winnie.'

'Sam will be so grateful,' Susie said. 'He didn't know who to turn to, my lady.'

Lady Diane dismissed her thanks with unconcern. 'It was an easy thing for me and Hugo will be delighted to do this little thing for us. He is a charming man and an excellent lawyer, I assure you.'

'I can't thank you enough,' Susie said. 'May I tell Sam someone will visit the police station this morning?'

'I imagine Hugo will already be on the telephone and I do not doubt they will release Winnie quite soon. They can have no evidence or they would have charged her immediately.' Her calm manner was reassuring and Susie felt relieved.

'I do not believe she is capable of such a thing,' Susie replied with a little shudder. 'How anyone could even think it, I cannot imagine.'

'Well, go and tell your brother not to concern himself – and he should not worry about the cost either. Hugo will do this for me as a favour.' Lady Diane smiled confidently. 'And when you are finished, please return to me. I want to complete the dress we were working on yesterday.'

Susie thanked her and returned to Sam. He had been left waiting in a downstairs parlour and she saw he was staring out at the courtyard to the rear of the house, frowning. He turned as he heard her footsteps, fear and worry in his face.

'Lady Diane has instructed her lawyer. She says Winnie

should be released today. She says he will act as a favour to her
and there will be no cost.'

'That's quite a favour,' Sam said, frowning. 'I hope you told
her ladyship I was ready to pay for his services. I only asked for a
name.' He had flushed to his roots. 'I'm not one to ask for
favours.'

'It was nothing to her,' Susie assured him. 'Merely a phone
call. Let's hope it ends there, Sam.' Even if the lawyer secured
Winnie's immediate release, it didn't mean the nightmare was
over. The police would continue to investigate the murder of
Winnie's mother; it was their duty and their job, and it might be
that Winnie would be questioned again before the real
murderer was found.

Sam nodded, prepared to leave, and then looked straight at
Susie. 'Will her ladyship still want Winnie to come to the house
for tea?'

'She will tell me if she doesn't,' Susie replied. 'Don't look so
worried, Sam – no one thinks Winnie would do such a wicked
act.' She gave a little shiver. 'It was a terrible thing to happen.
Poor Winnie – to be told her mother had died and then the next
moment, be arrested...'

'She didn't get on with her mother – and I know she was a
right tartar to Winnie when she lived at home, but I can't believe
she would do it, Susie. I know she didn't.'

'Of course not. It is just some officious police officer over-
stepping his duty,' Susie told him. 'I must go now, Sam. My lady
needs me.'

'You will thank her. Tell her I'll never forget this,' Sam said
earnestly. 'It might be a small thing to her – but it is everything
to me. One day I'll do something for her...'

Susie smiled. 'Just go and be there when Winnie needs you,

Sam. I think she will be much in need of some love and comfort. Imagining all kinds of things...'

* * *

Winnie was sitting with her back to the wall when Constable Winston came to the door of the cell and unlocked it. She felt numb and exhausted, her head ached and her eyes felt gritty. Her emotions had run the gamut of shock, grief, anger and despair, as it became clear to her that she was the prime suspect in the case. All her protestations of innocence had not been believed and she had begun to think that they intended to charge her with murder.

'Come on, Winnie, you can come home now,' Constable Winston told her. She looked up at him then, hopefully, yet not moving, hardly daring to believe she was being allowed to leave.

'Have they found the murderer?'

'No – but you are being released pending further investigation.' He saw her start of alarm. 'It's all right, Winnie. It's just legal jargon. They will tell you not to leave town, but you've been bailed and you've got a good lawyer on your side now.'

She looked at him in wonder as she was released, following him up to the reception desk, where she was formally given the news that she was being released but the charges against her were still being investigated.

Leaving the station with Constable Winston, she walked in silence for a while.

'What happens if they don't discover who killed Mum?' she asked him eventually. 'Will I still be under suspicion?'

'They need to come up with some evidence,' he told her. 'Seems they've got nothing – except what the neighbour told them.'

'I did go with Sam to see Mum – and I intended to visit her again, but then I couldn't make up my mind to it, so I didn't—' Winnie gulped back a sob. 'We didn't get on – but I never wanted this to happen. You must believe me...' Tears trickled down her cheeks. She hadn't cried at the police station, bolstered by her anger and fear, but now the storm of grief hit her. She leaned against the wall as the sobs broke from her.

'I'm sorry for your loss, Winnie,' Constable Winston began. 'And sorrier that I was the one they sent to bring you in. I don't like the way you were treated and that's a fact.'

Winnie shook her head. For a moment, she just felt she couldn't walk another step, her head spinning, nauseated, and her knees weak. To be suspected of murder – of her own mother! It was so awful, she couldn't even bear to think about it. 'I should have gone to see her sooner, more often...' Regret swept through her in a great wave as realisation hit. Her mother was dead, murdered. She would never see her again. Tears ran down her cheeks as she leaned against the wall, her heart breaking. How could it have happened?

All kinds of thoughts rushed through Winnie's head. She hadn't killed her mother but someone had – why? What of the man her mother had been about to marry? Had the police spoken to him? Was he a suspect? Was he grieving – had he loved her? Her head was whirling as the tears came and she closed her eyes, unable to move on.

* * *

It was to this scene, of Winnie sobbing in the street with Constable Winston trying to comfort her and encourage her to come to his home, that Sam emerged from his bus, having seen them as it was passing, and rung the bell to stop it. He'd been taken past them to the next stop, but he had jumped off and came haring back to them.

'Winnie love,' he said and then swept her into his arms right there in the street. He held her to him protectively and she leaned into him, giving way to her distress against his broad shoulder. Sam looked at Constable Winston for a brief moment as he stroked Winnie's hair. 'I'll take her home to my mother.'

'Aye, you do that.' Constable Winston looked relieved. 'I'll tell Mary what's happened. Now, don't you worry, Winnie. I'm sure it will all be sorted soon enough…'

He watched Sam lead her away, his arm supporting her. It was a right turn-up and no mistake. He'd like to give that officious officer who had insisted that the most obvious culprit was Winnie a facer, if he dared, but it wouldn't help her if he got himself stood down for insubordinate behaviour. If he knew anything at all, it was that there was something smoky about the way that neighbour had reported the incident so neatly. If Constable Winston was any judge, *she* knew more than she was saying.

36

'I can't go to Lady Diane's to tea,' Winnie told Susie when she called the following Sunday evening to see how she was. 'It was so kind of her to help me – but I feel ashamed that I was accused of... doing that, and they haven't said I'm in the clear even now.'

'Her ladyship wants to see you,' Susie insisted. 'She doesn't make much fuss about things, but she was concerned that a young woman should be exposed to such distress after what happened. I was in shock when Sam first told me, but now I feel so angry I can't tell you. After all you did to help the police when those poor girls were being so abused – and they might never have caught Mr Sinclair if it hadn't been for you. They should have known you wouldn't do such a wicked thing...'

'Apparently, the fact that I attacked that man with the fire tongs made them think I might have a violent streak,' Winnie said. 'I fought back when a man tried to molest me last year, too – and I smashed Harpers' shop window...' She blushed fiery red. 'I knocked a policeman's helmet off once when we were demonstrating. I didn't do it on purpose. I was struggling when they tried to arrest some of us... but it seems I have a bit of a record with the police. I suppose that was why they thought...' She swallowed hard. 'I do have a temper, I know that – but I wouldn't do anything really wicked.'

'Of course you wouldn't. Smashing a window and knocking a policeman's hat off is nothing like being able to commit murder. Besides, my lady agrees with your Movement, and the demonstrations for women's rights, too, though she isn't a member. None of us believe you did it, so don't let a few stupid people ruin your life.'

Winnie was uncertain, but after some coaxing from Sam and his mother, she agreed that she would keep the appointment to have tea with her ladyship and hear what she had to say, but it didn't stop her worrying. It was all very well to say she must just get on with her life – but supposing they arrested her again? Winnie had been frightened when she was locked in a cell and understood that people actually thought her capable of violently striking and harming her mother. It was true that they had quarrelled often in the past, and Winnie felt sorry she had not let her mother know she was safe and doing well – above sending her one postcard – but she had never considered raising her hand to her mother. In fact, it was the other way for she'd been struck a hard smack on the ear more than once when she lived at home.

In the end, Winnie gave in to Susie's demands and Sam's soft persuasion. 'You owe it to her ladyship for what she did,' he told her and that was what changed her mind. She did owe Lady Diane her thanks and she might as well see what commissions she had for her because she'd given her notice at the office and had little else to do.

* * *

In the event, Lady Diane was so matter-of-fact about the whole thing, dismissing it as just a foolish mistake on the part of an overzealous police officer that Winnie was able to face her calmly and to agree to make the garments she required. It was then that her ladyship told them what she had in mind for the future.

'It is my intention to offer you a position as the receptionist at Miss Susie's,' she told Winnie. 'You will be able to keep an eye on things – and to judge if standards are slipping. Although you will be officially the receptionist, you will report to Susie if you suspect anything untoward happening... We do not want shoddy work but neither do we require the girls to be treated unfairly as they were before. Susie thinks we should give Mrs Ford a trial at her old job because her knowledge of the clothing trade may be useful – but neither of us is sure we can trust her.'

'So I am not to be a seamstress...' Winnie was surprised, but pleased as her ladyship expanded on her plans to have a show-room upstairs and to model the new designs to potential customers. 'I had thought... but are you sure you still wish to employ me, my lady? If I were to be arrested again and charged...'

'I should say Hugo had failed me and I do not think it,' Lady Diane replied with a smile. 'He will not be idle in the meantime, I assure you. Since we know you to be innocent – and now that I have met you, I am convinced of it – it behoves us to do what we can to establish that, Winnie. Please do not worry. I am certain it will all be settled satisfactorily before long. Now, will you oblige me? I do need people I can trust in this venture, for I am unable to be at the workshop myself... at least for the foreseeable future.'

Her calm assurance did much to ease Winnie's anxiety, in a

way that Sam and Susie's had been unable to, and Winnie found herself willing to accept her ladyship's kind offer.

* * *

When Winnie met Sam that evening, she was in a much better frame of mind and beginning to look forward to the future again. Yet, later, when she settled into the bedroom that had been Sam's and which they would share once married, the doubts and fears came back to haunt her. The penalty for murder would be hanging – especially for such a heinous crime as the brutal murder of her own mother.

Who had killed Winnie's mother? It was a question she knew would haunt her until the police found the guilty person. She shuddered as the thoughts tormented her. Had her mother suffered? Had it been a robbery or something else?

Tears came to her eyes again – tears for herself and her mother. Winnie regretted that she had not visited her mother more; she had dwelled too long on their quarrels, but as she lay reflecting on the past, the unhappy memories returned. She could not forget that her mother had resented her, though she'd never known why. Once she had asked her mother why she disliked her so much, for it had seemed to Winnie after several days of being unable to please her that she must hate her.

'Stupid girl,' her mother had retorted harshly. 'It's my life I hate, not you. If it hadn't been for— but I don't hate you.'

There had, Winnie reflected, always been a barrier between them. She'd never known why. Sighing, Winnie buried her damp face in the pillows. She would never know the answer now.

* * *

Winnie stayed at home with Mrs Collins for two days, feeling as if she needed to hide away to lick her wounds. Perhaps she was grieving for something she'd never had – her mother's love. On the third day, Mrs Collins asked her if she would pop down to the market for her and buy some fresh vegetables.

'Cabbage, if you can get it, carrots, onions and maybe a cauliflower, if it isn't too expensive,' she said. 'On your way back, you can buy a bit of neck of lamb. We'll make a nice stew this evening, Winnie. I'll show you how to make dumplings if you bring me a bit of suet.'

'Sam loves your dumplings,' Winnie agreed, knowing that she couldn't refuse the errand. 'I'll put my jacket on as it's getting a bit chilly now the weather has changed.'

'Yes, more's the pity,' Mrs Collins agreed. 'Let's hope the summer hasn't gone for good. Sometimes we get a lovely autumn.'

Winnie agreed to it, slipped on her jacket, and accepted the basket and the five shillings Mrs Collins gave her and went out. She felt a bit self-conscious as she walked down the street. People would know who she was. Would she meet with hostile stares? It was bound to happen if gossip about her being arrested had spread.

However, she reached the small market without incident, bought the vegetables and then stopped on the way back to purchase the meat. She met with some curious stares in the butcher, but the only person who spoke to her was Mrs Collins' next-door neighbour and she asked her how she was getting on in a friendly way.

* * *

Winnie was aware of being watched as she left the shop and walked the short distance home. As she went into the kitchen, she heard voices and stopped, her heart racing as she recognised one of them – Constable Winston! For one dreadful moment as he looked at her, she thought he'd come to arrest her again and then he smiled.

'Ah, Winnie,' he said. 'I was asked to come along this morning by Mr Montford – he is the lawyer who arranged for you to be released on bail.'

'Oh...' Winnie's heart was pounding as she looked at the stranger. He was tall, lean, and attractive with a serious manner. Her throat was tight, her mouth dry as she stammered, 'I... I wanted to thank you.'

Mr Montford stood up and offered his hand. 'Miss Winnie Brown? I wanted to see you myself because we have good news.'

Winnie let out a sigh of relief as she shook hands. 'Have they caught the person who... killed my mother?' she asked with a catch in her voice.

'Not yet,' he said, 'but Constable Winston has managed to confirm your story, Miss Brown. He says the stallholder you bought that material from remembers you, because you had bought from him before, and he also remembers the time. It was twelve-fifteen exactly. He knows because he was expecting the young lad who works for him back from an errand, and he was late, so he consulted his watch. Constable Winston has checked the bus route to your mother's house. Your colleague has confirmed that you were back at work at one-thirty so that she could take her break – and it isn't possible for you to have gone to your mother's house, committed a crime and returned to the office in the time. You would have needed at least two hours, or longer. It is also not possible for you to have gone from your office to your mother's, kill her and then to be at the market at twelve-fifteen. Therefore, you are eliminated from the investigation and no longer a suspect.'

'Oh, thank goodness,' Winnie cried, tears starting to her eyes. She blinked them away and looked at Constable Winston. 'Thank you so much for helping me – and you, sir.'

Mr Montford inclined his head. 'I did very little – except impress on a certain officer that the wife of a close friend of his chief constable would be most displeased if you were harassed in future. I imagine you will have no further trouble, Miss Brown.' He glanced at Constable Winston. 'I believe a certain police sergeant may find himself reprimanded for his treatment of an innocent young woman.'

'Lady Diane has been so kind...' Winnie sniffed, holding back the tears.

'Well, I shall take my leave,' Mr Montford said and stood up. He turned to Mrs Collins, who had attempted to rise. 'Please remain seated, ma'am. It was a pleasure to meet you – and I've seldom eaten a better treacle tart.'

'It's kind of you to say so, sir – and even kinder to come here yourself to tell Winnie the outcome of this sad business, for I know she has been worried and would not have left the house if I hadn't asked her to do my shopping.'

'It was my pleasure, I assure you,' he said, then smiled at Winnie and took his leave.

Constable Winston remained after shaking hands with him and there was silence for a moment in the kitchen, then, 'I wouldn't say it while the lawyer was here, Winnie, but there's a new suspect in the case...'

'You know who killed Mum?' Winnie's heart soared with hope.

'Not for certain,' he said, 'and I can't tell you too much just yet – but I've been making some enquiries and I believe I have a good idea.' He paused, then, 'Did your mum have anything much of value in the house, Winnie?'

She shook her head and then looked thoughtful. 'There was a silver coffee pot her mother gave her. It was a good one – had belonged to a very generous lady my grandmother worked for...'

His eyes gleamed. 'An old one was it – possibly a hundred years old or so?'

Winnie hesitated, then, 'Yes, I think it might have been. Mum said it was her only good thing... but I never took much notice.'

'Would you know it if you saw it again?'

'Oh yes, I think so...' Winnie bit her lip. 'I dropped it once when I was cleaning it for her and there is a tiny dent on—'

'On the handle?' he asked and she nodded. A look of satisfaction entered his eyes. 'If you can identify the pot, I think we've got him bang to rights.'

'He killed her for a silver pot?' Winnie cried, shocked and distressed.

'Some of them will kill for a shilling,' Constable Winston said. 'Now, don't ask any more, Winnie. If you'd like to step down to the station tomorrow morning, you may be asked to pick out your pot from amongst some other stuff.'

She hesitated and then agreed. 'I'll ask Mary to come with me,' she said. 'If you're sure they won't start accusing me again?'

'Oh, they won't do that,' he said with a grim smile. 'That's one thing you can be certain of.'

37

Winnie's treatment at the police station the next morning was entirely different – respectful and polite, though no apology was made. She quite easily picked out her mother's coffee pot from amongst three similar ones and was asked to sign a form stating it belonged to her mother and then she was allowed to leave, after being informed she could arrange the funeral.

'Well, I am glad that is all over,' Mary said as they walked home together. 'So what will you do now that this is finished?'

'I am going to make some things for Lady Diane. I'll be visiting her house to do some sewing and then I'll be working with Susie Collins, that's Sam's sister, at the new workshop in Dressmakers' Alley. I am to be the receptionist.'

'That's good,' Mary said, nodding. 'I was thinking more on a personal level, Winnie. You've a funeral to arrange for your mother. If you need some help, you know you only have to ask...'

'I think I shall call in at the funeral parlour just around the corner from Sam's shop and ask them to arrange it.'

'What about the money?' Mary asked. 'Can you manage to pay for the funeral? I could help if you need to borrow it.'

'I think Mum had an insurance policy. A man used to call twice a year. It should be enough to cover the costs – and there may be a small amount of money in her savings. I have some put by, too, not much, but I think I'll manage.'

'You'll need to clear the house and give notice to the landlord, too,' Mary reminded her. 'Otherwise you'll need to keep paying rent.'

Winnie nodded. She would have to wait until the police gave her permission to clear her mother's house, but she could give the landlord notice of her intention to give up the tenancy as soon as she was able. A little shudder went through her because she wasn't sure she wanted to visit the house again. 'I may have to ask someone to clear it for me...'

Mary looked at her in concern. 'I didn't mean to upset you, love, but it needs to be done.'

'Yes... I might speak to Lilly at the flower shop. I think her husband clears houses. He could do it for me.'

'It's probably best – if there's nothing you want to keep?'

'I don't think so,' Winnie replied thoughtfully. 'Mum never had much jewellery, just her wedding ring. If she ever had anything of value, I think she sold it – though she did keep the silver pot. I might keep that – it was the thing that proved my innocence in a way, though Constable Winston went to a lot of trouble to check my alibi...'

'Did you think he wouldn't?' Mary asked her. 'We are both fond of you, Winnie. I know you felt the police were slow to act before – but that was the fault of those in higher offices. My Bill is a dogged plodder, but he usually gets there in the end.'

'Yes, he does,' Winnie agreed and smiled at her. 'You've both been good friends to me. I've been very lucky since he brought me to you...'

Mary studied her for a moment, then, 'You're a different girl to the one I first met. You've got purpose in your step and you want to get on in life, but you've learned the meaning of love and kindness, haven't you?'

'That's due to you, Mary – and Sam, but I might never have met him if you hadn't sent me to work at Madame Pauline's.'

'I'm glad that I did then – though it led to terrible things; but there's no sense in thinking about it. We all have to live with the past, Winnie, and to move on. You have a new life to look forward to, my dear. You've lost your mum and that is sad, especially because of what happened. I know she was a tartar and you weren't happy at home, but I also know you feel guilty and upset over it.'

Winnie blinked hard. 'Yes, I do. I ought to have visited her sooner – though she wouldn't have wanted to see me. I don't know why she never liked me and now I never shall.'

'You do have an aunt, don't you?'

'Yes, she works for Mrs Sally Harper... you met her once, when I went there to apologise.'

'Then talk to her,' Mary advised. 'Ask her if she knows anything – she might be able to set your mind at rest. And you will need to tell her of your mother's death, and to invite her to the funeral.'

'Yes, I shall,' Winnie agreed. 'I'd like you to come, too, Mary. It will just be my aunt, if she comes, Sam, you and me. His mother would find it too tiring – and Mum had no friends. She didn't get on well with anyone for long, even my aunt... although she was to have married. I should try to let him know... though she only told me he was Mr Robinson from the country...' Winnie wondered if the police had discovered his whereabouts. She ought perhaps to write to him, invite him to the funeral.

'Are you coming in for a cup of tea or do you want to get off?' Mary said as they reached her home.

'I think I'll just go,' Winnie replied and impulsively kissed her cheek. 'Thank you for coming with me, Mary. I didn't fancy going alone.'

'I'm always here for you, my dear. Let me know the arrangements.'

They parted then, Winnie walking on alone. She was lost in thought for a while, reflecting on what Mary had said to her, but then she stood up straighter and squared her shoulders. Life hadn't always been fair to her, but she wouldn't let it get her down. The future looked so much brighter and, as Mary had said, there was no point in dwelling on the past. Perhaps her aunt might know more about what had turned her mother sour – but perhaps she'd always been that way.

* * *

Winnie walked down Dressmakers' Alley and stopped to speak to Lilly, who had come to the door. She explained about her mother's house needing to be cleared and Lilly looked at her with sympathy.

'Sam told me some of it,' she said. 'As if you'd do such a thing, Winnie. I'll speak to my husband for you. He'll clear the house when you're ready and pay you as much as he can for anything that he can sell...'

'That is so kind of you. I'll need her insurance book; she paid monthly – and any letters he finds,' Winnie said, blinking back a sudden rush of tears. To think she'd once been jealous of Lilly, and all for nothing. She had proved herself a friend, and Winnie thought that if ever she could, she would do something nice for her in return.

As she passed the workshop where she would be spending her future working life, Winnie watched as the builders went in and out carrying wood and new windows. They were clearly making a proper job of it and she had been told by Susie that it would be much brighter and nicer to work in when it was finished. Across the road, she saw that what had been a boarded-up building was now open and there was a display of children's clothing in the window.

Turning the corner, Winnie walked past Sam's shop and noticed that he had customers inside. She would call in and tell him her news when her business at the undertakers was done, but for now she just waved and walked on. Once she'd made the arrangements, she could begin to put the past behind her and move on to a brighter time ahead.

Winnie's mood had begun to lighten and she was looking forward to all the future heralded. Her new job was exciting and tomorrow she was to visit Lady Diane and begin work on the sewing of some maternity dresses. Lady Diane was a warm, generous lady and she too was excited at the new venture. It was a pity, Winnie thought, that convention made it impossible for her to be more involved in the day-to-day running of the business. Susie would visit most days, but even she could not be there all day, for she had other duties. Winnie would be her eyes and ears when she was busy elsewhere.

When Lady Diane had proposed the job to her, Winnie had not at first taken it all in – but now she realised that she would play an important part in the success of Lady Diane's venture – though her name was not to be mentioned; Susie was the owner of the business to all intents and purposes. Yvonne was their head seamstress, but Betty would be the supervisor. Winnie wondered at their taking Betty on, for she had not made a good impression on her – or on them either. It would be interesting to see if she could change her ways and adapt to the new regime.

Winnie thought the clothes they had so far produced were

beautiful. An evening dress of midnight-blue velvet had taken her breath away, for she had not seen gowns as lovely, other than in the windows of exclusive dress shops that she'd never dared to enter. Lady Diane said it would be within the budget of women who were comfortably off, though Winnie knew it would still be beyond her reach. Perhaps one day now that she would be earning more... though she would have no occasion to wear it. However, there were other lovely clothes that might be obtainable once she started to earn more.

It would be an adventure. Truly, it was Lady Diane's adventure, but Winnie was privileged to share it and it was a wonderful chance. Once before, she'd been given an opportunity, but in her childish jealousy, she'd thrown it away. She would make certain she did not throw away her good fortune this time. Winnie had a job she would enjoy and quite soon she would be Sam's wife. All of a sudden, her spirits soared. The past few weeks had been tense and ended in heartache for Winnie, but now she had everything to look forward to.

Her thoughts came to an abrupt halt as she stopped outside the discreet exterior of the undertakers. First, she had to do this for her mother and then she could get on with *her* life. Tomorrow was waiting just around the corner, tomorrow and tomorrow. Lifting her head proudly, she took a deep breath and went in.

38

'So Winnie's name has been cleared, as it ought to be,' Lady Diane said as she listened to Susie's account the following day. Sam had sent Susie a note telling her of their relief and gratitude for the lawyer's help. 'Well, that is as it should be, of course.' She looked at Susie consideringly. 'We have been so busy with the collection of late – and my maternity clothes...' She placed a gentle hand on her stomach. 'She kicked me – although by the feel of that kick, it might well be a boy...'

'Not long to go now, my lady,' Susie said and smiled as Lady Diane settled comfortably against her pillows. 'How are you feeling?'

'Very well, but tired,' she said and yawned behind her hand. 'I was thinking you need some new clothes, too, Susie. Ask Winnie to help you make them, if you wish. You may send the bill for material to me, of course.'

'I'm not one to take advantage,' Susie said. 'I'll get by with what I have for the time being – we are supposed to open next month. I can manage until—' She stopped and looked at Lady Diane as she winced. 'Kicking again?'

'No – that was more of a pain,' Lady Diane said, a startled look in her eyes. 'I felt it earlier this morning, but thought it might have been indigestion... Ohhh...'

Susie was suddenly anxious. 'It isn't the baby?' she said. 'It isn't due for another month...'

'I know but...' Lady Diane gave a little moan of pain. 'I think something is wrong, Susie. Please ask Lord Henry to summon my doctor...'

'His lordship had a meeting. I am not sure if he is back...'

'Then tell Molton to send someone to fetch my doctor and the midwife, because I think my baby is in a hurry to be born – and tell him to request his lordship to come home as soon as he can...'

'Yes, my lady.' Susie walked quickly to the door, only to be stopped by a little cry from Lady Diane.

'Come back quickly, Susie. I need you.'

'Yes, my lady,' Susie replied. 'I'll be with you all the time. I promise.'

* * *

Lady Diane's doctor arrived promptly, but the baby did not. Despite the pains that wracked her young body, it seemed the child would never come. Susie stayed by her side, holding her hands, bathing her brow and stroking her damp hair as she struggled to give her child birth.

Lord Henry came home three hours after his wife's ordeal began and sat by her bed until well into the night when he was ordered from the room by the doctor.

'Get some rest, man,' Mr Griffin, the renowned physician, said gruffly. 'You won't make the child come any sooner, nor can you ease her pain. Come back in a few hours.'

'You will call me if...' Lord Henry said, running his hands through his hair. His face looked tired and suddenly old, as if all the life had drained out of him. 'I would give my life for hers...'

'Nonsense,' his friend told him brusquely. 'She is young and healthy and isn't going to die if I can prevent it – but if it should be a choice between the mother or the baby...'

'You will save my wife,' his lordship said in no uncertain tones. 'She means the world to me – but I know she longs for a child of her own.'

'She may not be able to bear the pain, and then I shall have to cut her,' the physician replied in a flat tone. 'I shall save both if it is possible – but if it comes to it, they may both die.'

'You may as well stick the knife in my guts,' his lordship said angrily and then left the room before he ruined an old friendship.

Susie had heard their conversation and hoped her mistress was too far out of it to hear. She applauded Lord Henry for wanting to save his wife, but understood that the loss of her child – and the knowledge that she would almost certainly not be able to have another – would be devastating for her mistress.

She bent over Lady Diane, gently wiping away the sweat from her eyes, and then kissed her brow. Placing her face against her cheek, she whispered, 'Try again, my lady. I know you are exhausted. I know it hurts, but you *must* try again.'

'Can't...' Lady Diane muttered, thrashing in her agony. 'Can't... too tire—' Even as she denied it, a scream of agony left her lips and her body bucked and writhed as Susie held her hand tighter and encouraged her.

'Yes, you can – one more...' It was enough, as the tiny little body suddenly came slithering out of her to be caught up in triumph and carried away by the midwife.

Lady Diane's eyes flickered open and she looked at Susie. 'Is it a girl?' she asked croakily.

'Yes, my lady,' the midwife told her in a loud voice that seemed to boom in the suddenly quiet room. There was the sound of a loud smack and then an indignant cry. 'And she's perfectly formed and has good lungs,' she said and brought the babe for Lady Diane to see.

Lady Diane tried to sit up but couldn't. She fell back against the pillows, her face pale and her eyes closed. Her breathing was slow and tortured, her body exhausted by her ordeal.

'Is she all right?' Susie cried in fear and the doctor hurried to the bed.

He bent over her and shook his head. 'She breathes, but it is touch-and-go whether she survives, Miss Collins. Delicate women like her ladyship ought not to have children.' He tutted to himself. 'You'll need a wet nurse for the child. She won't be able to nurse her herself – and her ladyship will need constant care.'

'She will get that, but you will need to arrange the wet nurse,' Susie glanced at the midwife, who was making Lady Diane as comfortable as she could, and received a brief nod of acceptance.

'If she develops the childbed fever, you must send for me,' Mr Griffin said. 'There is nothing more I can do for her at the moment. You must care for your mistress, Miss Collins.'

'Yes, of course,' Susie said. 'Do you think—' She was about to ask further questions when the bedroom door opened to admit Lord Henry. The scent of fresh soap told her he had washed and shaved, though by the look of his haggard face, he had not slept.

'The child is born?' he asked hoarsely and glanced towards the babe in its cot briefly as he crossed to the bed. 'Diane...' His eyes were wide with fear as he looked from the physician to Susie. 'Is she... Will she recover?'

'That is in God's hands,' Mr Griffin replied. 'She will need a lot of nursing – and may never recover her full health.'

Susie's heart caught as she saw a look of such grief on his lordship's face that she felt choked with tears. She bent to wipe the sweat from Lady Diane's face as Lord Henry escorted the physician to the bedroom door, where they spoke in whispers for a few minutes, then he returned and sat down by the bed.

'We shall send for Nanny,' he said after a few moments silence. 'She shall come up from the country to nurse her.'

'Is Nanny not a little elderly for the task?' Susie asked. 'I shall care for her, my lord, and we could get a nurse to help as well if you wished.'

His eyes met hers, and there was a glimmer of a smile. 'You might not think it, but I was a sickly child, Miss Collins. The doctors said I would not live beyond childhood, but Nanny pulled me through. She was already insisting that she come up to nurse the child...' His head went up, his shoulders squared, and his gaze was steady. 'Besides, you will not have time. Are you not to open the new workshop within a matter of days?'

'I was...' Susie faltered. 'But... how can I...?'

'Did you not give her your promise, Miss Collins?'

'Yes, but it was to be her adventure... her dream...'

'Exactly.' He nodded. 'You must make her dream live... whatever happens. It is what she would want.'

Susie stared at him in stunned disbelief. How could she do it alone? Lady Diane was the driving force. Hers was the talent to create beautiful gowns. It was impossible. 'My lord, I'm not sure... Lady Diane—'

'Will you let down those people you have promised a new job with better pay and conditions – the seamstress who comes here to help with the collection, and the other young woman my wife helped when she was falsely arrested? She would be disappointed in you, Susie.'

Susie hardly knew what to say or think. His lordship had never addressed her by her first name and probably never would again. It seemed he'd known exactly what was going on in his house all the time, though they'd tried to keep it secret. 'I'm not sure...' she began and he smiled.

'My wife has done hundreds of sketches. I will give you her folder. I am certain there is enough material to keep you busy for months, if not years – and by then she will be well enough to continue or she will tell you what she wants.'

Susie's eyes brimmed with tears as she looked at him. 'She will get better, won't she?'

'Yes,' he said firmly. 'Don't listen to Griffin, he is an old fool. I should've got one of the younger men in – and I shall ask another physician to see her, but she will be all right when Nanny gets here.' He smiled and she knew that he had set his faith in the woman who had nursed him as a child. 'And now, Miss Collins, you should rest. I am with my wife and I shall not leave her. You must sleep because you will be needed later... until Nanny arrives.' He nodded, convinced that all would be well once Nanny was here.

Susie knew it was true; she needed to rest and it would be at least a day before the car could return with Nanny. She bent over Lady Diane and touched her. She was still hot but perhaps a little cooler. 'You will send for me if I am needed?'

'Of course.' Lord Henry inclined his head, but he was no longer looking at her. His gaze was firmly on his beloved wife.

Susie left them together. They were alone now. The midwife had followed the doctor from the room, though she was probably still in the house, resting until the morning.

* * *

Alone in her bedroom, Susie lay down on the bed. She didn't
bother with undressing. Her body ached with tiredness, but her
mind was whirling, her fear for Lady Diane and the future inter-
mixing in swirls as she closed her eyes.

Could she do as Lord Henry said she must? Could she run
this huge new venture if Lady Diane was not well enough to
direct her or...? But, no, she would not think of the worst
outcome. Lady Diane would live. She must, because they all
loved her so much and she had the little girl she'd longed for. In
that moment, Susie felt that her lady *would* live, because some-
how, despite her exhaustion and her pain, she would know her
child needed her.

The future was uncertain and it would be difficult, but Susie
knew she had to try. She couldn't let down the girls she'd
promised new jobs to; Betty, who was so sceptical, Yvonne, who
was so excited, and Winnie, who had been through enough
trauma of late. It was frightening but it was also exciting and she
had to do it, for their sakes' – but most of all for the young
woman she loved.

Susie's mind was set as she finally drifted into sleep. She
would do it for her lady...

ABOUT THE AUTHOR

Rosie Clarke is a #1 bestselling saga writer whose most recent books include *The Mulberry Lane* series. She has written over 100 novels under different pseudonyms and is a RNA Award winner. She lives in Cambridgeshire.

Sign up to Rosie Clarke's mailing list for news, competitions and updates on future books.

Visit Rosie's website: https://www.rosieclarke.co.uk/

Follow Rosie on social media here:

 facebook.com/Rosie-clarke-119457351778432

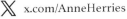 x.com/AnneHerries

BB bookbub.com/authors/rosie-clarke

ALSO BY ROSIE CLARKE

Welcome to Harpers Emporium Series

The Shop Girls of Harpers

Love and Marriage at Harpers

Rainy Days for the Harpers Girls

Harpers Heroes

Wartime Blues for the Harpers Girls

Victory Bells For The Harpers Girls

Changing Times at Harpers

The Mulberry Lane Series

A Reunion at Mulberry Lane

Stormy Days On Mulberry Lane

A New Dawn Over Mulberry Lane

Life and Love at Mulberry Lane

Last Orders at Mulberry Lane

Blackberry Farm Series

War Clouds Over Blackberry Farm

Heartache at Blackberry Farm

Love and Duty at Blackberry Farm

The Trenwith Collection Series

Sarah's Choice

Sixpence Stories

Introducing Sixpence Stories!

Discover page-turning historical novels from your favourite authors, meet new friends and be transported back in time.

Join our book club Facebook group

https://bit.ly/SixpenceGroup

Sign up to our newsletter

https://bit.ly/SixpenceNews

Boldwood

Boldwood Books is an award-winning fiction
publishing company seeking out the best
stories from around the world.

Find out more at www.boldwoodbooks.com

Join our reader community for brilliant books,
competitions and offers!

Follow us
@BoldwoodBooks
@TheBoldBookClub

Sign up to our weekly
deals newsletter

https://bit.ly/BoldwoodBNewsletter